North Wood

Ruins of House

Library

Northern Swamp

West Bridge

Field

Eastern Ridge

Power Station

Eastern Wood

Quarter

Also by
Haruki Murakami

A WILD SHEEP CHASE
(1989)

HARD-BOILED WONDERLAND
AND THE END OF THE WORLD

HARD-BOILED WONDERLAND AND THE END OF THE WORLD

A Novel

HARUKI MURAKAMI

Translated by
ALFRED BIRNBAUM

KODANSHA INTERNATIONAL
Tokyo · New York · London

Translated and adapted by Alfred Birnbaum with the
participation of the author.

The translator wishes to acknowledge the assistance of
editor Elmer Luke.

Originally published in Japanese under the title
Sekai no owari to hādo-boirudo wandārando
by Shinchosha Ltd.

Distributed in the United States by Kodansha America, Inc.,
114 Fifth Avenue, New York, NY 10011.
Published by Kodansha International Ltd.,
1-17-14 Otowa, Bunkyo-ku, Tokyo 112, and
Kodansha America, Inc.

First edition, 1991.
91 92 93 10 9 8 7 6 5 4 3 2 1

Library of Congress Cataloging-in-Publication Data
Murakami, Haruki. 1949–
  [Sekai no owari to hādo-boirudo wandārando. English]
  Hard-boiled wonderland and the end of the world : a novel / by
Haruki Murakami ; translated by Alfred Birnbaum.
     p.   cm.
  Translation of: Sekai no owari to hādo-boirudo wandārando.
  ISBN 4-7700-1544-5
PL856.U673S4513   1991
895.6'35—dc20   91-23818
                                                        CIP

CONTENTS

HARD-BOILED WONDERLAND
AND THE END OF THE WORLD

1

Elevator, Silence, Overweight

THE elevator continued its impossibly slow ascent. Or at
least I imagined it was ascent. There was no telling for
sure: it was so slow that all sense of direction simply
vanished. It could have been going down for all I knew, or
maybe it wasn't moving at all. But let's just assume it was
going up. Merely a guess. Maybe I'd gone up twelve stories,
then down three. Maybe I'd circled the globe. How would I
know?

Every last thing about this elevator was worlds apart from
the cheap die-cut job in my apartment building, scarcely one
notch up the evolutionary scale from a well bucket. You'd
never believe the two pieces of machinery had the same name
and the same purpose. The two were pushing the outer limits
conceivable as elevators.

First of all, consider the space. This elevator was so spacious it could have served as an office. Put in a desk, add a

cabinet and a locker, throw in a kitchenette, and you'd still have room to spare. You might even squeeze in three camels and a mid-range palm tree while you were at it. Second, there was the cleanliness. Antiseptic as a brand-new coffin. The walls and ceiling were absolutely spotless polished stainless steel, the floor immaculately carpeted in a handsome moss-green. Third, it was dead silent. There wasn't a sound—literally not one sound—from the moment I stepped inside and the doors slid shut. Deep rivers run quiet.

Another thing, most of the gadgets an elevator is supposed to have were missing. Where, for example, was the panel with all the buttons and switches? No floor numbers to press, no DOOR OPEN and DOOR CLOSE, no EMERGENCY STOP. Nothing whatsoever. All of which made me feel utterly defenseless. And it wasn't just no buttons; it was no indication of advancing floor, no posted capacity or warning, not even a manufacturer's nameplate. Forget about trying to locate an emergency exit. Here I was, sealed in. No way this elevator could have gotten fire department approval. There are norms for elevators after all.

Staring at these four blank stainless-steel walls, I recalled one of Houdini's great escapes I'd seen in a movie. He's tied up in how many ropes and chains, stuffed into a big trunk, which is wound fast with another thick chain and sent hurtling, the whole lot, over Niagara Falls. Or maybe it was an icy dip in the Arctic Ocean. Given that I wasn't all tied up, I was doing okay; insofar as I wasn't clued in on the trick, Houdini was one up on me.

Talk about not clued in, I didn't even know if I was moving or standing still.

I ventured a cough, but it didn't echo anything like a cough. It seemed flat, like clay thrown against a slick concrete wall. I could hardly believe that dull thud issued from my own body. I tried coughing one more time. The result was the same. So much for coughing.

I stood in that hermetically sealed vault for what seemed an eternity. The doors showed no sign of ever opening. Sta-tionary in unending silence, a still life: *Man in Elevator*.

I started to get nervous. What if the machinery had malfunctioned? Or suppose the elevator operator—assuming there was one in the building—forgot I was here in this box? People have lost track of me before.

I strained to hear something, anything, but no sound reached my ears. I pressed my ear against the stainless-steel wall. Sure enough, not a sound. All I managed was to leave an outline of my ear on the cold metal. The elevator was made, apparently, of a miracle alloy that absorbed all noise. I tried whistling *Danny Boy*, but it came out like a dog wheezing with asthma.

There was little left to do but lean up against a wall and count the change in my pockets. For someone in my profession, knowing how to kill time is as important a method of training as gripping rubber balls is for a boxer. Although, in any strict sense, it's not killing time at all. For only through assiduous repetition is it possible to redistribute skewed tendencies.

I always come prepared with pockets full of loose change. In my right pocket I keep one-hundred- and five-hundred-yen coins, in my left fifties and tens. One-yen and five-yen coins I carry in a back pocket, but as a rule these don't enter into the count. What I do is thrust my hands simultaneously into both pockets, the right hand tallying the hundreds and five-hundreds in tandem with the left hand adding up the fifties and tens.

It's hard for those who've never attempted the procedure to grasp what it is to calculate this way, and admittedly it is tricky at first. The right brain and the left brain each keep separate tabs, which are then brought together like two halves of a split watermelon. No easy task until you get the hang of it.

Whether or not I really do put the right and left sides of my brain to separate accounts, I honestly can't say. A specialist in neurophysiology might have insights to offer on the matter. I'm no neurophysiologist, however. All I know is that when I'm actually in the midst of counting, I feel like I'm using the right side and left side of my brain differently. And when I'm through counting, it seems the fatigue that sets in is qualitatively quite distinct from what comes with normal counting. For convenience sake, I think of it as right-brain-totals-right-pocket, left-brain-totals-left-pocket.

On the whole, I think of myself as one of those people who take a convenience-sake view of prevailing world conditions, events, existence in general. Not that I'm such a blasé, convenience-sake sort of guy—although I do have tendencies in that direction—but because more often than not I've observed that convenient approximations bring you closest to comprehending the true nature of things.

For instance, supposing that the planet earth were not a sphere but a gigantic coffee table, how much difference in everyday life would that make? Granted, this is a pretty far-fetched example; you can't rearrange facts of life so freely. Still, picturing the planet earth, for convenience sake, as a gigantic coffee table does in fact help clear away the clutter—those practically pointless contingencies such as gravity and the international dateline and the equator, those nagging details that arise from the spherical view. I mean, for a guy leading a perfectly ordinary existence, how many times in the course of a lifetime would the equator be a significant factor?

But to return to the matter at hand—or rather, hands, the right and the left each going about its own separate business—it is by no means easy to keep running parallel counts. Even for me, to get it down took the longest time. But once you do, once you've gotten the knack, it's not something you lose. Like riding a bike or swimming. Which isn't to say you can't always use a little more practice. Repetition can improve your technique and refine your style. If for no other reason than this, I always keep my hands busy.

This time I had three five-hundred-yen coins and eighteen hundreds in the one pocket, and seven fifties and sixteen tens in the other. Making a grand total of three-thousand eight-hundred-ten yen. Calculations like this are no trouble at all.

Simpler than counting the fingers on my hands. Satisfied, I leaned back against the stainless-steel wall and looked straight ahead at the doors. Which were still not opening.

What could be taking so long? I tentatively wrote off both the equipment-malfunction theory and the forgotten-by-operator theory. Neither very realistic. This was not to say that equipment malfunction or operator negligence couldn't realistically occur. On the contrary, I know for a fact that such accidents are all too common in the real world. What I mean to say is that in a highly exceptional reality—this ridiculously slick elevator a case in point—the non-exceptional can, for convenience sake, be written off as paradoxically exceptional. Could any human being capable of designing this Tom Swift elevator fail to keep the machinery in working order or forget the proper procedures once a visitor stepped inside?

The answer was obvious. No.

Never happen.

Not after *they* had been so meticulous up to that point. They'd seen to minute details, measuring each step I'd taken virtually to the millimeter. I'd been stopped by two guards at the entrance to the building, asked whom I was there to see, matched against a visitors' list, made to produce my driver's license, logged into a central computer for verification, after which I was summarily pushed into this elevator. You don't get this much going over when you visit the Bank of Japan. It was unthinkable that they, having done all that, should slip up now.

The only possibility was that they had intentionally placed me in this particular situation. They *wanted* the elevator's motions to be opaque to me. They *wanted* the elevator to move so slow I wouldn't be able to tell if it were going up or down. They were probably watching me with a hidden TV camera now.

To ward off the boredom, I thought about searching for the camera lens. But on second thought, what would I have to gain if I found it? That would alert them, they'd halt the elevator, and I'd be even later for my appointed hour.

So I decided to do nothing. I was here in proper accordance with my duties. No need to worry, no cause for alarm.

I leaned against the elevator wall, thrust my hands in my pockets, and once more counted my change. Three-thousand seven-hundred-fifty yen. Nothing to it. Done in a flash.

Three-thousand seven-hundred-fifty yen?

Something was wrong.

I'd made a mistake somewhere.

My palms began to sweat. In three years of counting, never once had I screwed up. This was a bad sign.

I shut my eyes and made my right brain and left brain a blank, in a way you might clean your glasses. Then withdrawing both hands from my pockets, I spread my fingers to dry the sweat. Like Henry Fonda in *Warlock*, where he steels himself before a gunfight.

With palms and fingers completely dry, both hands dived into my pockets to do a third count. If the third sum corresponded to either of the other sums I'd feel better. Everybody makes mistakes. Under the peculiar conditions I found myself, I may have been anxious, not to mention a little over-confident. That was my first mistake. Anyway, an accurate recount was all I needed to remedy the situation, to put things right.

But before I could take the matter in hand, the elevator doors opened. No warning, no sound, they just slid open to either side. I was concentrating so hard on the critical recount that I didn't even notice. Or more precisely, my eyes had seen the opening doors, but I didn't fully grasp the significance of the event. Of course, the doors' opening meant the linking of two spaces previously denied accessible continuity by means of those very doors. And at the same time, it meant the elevator had reached its destination.

I turned my attention to what lay beyond the doors. There was a corridor and in the corridor stood a woman. A young woman, turned out in a pink suit, wearing pink high heels. The suit was coutured of a polished material, her face equally polished. The woman considered my presence, then nodded succinctly. "Come this way," she seemed to indicate. I gave up all hope of that recount, and removing my hands from my pockets, I exited the elevator. Whereupon the elevator doors closed behind me as if they'd been waiting for me to leave.

Standing there in the corridor, I took a good look around, but I encountered no hint of the nature of my current circumstances. I did seem to be in an interior passage of a building, but any school kid could have told you as much.

The interior was gloomy, featureless. Like the elevator. Quality materials throughout; no sign of wear. Marble floors buffed to a high luster; the walls a toasted off-white, like the muffins I eat for breakfast. Along either side of the corridor were tall wooden doors, each affixed with metal room numbers, but out of order. <936> was next to <1213> next to <26>. Something was screwy. Nobody numbers rooms like that.

The young woman hardly spoke. "This way, please," was all she told me, but it was more her lips forming the words than speaking, because no sound came out. Having taken two months of lipreading since starting this line of work, I had no problem understanding what she said. Still, I thought there was something wrong with my ears. After the dead silence of the elevator, the flattened coughs and dessicated whistling, I had to be losing my hearing.

So I coughed. It sounded normal. I regained some confidence in my hearing. Nothing's happened to my ears. The problem must be with the woman's mouth.

I walked behind her. The clicks of her pointy high heels echoed down the empty corridor like an afternoon at the quarry. Her full, stockinged legs reflected clearly in the marble.

The woman was on the chubby side. Young and beautiful and all that went with it, but chubby. Now a young, beautiful woman who is, shall we say, plump, seems a bit off. Walking behind her, I fixated on her body.

Around young, beautiful, fat women, I am generally thrown into confusion. I don't know why. Maybe it's because an image of their dietary habits naturally congeals in my mind. When I see a goodly sized woman, I have visions of her mopping up that last drop of cream sauce with bread, wolfing down that final sprig of watercress garnish from her plate. And once that happens, it's like acid corroding metal: scenes of her eating spread through my head and I lose control.

Your plain fat woman is fine. Fat women are like clouds in the sky. They're just floating there, nothing to do with me. But your young, beautiful, fat woman is another story. I am demanded to assume a posture toward her. I could end up sleeping with her. That is probably where all the confusion comes in.

Which is not to say that I have anything against fat women. Confusion and repulsion are two different things. I've slept with fat women before and on the whole the experience wasn't bad. If your confusion leads you in the right direction, the results can be uncommonly rewarding. But of course, things don't always take the right course. Sex is an extremely subtle undertaking, unlike going to the department store on Sunday to buy a thermos. Even among young, beautiful, fat women, there are distinctions to be made. Fleshed out one way, they'll lead you in the right direction; fleshed out another way, they'll leave you lost, trivial, confused.

In this sense, sleeping with fat women can be a challenge. There must be as many paths of human fat as there are ways of human death.

This was pretty much what I was thinking as I walked down the corridor behind this young, beautiful, fat woman.

A white scarf swirled around the collar of her chic pink suit. From the fullness of her earlobes dangled square gold earrings, glinting with every step she took. Actually, she moved quite lightly for her weight. She may have strapped herself into a girdle or other paraphernalia for maximum visual effect, but that didn't alter the fact that her wiggle was tight and cute. In fact, it turned me on. She was my kind of chubby.

Now I'm not trying to make excuses, but I don't get turned on by that many women. If anything, I think of myself as more the non-turn-on type. So when I do get turned on, I don't trust it; I have to investigate the source.

I scooted up next to her and apologized for being eight or nine minutes late for the appointment. "I had no idea the entrance procedures would take so long," I said. "And then the elevator was so slow. I was ten minutes early when I got to the building."

She gave me a brisk I-know sort of nod. A hint of *eau de cologne* drifted from her neckline. A scent reminiscent of standing in a melon patch on a summer's morn. It put me in a funny frame of mind. A nostalgic yet impossible pastiche of sentiments, as if two wholly unrelated memories had threaded together in an unknown recess. Feelings like this sometimes come over me. And most often due to specific scents.

"Long corridor, eh?" I tried to break the ice. She glanced at me, but kept walking. I guessed she was twenty or twenty-one. Well-defined features, broad forehead, clear complexion.

It was then that she said, "Proust".

Or more precisely, she didn't pronounce the word "Proust", but simply moved her lips to form what ought to have been "Proust". I had yet to hear a genuine peep out of her. It was as if she were talking to me from the far side of a thick sheet of glass.

Proust?

"*Marcel* Proust?" I asked her.

She gave me a look. Then she repeated, "Proust." I gave up on the effort and fell back in line behind her, trying for the life of me to come up with other lip movements that corresponded to "Proust". *Truest? . . . Brew whist? . . . Blue is it?* . . . One after the other, quietly to myself, I pronounced strings of meaningless syllables, but none seemed to match. I could only conclude that she had indeed said, "Proust". But what I couldn't figure was, what was the connection between this long corridor and Marcel Proust?

Perhaps she'd cited Marcel Proust as a metaphor for the length of the corridor. Yet, supposing that were the case, wasn't it a trifle flighty—not to say inconsiderate—as a choice of expression? Now if she'd cited this long corridor as a metaphor for the works of Marcel Proust, that much I could accept. But the reverse was bizarre.

A corridor as long as Marcel Proust?

Whatever, I kept following her down that long corridor. Truly, a long corridor. Turning corners, going up and down short flights of stairs, we must have walked five or six ordinary buildings' worth. We were walking around and around, like in an Escher print. But walk as we might, the surroundings never seemed to change. Marble floors, muffin-white walls, wooden doors with random room numbers. Stainless-steel door knobs. Not a window in sight. And through it all, the same staccato rhythm of her heels, followed by the melted rubber gumminess of my jogging shoes.

Suddenly she pulled to a halt. I was now so tuned in to the sound of my jogging shoes that I walked right into her backside. It was wonderfully cushioning, like a firm rain cloud. Her neck effused that melon *eau de cologne*. She was tipping forward from the force of my impact, so I grabbed her shoulders to pull her back upright.

"Excuse me," I said. "I was somewhere else in my thoughts."

The chubby young woman blushed. I couldn't say for sure, but she didn't seem at all bothered. "*Tozum'sta,*" she said with a trace of a smile. Then she shrugged her shoulders and added, "*Sela.*" She didn't actually say that, but need I repeat, her lips formed the words.

"*Tozum'sta?*" I pronounced to myself. "*Sela?*"

"*Sela,*" she said with conviction.

Turkish perhaps? Problem was, I'd never heard a word of Turkish. I was so flustered, I decided to forget about holding a conversation with her. Lipreading is very delicate business and not something you can hope to master in two months of adult education classes.

She produced a lozenge-shaped electronic key from her suit pocket and inserted it horizontally, just so, into the slot of the door bearing the number <728>. It unlocked with a click. Smooth.

She opened the door, then turned and bid me, "*Saum'te, sela.*"

Which, of course, is exactly what I did.

2

Golden Beasts

WITH the approach of autumn, a layer of long golden fur grows over their bodies. Golden in the purest sense of the word, with not the least intrusion of another hue. Theirs is a gold that comes into this world as gold and exists in this world as gold. Poised between all heaven and earth, they stand steeped in gold.

When I first came to the Town—it was in the spring—the beasts had short fur of varying colors. Black and sandy gray, white and ruddy brown. Some were a piebald of shadow and bright. These beasts of every imaginable shade drifted quietly over the newly greening countryside as if wafted about on a breeze. Almost meditative in their stillness, their breathing hushed as morning mist, they nibbled at the young grass with not a sound. Then, tiring of that, they folded their legs under them to take a short rest.

Spring passed, summer ended, and just now as the light

takes on a diaphanous glow and the first gusts of autumn ripple the waters of the streams, changes become visible in the beasts. Golden hairs emerge, in scant patches at first, chance germinations of some unseasonal herb. Gradually whole fields of feelers knit out through the shorter fur, until at length the whole coat is gleaming gold. It takes not more than a week from start to finish for this ritual to transpire. They commence their metamorphosis almost at the same time; almost at once they are done. Within a week every animal has been completely transformed into a beast of gold. When the morning sun rises and casts newly golden over the world, autumn has descended upon the earth.

Only that long, single horn protruding from the middle of their forehead stays white from base to slender tip. It reminds one less of a horn than a broken bone that has pierced the skin and lodged in place. But for the white of their horns and the blue of their eyes, the beasts are gold. They shake their heads, as if trying on a new suit, thrusting horns into the high autumn sky. They wade into the streams; they stretch their necks to nibble on the autumnal bounty of red berries.

As dusk falls over the Town, I climb the Watchtower on the western Wall to see the Gatekeeper blow the horn for the herding of the beasts. One long note, then three short notes —such is the prescribed call. Whenever I hear the horn, I close my eyes and let the gentle tones spread through me. They are like none other. Navigating the darkling streets like a pale transparent fish, down cobbled arcades, past the enclosures of houses and stone walls lining the walkways along the river, the call goes out. Everything is immersed in the call. It cuts through invisible airborne sediments of time, quietly penetrating the furthest reaches of the Town.

When the horn sounds, the beasts look up, as if in answer to primordial memories. All thousand or more, all at once assume the same stance, lifting their heads in the direction of the call. Some reverently cease chewing the leaves of the broom trees, others pause their hoofs on the cobblestones, still others awaken from their napping in that last patch of sun; each lifts its head into the air.

For that one instant, all is still, save their golden hair which stirs in the evening breeze. What plays through their heads at this moment? At what do they gaze? Faces all at one angle, staring off into space, the beasts freeze in position. Ears trained to the sound, not twitching, until the dying echoes dissolve into twilight. Then suddenly, as if some memory beckons, the beasts rise and walk in the same direction. The spell is broken and the streets resound with countless hooves. I imagine flumes of foam rising from underground, filling the alleyways, climbing over house walls, drowning even the Clocktower.

But on opening my eyes, the flow immediately vanishes. It is only hoofbeats, and the Town is unchanged. The beasts pour through the cobbled streets, swerving in columns hither and yon, like a river. No one animal at the fore, no one animal leading. The beasts lower their eyes and tremble at the shoulders as they follow their unspoken course. Yet among the beasts registers some unshakable inner bond, an indelible intimacy of memories long departed from their eyes.

They make their way down from the north, crossing the Old Bridge to the south bank, where they meet with others of their kind coming in from the east, then proceed along the Canals through the Industrial Sector, turn west and file into a passageway under a foundry, emerging beyond the foot of the Western Hill. There on the slopes they string along the elderly beasts and the young, those unable to stray far from the Gate, waiting in expectation of the procession. Here the group changes directions and goes north across the West Bridge until they arrive at the Gate.

No sooner have the first animals plodded up to the Gate than the Gatekeeper has it opened. Reinforced with thick horizontal iron bands, the doors are rugged and heavy. Perhaps fifteen feet high, crowned with a bristle of spikes. The

Gatekeeper swings the right of these massive doors toward
him effortlessly, then herds the gathered beasts out through
the Gate. The left door never opens. When all the animals
have been ushered out, the Gatekeeper closes the right door
again and lowers the bolt in place.

This West Gate is, to my knowledge, the sole passage in
and out of the Town. The entire community is surrounded by
an enormous Wall, almost thirty feet high, which only birds
can clear.

Come morning, the Gatekeeper once again opens the gate,
sounds the horn, and lets the beasts in. When they are back
within the dominion, he closes the door and lowers the bolt.

"Really no need for the bolt," the Gatekeeper explains to
me. "Nobody but me is strong enough to open a gate this
heavy. Even if people try teaming up. But rules are rules."

The Gatekeeper pulls his wool cap down to his eyebrows,
and there is not another word out of him. The Gatekeeper is
a giant of a man, thick-skinned and brawny, as big as I have
ever seen. His shirt would seem ready to rip at a flex of his
muscles. There are times he closes his eyes and sinks into a
great silence. I cannot tell if he is overcome by melancholy, or
if this is simply the switch of some internal mechanism. Once
the silence envelops him, I can say nothing until he regains
his senses. As he slowly reopens his eyes, he looks at me
blankly, the fingers of his hands moving vaguely on his lap as
if to divine why I exist there before him.

"Why do you round up the beasts at nightfall and send
them outside the walls, only to let them back in again in the
morning?" I ask the Gatekeeper as soon as he is conscious.

The Gatekeeper stares at me without a trace of emotion.

"We do it that way," he says, "and that is how it is. The
same as the sun rising in the east and setting in the west."

Apart from opening and closing the Gate, the Gatekeeper
seems to spend his time sharpening tools. The Gatehouse is
arrayed with all manner of hatchets, adzes, and knives, so

that his every free moment is devoted to honing them on his whetstone. The honed blades attain an unnatural gleam, frozen white, aglow from within.

When I look at the rows of blades, the Gatekeeper smiles with satisfaction, attentively following my gaze.

"Careful, one touch can cut," says the Gatekeeper, pointing a stocky finger at his arsenal. "These are not toys. I made them all, hammered each one out. I was a blacksmith, and this is my handiwork. Good grip, perfect balance. Not easy to match a handle to a blade. Here, hold one. But be careful about the blade."

I lift the smallest hatchet from the implements on the table and swing it through the air. Truly, at the slightest flick of the wrist—at scarcely my thought of it—the sharpened metal responds like a trained hunting dog. The Gatekeeper has reason to be proud.

"I made the handle, too. Carved it from ten-year-old ash. Some people like other wood, but my choice is ten-year ash. No younger, no older. Ten-year is prime grain. Strong and moist, plenty of flex. The Eastern Woods is my ash stock."

"What ever do you need so many knives for?"

"Different things," says the Gatekeeper. "In winter, I use them the most. Wait till winter, I can show you. Winter is mighty long here."

There is a place for the beasts outside the Gate. An enclosure where they sleep at night, transversed by a stream that gives them drink. Beyond that are apple trees, as far as the eye can see, vast wooded seas that stretch on and on.

"Nobody but you watches the animals," says the Gatekeeper. "You just got here, though. You get used to living here, and things fall into place. You lose interest in them. Everybody does. Except for one week at the beginning of spring."

For one week at the beginning of spring, the Gatekeeper tells me, people climb the Watchtower to see the beasts fight.

This is the time when instinct compels the males to clash—after they have shed their winter coats, a week before the females bear young. They become so fierce, wounding each other viciously, one would never imagine how peaceful they usually are.

These autumn beasts crouch in a hush, each to each, their long golden fur radiant in the sunset. Unmoving, like statues set in place, they wait with lifted heads until the last rays of the day sink into the apple trees. When finally the sun is gone and the gloom of night draws over them, the beasts lower their heads, laying their one white horn to earth, and close their eyes.

So comes to an end one day in the Town.

3

Rain Gear, INKlings, Laundry

I WAS conducted into a big, empty room. The walls were a white, the ceiling a white, the carpet a mocha brown—all decorator colors. Yes, even in whites, there are tasteful whites and there are crass whites, shades that might as well not be white.

The opaque windows blocked all view to the world outside, but the light that was filtering in could only be sunlight. Which placed us somewhere above ground. So the elevator *had* risen. Knowing this put me at ease: it was as I had imagined after all.

The woman motioned for me to sit on the leather sofa in the center of the room. I obliged, and crossed my legs, whereupon she exited by a different door.

The room had very little furniture. Before the sofa was a low coffee table set with a ceramic ashtray, lighter, and cigarette case. I flipped open the cigarette case; it was empty.

On the walls, not a painting, nor a calendar, nor a photo. Pretty bleak.

Next to the window was a large desk. I got up from the sofa and walked over to the window, inspecting the desk as I passed by. A solid affair with a thick panel top, ample drawers to either side. On the desk were a lamp, three ballpoint pens, and an appointment book, beside which lay scattered a handful of paperclips. The appointment book was open to today's date.

In one corner of the room stood three very ordinary steel lockers, entirely out of keeping with the interior scheme. Straight-cut industrial issue. If it had been up to me, I would have gone for something more elegant—say, designer wardrobes. But no one was asking me. I was here to do a job, and gray steel lockers or pale peach jukebox was no business of mine.

The wall to my left held a built-in closet fitted with an accordion door. That was the last item of furnishing of any kind in the room. There was no bookcase, no clock, no phone, no pencil sharpener, no letter tray, no pitcher of water. What the hell kind of room was it supposed to be? I returned to the sofa, recrossed my legs, and yawned.

Ten minutes later, the woman reappeared. And without so much as a glance in my direction, she opened one of the lockers and removed an armload of some shiny black material, which she brought over to the coffee table.

The black material turned out to be a rubberized slicker and boots. And topping the lot was a pair of goggles, like the ones pilots in World War I wore. I hadn't the foggiest what all this was leading up to.

The woman said something, but her lips moved too fast for me to make it out.

"E . . . excuse me? I'm only a beginner at lipreading," I said.

This time she moved her lips slowly and deliberately: "Put these on over your clothes, please."

Really, I would have preferred not to, but it would have

been more bothersome to complain, so I shut up and did as told. I removed my jogging shoes and stepped into the boots, then slipped into the slicker. It weighed a ton and the boots were a couple of sizes too big, but did I have a choice? The woman swung around in front of me and did up the buttons of my slicker, pulling the hood up over my head. As she did so, her forehead brushed the tip of my nose.

"Nice fragrance," I complimented her on her *eau de cologne.*

"Thanks," she mouthed, doing the hood snaps up to right below my nose. Then over the hood came the goggles. And there I was, all slicked up and nowhere to go—or so I thought.

That was when she pulled open the closet door, led me by the hand, and shoved me in. She turned on the light and pulled the door shut behind her. Inside, it was like any clothes closet—any clothes closet without clothes. Only coat hangers and mothballs. It probably wasn't even a clothes closet. Otherwise, what reason could there be for me getting all mummied up and squeezed into a closet?

The woman jiggled a metal fitting in the corner, and presently a portion of the facing wall began to open inward, lifting up like the door of the trunk of a compact car. Through the opening it was pitch black, but I could feel a chill, damp air blowing. There was also the deep rumble of water.

"There's a river in there," she appeared to say. The sound of the water made it seem as if her speaking were simply drowned out. Somehow I found myself understanding what she was saying. Odd.

"Up toward the headwaters, there's a big waterfall which you pass right under. Beyond that's Grandfather's laboratory. You'll find out everything once you get there."

"Once I get there? Your *grand*father's waiting for me?"

"That's right," she said, handing me a large waterproof flashlight with a strap. Stepping into total blackness wasn't my idea of fun, but I toughened up my nerve and planted one foot inside the gaping hole. I crouched forward to duck head and shoulders through, coaxing my other foot along. With all the bulky rain gear, this proved no mean effort. I turned and looked back though my goggles at the chubby woman standing inside the closet. She was awfully cute.

"Be careful. You mustn't stray from the river or go down a side path," she cautioned, stooping down to peer at me.

"Straight ahead, waterfall?" I shouted.

"Straight ahead, waterfall," she repeated.

As an experiment, I mouthed the word "*sela*". This brought a smile and a "*sela*" from her, before she slammed the wall panel shut.

All at once I was plunged into darkness, literally, without a single pinprick of light. I couldn't see a thing. I couldn't even make out my hand raised up to my face. I stood there dumbfounded, as if I'd been hit by a blunt object, overcome by the chilling realization of my utter helplessness. I was a leftover wrapped in black plastic and shoved into the cooler. For an instant, my body went limp.

I felt for the flashlight switch and sent a welcome beam of light straight out across nowhere. I trained the light on my feet, then slowly took my bearings. I was standing on a three-meter-square concrete platform jutting out over bottomless nothingness. No railing, no enclosure. Wish she'd told me about this, I huffed, just a tad upset.

An aluminum ladder was propped against the side of the platform, offering a way down. I strapped the flashlight diagonally across my chest, and began my descent, one slippery rung at a time. The lower I got, the louder and more distinct the sound of water became. What was going on here? A closet in an office building with a river chasm at the bottom? And smack in the middle of Tokyo!

The more I thought about it, the more disturbed I got. First that eerie elevator, then that woman who spoke without ever saying anything, now this leisurely jaunt. Maybe I should have turned down the job and gone home. But no, here I was, descending into the abyss. And for what? Professional pride? Or was it the chubby woman in the pink suit? Okay, I confess: she'd gotten to me, and now I had to go through with this nonsense.

Twenty rungs down the ladder I stopped to catch my breath, then continued another eighteen rungs to the ground. At the bottom, I cautiously shined my light over the level stone slab beneath my feet and discovered the river ahead. The surface of the water rippled in the flashlight beam. The current was swift, but I could get no sense of the depth or even the color of the water. All I could tell was that it flowed from left to right.

Pouring light into the ground at my feet, I slowly made my way upstream. Now and again I could swear something was moving nearby, but I saw nothing. Only the vertical hewn-rock walls to either side of the river. I was probably anxious from the darkness.

After five or six minutes of walking, the ceiling dropped low—or so it seemed from the echo. I pointed my flashlight beam up but could not discern anything above me. Next, just as the woman had warned, I saw what seemed to be tunnels branching off to either side. They weren't so much side paths as fissures in the rock face, from which trickled veins of water that fed into the river. I walked over and shined my flashlight into one of the cracks. A black hole that got bigger, much bigger, further in. Very inviting.

Gripping the flashlight tightly in my right hand, I hurried upstream like a fish mid-evolution. The stone slab was wet, so I had to step carefully. If I slipped now or broke my flashlight, that'd be it.

All my attention was on my feet. When I happened to glance up, I saw a light closing in, a mere seven or eight meters away. I immediately switched off the flashlight. I reached into the slicker for my knife and got the blade open, the darkness and the roar of the water making a perfect cover.

The instant I switched off my flashlight, the yellowish beacon riveted to a pinpoint stop. It then swung around in an
arc to describe two large circles in the air. This seemed to be
a signal: "Everything all right—not to worry." Nonetheless, I
stood poised on guard and waited for *them* to move.
Presently, the light began to come toward me, waving
through empty space like a giant glowbug coupled to a
higher brain. I stared at it, right hand clutching the knife, left
hand on the switched-off flashlight.

The light stopped its advance scarcely three meters from
me. It motioned upward and downward. It was weak. I eventually realized it was trying to illuminate a face. The face of a
man wearing the same crazy goggles and slicker as I had on.
In his hand was the light, a small lantern like the kind they
sell in camping supply shops. He was yelling to me over the
noise of the water, but I couldn't hear him; and because it
was too dark, I couldn't I read his lips.

". . . ing except that . . . time. Or you'd . . . in that regard,
since . . . ," the man appeared to be saying. Indecipherable.
But he seemed to pose no threat, so I turned my flashlight
back on and shined it on my face, touching a finger to my ear
to signal that I could barely hear him.

The man nodded several times, then he set down his lantern and fumbled with both hands in his pockets. Suddenly,
the roar subsided from all around me, like a tide receding. I
thought I was passing out. Expecting unconsciousness—
though why I should be passing out, I had no idea—I braced
myself for a fall.

Seconds passed. I was still standing. In fact, I felt just fine.
The noise of the water, however, had faded.

"I came t'meet you," the man said. Perfectly clear.

I shook my head, tucked the flashlight under my arm,
folding the knife and pocketing it. Going to be one of those
days, I could just tell.

"What happened to the sound?" I asked the man.

"Oh yes, the sound. It was loud, wasn't it? I turned it
down. Sorry about that. It's all right now," said the man,

nodding repeatedly. The roar of the river was now the babble of a brook. "Well then, shall we?" he said with an abrupt about-face, then began walking back upstream with sure-footed ease. I followed, shining my flashlight in his steps.

"You turned the sound down? Then it's artificial, I take it?"

"Not at all," the man said. "That's natural sound, that is."

"But how do you turn down natural sound?" I asked.

"Strictly speaking, I don't turn it down," the man replied. "I take it out."

Well, I guess, if he said so. I kept walking, saying nothing. Everything was very peaceful now, thanks to his softening the sound of the water. I could even hear the squish-squish of my rubber boots. From overhead there came a weird grinding as if someone were rubbing pebbles together. Twice, three times, then it stopped.

"I found signs that those INKlings were sneakin' in here. I got worried, so I came t'fetch you. By rights INKlings shouldn't ever make it this far in, but sometimes these things happen. A real problem," the man said.

"INKlings?" I said.

"Even someone like you, bet y'wouldn't fancy runnin' into an INKling down here, eh?" said the man, bursting into a loud guffaw.

"I suppose not," I said. INKling or whatling, I wasn't up for a rendezvous in a dark place like this.

"That's why I came t'get you," the man repeated. "Those INKlings are bad news."

"Much obliged," I said.

We walked on until we came within hearing of what sounded like a faucet running full blast. The waterfall. With only a quick shine of my flashlight, I could see it wasn't your garden variety. If the sound hadn't been turned down, it would have made a mean rumble. I moved forward, my goggles wet with spray.

"Here's where we go under, right?" I asked.

"That's right, son," said the man. And without further explanation, he headed straight into the waterfall and disappeared. I had little choice but to head straight into the waterfall, too.

Fortunately, our route took us through what proved to be a "dry" part of the waterfall, but this was becoming absurd. Even all suited up in this rain gear, I was getting drenched under sheets of water. And to think the old man had to do this every time he entered or left the laboratory. No doubt this was for information-security purposes, but there had to be a more graceful way.

Inside the waterfall, I stumbled and struck my kneecap on a rock. With the sound turned down, I had gotten confused by the sheer discrepancy between the non-sounds and the reality that would have produced them had they been audible. Which is to say, a waterfall ought to have a waterfall's worth of sound.

On the far side of the falls was a cave barely big enough for one man. Dead center was an iron door. The man pulled what looked like a miniature calculator out of his pocket, inserted it into a slot, and after he maneuvered it a bit, the door opened silently inward.

"Well, here we are. After you," said the man. He stepped in after me and locked the door. "Rough goin', eh?"

"No, uh . . . that wasn't . . ."

The man laughed, lantern hanging by a cord around his neck, goggles and hood still in place. A jolly ho-ho-ho sort of laugh.

The room we'd entered was like a swimming pool locker room, the shelves stacked with a half dozen sets of the same gear we had on. I took off my goggles and climbed out of the slicker, draping it over a hanger, then placed my boots on the shelf. The flashlight I hung on a hook.

"Sorry t'cause you so much trouble," the man apologized, "but we can't be slack on security. Got t'take the necessary precautions. There's types out there lyin' in wait for us."

"INKlings?" I prompted.

"Yessir. And those INKlings, in case you were wonderin', aren't the only ones," said the man, nodding to himself.

He then conducted me to a reception room beyond the lockers. Out of his slicker, my guide proved to be a kindly old man. Short and stout; not fat so much as sturdily built. He had good color to his complexion and when he put on his rimless spectacles, he was the very image of a major pre-War political figure.

He motioned for me to sit on the leather sofa, while he himself took a seat behind the desk. This room was of exactly the same mold as the other room. The carpet, the walls, the lighting, everything was the same. On the coffee table in front of the sofa was an identical smoking set, on the desk an identical appointment book and an identical scattering of paperclips. Had I been led around in a circle back to the same room? Maybe in fact I had; maybe in fact I hadn't. Hard to memorize the precise position of each scattered paperclip.

The old man looked me over. Then he picked up a paperclip and unbent it to scrape at a fingernail cuticle. His left index finger cuticle. When he'd finished with the cuticle, he discarded the straightened paperclip into the ashtray. If I ever get reincarnated, it occurred to me, let me make certain I don't come back as a paperclip.

"Accordin' t'my information, those INKlings are like this with the Semiotecs," said the old man. "Not that they're in cahoots, mind you. INKlings're too wary, and your Semiotec's got his own agenda planned out way ahead. So cooperation's got t'be limited to the very few. Still, it doesn't bode well. The fact that we've got INKlings pokin' around right here, where there oughn't t'be INKlings 'tall, just shows how bad things are. If it keeps on like this, this place's goin' t'be swarmin' with INKlings day and night. And that'll make real problems for me."

"Quite," I concurred, "quite." I hadn't the vaguest idea what sort of operants these INKlings were, but if for any reason they'd joined forces with the Semiotecs, then the outlook wasn't too bright for me either. Which was to say that the contest between our side and the Semiotechnicians was already in a delicate balance, and the slightest tampering could overturn the whole thing. For starters, I knew nothing about these INKlings, yet they knew about me. This already tipped the scales in their favor. Of course, to a lower-echelon field independent like myself, not knowing about INKlings was only par for the course, whereas the Brass at the top were probably aware of them ages ago.

"Well, if it's all right with you, let's get hoppin'," said the old man.

"Absolutely," I said.

"I asked them t'send 'round their crackest Calcutec, and seems you've got that reputation. Everyone speaks mighty highly of you. You got the knack, got the gumption, you do a crack job. Other than a certain lack of team spirit, you got no strikes against you."

"An exaggeration, I'm sure," I said.

The old man guffawed again. "And team spirit's no great shakes. The real question is gumption. You don't get t'be a first-string Calcutec without your share of spunk. That's how you command such high wages, eh?"

Yet another guffaw. Then the old man guided me into an adjoining workroom.

"I'm a biologist," he said. "But the word biology doesn't begin t'cover all that I do. Everythin' from neurophysiology to acoustics, linguistics to comparative religion. Not your usual bag of tricks, if I do say so myself. These days I'm researchin' the mammalian palate."

"Palate?"

"The mouth, son. The way the mouth's put together. How the mouth works, how it gives voice, and various related topics. Here, take a look at this."

Whereupon he flicked a switch on the wall and the lab lights came on. The whole back of the room was flush with shelves, each lined with skulls. Giraffe, horse, panda, mouse, every species of mammal imaginable. There must have been three hundred or four hundred skulls. Naturally, there were human skulls, too. Caucasoid, Negroid, Asiatic, Indian, one male and one female of each.

"Got the whale and elephant in the storeroom downstairs. Take up a lot of space, they do," said the old man.

"Well, I guess," I said. A few whale skulls and there goes the neighborhood.

All the skulls had their mouths propped open, a chorus ready for inspection; all stared at the opposite wall with empty sockets. Research specimens or no, the atmosphere in the room was not exactly pleasant. On other shelves, although not so numerous as the skulls, were jars of tongues and ears and lips and esophagi.

"What d'y' think? Quite a collection, eh?" twinkled the old man. "Some folks collect stamps, some folks collect records. Me, I collect skulls. Takes all kinds t'make a world, eh?"

"Er, yes."

"From early on, I had this interest in mammalian skulls, and I've been buildin' up the collection bit by bit. Been at it close t'forty years. Unscramblin' the skulls has taken me longer than I ever thought possible. Would've been easier t'figure out living flesh-and-blood human beings. I really think so. Granted, of course, someone young as yourself's probably more interested in the flesh and nothing but, eh?" the old man laughed. "For me, it's taken thirty years t'get t'where I can hear the sounds bones make. Thirty years, now that's a good long time."

"Sounds?" I said. "Bones produce sounds?"

"Of course they do," said the old man. "Every bone has unique sound. It's the hidden language of bones. And I don't mean metaphorically. Bones literally speak. Research I'm engaged in proposes t'decode that language. Then, t'render it artificially controllable."

The details escaped me, but if what the old man said were true, he had his work cut out for him. "Very valuable research," I offered.

"Truly," said the old man with a nod. "That's why those types have all got designs on my findings. 'Fraid the word's out. They all want my research for their own ends. F'r instance, suppose you could draw out the memories stored in bones; there'd be no need for torture. All you'd have t'do is kill your victim, strip the meat clean off the skull, and the information would be in your hands."

"Lovely," I said.

"Granted, for better or worse, research hasn't gotten that far. At this stage, you'd get a clearer memory log taking the brain out."

"Oh." Remove the skull, remove the brain, some difference.

"That's why I called for your services. So those Semiotecs can't steal my experiment data. Civilization," the old man pronounced, "faces serious crises because science is used for evil—or good. I put my trust in science for the sake of pure science."

"I can't say I understand," I said. "I'm here on a matter of pure business. Except my orders didn't come from System Central and they didn't come from any official agent. They came directly from you. Highly irregular. And more to the point, probably in violation of professional regulations. If reported, I could lose my license. I hope you understand this."

"I do indeed," said the old man. "You're not without cause for concern. But rest assured, this request was cleared through the proper System channels. Only the business procedures were dropped. I contacted you directly t'keep everything undercover. You won't be losin' any license."

"Can you guarantee this?"

The old man pulled out a folder and handed it to me. I leafed through it. Official System request forms, no mistake about it. The papers, the signatures, all in order.

"Well enough," I said, returning the folder. "I pull double-scale at my rank, you realize. Double-scale means—"

"Twice the standard fee, right? Fine by me. Fact is, as a

bonus, I'm willin' t'go to a full triple-scale."

"Very trusting of you, I must say."

"This is an important job. Plus I already had you go under the waterfall. Ho-ho-ho."

"Then may I see the data," I said. "We can decide the calc-scheme after I see the figures. Which of us will do the computer-level tabulations?"

"I'll be usin' my computer here. You just take care of the before and after. That is, if you don't mind."

"So much the better. Saves me a lot of trouble."

The old man stood up from his chair and pressed a coordinate on the wall behind him. An ordinary wall—until it opened. Tricks within tricks. The old man took out another folder and closed the wall. Resealed, it looked like any other plain white wall. No distinguishing features or seams, no nothing.

I skimmed the seven pages of numerics. Straightforward data.

"This shouldn't take too much time to launder," I said. "Infrequent number series like these virtually rule out temporary bridging. Theoretically, of course, there's always that possibility. But there'd be no proving the syntactical validity, and without such proof you couldn't shake the error tag. Like trying to cross the desert without a compass. Maybe Moses could do it."

"Moses even crossed the sea."

"Ancient history. To my knowledge, at this level, never once has a Semiotec succeeded in securing illegal access."

"You're sayin' a single-conversion trap's sufficient, eh?"

"A double-conversion trap is too risky. It would effectively reduce the possibility of temporary bridging to zero, but at this point it's still a freak stunt. The trapping process isn't solidly grounded. The research isn't complete."

"Who said anything 'bout double-conversion trapping?" said the old man, working another paperclip into his cuticle. The right index finger this time.

"What is it you're saying, then?"

"Shuffling, son. I'm talkin' shuffling. I want you to launder and shuffle. That's why I called on you. If it was simple brainwash laundry, there wouldn't have been any need t'call you."

"I don't get it," I said, recrossing my legs. "How do you know about shuffling? That's classified information. No outsider's supposed to know about it."

"Well, I do. I've got a pretty open pipeline to the top of the System."

"Okay, then run this through your pipeline. Shuffling procedures are completely frozen at this time. Don't ask me why. Obviously some kind of trouble. Whatever the case, shuffling is now prohibited."

The old man handed me the request folder once again.

"Have yourself a good look at the last page. Should be shuffling procedure clearance there somewhere."

I opened the folder to the last page and ran my eyes over the documentation. Sure enough, shuffling clearance authorized. I read it over several times. Official. Five signatures, no less. What the hell could the Brass be thinking? You dig a hole and the next thing they say is fill it in; fill it in and they tell you to dig a hole. They're always screwing with the guy in the field.

"Could I ask you to make color copies of all pages of this request. I might find myself driven into a nasty corner without them."

"Fine," said the old man. "Glad to make you your copies. Nothing to worry 'bout. Everything's on the up and up. I'll give you half your fee today, the other half on final receipt. Fair and square?"

"Fair enough. Now, to get on with the laundry. After I'm done, I'll take the wash home with me and do the shuffling there. Shuffling requires special precautions. I'll be back with the shuffled data when I'm through."

"Noon, four days from now. It can't be any later."

"Plenty of time."

"I beg of you, son, whatever you do, don't be late," the

old man pleaded. "If you're late, something terrible will happen."

"World going to fall apart?" I kidded.

"In a way," said the old man, "yes."

"Not this time. I never come in late," I said. "Now, if it's not too much to ask, could I please trouble you for some ice water and a thermos of hot black coffee. And maybe a small snack. Please. Something tells me this is going to be a long job."

Something told me right. It was a long, hard job. The numerics themselves were the proverbial piece of cake, but with so many case-determinant step-functions, the tabulations took much more doing than they first appeared to require. I input the data-as-given into my right brain, then after converting it via a totally unrelated sign-pattern, I transfer it to my left brain, which I then output as completely recoded numbers and type up on paper. This is what is called laundering. Grossly simplified, of course. The conversion code varies with the Calcutec. This code differs entirely from a random number table in its being diagrammatic. In other words, the way in which right brain and left brain are split (which, needless to say, is a convenient fiction; left and right are never actually divided) holds the key. Drawn, it might look something like this:

LEFT BRAIN   RIGHT BRAIN

Significantly, the way the jagged edges do not precisely match up means that it is impossible to reconvert data back into its original form. Nonetheless, Semiotecs can occasionally decode stolen data by means of a temporary bridge. That is, they holographically reproduce the jagged edges from an analysis of the data-as-retrieved. Sometimes it works, sometimes it doesn't. The more we Calcutecs up our technologies, the more they up their counter-technologies. We safeguard the data, they steal it. Your classic cops-and-robbers routine.

Semiotecs traffic illegally obtained data and other information on the black market, making megaprofits. And what's worse, they keep the most valuable bits of information for themselves and the benefit of their own organization.

Our organization is generally called the System, theirs the Factory. The System was originally a private conglomerate, but as it grew in importance it took on quasi-governmental status. In the same way as, say, Ma Bell in America. We rank-and-file Calcutecs work as individual independents not unlike tax accountants or attorneys, yet we need licenses from the state and can only take on jobs from the System or through one of the official agents designated by the System. This arrangement is intended to prevent misuse of technologies by the Factory. Any violation thereof, and they revoke your license. I can't really say whether these preventative measures make sense or not. The reason being that any Calcutec stripped of his qualifications eventually ends up getting absorbed into the Factory and going underground to become a Semiotec.

As for the Factory, much less is known. It apparently started off as a small-scale venture and grew by leaps and bounds. Some refer to it as the Data Mafia, and to be certain, it does bear a marked resemblance in its rhizomic penetration to various other underworld organizations. The difference is that this Mafia deals only in information. Information is clean and information makes money. The Factory stakes out a computer, hacks it for all its worth, and makes off with its information.

I drank a whole pot of coffee while doing the laundry. One hour on the job, thirty minutes rest—regular as clockwork. Otherwise the right-brain–left-brain interface becomes muddled and the resulting tabulations glitched.

During those thirty-minute breaks, I shot the breeze with the old man. Anything to keep my mouth moving. Best method for repolarizing a tired brain.

"What *are* all these figures?" I asked.

"Experiment data," said the old man. "One-year's worth of findings. Numeric conversions of 3-D graphic-simulated volume mappings of the skulls and palates of various animals, combined with a three-element breakdown of their voices. I was tellin' you how it took me thirty years t'get t'where I could tune in each bone's waveform. Well, when this here calculation's completed, we'll finally be able t'extract that sound—not empirically, but theoretically."

"Then it'll be possible to control things artificially?"

"Right on the mark," said the old man.

"So we have artifical control—where does that get us?"

The old man licked his upper lip. "All sorts of things could happen," he said after a moment. "Truly all sorts of things. I can't go spoutin' off about them, but things you can't begin t'imagine."

"Sound removal being only one of them?"

The old man launched into another round of his belly laugh. "Oh-ho-ho, right you are, son. Tunin' in the signal of the human skull, we'll take the sound out or turn it up. Each person's got a different shaped skull, though, so we won't be able t'take it out completely. But we can turn it down pretty low, eh? Ho-ho-ho. We match the sound-positive to a sound-negative and make them resonate together. Sound removal's just one of the more harmless applications."

Harmless? Fiddling with the volume was screwy enough. What was the rest going to be like?

"It's possible t'remove sound from both speakin' and

hearin'," resumed the old man. "In other words, we can erase the sound of the water from hearing—like I just did—or we can erase speech."

"You plan to present these findings to the world?"

"*Tosh*," said the old man, wiping his hands, "now why would I want t'let others in on something this much fun? I'm keepin' it for my own personal enjoyment."

The old man burst out laughing some more. Ho-ho-ho.

He even had me laughing.

"My research is purely for the specialist. Nobody's got any interest in acoustics anyway," the old man said. "All the idiot savants in the world couldn't make head or tail of my theories if they tried. Only the world of science pays me any mind."

"That may be so, but your Semiotec is no idiot. When it comes to deciphering, they're genius class, the whole lot of them. They'll crack your findings to the last digit."

"I know, I know. That's why I've withheld all my data and processes, so they wouldn't be pokin' into things. Probably means even the world of science doesn't take me seriously, but what of that? *Tosh*, a hundred years from now my theories will all've been proved. That's enough, isn't it?"

"Hmm."

"Okay, son, launder and shuffle everything."

"Yessir," I said, "yessir."

For the next hour, I concentrated on tabulations. Then took another rest.

"One question, if I might," I said.

"What's that?" asked the old man.

"That young woman at the entrance. You know, the one with the pink suit, slightly plump . . . ?"

"That's my granddaughter," said the old man. "Extremely bright child. Young's she is, she helps me with my research."

"Well, uh, my question is . . . was she born mute that way?"

"Darn," said the old man, slapping his thigh. "Plum for-got. She's still sound-removed from that experiment. Darn, darn, darn. Got t'go and undo it right now."

"Oh."

4

The Library

HE Town centers around a semicircular plaza
directly north of the Old Bridge. The other semicircular fragment, that is, the lower half of the circle, lies across the river to the south. These two half-circles
are known as the North and South Plazas respectively.
Regarded as a pair, the two can impress one only as complete
opposites, so unlike each other as they are. The North Plaza
is heavy with an air of mystery, laden with the silence of the
surrounding quarter, whereas the South Plaza seems to lack
any atmosphere at all. What is one meant to feel here? All is
adrift in a vague sense of loss. Here, there are relatively fewer
households than north of the Bridge. The flowerbeds and
cobblestones are not well kept.

In the middle of the North Plaza stands a large Clocktower piercing skyward. To be precise, one should say it is
less a clocktower than an object retaining the form of a

clocktower. The clock has long forfeited its original role as a timepiece.

It is a square stone tower, narrowing up its height, its faces oriented in compass fashion toward the cardinal directions. At the top are dials on all four sides, their hands frozen in place at thirty-five minutes past ten. Below, small portals give into what is likely a hollow interior. One might imagine ascending by ladder within but for the fact that no entrance is to be found at the base. The tower climbs so high above the plaza that one has to cross the Old Bridge to the south even to see the clock.

Several rings of stone and brick buildings fan out from the North Plaza. No edifice has any outstanding features, no decorations or plaques. All doors are sealed tight; no one is seen entering or leaving. Here, is this a post office for dead letters? This, a mining firm that engages no miners? This, a crematorium without corpses to burn? The resounding stillness gives the structures an impression of abandonment. Yet each time I turn down these streets, I can sense strangers behind the façades, holding their breath as they continue pursuits I will never know.

The Library stands in one block of this quarter. None the more distinguished for being a library, it is an utterly ordinary stone building. There is nothing to declare it a library. With its old stone walls faded to a dismal shade, the shallow eaves over the iron-grilled windows and the heavy wooden doors, it might be a grain warehouse. If I had not asked the Gatekeeper to explain the way there in some detail, I would never have recognized it as a library.

"Soon as you get settled, go to the Library," the Gatekeeper tells me my first day in town. "There is a girl who minds the place by herself. Tell her the Town told you to come read old dreams. She will show you the rest."

"Old dreams?" I say. "What do you mean by 'old dreams'?"

The Gatekeeper pauses from whittling a round peg, sets down his penknife, and sweeps the wood shavings from the table. "Old dreams are . . . old dreams. Go to the Library. You will find enough of them to make your eyes roll. Take out as many as you like and read them good and long."

The Gatekeeper inspects the pointed end of his finished peg, finds it to his approval, and puts it on the shelf behind him. There, perhaps twenty of the same round pegs are lined.

"Ask whatever questions you want, but remember, I may not answer," declares the Gatekeeper, folding his arms behind his head. "'There are things I cannot say. But from now on you must go to the Library every day and read dreams. That will be your job. Go there at six in the evening. Stay there until ten or eleven at night. The girl will fix you supper. Other times, you are free to do as you like. Understand?"

"Understood," I tell him. "How long am I to continue at that job?"

"How long? I cannot say," answers the Gatekeeper. "Until the right time comes." Then he selects another scrap of wood from a pile of kindling and starts whittling again.

"This is a poor town. No room for idle people wandering around. Everybody has a place, everybody has a job. Yours is in the library reading dreams. You did not come here to live happily ever after, did you?"

"Work is no hardship. Better than having nothing to do," I say.

"There you are," says the Gatekeeper, nodding squarely as he eyes the tip of his knife. "So the sooner you get yourself to work, the better. From now on you are the Dreamreader. You no longer have a name. Just like I am the Gatekeeper. Understand?"

"Understood," I say.

"Just like there is only one Gatekeeper in this Town, there is only one Dreamreader. Only one person can qualify as Dreamreader. I will do that for you now."

The Gatekeeper takes a small white tray from his cupboard, places it on the table, and pours oil into it. He strikes a match and sets the oil on fire. Next he reaches for a dull, rounded blade from his knife rack and heats the tip for ten minutes. He blows out the flame and lets the knife cool.

"With this, I will give you a sign," says the Gatekeeper. "It will not hurt. No need to be afraid."

He spreads wide my right eye with his fingers and pushes the knife into my eyeball. Yet as the Gatekeeper said, it does not hurt, nor am I afraid. The knife sinks into my eyeball soft and silent, as if dipping into jelly.

He does the same with my left eye.

"When you are no longer a Dreamreader, the scars will vanish," says the Gatekeeper, putting away the tray and knife. "These scars are the sign of the Dreamreader. But as long as you bear this sign, you must beware of light. Hear me now, your eyes cannot see the light of day. If your eyes look at the light of the sun, you will regret it. So you must only go out at night or on gray days. When it is clear, darken your room and stay safe indoors."

The Gatekeeper then presents me with a pair of black glasses. I am to wear these at all times except when I sleep.

So it was I lost the light of day.

It is in the evening a few days later that I go my way to the Library. The heavy wooden door makes a scraping noise as I push it open. I find a long straight hallway before me. The air is dusty and stale, an atmosphere the years have forsaken. The floorboards are worn where once tread upon, the plaster walls yellowed to the color of the light bulbs.

There are doors on either side of the hallway, each door-knob with a layer of white dust. The only unlocked door is at the end, a delicate frosted glass panel behind which shines lamplight. I rap upon this door, but there is no answer. I place my hand on the tarnished brass knob and turn it, whereupon the door opens inward. There is not a soul in the room. A great empty space, a larger version of a waiting room in a train station, exceedingly spare, without a single window, without particular ornament. There is a plain table and three chairs, a coal-burning iron stove, and little else besides an upright clock and a counter. On the stove sits a steaming, chipped black enamel pot. Behind the counter is another frosted glass door, with lamplight beyond. I wonder whether to knock, but decide to wait for someone to appear.

The counter is scattered with paperclips. I pick up a handful, then take a seat at the table.

I do not know how long it is before the Librarian appears through the door behind the counter. She carries a binder with various papers. When she sees me, her cheeks flush red with surprise.

"I am sorry," she says to me. "I did not know you were here. You could have knocked. I was in the back room, in the stacks. Everything is in such disorder."

I look at her and say nothing. Her face comes almost as a reminiscence. What about her touches me? I can feel some deep layer of my consciousness lifting toward the surface. What can it mean? The secret lies in distant darkness.

"As you can see, no one visits here. No one except the Dreamreader."

I nod slightly, but do not take my eyes off her face. Her eyes, her lips, her broad forehead and black hair tied behind her head. The more closely I look, as if to read something, the further away retreats any overall impression. Lost, I close my eyes.

"Excuse me, but perhaps you have mistaken this for another building? The buildings here are very similar," she says, setting her binder down by the paperclips. "Only the Dreamreader may come here and read old dreams. This is forbidden to anyone else."

"I am here to read dreams," I say, "as the Town tells me to."

"Forgive me, but would you please remove your glasses?"

I take off my black glasses and face the woman, who peers

into the two pale, discolored pupils that are the sign of the Dreamreader. I feel as if she is seeing into the core of my being.

"Good. You may put your glasses on."

She sits across the table from me.

"Today I am not prepared. Shall we begin tomorrow?" she says. "Is this room comfortable for you? I can unlock any of the other reading rooms if you wish."

"Here is fine," I tell her. "Will you be helping me?"

"Yes, it is my job to watch over the old dreams and to help the Dreamreader."

"Have I met you somewhere before?"

She stares at me and searches her memory, but in the end shakes her head. "As you may know, in this Town, memory is unreliable and uncertain. There are things we can remember and things we cannot remember. You seem to be among the things I cannot. Please forgive me."

"Of course," I say. "It was not important."

"Perhaps we have met before. This is a small town."

"I arrived only a few days ago."

"How many days ago?" she asks, surprised. "Then you must be thinking of someone else. I have never been out of this Town. Might it have been someone who looks like me?"

"I suppose," I say. "Still, I have the impression that elsewhere we may all have lived totally other lives, and that somehow we have forgotten that time. Have you ever felt that way?"

"No," she says. "Perhaps it is because you are a Dreamreader. The Dreamreader thinks very differently from ordinary people."

I cannot believe her.

"Or do you know where this was?"

"I wish I could remember," I say. "There was a place, and you were there."

The Library has high ceilings, the room is quiet as the ocean floor. I look around vacantly, paperclips in hand. She remains seated.

"I have no idea why I am here either," I say.

I gaze at the ceiling. Particles of yellow light seem to swell and contract as they fall. Is it because of my scarred pupils that I can see extraordinary things? The upright clock against the wall metes out time without sound.

"I am here for a purpose, I am told."

"This is a very quiet town," she says, "if you came seeking quiet."

I do not know.

She slowly stands. "You have nothing to do here today. Your work starts tomorrow. Please go home to rest."

I look up at the ceiling again, then back at her. It is certain: her face bears a fatal connection to something in me. But it is too faint. I shut my eyes and search blindly. Silence falls over me like a fine dust.

"I will return tomorrow at six o'clock in the evening," I say.

"Good-bye," she says.

On leaving the Library, I cross the Old Bridge. I lean on the handrail and listen to the the River. The Town is now devoid of beasts. The Clocktower and the Wall that surrounds the Town, the buildings along the riverbank, and the sawtooth mountains to the north are all tinged with the blue-gray gloom of dusk. No sound reaches my ears except for the murmur of the water. Even the birds have taken leave.

If you came seeking quiet—I hear her words.

Darkness gathers all around. As the streetlights by the River blink on, I set out down the deserted streets for the Western Hill.

5

Tabulations, Evolution, Sex Drive

WHILE the old man went back above ground to rectify the sound-removed state in which he'd left his granddaughter, I plugged away in silence at my tabulations.

How long the old man was gone, I didn't really know. I had my digital alarm clock set to an alternating one-hour–thirty-minutes–one-hour–thirty-minutes cycle by which I worked and rested, worked and rested. The clock face was covered over so I couldn't read it. Time gets in the way of tabulations. Whatever the time was now, it had no bearing on my work. My work begins when I start tabulating and it ends when I stop. The only time I need to know about is the one-hour–thirty-minutes–one-hour–thirty-minutes cycle.

I must have rested two or three times during the old man's absence. During these breaks, I went to the toilet, crossed my arms and put my face down on the desk, and stretched out on the sofa. The sofa was perfect for sleeping. Not too soft, not too hard; even the cushions pillowed my head just right. Doing different tabulation jobs, I've slept on a lot of sofas, and let me tell you, the comfortable ones are few and far between. Typically, they're cheap deadweight. Even the most luxurious-looking sofas are a disappointment when you actually try to sleep on them. I never understand how people can be lax about choosing sofas.

I always say—a prejudice on my part, I'm sure—you can tell a lot about a person's character from his choice of sofa. Sofas constitute a realm inviolate unto themselves. This, however, is something that only those who have grown up sitting on good sofas will appreciate. It's like growing up reading good books or listening to good music. One good sofa breeds another good sofa; one bad sofa breeds another bad sofa. That's how it goes.

There are people who drive luxury cars, but have only second- or third-rate sofas in their homes. I put little trust in such people. An expensive automobile may well be worth its price, but it's only an expensive automobile. If you have the money, you can buy it, anyone can buy it. Procuring a good sofa, on the other hand, requires style and experience and philosophy. It takes money, yes, but you also need a vision of the superior sofa. That sofa among sofas.

The sofa I presently stretched out on was first-class, no doubt about it. This, more than anything, gave me a warm feeling about the old man. Lying there on the sofa with my eyes closed, I thought about him and his quirks, his hokey accent, that outlandish laugh. And what about that sound-removal scheme of his? He *had* to be a top-rank scientist. Sound removal wouldn't even occur to your ordinary researcher. And another thing—you always hear about these oddball scientificos, but what kind of eccentric or recluse would build a secret laboratory behind a subterranean waterfall just to escape inquisitive eyes? He was one strange individual.

As a commercial product, his sound-alteration technolo-

gies would have all sorts of applications. Imagine, concert
hall PA equipment obsolete—no more massive amps and
speakers. Then, there was noise reduction. A sound-removal
device would be ideal for people living near airports. Of
course, sound-alteration would be ripe for military or criminal abuse. I could see it now: silent bombers and noiseless
guns, bombs that explode at brain-crushing volumes, a whole
slew of toys for destruction, ushering in a whole new generation of refinements in mass slaughter. The old man had obviously seen this too, giving him greater reason to hide his
research from the world. More and more, I was coming to
respect the old guy.

I was into the fifth or sixth time around in the work cycle
when the old man returned, toting a large basket.

"Brought you fresh coffee and sandwiches," he said.
"Cucumber, ham, and cheese. Hope that's all right."

"Thanks. Couldn't ask for more," I said.

"Want t'eat right away?"

"No, after the next tab-cycle."

By the time the alarm went off, I'd finished laundering five
of the seven pages of numeric data lists. One more push. I
took a break, yawned, and turned my attention to food.

There were enough sandwiches for a small crowd. I
devoured more than half of them myself. Long-haul tabulations work up a mean appetite. Cucumber, ham, cheese, I
tossed them down in order, washing the lot down with coffee.

For every three I ate, the old man nibbled at one, looking
like a terribly well-mannered cricket.

"Have as many as you like," said the old man. "When
you get t'my age, your eatin' declines. Can't eat as much,
can't work as much. But a young person ought t'eat plenty.
Eat plenty and fatten up plenty. People nowadays hate t'get
fat, but if you ask me, they're looking at fat all wrong. They
say it makes you unhealthy or ugly, but it'd never happen
'tall if you fatten up the right way. You live a fuller life, have
more sex drive, sharpen your wits. I was good and fat when I
was young. Wouldn't believe it t'look at me now. Ho-ho-ho."

The old man could hardly contain his laughter. "How 'bout it? Terrific sandwiches, eh?"

"Yes, indeed. Very tasty," I said. The sandwiches really were very tasty. And I'm as demanding a critic of sandwiches as I am of sofas.

"My granddaughter made them. She's the one deserves your compliments," the old man said. "The child knows the finer points of making a sandwich."

"She's definitely got it down. Chefs can't make sandwiches this good."

"The child'd be overjoyed to hear that, I'm sure. We don't get many visitors, so there's hardly any chance t'make a meal for someone. Whenever the child cooks, it's just me and her eatin'."

"You two live alone?"

"Yessiree. Just us two loners, but I don't think it's so healthy for her. She's bright, strong as can be, but doesn't even try t'mix with the world outside. That's no good for a young person. Got t'let your sex drive out in some constructive way. Tell me now, the child's got womanly charms, hasn't she?"

"Well, er, yes, on that account," I stammered.

"Sex drive's decent energy. Y' can't argue about that. Keep sex drive all bottled up inside and you get dull-witted. Throws your whole body out of whack. Holds the same for men and for women. But with a woman, her monthly cycle can get irregular, and when her cycle goes off, it can make her imbalanced."

"Uh, yes."

"That child ought t'have herself relations with the right type of man at the earliest opportunity. I can say that with complete conviction, both as her guardian and as a biologist," said the old man, salting his cucumbers.

"Did you manage with her to . . . uh . . . did you get her sound back in?" I asked. I didn't especially feel like hearing about people's sex drive, not while I was still in the middle of a job.

"Oh yes, I forgot t'tell you," said the old man. "I got her sound back t'normal, no trouble. Sure glad you thought t'remind me. No telling how many more days she would've had t'be without sound like that. Once I hole up down here, I don't generally go back up for a few days. Poor child, livin' without sound."

"I can imagine."

"Like I was sayin', the child's almost totally out of contact with society. Shouldn't make much difference for the most part, but if the phone were t'ring, could be trouble."

"She'd have a hard time shopping if she couldn't speak."

"*Tosh*, shoppin' wouldn't be so bad," said the old man. "They've got supermarkets out there where you can shop and not say a word. The child really likes supermarkets, she's always going to them. Office to supermarket, supermarket to office. That's her whole life."

"Doesn't she go home?"

"The child likes the office. It's got a kitchen and a shower, everything she needs. At most she goes home once a week."

I drank my coffee.

"But say, you managed t'talk with her all right," the old man said. " How'd you do it? Telepathy?"

"Lipreading. I studied it in my spare time."

"Lipreading, of course," the old man said, nodding with approval. "A right effective technique. I know a bit myself. What say we try carrying on a silent conversation, the two of us?"

"Mind if we don't?" I hastened to reply.

"Granted, lipreading's an extremely primitive technique. It has shortcomings aplenty, too. Gets too dark and you can't understand a thing. Plus you have t'keep your eyes glued to somebody's mouth. Still, as a halfway measure, it works fine. Must say you had uncanny foresight t'learn lipreading."

"Halfway measure?"

"Right-o," said the old man with another nod. "Now listen up, son. I'm tellin' this to you and you alone: The world ahead of us is goin' t'be sound-free."

"Sound-free?" I blurted out .

"Yessir. Completely sound-free. That's because sound is of no use to human evolution. In fact, it gets in the way. So we're going t'wipe sound out, morning to night."

"Hmph. You're saying there'll be no birds singing or brooks babbling. No music?"

"'Course not."

"It's going to be a pretty bleak world, if you ask me."

"Don't blame me. That's evolution. Evolution's always hard. Hard and bleak. No such thing as happy evolution," said the old man. He stood up and walked around his desk to retrieve a pair of nail clippers from a drawer. He came back to the sofa and set at trimming all ten fingernails. "The research is underway, but I can't give you the details. Still, the general drift of it is . . . well, that's what's comin'. You musn't breathe a word of this to anyone. The day this reaches Semiotec ears, all pandemonium's goin' t'break loose."

"Rest easy. We Calcutecs guard our secrets well."

"Much relieved t'hear that," said the old man, sweeping up his nail clippings with an index card and tossing them into the trash. Then he helped himself to another cucumber sandwich. "These sure are good, if I do say so myself."

"Is all her cooking this good?"

"Mmm, not cspecially. It's sandwiches where she excels. Her cooking's not bad, mind you, but it just can't match her sandwiches."

"A rare gift," I said.

"'Tis," the old man agreed. "I must say, I do believe it takes someone like you to fully appreciate the child. I could entrust her to a young man like you and know I'd done the right thing."

"Me?" I started. "Just because I said I liked her sandwiches?"

"You don't like her sandwiches?"

"I'm very fond of her sandwiches."

"The way I see it, you've got a certain quality. Or else,

you're missin' something."

"I sometimes think so myself."

"We scientists see human traits as being in the process of evolution. Sooner or later you'll see it yourself. Evolution is mighty gruelin'. What do you think the most gruelin' thing about evolution is?"

"I don't know. Tell me," I said.

"It's being unable to pick and choose. Nobody chooses to evolve. It's like floods and avalanches and earthquakes. You never know what's happening until they hit, then it's too late."

I thought about this for a bit. "This evolution," I began, "what does it have to do with what you mentioned before? You mean to say I'm going to lose my powers of speech?"

"Now that's not entirely accurate. It's not a question of speaking or not speaking. It's just a step."

"I don't understand." In fact, I *didn't* understand. On the whole, I'm a regular guy. I say I understand when I do, and I say I don't when I don't. I try not to mince words. It seems to me a lot of trouble in this world has its origins in vague speech. Most people, when they go around not speaking clearly, somewhere in their unconscious they're asking for trouble.

"What say we drop the subject?" said the old man. "Too much complicated talk. It'll spoil your tabulations. Let's leave it at that for now."

No complaints from this department. Soon after, the alarm rang and I went back to work. Whereupon the old man opened a drawer and pulled out what looked like a pair of stainless-steel fire tongs. He walked over to the shelves of skulls and, like a master violinist examining his Stradivarius collection, picked up one or another of them, tapping them with the fire tongs to listen to their pitch. They gave out a range of timbre and tones, everything from the clink you might get from tapping a whiskey glass, to the dull thud from an oversized flower pot. To think that each skull once had skin and flesh and was stuffed with gray matter—in varying quantities—teeming with thoughts of food and sex and dominance. All now vanished.

I tried to picture my own head stripped of skin and flesh, brains removed and lined up on a shelf, only to have the old guy come around and give me a rap with stainless-steel fire tongs. Wonderful. What could he possibly learn from the sound of my skull? Would he be able to read my memories? Or would he be tapping into something beyond memory?

I wasn't particularly afraid of death itself. As Shakespeare said, die this year and you don't have to die the next. All quite simple, if you want to look at it that way. Life's no piece of cake, mind you, but the recipe's my own to fool with. Hence I can live with it. But after I'm dead, can't I just lie in peace? Those Egyptian pharoahs had a point, wanting to shut themselves up inside pyramids.

Several hours later, the laundry was finally done. I couldn't say how many hours it had taken, but from the state of my fatigue I would guess a good eight or nine hours. I got up from the sofa and stretched my stressed muscles. The Calcutec manual includes how-to illustrations for limbering up a total of twenty-six muscle groups. Mental wear-and-tear takes care of itself if you relieve these stress points after a tab-session, and the working life of your Calcutec is extended that much longer.

It's been less than ten years since the whole Calcutec profession began, so nobody really knows what that life expectancy ought to be. Some say ten years, others twenty; either way you keep at it until you the day you die. Did I really want to know how long? If it's only a matter of time before you burn yourself out, all I can do is keep my muscles loose and my fingers crossed.

After working the knots in my body out, I sat back down on the sofa, closed my eyes, and slowly brought my right brain and left brain together again. Thus concluded all work for the day. Manual-perfect.

The old man had a large canine skull set out on his desk and was taking measurements with slide calipers, noting the figures on a photo of the specimen.

"Finished, have you?" asked the old man.

"All done."

"You put in a very hard day," he said.

"I'll be heading home to sleep now. Tomorrow or the next day I'll shuffle the data and have it back to you by noon two days later. Without fail. Is that satisfactory?"

"Fine, fine," said the old man, nodding. "But remember, time is absolutely critical. If you're later than noon, there'll be trouble. There'll be real trouble."

"I understand."

"And I beg of you, make certain no one steals that list. If it gets stolen, it'll be both our necks."

"Don't worry. We receive quite thorough training on that count. There'll be no inadvertent straying of tabulated data."

I withdrew a flex-metal document cache from a pocket behind my left knee, inserted the data list, and locked it.

"I'm the only one who can open this. If someone tampers with the lock, the contents are destroyed."

"Mighty clever," the old man said.

I slipped the document cache back behind my knee.

"Say now, sure you won't have any more to eat? There're a few sandwiches left. I don't eat much when I'm caught up in research. Be a shame t'let them go to waste."

I was still hungry, so I squared away the remaining sandwiches. The old man poured me a fresh cup of coffee.

I climbed back into rain gear, pulled on my goggles, took flashlight in hand, and headed back into the subterranean passage. This time the old man didn't come along.

"Already put out ultrasonic waves t'drive those INKlings away, so shouldn't be any of them sneakin' around for the time bein'," the old man reassured me.

Apparently, these INKlings were some kind of subterranean

entity, which made me feel a bit squeamish about walking all alone out there in the dark. It didn't help that I didn't know a thing about INKlings, not their habits nor what they looked like nor how to defend myself against them. Flashlight in my left hand, knife in my right, I braced myself for the return trip.

When I saw the chubby pink-suited young woman waving her flashlight and coming my way, I felt saved. I made it over toward her. She was saying something which I couldn't hear over the rumble of the de-sound-removed river. Nor could I see her lips in the darkness.

Up the long aluminum ladder we went, to where there was light. I climbed first, she followed. Coming down, I hadn't been able to see anything, so there was nothing to be afraid of, relatively speaking, but going back up was something else entirely. I could picture the height only too well—a two- or three-story drop. I wanted to stop to regather my wits, but she was on my tail. Safety first, I always say, so I kept climbing.

We made it through the closet back into the first room and stripped off our rain gear.

"Work go well?" she asked. Her voice, now audible for the first time, was soft and clear.

"Well enough, thanks."

"I really appreciate your telling Grandfather about my sound-removal. I would have been like that for a whole week."

"Why didn't you tell me that in writing? You could have been straightened up a lot sooner, and I wouldn't have been so confused."

She did a quick turn around the table without a word, then adjusted both of her earrings.

"Rules are rules," she said.

"Against communicating in writing?"

"That's one of them."

"Hmph."

"Anything that might lead to devolution."

"Oh," I said. Talk about precautions.

"How old are you?" she asked out of the blue.

"Thirty-five. And you?"

"Seventeen. You're the first Calcutec I've ever met. But then, I've never met any Semiotecs either."

"You're really only seventeen?" I asked, surprised.

"Yes, why should I lie? I'm really seventeen. I don't look seventeen, though, do I?"

"No, you look about twenty."

"It's because I don't want to look seventeen," she said. "Tell me, what's it like to be a Calcutec?"

"We're normal ordinary people, just like everyone else."

"Everyone may be ordinary, but they're not normal."

"Yes, there is that school of thought," I said. "But there's normal and then there's *normal*. I mean the kind of normal that can sit down next to you on the train and you wouldn't even notice. Normal. We eat food, drink beer—oh, by the way, the sandwiches were great."

"Really?" she said, beaming.

"I don't often get good sandwiches like that. I practically ate them all myself."

"How about the coffee?"

"The coffee wasn't bad either."

"Really? Would you like some now? That way we could sit and talk a little while longer."

"No thanks, I've had more than enough already," I said. "I don't think I can manage another drop. And besides, I need to get myself home to bed quick."

"That's too bad."

"Too bad for me, too."

"Well, let me at least walk you to the elevator. The corridors are extremely complex. I bet you couldn't find your way on your own."

"I doubt it myself."

The girl picked up what looked like a round hatbox, sealed several times over with wide adhesive tape, and handed it to me.

"What's this?" I asked.

"A gift for you from Grandfather. Take it home and open it."

I weighed the box in my hands. It was much lighter than I would have guessed, and it would have had to be an awfully big hat. I shook the box. No sound.

"It's fragile, so please be careful with it," the girl cautioned.

"Some kind of souvenir?"

"I don't know. You'll find out when you open it, won't you?"

Then the girl opened her pink handbag and gave me an envelope with a bank check. Filled out for an amount slightly in excess of what I'd expected. I slipped it into my wallet.

"Receipt?"

"No need," she said.

We exited the room and walked the same long maze of corridors back to the elevator. Her high heels made the same pleasant clicking on the floor, but her plumpness didn't make as strong an impression as it had at first. As we walked along together, I almost forgot about her weight. Given time, I'd probably even get used to it.

"Are you married?" she asked, turning to me.

"No, I'm not," I said. "I used to be, but not now."

"Did you get divorced because you became a Calcutec? I always hear how Calcutecs don't have families."

"That's not true. Some Calcutecs are fine family men. Though certainly, most seem to pursue their careers without a home life. It's a nerve-racking line of work, sometimes very risky. You wouldn't want to endanger a wife and kids."

"Is that how it was with you?"

"I became a Calcutec after I got divorced. The two had nothing to do with each other."

"Sorry for prying. It's just that you're my first Calcutec and there're so many things I don't know."

"I don't mind."

"Well then, I've also heard that Calcutecs, when they've

finished a job, that they get all pumped up with sex drive."

"I couldn't . . . umm . . . really say. Maybe so. We do work ourselves into a very peculiar mental condition on the job."

"At those times, who do you sleep with? A special somebody?"

"I don't have 'a special somebody'."

"So then, who do you sleep with? You're not one of those people who have no interest in sex. You're not gay or anything, are you?"

"No, I'm not," I said.

"So who do you sleep with?"

"I guess I sleep with different women."

"Would you sleep with me?"

"No. Probably not."

"Why not?"

"That's just the way I am. I don't like to sleep with people I know. It only complicates things. And I don't sleep with business contacts. Dealing with other people's secrets like I do, you have to draw the line somewhere."

"Are you sure it's not because I'm fat or I'm ugly?"

"Listen, you're not that overweight, and you're not ugly at all," I said.

She pouted. "If that's the way you feel, then, do you simply pick up someone and go to bed with her?"

"Well . . . yes."

"Or do you just buy a girl?"

"I've done that too."

"If I offered to sleep with you for money, would you take me up on it?"

"I don't think so," I replied. "I'm twice your age. It wouldn't be right."

"It'd be different with me."

"Maybe so, but no offense intended, I'd really rather not. I think it's for the best."

"Grandfather says the first man I sleep with should be over thirty. He also says if sex drive builds up to a particular point, it affects your mental stability."

"Yes, I heard this from your grandfather."

"Do you think it's true?"

"I'm afraid I'm not a biologist."

"Are you well endowed?"

"I beg your pardon?" I nearly choked.

"Well, it's just that I don't know anything about my own sex drive yet," she explained. "So I'd like to try lots of different things."

We reached the elevator. It waited with open doors. What a relief!

"Until next time, then," she said.

I got in the elevator and the doors slid shut without a sound. I leaned against the stainless-steel wall and heaved a big sigh.

6

Shadow

THE first old dream she places on the table is nothing I know as an old dream. I stare at the object before me, then look up at her. She stands next to me looking down at it. How is this an "old dream"? The sound of the words "old dream" led me to expect something else—old writings perhaps, something hazy, amorphous.

"Here we have an old dream," says the Librarian. Her voice is distant, aimless; her tone wants not so much to explain to me as to reconfirm for herself. "Or it is possible to say, the old dream is inside of this."

I nod, but do not understand.

"Take it in your hands," she prompts.

I pick it up and run my eyes over the surface to see if I can find some trace of an old dream. But there is not a clue. It is only the skull of an animal, and not a very big animal. Dry and brittle, as if it had lain in the sun for years, the bone matter is leached of whatever color it might originally have had. The jutting jaw is locked slightly open, as if suddenly frozen when about to speak. The eye sockets, long bereft of their contents, lead to the cavernous recesses behind.

The skull is unnaturally light, with virtually no material presence. Nor does it offer any image of the species that had breathed within. It is stripped of flesh, warmth, memory. In the middle of the forehead is a small depression, rough to the touch. Perhaps this is the vestige of a broken horn.

"Is this a skull of one of the Town unicorns?" I ask her.

"Yes. The old dream is sealed inside."

"I am to read an old dream from this?"

"That is the work of the Dreamreader," says the Librarian.

"And what do I do with the dreams I read?"

"Nothing. You have only to read them."

"How can that be?" I say. "I know that I am to read an old dream from this. But then not to do anything with it, I do not understand. What can be the point of that? Work should have a purpose."

She shakes her head. "I cannot explain. Perhaps the dreamreading will tell you. I can only show you how it is done."

I set the skull down on the table and lean back to look at it. The skull is enveloped in a profound silence that seems nothingness itself. The silence does not reside on the surface, but is held like smoke within. It is unfathomable, eternal, a disembodied vision cast upon a point in the void.

There is a sadness about it, an inherent pathos. I have no words for it.

"Please show me," I say. I pick the skull up from the table once again and feel its weight in my hands.

Smiling faintly, she takes the skull from me and painstakingly wipes off the dust. She returns a whiter skull to the table.

"This is how to read old dreams," the Librarian begins.

"Watch carefully. Yet please know I can only imitate, I cannot actually read. You are the only one who can read the dreams. First, turn the skull to face you in this way, then gently place your hands on either side."

She touches her fingertips to the temples of the skull.

"Now gaze at the forehead. Do not force a stare, but focus softly. You must not take your eyes from the skull. No matter how brilliant, you must not look away."

"Brilliant?"

"Yes, brilliant. Before your eyes, the skull will glow and give off heat. Trace that light with your fingertips. That is how old dreams are read."

I go over the procedure in my head. It is true that I cannot picture what kind of light she means or how it should feel, but I understand the method. Looking at the skull beneath her slender fingers, I am overcome with a strong sense of déjà vu. Have I seen this skull before? The leached colorlessness, the depression in the forehead. I feel a humming, just as when I first saw her face. Is this a fragment of a real memory or has time folded back on itself? I cannot tell.

"What is wrong?" she asks.

I shake my head. "Nothing. I think I see how. Let me try."

"Perhaps we should eat first," she says. "Once you begin to work, there will not be time."

She brings out a pot of vegetable stew and warms it on the stove. The minestra simmers, filling the room with a wonderful aroma. She ladles it out into two bowls, slices walnut bread, and brings this simple fare to the table.

We sit facing each other and speak not a word as we eat. The seasoning is unlike anything I have ever tasted, but good nonetheless. By the time I finish eating, I am warmed inside. Then she brings us cups of hot tea. It is an herbal infusion, slightly bitter and green.

Dreamreading proves not as effortless as she has explained. The threads of light are so fine that despite how I concentrate the energies in my fingertips, I am incapable of unravelling the chaos of vision. Even so, I clearly sense the presence of dreams at my fingertips. It is a busy current, an endless stream of images. My fingers are as yet unable to grasp any distinct message, but I do apprehend an intensity there.

By the time I finally manage to extract two dreams, it is already past ten o'clock. I return to her the dream-spent skull, take off my glasses, and rub my eyes.

"Are you tired?" she asks.

"A little," I reply. "My eyes are not accustomed to this. Drinking in the light of the old dreams makes my eyes hurt. I cannot look too long for the pain."

"I am told it is this way at first," she says. "Your eyes are not used to the light; the readings are difficult. Work slowly for a while."

Returning the old dream to the vaults, the Librarian prepares to go home. She opens the lid of the stove, scoops out the red coals with a tiny shovel, and deposits them in a bucket of sand.

"You must not let fatigue set in," she warns. "That is what my mother said. Let your body work until it is spent, but keep your mind for yourself."

"Good advice."

"To tell the truth, I do not know this thing called 'mind', what it does or how to use it. It is only a word I have heard."

"The mind is nothing you use," I say. "The mind is just there. It is like the wind. You simply feel its movements."

She shuts the lid of the stove, takes away the enamel pot and cup to wash, and returns wrapped in a blue coat of coarse material. A remnant torn from a bolt of the sky, worn so many years that it too has lost memory of its origins. She stands, absorbed in thought, in front of the extinguished stove.

"Did you come from some other land?" she asks, as if the thought had only then occurred to her.

"I think so."

"And what was that land like?"

"I cannot remember," I say. "I cannot recall a single thing. They seem to have taken all memory of my old world when they took my shadow. I only know it was far, far away."

"But you understand these things of mind?"

"A little."

"My mother also had mind," she says. "But my mother disappeared when I was seven. Perhaps it was because she had this mind, the same as you."

"Disappeared?"

"Yes, she vanished. I do not want to talk about it. It is wrong to talk about people who have disappeared. Tell me about the town where you lived. You must remember something."

"I can only remember two things," I say. "That the town I lived in had no wall around it, and that our shadows followed us wherever we walked."

Yes, we all had shadows. They were with us constantly. But when I came to this Town, my shadow was taken away.

"You cannot come into Town with that," said the Gatekeeper. "Either you lose the shadow or forget about coming inside."

I surrendered my shadow.

The Gatekeeper had me stand in an open space beside the Gate. The three-o'clock afternoon sun fixed my shadow fast to the ground.

"Keep still now," the Gatekeeper told me. Then he produced a knife and deftly worked it in between the shadow and the ground. The shadow writhed in resistance. But to no avail. Its dark form peeled neatly away.

Severed from the body, it was an altogether poorer thing. It lost strength.

The Gatekeeper put away his blade. "What do you make of it? Strange thing once you cut it off," he said. "Shadows are useless anyway. Deadweight."

I drew near the shadow. "Sorry, I must leave you for now," I said. "It was not my idea. I had no choice. Can you accept being alone for a while?"

"A while? Until when?" asked the shadow.

I did not know.

"Sure you won't regret this later?" said the shadow in a hushed voice. "It's wrong, I tell you. There's something wrong with this place. People can't live without their shadows, and shadows can't live without people. Yet they're splitting us apart. I don't like it. There's something wrong here."

But it was too late. My shadow and I were already torn apart.

"Once I am settled in, I will be back for you," I said. "This is only temporary, not forever. We will be back together again."

The shadow sighed weakly, and looked up at me. The sun was bearing down on us both. Me without my shadow, my shadow without me.

"That's just wishful thinking," said the shadow. "I don't like this place. We have to escape and go back to where we came from, the two of us."

"How can we return? We do not know the way back."

"Not yet, but I'll find out if it's the last thing I do. We need to meet and talk regularly. You'll come, won't you?"

I nodded and put my hand on my shadow's shoulder, then returned to the Gatekeeper. While the shadow and I were talking, the Gatekeeper had been gathering up stray rocks and flinging them away.

As I approached, the Gatekeeper brushed the dust from his hands on his shirttails and threw a big arm around me. Whether this was intended as a sign of welcome or to draw my attention to his strength, I could not be certain.

"Trust me. Your shadow is in good hands," said the Gatekeeper. "We give it three meals a day, let it out once a day for exercise. Nothing to worry about."

"Can I see him from time to time?"

"Maybe," said the Gatekeeper. "If I feel like letting you, that is."

"And what would I have to do if I wanted my shadow back?"

"I swear, you are blind. Look around," said the Gatekeeper, his arm plastered to my back. "Nobody has a shadow in this Town, and anybody we let in never leaves. Your question is meaningless."

So it was I lost my shadow.

Leaving the Library, I offer to walk her home.

"No need to see me to my door," she says. "I am not frightened of the night, and your house is far in the opposite direction."

"I want to walk with you," I say. "Even if I went straight home, I would not sleep."

We walk side-by-side over the Old Bridge to the south. On the sandbar midstream, the willows sway in the chill spring breeze. A hard-edged moon shines down on the cobblestones at our feet. The air is damp, the ground slick. Her long hair is tied with twine and pulled around to tuck inside her coat.

"Your hair is very beautiful," I say.

"Is it?" she says.

"Has anyone ever complimented you on your hair before?"

"No," she says, looking at me, her hands in her pockets. "When you speak of my hair, are you also speaking about something in you?"

"Am I? It was just a simple statement."

She smiles briefly. "I am sorry. I suppose I am unused to your way of speaking."

Her home is in the Workers' Quarter, an area in disrepair at the southwest corner of the Industrial Sector. The whole of this district is singularly desolate. No doubt the Canals once conducted a brisk traffic of barges and launches, where now-stopped sluices expose dry channel beds, mud shriveling like the skin of a prehistoric organism. Weeds have rooted in cracks of the loading docks, broad stone steps descending to where the waterline once was. Old bottles and rusted machine parts poke up through the mire; a flat-bottom boat slowly rots nearby.

Along the Canals stand rows of empty factories. Their gates are shut, windowpanes are missing, handrails have rusted off fire escapes, walls a tangle of ivy.

Past these factory rows is the Workers' Quarter. Betraying a former opulence, the estate is a confusion of subdivided rooms parceled out to a mass occupation of impoverished laborers. Even now, she explains, the laborers have no trade to practice. The factories have closed, leaving the disowned with a meager livelihood, making small artifacts for the Town. Her father had been one of these craftsmen.

Crossing a short stone bridge over the last canal brings us to the precinct of her housing block. A nexus of passageways, like medieval battlements, entrenches the cramped grounds between one building and the next.

The hour approaches midnight. All but a few windows are dark. She takes me by the hand and leads me through this maze as if trying to evade predatory eyes. She stops in front of one building and bids me good-night.

"Good-night," I say.

Whereupon I climb the slope of the Western Hill alone and return to my own lodgings.

7

Skull, Lauren Bacall,
Library

OUTSIDE it was dark, it was drizzling, and the streets were filled with people going home from work. It took forever to catch a cab.

Even under usual circumstances I have a hard time catching cabs. By which I should explain that in order to avoid potentially dangerous situations, I make a point of not taking the first two empty cabs that come my way. The Semiotecs had fake taxis, and you sometimes heard about them swooping off with a Calcutec who'd just finished a job. Of course, these might have been rumors, since I don't know anyone it actually happened to. Still, you can't be too careful.

That's why I always take the subway or bus. But this time I was so tired and drowsy that I couldn't face the prospect of cramming into a rush-hour train. I decided to take a taxi, even if it took longer. Once in the cab, I nearly dozed off several times and panicked to false alert. As soon as I got home to my own bed, I could sleep to my heart's content. A cab was no place to sleep.

To keep myself awake, I concentrated on the baseball game being broadcast on the cab radio. I don't follow baseball, so for convenience sake I rooted for the team currently at bat and against the team in the field. My team was behind, 3–1. It was two outs with a man on second base when there was a hit, but the runner stumbled between second and third, ending the side without a run. The sportscaster called it rotten playing, and even I thought so too. Sure, anyone can take a spill, but you don't stumble between second and third in the middle of a baseball game. This blunder apparently so fazed my team's pitcher that he threw the opponent's lead-off batter an easy ball down the middle, which the guy walloped into the left-field bleachers for a home run.

When the taxi reached my apartment, the score was 4–1. I paid the fare, collected my hatbox and foggy brain, and got out. The drizzle had almost stopped.

There wasn't a speck of mail in the mailbox. Nor any message on the answering machine. No one had any business with me, it seemed. Fine. I had no business with anyone else either. I took some ice out of the freezer, poured myself a large quantity of whiskey, and added a splash of soda. Then I got undressed and, crawling under the covers, sat up in bed and sipped my drink. I felt like I was going to fade out any second, but I had to allow myself this luxury. A ritual interlude I like so much between the time I get into bed and the time I fall asleep. Having a drink in bed while listening to music and reading a book. As precious to me as a beautiful sunset or good clean air.

I'd finished half my whiskey when the telephone rang. The telephone was perched on a round table two meters away from the foot of the bed. I wasn't about to leave my nice warm bed and walk all the way over to it, so I simply watched the thing ring. Thirteen rings, fourteen rings, what did I care? If this had been a cartoon, the telephone would be vibrating midair, but of course that wasn't happening. The telephone remained humbly on the table ringing on and on. I drank my whiskey and just looked at it.

Next to the telephone were my wallet and knife—and that gift hatbox. It occurred to me that I should open it. Maybe it was something perishable that I should put in the refrigerator, something living, or even something "urgent". But I was too tired. Besides, if any of the above had been the giver's intention, you would think he'd have told me about it. When the telephone stopped ringing, I bottomed-up my whiskey, turned off the bedside light, and shut my eyes. A huge black net of sleep that had been poised in ambush fell over me. As I drifted off, I thought, do you really expect me to know what's going on?

When at last I awoke, it was half light out. The clock read six-fifteen, but I couldn't tell whether it was morning or evening. I pulled on a pair of slacks and leaned out my door to check the neighbor's doormat. The morning edition was lying there, which led me to conclude it was morning. Subscribing to a paper comes in handy at times like this. Maybe I ought to.

So I'd slept ten hours. My body still craved rest. With nothing particular that required my attention for the day, I could happily have gone back to bed. But on second thought, I got up. Rise and shine with the sun, I always say. I took a shower, scrubbing my body well, and shaved. I did my usual twenty-five minutes of calisthenics. I threw together breakfast.

The refrigerator was all but plundered of its contents. Time to restock. I sat down with my orange juice and wrote out a shopping list. It filled up one page and spilled over onto a second.

I dumped my dirty clothes into the washing machine and was busily brushing off my tennis shoes at the sink when I remembered the old man's mystery present. Dropping the shoes, I washed my hands and went to get the hatbox. Light as ever for its bulk—a nasty lightness somehow. Lighter than it had any need to be.

Something put me on edge. Call it occupational intuition. I did a quick scan of the room. It was unnervingly quiet. Almost sound-removed. But my test cough did sound like a cough. And when I flicked open my spring-action knife and whacked the handle on the table, the noise was right. Having experienced sound-removal, I had gotten suspicious. I opened a window onto the balcony. I could hear cars and birds. What a relief. Evolution or no evolution, a world ought to have sound.

I cut the tape, careful not to damage the contents of the box. On top was crumpled newspaper. I spread open a few sheets—the *Mainichi Shimbun*, three weeks old, no news of note. I crumpled the pages up again and tossed them away. There must have been two weeks' worth of wadded newspapers in the box, all of them *Mainichi*. With the newspapers out of the way, I now found a layer of those—polyethylene? styrofoam?—those pinkie-sized wormoids they use for packing. I scooped them up and into the garbage they went. This was getting to be one chore of a present. With half the plastic cheez puffs out of the way, there surfaced an item wrapped in more newspaper.

I didn't like the look of it. I went into the kitchen and returned with a can of Coke. I sat on the edge of the bed and drank the whole thing. I trimmed a fingernail. A black-breasted bird appeared on the balcony and hopped around on the deck table, pecking spryly at some crumbs. A peaceful morning scene.

Eventually, I turned my attention back to the newspaper-wrapped object and gently removed it from the box. The newspaper was wound with further orbits of tape, looking very much like a piece of contemporary art. An elongated watermelon in shape, though again, with hardly any weight to it. I cleared the table and undid the tape and newspaper.

It was an animal skull.

Great, I thought, just great. Did the old duffer really imagine I'd be overjoyed to receive this? He had to have a screw loose, giving a skull for a present.

The skull was similar to a horse's in shape, but considerably smaller. From my limited knowledge of biology, I deduced that the skull had been attached to the shoulders of a narrow-faced, hoofed, herbivorous, and not overly large species of mammal. Let's see now. I checked my mental catalogue of animals matching that description. Deer, goat, sheep, donkey, antelope, . . . I couldn't remember any others.

I placed the skull on top of the TV. Very stylish. If I were Ernest Hemingway, I'd have put it over the mantle, next to the moose head. But my apartment, of course, had no fireplace. No fireplace and no sideboard, not even a coat closet. So on top of the TV it was.

I dumped the rest of the packing material into the trash. There at the bottom of the box was a long object rolled up in newspaper. Unwrapping it, I found a pair of stainless-steel fire tongs exactly like the ones the old man had used on his skull collection. I was reminded of the ivory baton of a Berlin Philharmonic conductor.

"All right, all right, I'll play along," I said out loud. I went over to the skull on the TV and tapped it on the forehead. Out came a *mo-oan* like the nasal whine of a large dog. Not the hard clunk that I expected. Odd, yes, but nothing to get upset about. If that whiny moan was the noise it made, who was I to argue?

Tapping the skull got old quick. I sat down and dialed the System to check my schedule. My rep answered and told me he'd penciled in a job four days hence, was that okay? No problem, I told him. I thought about verifying the shuffling clearance, but decided not to. It would have entailed a lot of extra talk. The papers were all in order, the remuneration already squared away. Besides, the old man said he'd avoided going through agents to keep things secret. Better not complicate matters.

Added to which, I was none too enthused with my rep. Tall, trim, thirtyish, the type who thinks he's on top of everything. I try my best to avoid talking with guys like that any more than I have to.

I finished my business and hung up, then went into the living room and relaxed on the sofa with a beer to watch a video of Humphrey Bogart's *Key Largo*. I love Lauren Bacall in *Key Largo*. Of course, I love Bacall in *The Big Sleep* too, but in *Key Largo* she's practically allegorical.

Watching the TV screen, my eyes just naturally drifted up to the animal skull resting on top. Which robbed me of my usual concentration. I stopped the video where the hurricane hits, promising myself to see the rest later, and kicked back with the beer, gazing blankly at the item atop the TV. I got the sneaking suspicion that I'd seen the skull before. But where? And how? I pulled a T-shirt out of a drawer and threw it over the skull so I could finish watching *Key Largo*. Finally, I could concentrate on Lauren Bacall.

At eleven o'clock, I left the apartment, headed for the supermarket near the station, stopping next at the liquor store for some red wine, soda water, and orange juice. At the cleaners I claimed a jacket and two shirts; at the stationery shop I purchased a pen, envelopes, and letter paper; at the hardware store, the finest-grain whetstone in the place. Then to the bookshop for two magazines, the electrical goods store for light bulbs and cassette tapes, the photo store for a pack of Polaroid film. Last, it was the record shop, where I picked out a few disks. By now, the whole back seat of my tiny coupé was taken up with shopping bags. I must be a born shopper. Every time I go to town, I come back, like a squirrel in November, with mounds of little things.

Even the car I drove was purely for shopping. I only bought it because I was already buying too much stuff to carry home by myself. I was lugging a shopping bag when I happened to pass a used-car dealer and went in and saw all the different cars they had. Now I'm not particulary crazy about cars, nor do I know much about them. So I said simply: "I want a car, any make, nothing fancy, nothing big."

The middle-aged salesman started to pull out a catalog, but I didn't want to look at any catalog. I only wanted a car for shopping, I told the guy, pure and simple. It didn't need go fast for the highway, didn't need to look smart for dates. No family outings either. I had no use for a high-performance engine or air-conditioning. No car stereo, no sun roof, no super radials. All I wanted was a decent compact that cornered well, didn't belch exhaust, wasn't too noisy, and wouldn't break down on me. And if it came in dark blue, so much the better.

The car the guy showed me was yellow. I didn't think much of the color, but otherwise it was just what I described. And because it was an old model, the price was right.

"This is how cars were meant to be," said the salesman. "If you really want to know, I think people are nuts."

No argument from me.

That's how I came to own my shopping car.

I wound up my purchases and pulled into my convenient neighborhood fast-food restaurant. I ordered shrimp salad, onion rings, and a beer. The shrimp were straight out of the freezer, the onion rings soggy. Looking around the place, though, I failed to spot a single customer banging on a tray or complaining to a waitress. So I shut up and finished my food. Expect nothing, get nothing.

From the restaurant window I could see the expressway, with cars of all makes, colors, and styles barrelling along. I remembered the jolly old man and his chubby granddaughter. No matter how much I liked them, I couldn't help thinking they had to be living in the outer limits. That inane elevator, the open pit in the back of a closet, INKlings, and sound removal—I wouldn't believe it in a novel. And then, they give me an animal skull as a memento.

Waiting for my after-meal coffee, I thought about the chubby girl. I thought about her square earrings and pink suit and pink high heels. I thought about her body, her calves and the flesh around her neck and the build of her face and . . . well, things like that. I could recall each detail with alarming clarity, yet the composite was indistinct. Curious. Maybe it was because I hadn't slept with an overweight woman in a while that I just couldn't picture a heavyset woman in the altogether.

The last time I'd slept with a fat female was the year of the Japanese Red Army shoot-out in Karuizawa. The woman had extraordinary thighs and hips. She was a bank teller who had always exchanged pleasantries with me over the counter. I knew her from the midriff up. We became friendly, went out for a drink once, and ended up sleeping together. Not until we were in bed did I notice that the lower half of her body was so demographically disproportionate. It was because she played table tennis all through school, she had me know, though I didn't quite grasp the causal relationship. I didn't know table tennis led to below-the-belt corporeality.

Still, her plumpness was charming. Resting an ear on her hip was like lying in a meadow on an idyllic spring afternoon, her thighs as soft as freshly aired *futon*, the rolling flow of her curves leading gracefully to her pubis. When I complimented her on her qualities, though, all she said was, "Oh yeah?"

After I left the restaurant, I went to the library nearby. At the reference desk sat a slender young woman with long black hair, engrossed in a paperback book. "Do you have any reference materials pertaining to the mammalian skull?" I asked.

"Huh?" she said, looking up.

"References—on—mammalian—skulls," I repeated, saying each word separately.

"*Mam-ma-li-an-skulls?*" she repeated, almost singing. It sounded so lovely the way she said it, like the first line of a poem.

She bit her lower lip briefly and thought. "Just a minute, please. I'll check," she said, turned around to type the word MAMMAL on her computer keyboard. Some twenty titles appeared on the screen. She used a light pen and two-thirds of the titles disappeared at once. She then hit the MEMORY function, and this time she typed the word SKELETON. Seven or eight titles appeared, of which she saved two and then entered into the MEMORY alongside the previous selections. Libraries have certainly come a long way. The days of card pockets inside the backsleeves of books seemed like a faded dream. As a kid, I used to love all those withdrawal date stamps.

While she was nimbly operating her computer, I was looking down at her long hair and elegant backside. I didn't know exactly what to make of her. She was beautiful and seemingly quite intelligent, what with her pentameter search system. There wasn't a reason in the world not to find her appealing.

She pressed the COPY button for a printout of the screen data, which she handed to me.

"You have nine titles to select from," she said.

1. A GUIDE TO MAMMALS
2. PICTORIAL ATLAS OF MAMMALS
3. THE MAMMALIAN SKELETON
4. THE HISTORY OF MAMMALS
5. I, A MAMMAL
6. MAMMALIAN ANATOMY
7. THE MAMMALIAN BRAIN
8. ANIMAL SKELETONS
9. BONES SPEAK

I had an allowance of three books with my card. I chose nos. 2, 3, and 8. Nos. 5 and 9 did sound intriguing, but they didn't seem to have much to do with my investigation, so I left them for some other time.

"I'm sorry to say that *Pictorial Atlas of Mammals* is for

library use only and cannot be borrowed overnight," she said, scratching her temple with a pen.

"This is extremely important. Please, do you think it would be at all possible to lend it to me for just one day?" I begged. "I'll have it back tomorrow noon, I promise."

"I'm sorry, but the *Pictorial Atlas* series is very popular, and these are library rules. I could get in trouble for lending out reference materials."

"One day. Please. Nobody will find out."

She hesitated, teasing the tip of her tongue between her teeth. A cute pink tongue.

"Okay. But it has to be back here by nine-thirty in the morning."

"Thank you," I said.

"You're welcome," she said.

"Really, I'm very grateful. May I offer you some token of my thanks. Anything special I could do for you?"

"Yes, as a matter of fact. There's a Baskin-Robbins ice cream parlor across the way. I'd love a double cone of mocha chip on top of pistachio. Would you mind?"

"Mocha chip on pistachio—coming right up!"

Whereupon I left the library and headed for the Baskin-Robbins.

She was still not back with the books by the time I returned, so I stood there at her desk with ice cream cone in hand. Two old men reading newspapers took turns stealing looks at this curious sight. Luckily the ice cream was frozen solid. Having it drip all over the place was the only thing that could have made me feel more foolish.

The paperback she'd been reading was face-down on the desk. *Time Traveller*, a biography of H. G. Wells, volume two. It was not a library book. Next to it were three well-sharpened pencils and some paperclips. Paperclips! Everywhere I went, paperclips! What was this?

Perhaps some fluctuation in the gravitational field had suddenly inundated the world with paperclips. Perhaps it was mere coincidence. I couldn't shake the feeling that things weren't normal. Was I being staked out by paperclips? They were everywhere I went, always just a glance away.

Something went ding. Come to think of it, there'd been a couple of dings lately. First animal skulls, now paperclips. It seemed as if a pattern was establishing itself, but what relationship could there be between skulls and paperclips?

Before much longer, the woman returned carrying the three volumes. She handed them to me, accepting the ice cream cone in exchange.

"Thank you very much," she said.

"Thank *you*," I said.

She held the cone low behind the desk. Glimpsed from above, the nape of her neck was sweet and defenseless.

"By the way, though, why all the paperclips?" I asked.

"*Pa-per-clips?*" she sang back. "To keep papers together, of course. Everybody uses them. Don't you?"

She had a point. I thanked her again and left the library. Paperclips were indeed used by everyone. A thousand yen will buy you a lifetime supply. Sure, why not? I stopped into a stationery shop and bought myself a lifetime supply. Then I went home.

Back at the apartment, I put away the groceries. I hung my clothes in the wardrobe. Then, on top of the TV, right next to the skull, I spread a handful of paperclips.

Nice and artsy. Like a composition of down pillow with ice scraper, ink bottle with lettuce. I went out on the balcony to get a better look at my TV-top arrangement. There was nothing to suggest how the skull and the paperclips went together. Or was there?

I sat down on the bed. Nothing came to mind. Time passed. An ambulance, then a right-wing campaign sound-truck passed. I wanted a whiskey, but I passed on that too. I needed to have my brain absolutely sharp.

I went to the kitchen and sat down with the library books. First I looked up medium-sized herbivorous mammals and their skeletal structures. The world had far more medium-sized herbivorous mammals than I'd imagined. No fewer than thirty varieties of deer alone.

I fetched the skull from the TV, set it on the table, and began the long, laborious process of comparing it with each of the pictures in the books. One hour and twenty minutes and ninety-three species later, I had made no progress. I shut all three books and piled them up in one corner of the table. Then I threw up my arms and stretched.

What to do?

Put on a video of John Ford's *Quiet Man*.

I was sprawled on the bed, hash-browned, when the doorbell rang. I looked through the peephole and saw a middle-aged man in a Tokyo Gas uniform. I cracked open the door with the chain still bolted.

"Routine safety check," said the man.

"One moment please," I replied, slipping into the bedroom to pocket my knife before opening the door. I smelled something fishy. There'd been a gas inspector visit the month before.

I let the guy in and went on watching *The Quiet Man*. The inspector pulled out a pressure gauge and proceeded to check the water heater for the bath, then went into the kitchen where the skull was sitting on the table. I left the TV on and tiptoed to the kitchen in time to catch him whisking the skull into a black plastic bag. I flicked open my knife and dived at him, circling around to clamp him in an armlock, the blade thrust right under his nose. The man immediately threw the bag down.

"I . . . I didn't mean any harm," he stammered. "I just saw the thing and suddenly wanted it. A sudden impulse. Forgive me."

"Like hell," I sneered. "Tell me the truth or I'll slit your throat," I said. It sounded unbelievably phony—especially since the knife wasn't under his chin—but the man was convinced.

"Okay, okay, don't hurt me. I'll tell the truth," he whimpered. "The truth is, I got paid to come in here and steal the thing. Two guys came up to me on the street and asked if I wanted to make a quick fifty-thousand yen. If I came through, I'd get another fifty thousand. I didn't want to do it, but one of the guys was a gorilla. Honest. Please, don't kill me. I've got two daughters in high school."

"Two daughters in high school?"

"Y . . . yeah."

"Which high school?"

"The older one's a junior at Shimura Metropolitan. The younger one just started at Futaba in Yotsuya," he said.

The combination was odd enough to be real. I decided to believe him.

As a precaution, I fished the man's wallet out of his pocket and checked its contents. Five crisp ten-thousand-yen bills. Also a Tokyo Gas ID and a color photo of his family. Both daughters were done up in fancy New Year's *kimono*, neither of them exactly a beauty. I couldn't tell which was Shimura and which Futaba. Other than that, there was only a Sugamo-Shinanomachi train pass. The guy looked harmless, so I folded the knife up and let him go.

"All right, get out of here," I said, handing back his wallet.

"Thank you, thank you," the gas inspector said. "But what do I do now? I took their money but didn't come through with the goods."

I had no idea. Those Semiotecs—I'm sure that's who they were—weren't what you could call gentlemen. They did whatever they felt like, whenever. Which is why no one could read their modus operandi. They might gouge this guy's eyes out, or they might hand him the other fifty thousand yen and wish him better luck next time.

"One guy's a real gorilla, you say?" I asked.

"That's right. A monster. The other guy's small, only about a meter and a half; he was wearing a tailor-made suit. Both looked like very tough characters."

I instructed the man to leave the building through the

parking garage. There was a narrow passage out back, which was not easy to detect. Probably he'd get away without incident.

"Thank you very much," said the gas inspector. "Please don't tell my company about this."

Fine, I told him. Then I pushed him out, locked the door, and bolted the chain. I went into the kitchen and removed the skull from the plastic bag. Well, at least I'd learned one thing: the Semiotecs wanted the skull.

I considered the circumstances. I had the skull, but didn't know what it meant. They knew what it meant—or had a vague notion of what it meant—but didn't have the skull. Even-steven. At this point, I had two options: one, explain everything to the System, so they'd protect me from the Semiotecs and safeguard the skull; or two, contact the chubby girl and get the lowdown on the skull.

I didn't like option no. 1. There'd be pointless debriefings and investigations. Huge organizations and me don't get along. They're too inflexible, waste too much time, have too many stupid people.

Option no. 2, however, was impossible. I didn't know how to go about contacting the chubby girl. I didn't have her phone number. Of course, I could have gone to the building, but leaving my own apartment now was dangerous. And how was I going to talk my way into that top-security building?

I made up my mind: I would do nothing.

I picked up the stainless-steel tongs and once again tapped the crown of the skull lightly. It made the same *mo-oan* as before. A hollow, pathetic cry, almost as if it were alive. How was this possible? I picked up the skull. I tapped it again. That *mo-oan* again. Upon closer scrutiny, the sound seemed to emanate from one particular point on the skull.

I tapped again and again, and eventually located the exact position. The moaning issued from a shallow depression of about two centimeters in diameter in the center of the forehead. I pressed my fingertip into the depression. It felt slightly rough. Almost as if something had been broken off. Something, say, like a horn . . .

A horn?

If it really were a horn, that'd make it a one-horned animal. A one-horned animal? I flipped through the *Pictorial Atlas of Mammals* again, looking for any mammal with a single horn in the middle of its forehead. The rhinoceros was a possibility, but this was not a rhinoceros skull. Wrong size, wrong shape.

I got some ice out of the refrigerator and poured myself an Old Crow. It was getting late in the day, and a drink seemed like a good idea. I opened a can of asparagus, which I happen to like. I canapéed some smoked oysters on crispbread. I had another whiskey.

Okay. For convenience sake, I agreed to entertain the remote hypothesis that the owner of said skull might be, conceivably, a unicorn.

What else did I have to go on?

I had a unicorn skull on my hands.

Great, I thought, just great. Why were all these bizarre things happening to me? What had I ever done to deserve this? I was just your practical-minded, lone-wolf Calcutec. I wasn't overly ambitious, wasn't greedy. Didn't have family, friends, or lovers. I saved my money. When I retired, I was planning to settle down and learn the cello or Greek. How on earth did I get mixed up in this?

After that second whiskey, I opened the telephone book and dialed the number. "Reference desk, please," I said.

Ten seconds later, the long-haired librarian was on the line.

"*Pictorial Atlas of Mammals* here," I said.

"Hello. Thank you for the ice cream," she said.

"You're welcome," I said. "But could I ask you for another favor?"

"A favor?" she said. "Depends on the species of favor."

"Can you look up what you've got on unicorns?"

"*U-ni-corns?*" she repeated.

"Is that too much to ask?"

Silence. She was probably biting her lip.

"You want me to look up *what* about unicorns?"

"Everything," I said.

"Please, it's four-fifteen. The library gets very busy around closing time. Why don't you come around first thing tomorrow morning? Then you could look up all about unicorns or tricorns or whatever you like."

"This can't wait. I'm afraid it's exceedingly urgent."

"Oh, really?" she said. "How urgent?"

"It's a matter of evolution," I said.

"*E-vo-lu-ti-on?*" She seemed to be caught off guard. "By evolution, you wouldn't be referring to the evolving-over-millions-of-years kind of evolution, would you? Excuse me if I misunderstand, but why then do you need things so quickly? What's one more day?"

"There's evolution that takes millions of years and there's evolution that only takes three hours. I can't explain over the phone. But I want you to believe me, this is dead urgent. This will affect the next step in human evolution."

"Like in *2001: A Space Odyssey?*"

"Exactly," I said. I'd watched it countless times on video.

She didn't say anything.

"Can't decide if I'm some kind of a maniac or a harmless nut?" I took a shot.

"You got it," she said.

"I don't know how I'm going to convince you, but I'm really not crazy. A little narrow-minded or stubborn maybe, but crazy I'm not."

"Hmph," was all she said to that. "Well, you talk normal enough. And you didn't seem too weird. You even bought me ice cream. All right, at six-thirty, meet me at the café across from the library. I'll bring you the books. Fair enough?"

"Unfortunately, it's not so simple. I, uh, can't go into details, but I can't leave my place unattended just now. Sorry, but—"

"You mean. . . ," she trailed off. I could her hear drumming her front teeth with her nails. "Let me get this straight. You want me—to bring the books—to your doorstep? You must be crazy."

"That's the general idea," I said sheepishly. "Though, of course, I'm not demanding. I'm requesting."

"You're requesting an awful lot."

"I know, I know," I said. "But you wouldn't believe what's been going on."

Another lengthy silence.

"I've worked in this library for five years now and never have I come across any borrower as impudent as you," she fumed. "Nobody asks to have books hand-delivered. And with no previous record! Don't you think you're being just a little high-handed?"

"Actually, I do think so, too. I'm very sorry. I realize it's highly irregular, but I have no other choice."

"I don't know why I'm doing this," she said, "but I don't suppose you'd want to tell me the way to your place?"

8

The Colonel

I DOUBT you can regain your shadow," speaks the Colonel as he sips his coffee.

Like most persons accustomed to years of giving orders, he speaks with his spine straight and his chin tucked in. It is greatly to his credit that his long career in the military has not made him officious. Rather, it has bestowed an order to his life, along with many decorations. Exceedingly quiet and thoughtful, the Colonel is an ideal neighbor for me. He is also a veteran chessplayer.

"As the Gatekeeper warned you," the old officer continues, "one of the conditions of this Town is that you cannot possess a shadow. Another is that you cannot leave. Not as long as the Wall surrounds the Town."

"I did not know I would forfeit my shadow forever," I say. "I thought it would be temporary. No one told me about this."

"No one tells you anything in this Town," says the Colonel. "The Town has its own protocol. It has no care for what you know or do not know. Regrettable . . ."

"What will become of my shadow?"

"Nothing at all. It waits and then it dies. Have you seen it since your arrival?"

"No. I tried several times and the Gatekeeper turned me away. For security reasons, he said."

"Predictable," the Colonel says, shaking his head. "The Gatekeeper is entrusted with the care of shadows. He shoulders the entire responsibility. The Gatekeeper can be a difficult man; harsh when not called for, blind to his own faults. Your only move is to wait for his mood to change."

"Then I will wait," I say. "Yet what does he have to fear from me?"

The Colonel finishes his coffee, then takes out a handkerchief to wipe his mouth. The white square of cloth, like his uniform, is worn but clean and pressed.

"He fears that you and your shadow will become one again."

At that, he returns his attention to the chessboard. This chess differs from the game I know in its pieces and their movements. Hence the old officer always wins.

"Ape takes High Priest, you realize?"

"Go ahead," I say. I move a Parapet to cover the Ape's retreat.

The Colonel nods, then glares again at the board. The tides of fortune have almost swept victory to the old officer's feet. Even so, he does not rush into the fray as he compounds strategem upon strategem. For him, the game is not to defeat the opponent, but to challenge his own abilities.

"It is not easy to surrender your shadow and simply let it die," he says, deftly maneuvering his Knight between the Parapet and my King. This leaves my King vulnerable. He will have checkmate in three moves.

"No, it is not easy," stresses the Colonel. "The pain is the same for everyone, though it is one thing to tear the shadow away from an innocent child who has not gotten attached to it, and quite another to do it to an old fool. I was in my sixty-fifth year when they put my shadow to death. By that age we already had had a lifetime together."

"How long do shadows live once they have been torn away?"

"That depends on the shadow," says the old officer. "Some shadows are fit and some are not. In this Town, severed shadows do not live long. The climate is harsh and the winters long. Few shadows live to see the spring."

I study the chessboard and concede defeat.

"You can gain yourself five moves," says the Colonel. "Worth fighting to the end. In five moves your opponent can err. No war is won or lost until the final battle is over."

"Then give me a moment," I say.

While I reassess my options, the Colonel walks over to the window and parts the thick curtains slightly to peer out.

"These few weeks will be the hardest for you. It is the same as with broken bones. Until they set, you cannot do anything. Believe me."

"You mean to say I am anxious because my shadow still is not dead?"

"I do," the old officer nods. "I, too, remember the feeling. You are caught between all that was and all that must be. You feel lost. Mark my words: as soon as the bones mend, you will forget about the fracture."

"You mean to say, as soon as my mind vanishes?"

The Colonel does not answer.

"Excuse me for asking so many questions," I say. "I know nothing about this Town. How it works, why it needs the Wall, why the beasts are herded in and out every day. I do not understand any of it. You are the only one I can ask."

"Not even I know all the rules," says the old officer under his breath. "There are things that cannot and should not be explained. But there is no cause for concern. The Town is fair in its own way. The things you need, the things you need to know, one by one the Town will set these before you. Hear me now: this Town is perfect. And by perfect, I mean complete. It has everything. If you cannot see that, then it has nothing. A perfect nothing. Remember this well. That is as much as anyone can tell you; the rest you must learn for yourself. Open your eyes, train your ears, use your head. If a mind you have, then use it while you can."

If the Workers' Quarter, where the Librarian lives, is a place of past brilliance, then the Bureaucratic Quarter, which spreads to the southwest, is a place of color fading into parched light. Here, the spectacle of spring has dissolved into summer, only to be eroded by the winter winds. All along the gentle slope known as the Western Hill stand rows of two-story Official Residences. The buildings, originally three-family dwellings with common entrance halls, are painted white. The siding and doors and window frames—every detail is white. None of the these Official Residences have hedges, only narrow flower beds below tiny porches. The flower beds are carefully tended, with plantings of crocus and pansy and marigold in spring, cosmos in autumn. The flowers in bloom make the buildings look all the more tawdry.

Strolling the Hill, one can imagine its former splendor: children playing gaily in the streets, piano music in the air, warm supper scents. Memories feign through scarcely perceived doors of my being.

Only later did this slope become the Bureaucratic Quarter, which, as the name suggests, was an area for government officials, undistinguished ranks of officialdom lodged in mediocrity. They too have gone, but to where?

After the bureaucrats came the retired military. Surrendering their shadows, cast off like molted insect shells, each pursues his own end on the windswept Western Hill. With little left to protect, they live a half dozen old majordomos to a house.

The Gatekeeper indicated that I was to find my room in one of these Official Residences. My cohabitants proved to be the Colonel, four commissioned officers under him, and a sergeant, who cooks the meals and does the chores. The Colonel passes judgment on everything, as was his duty in the army. These career soldiers have known numerous battle preparations and maneuvers, revolutions and counterrevolutions and outright wars. They who had never wanted family are now lonely old men.

Rising early each morning, they charge through breakfast before going their own way, as if by tacit order, to their respective tasks. One scrapes peeling paint from the building, one repairs furniture, one takes a wagon down the Hill to haul food rations back up. Their morning duties done, they reassemble to spend the rest of the day sitting in the sun, reminiscing about past campaigns.

The room assigned to me is on the upper story facing east. The view is largely blocked by hills in the foreground, although I can see the River and the Clocktower. The plaster walls of the room are stained, the window sills thick with dust. There is an old bed, a small dining table, and two chairs. The windows are hung with mildewed curtains. The floorboards are badly damaged and creak when I walk.

In the morning, the Colonel appears from the adjacent room. We eat breakfast together, then repair to a dark, curtained room for a session of chess. There is no other way to pass the daylight hours.

"It must be frustrating. A young man like you should not be shut indoors on such a beautiful day," says the Colonel.

"I think so too."

"Though I must say, I appreciate gaining a chess companion. The rest of the men have no interest in games. I suppose I am the only one with any desire to play chess at this late date."

"Tell me, why did you give up your shadow?"

The old officer examines his fingers, sun-strafed against the curtains, before leaving the window to reinstall himself across the table.

"I wish I could say. It may have been that I spent so long defending this Town I could not walk away. If I left, my whole life would have been for nothing. Of course, it makes no difference now."

"Do you ever regret giving up your shadow?"

"I have no regrets," speaks the old officer, shaking his head. "I never do anything regrettable."

I crush his Ape with my Parapet, creating an opening for my King.

"Good move," says the Colonel. "Parapet guards against penetration and frees up the King. At the same time, it allows my Knight greater range."

While the old officer contemplates his next move, I boil water for a new pot of coffee.

9

Appetite, Disappointment, Leningrad

WHILE I waited for her, I fixed supper. I mashed an *umeboshi* salt plum with mortar and pestle to make a sour-sweet dressing; I fried up a few sardines with *abura-agé* tofu-puffs in grated *yama-imo* taro batter; I sautéed a celery-beef side dish. Not a bad little meal.

There was time to spare, so I had a beer as I tossed together some soy-simmered *myoga* wild ginger and green beans with tofu-sesame sauce. After which I stretched out on my bed, gazed at the ceiling, and listened to old records.

The hour was well past seven, and outside it was quite dark. But still no sign of her. Maybe she thought better of the whole proposition and decided not to come. Could I blame her? The reasonable thing would have been not to come.

Yet, as I was choosing the next record, the doorbell rang. I checked through the fisheye lens, and there stood the woman from the library with an armload of books. I opened the door with the chain still in place.

"See anyone milling around in the hall?" I asked.

"Not a soul," she said.

I undid the chain, let her in, and quickly relocked the door.

"Something sure smells good," she said. "Mind if I peek in the kitchen?"

"Go right ahead. But are you sure there weren't any strange characters hanging around the entrance? No one doing street repairs, or just sitting in a parked car?"

"Nothing of the kind," she said, plunking the books down on the kitchen table. Then she lifted the lid of each pot on the range. "You make all this yourself?"

"Sure thing. I can dish some up if you want. Pretty every-day fare, though."

"Not at all. I'm wild about this sort of food."

I set out the dishes on the kitchen table.

We sat down to eat, and I watched awestruck as she, with casual aplomb, lay the entire spread to waste. She had a stunning appetite.

I made myself a big Old Crow on the rocks, flash-broiled a block of *atsu-agé* fried tofu, and topped it with grated *daikon* radish to go along with my drink. I offered her a drink, but she wasn't interested.

"Could I have a bit of that *atsu-agé*, though?" she asked. I pushed the remaining half-block over to her and just drank my bourbon.

"There's rice, if you like. And I can whip up some *miso* soup in a jiff," I said.

"Fabulous!" she exclaimed.

I prepared a *katsuobushi* dried-bonito broth and added *wakame* seaweed and scallions for the *miso* soup. I served it alongside a bowl of rice and *umeboshi*. Again she leveled it all in no time flat. All that remained was a couple of plum pits.

Then she sighed with satisfaction. "Mmm, that was good. My compliments to the chef," she said.

Never in my life had I seen such a slim nothing of a figure eat like such a terror. As the cook, I was gratified, and I had to hand it to her—she'd done the job with a certain all-consuming beauty. I was overwhelmed. And maybe a little disgusted.

"Tell me, do you always eat this much?" I blurted out.

"Why, yes. This is about normal for me," she said, unembarrassed.

"But you're so thin."

"Gastric dilation," she confessed. "It doesn't matter matter how much I eat. I don't gain weight."

"Must run up quite a food bill," I said. Truth was, she'd gastrically dilated her way through tomorrow's dinner in one go.

"It's frightening," she said. "Most of my salary disappears into my stomach."

Once again, I offered her something to drink, and this time she agreed to a beer. I pulled one out from the refrigerator and, just in case, a double ration of frankfurter links, which I tossed into the frying pan. Incredible, but except for the two franks I fended for myself, she polished off the whole lot. A regular machine gun of a hunger, this girl!

As a last resort, I set out ready-made potato salad, then dashed off a quick *wakame*-tuna combo for good measure. Down they went with her second beer.

"Boy, this is heaven!" she purred. I'd hardly touched a thing and was now on my third Old Crow on the rocks.

"While you're at it, there's chocolate cake for dessert," I surrendered. Of course, she indulged. I watched in disbelief, almost seeing the food backing up in her throat.

Probably that was the reason I couldn't get an erection.

It was the first time I hadn't risen to the occasion since the Tokyo Olympic Year.

"It's all right, nothing to get upset about," she tried to comfort me.

After dessert, we'd had another round of bourbon and beer, listened to a few records, then snuggled into bed. And like I said, I didn't get an erection.

Her naked body fit perfectly next to mine. She lay there stroking my chest. "It happens to everyone. You shouldn't get so worked up over it."

But the more she tried to cheer me, the more it only drove home the fact that I'd flopped. Aesthetically, I remembered reading, the flaccid penis is more pleasing than the erect. But somehow, under the circumstances, this was little consolation.

"When was the last time you slept with someone?" she asked.

"Maybe two weeks ago," I said.

"And that time, everything went okay?"

"Of course," I said. Was my sex life to be questioned by everyone these days?

"Your girlfriend?"

"A call girl."

"A call girl? Don't you feel, how shall I put it, guilt?"

"Well . . . no."

"And nothing . . . since then?"

What was this cross-examination? "No," I said. "I've been so busy with work, I haven't had time to pick up my dry-cleaning, much less wank."

"That's probably it," she said, convinced.

"What's probably it?"

"Overwork. I mean, if you were really that busy . . ."

"Maybe so." Maybe it was because I hadn't slept in twenty-six hours the night before.

"What's your line of work?"

"Oh, computer-related business." My standard reply. It wasn't really a lie, and since most people don't know much about computers, they generally don't inquire any further.

"Must involve long hours of brain work. I imagine the

stress just builds up and knocks you temporarily out of service."

That was a kind enough explanation. All this craziness all over the place. Small wonder I wasn't worse than impotent.

"Why don't you put your ear to my tummy," she said, rolling the blanket to the foot of the bed.

Her body was sleek and beautiful. Not a gram of fat, her breasts cautious buds. I placed my ear against the soft, smooth expanse above her navel, which, uncannily, betrayed not the least sign of the quantities of food within. It was like that magic coat of Harpo Marx, devouring everything in sight.

"Hear anything?" she asked.

I held my breath and listened. There was only the slow rhythm of her heartbeat.

"I don't hear a thing," I said.

"You don't hear my stomach digesting all that food?" she asked.

"I doubt digestion makes much sound. Only gastric juices dissolving things. Of course, there should be some peristaltic activity, but that's got to be quiet, too."

"But I can really feel my stomach churning. Why don't you listen again?"

I was content to keep in that position. I lazily eyed the wispy mound of pubic hair just ahead. I heard nothing that sounded like gastrointestinal action. I recalled a scene like this in *The Enemy Below*. Right below my ear, her iron stomach was stealthily engaged in digestive operations, like that U-boat with Curt Jurgens on board.

I gave up and lifted my head from her body. I leaned back and put my arm around her. I smelled the scent of her hair.

"Got any tonic water?" she asked.

"In the refrigerator," I said.

"I have an urge for a vodka tonic. Could I?"

"Why not?"

"Can I fix you one?"

"You bet."

She got out of bed and walked naked to the kitchen to mix
two vodka tonics. While she did that, I put on my favorite
Johnny Mathis album. The one with *Teach Me Tonight*. Then
I hummed my way back to bed. Me and my limp penis and
Johnny Mathis.

"How old are you?" she asked, returning with the drinks.

"Thirty-five," I said. "How about you?"

"Almost thirty. I look young, but I'm really twenty-nine,"
she said. "Honestly, though, aren't you a baseball player or
something?"

I was so taken aback, I spit out vodka tonic all over my
chest.

"Where'd you get an idea like that?" I said. "I haven't
even touched a baseball in fifteen years."

"I don't know, I thought maybe I'd seen your face on TV.
A ball game. Or maybe you were on the News?"

"Never done anything newsworthy."

"A commercial?"

"Nope," I said.

"Well, maybe it was your double. You sure don't look like
a computer person," she said, pausing. "You're hard to figure. You go on about evolution and unicorns, and you carry
a switchblade."

She pointed to my slacks on the floor. The knife was sticking out of the back pocket.

"Oh," I said, "in my line of work, you can't be too careful. I process data. Biotechnology, that sort of thing. Corpo-
rate interests involved. Lately there's been a lot of data
piracy."

She didn't swallow a word of it. "Why don't we deal with
our unicorn friends. That was your original purpose in calling me over here, wasn't it?"

"Now that you mention it," I said.

She unhanded me and picked up the two volumes from the
bedside. One was *Archaeology of Animals*, by Burtland
Cooper, and the other Jorge Luis Borges's *Book of Imaginary
Beings*.

"Let me give you a quick gloss," she began. "Borges treats the unicorn as a product of fantasy, not unlike dragons and mermaids. Whereas Cooper doesn't rule out the possibility that unicorns might have existed at one time, and approaches the matter more scientifically. Unfortunately neither one has much to report about the subject. Even dragons and trolls fare better. My guess is that unicorns never made much noise, so to speak. That's about all I could come up with at the library."

"That's plenty. I really appreciate it. Now I have another request. Do you think you could read a few of the better parts and tell me about them?"

She first opened *The Book of Imaginary Beings*. And this is what we learned:

There are two types of unicorns: the Western variety, which originates in Greece, and the Chinese variety. They differ completely in appearance and in people's perception of them. Pliny, for instance, described the unicorn of the Greeks like this:

> *His body resembles a horse, his head a stag, his feet an Elephant, his taile a boar; he loweth after an hideous manner, one black horne he hath in the mids of his forehead, bearing out two cubits in length: by report, this wild beast cannot possibly be caught aliue.*

By contrast, there is the Chinese unicorn:

> *It has the body of a deer, the tail of an ox, and the hooves of a horse. Its short horn, which grows out of its forehead, is made of flesh; its coat, on its back, is of five mixed colours, while its belly is brown or yellow.*

The difference was not simply one of appearance. East and West could not agree on character and symbolism either. The West saw the unicorn as fierce and aggressive. Hence a horn one meter long. Moreover, according to Leonardo da Vinci, the only way to catch a unicorn was to snare its passions. A young virgin is set down in front of it and the beast is so overcome with desire that it forgets to attack, and instead rests its head on the lap of the maiden. The significance of the horn is not easily missed.

The Chinese unicorn, on the other hand, is a sacred animal of portent. It ranks along with the dragon, the phoenix, and the tortoise as one of the Four Auspicious Creatures, and merits the highest status amongst the Three-Hundred-Sixty-Five Land Animals. Extremely gentle in temperament, it treads with such care that even the smallest living thing is unharmed, and eats no growing herbs but only withered grass. It lives a thousand years, and the visitation of a unicorn heralds the birth of a great sage. So we read that the mother of Confucius came upon a unicorn when she bore the philosopher in her womb:

> *Seventy years later, some hunters killed a qilin, which still had a bit of ribbon around its horn that Confucius' mother had tied there. Confucius went to look at the Unicorn and wept because he felt what the death of this innocent and mysterious animal foretold, and because in that ribbon lay his past.*

The *qilin* appears again in Chinese history in the thirteenth century. On the eve of a planned invasion of India, advance scouts of Genghis Khan encounter a unicorn in the middle of the desert. This unicorn has the head of a horse and the body of a deer. Its fur is green and it speaks in a human tongue: "Time is come for you to return to the kingdom of your lord."

One of the Genghis's Chinese ministers, upon consultation, explained to him that the animal was a jiao-shui, a variety of the qilin. "For four hundred years the great army has been warring in western regions," he said. "Heaven, which has a horror of bloodshed, gives warning through the jiao-shui. Spare the Empire for Heaven's sake; moderation will give boundless pleasure." The Emperor desisted in his war plans.

In the East, peace and tranquility; in the West, aggression and lust. Nonetheless, the unicorn remains an imaginary animal, an invention that can embody any value one wishes to project.

There is, however, one species of porpoise called the narwhal or "sea unicorn". It does not have a horn so much as an overgrown fang of the upper jaw protruding from the top of its head. The "horn" measures an average of two-and-half meters and is spiralled with a drill-like threading. This cetacean is rather rare and does not figure in medieval records.

Other mammals resembling the unicorn existed in the Mesozoic, but gradually died out.

She picked up the *Archaeology of Animals* and continued:

Two species of ruminants existed during the Mesozoic Period, approximately twenty million years ago, on the North American continent. One is the cyntetokerus, the other is the curanokerus. Both have three horns, although clearly one of the horns is freestanding.

The cyntetokerus is a smallish horse cum deer with a horn on either temple and a long Y-shaped prong at the end of its nose. The curanokerus is slightly rounder in the face, and sprouts two deer-like antlers from its crown and an addi-

tional horn that curves up and out in back. Grotesque creatures on the whole.

Within the mammal class, single-horned or odd-number-
horned animals are a rarity and even something of an evolutionary anomaly. That is to say, they are evolutionary
orphans, and for the most part, odd-horned species like these
have virtually perished from the earth. Even among
dinosaurs, the three-horned giant tricerotops was an exception.

Considering that horns are close-range weapons, three
would be superfluous. As with the tines of forks, the larger
number of horns serves to increase surface resistance, which
would in turn render the act of thrusting cumbersome. Furthermore, the laws of dynamics dictate a high risk of triadic
horns becoming wedged into mid-range objects, so that none
of the three horns might actually penetrate the body of the
opponent.

In the event of an animal confronting several predators,
having three horns could hamper fluidity of motion; extracting horns from the body of one for redirection to the next
could be awkward. These drawbacks proved the downfall of
the three-horned animal: the twin horn or single horn was a
superior design.

The advantage of two horns rests with the bilateral symmetry of the animal body. All animals, manifesting a right-left
balance that parcels their strength into two ligatures, regulate
their patterns of growth and movement accordingly. The nose
and even the mouth bear this symmetry that essentially
divides functions into two. The navel, of course, is singular,
though this is something of a retrograde feature. Conversely,
the penis and vagina form a pair.

Most important are the eyes. Both for offense and defense,
the eyes act as the control tower, so a horn located in close
proximity to the eyes has optimum effectiveness. The prime
example is the rhinoceros, which in principle is a "unicorn".
It is also extremely myopic, and that single horn is the very

cause. For all practical purposes, the rhinoceros is a cripple. In spite of this potentially fatal flaw, the rhinoceros has survived for two unrelated reasons: it is an herbivore and its body is covered with thick armor plating. Hence it does not want for defense. And for that reason, the rhinoceros falls by body-type to the tricerotops category.

Nonetheless, all pictures that exist of unicorns show the breed to be of a different stripe. It has no armor; it is entirely defenseless, not unlike a deer. If the unicorn were then also nearsighted, the defect could be disastrous. Even highly developed senses of smell or hearing would be inadequate to save it. Hunters would find it easy prey. Moreover, having no horn to spare, as it were, could severely disadvantage the unicorn in the event of an accident.

Still another failing of the single horn is the difficulty of wielding it with force, just as incisors cannot distribute a force equivalent to that of molars due to principles of balance. The heavier the mass, the greater the stability when force is applied. Obviously, the unicorn suffers physiodynamic defects.

"You're a real whiz at these explanations, aren't you?" I interrupted her.

She burst into a smile and trekked two fingers up my chest.

"Logically," she continued, "there's only one thing that could have saved the unicorn from extinction. And this is very important. Any idea?"

I folded my hands where her fingers were and thought it over a bit, inconclusively. "No natural predators?" I ventured.

"Bingo," she said, and gave me a little peck on the lips. "Now think: what conditions would give you no natural predators?"

"Well, isolation, for one thing. Somewhere no hunter could

get to," I hypothesized. "Someplace, say, on a high plateau, like in Conan Doyle's *Lost World*. Or down deep, like a crater."

"*Brill!*" she exclaimed, tapping her index finger now on my heart. "And in fact, there is a recorded instance of a unicorn discovered under exactly such circumstances."

I gulped. Uh-oh.

She resumed her exposition:

In 1917, the very item was discovered on the Russian front. This was September, one month prior to the October Revolution, during the First World War, under the Kerensky Cabinet, immediately before the start of the Bolshevik Coup.

At the Ukranian front line, a Russian infantryman unearthed a mysterious object while digging a trench. He tossed it aside, thinking it a cow or an elk skull. Had that been the end of it, the find would have remained buried in the obscurity of history. It happened, however, that the soldier's commanding lieutenant had been a graduate student in biology at the University of Petrograd. He noted a peculiarity to the skull and, returning with it to his quarters, he subjected it to thorough examination. He determined the specimen to be the skull of a species of animal as yet unknown. Immediately, he contacted the Chairman of the Faculty of Biology at the University and requested that a survey team be dispatched. None, of course, was forthcoming. Russia was in upheaval at the time. Food, gunpowder, and medicine had first priority. With communications crippled by strikes, it was impossible for a scientific team to reach the front. Even if they had, the circumstances would not have been conducive to a site survey. The Russian army was suffering defeat after defeat; the front line was being pushed steadily back. Very probably the site was already German territory.

The lieutenant himself came to an ignoble end. He was hanged from a telegraph pole in November that year. Many bourgeois officers were disposed of similarly along the Ukraine-Moscow telegraph line. The lieutenant had been a simple biology major without a shred of politics in him.

Nonetheless, immediately before the Bolshevik army seized control, the lieutenant did think to entrust the skull to a wounded soldier being sent home, promising him a sizable compensation upon delivery of the skull, packed securely in a box, to the Faculty Chairman in Petrograd. The soldier was released from military hospital but waited until February of the following year before visiting the University, only to find the gates closed indefinitely. Most of the lecturers either had been driven away or had fled the country. Prospects for the University reopening were not very promising. He had little choice but to attempt to claim his money at a later date. He stored the skull with his brother-in-law who kept a stable in Petrograd, and returned to his home village some three hundred kilometers from the former Imperial Capital. The soldier, for reasons undetermined, never visited Petrograd again, and the skull lay in the stable, forgotten.

The skull next saw the light of day in 1935. Petrograd had since become Leningrad. Lenin was dead, Trotsky was in exile, and Stalin was in power. No one rode horses in Leningrad. The old stablemaster had sold half his premises, and in the remaining half he opened a small hockey goods shop.

"Hockey?" I dropped my jaw. "In the Soviet thirties?"

"Don't ask me. That's just what I read. But who knows? Post-Revolution Leningrad was quite your modern *grad*. Maybe hockey was all the rage."

In any case, while inventorying his storeroom, the former stablemaster happened upon the box his brother-in-law had left with him in 1918. There in the box was a note addressed to the Chairman of the Faculty of Biology, Petrograd University. The note read: "Please bestow fair compensation upon the bearer of this item." Naturally, the purveyor of hockey goods took the box to the University—now Leningrad University—and sought a meeting with the Chairman. This proved impossible. The Chairman was a Jew who had been sent to Siberia after Trotsky's downfall.

This former stablemaster, however, was no fool. With no other prospect, rather than hold onto an unidentified animal skull for the remainder of his days and not receive a kopek, he found another professor of biology, recounted the tale, and prevailed upon him for a likely sum. He went home a few rubles richer.

The professor examined every square millimeter of the skull, and ultimately arrived at the same conclusion as had the lieutenant eighteen years earlier—to wit, that the skull did not correspond to any extant animal, nor did it correspond to any animal known to have existed previously. The morphology most closely resembled that of a deer. It had to have been a hoofed herbivore, judging by the shape of the jaw, with slightly fuller cheeks. Yet the greatest difference between this species and the deer was, lo and behold, the single horn that modified the middle of its forehead.

The horn was still intact. It was not in its entirety, to be sure, but what remained sufficed to enable the reconstruction of a straight horn of approximately twenty centimeters in length. The horn had been broken off close to the three-centimeter mark, its basal diameter approximately two centimeters.

"Two centimeters," I repeated to myself. The skull I'd received from the old man had a depression of exactly two centimeters in diameter.

"Professor Petrov—for that was his name—summoned several assistants and graduate students, and the team departed for the Ukraine on a one-month dig at the site of the young lieutenant's trenches. Unfortunately, they failed to find any similar skull. They did, however, discover a number of curious facts about the region, a tableland commonly known as the Voltafil. The area rose to a moderate height and as such formed one of the few natural strategic vantage points over the rolling plains. During the First World War, the German and Austro-Hungarian armies repeatedly engaged the Russians in bloody confrontations on all sides. During the Second World War, the entire plateau was bombarded beyond recognition, but that was years later.

What interested Professor Petrov about the Voltafil was that the bones unearthed there differed significantly from the distribution of species elsewhere in that belt of land. It prompted the professor to conjecture that the present tableland had in ancient times not been an outcropping at all, but a crater, the cradle for untold flora and fauna. In other words, a *lost world*.

A plateau out of a crater might tax the imagination, but that is precisely what occurred. The walls of the crater were perilously steep, but over millions of years the walls crumbled due to an intractable geological shift, convexing the base into an ordinary hill. The unicorn, an evolutionary misfit, continued to live on this outcropping isolated from all predation. Natural springs abounded, the soil was fertile, conditions were idyllic. Professor Petrov submitted these findings to the Soviet Academy of Sciences in a paper entitled "A Consideration of the Lifeforms of the Voltafil Tableland," detailing a total of thirty-six zoological, botanical, and geological proofs for his lost world thesis. This was August 1936.

It was dismally received. No one in the Academy took him seriously. His defense of his paper coincided with a power struggle within this august institution between Moscow University and Leningrad University. The Leningrad faction was not faring well; their purportedly non-dialectical research incurred a summary trouncing. Still, Petrov's hypothesis aside, there was the undeniably physical evidence of the skull itself. A cadre of specialists devoted the next year to excruciating study of the object in question. They were forced to conclude that it, indeed, was not a fabrication but the unadulterated skull of a single-horned animal. Ultimately, the Committee at the Soviet Academy of Sciences pronounced the embarrassing artifact a spontaneous mutation in *Cervidæ odocoileus* with no evolutionary consequence, and as such not a subject fit for research. The skull was returned to Professor Petrov at Leningrad University.

Thereafter, Professor Petrov waited valiantly for the winds of fortune to shift and his research to achieve recognition, but the onslaught of the German-Soviet War in 1940 dashed all such hopes and he died in 1943, a broken man. It was during the 1941 Siege of Leningrad that the skull vanished. Leningrad University was reduced to rubble by German shelling. Virtually the entire campus—let alone a single animal skull—was destroyed. And so the one piece of solid evidence proving the existence of the unicorn was no more.

"So there's not one concrete thing that remains?" I said.

"Nothing except for photographs."

"Photographs?"

"That's right, photographs of the skull. Professor Petrov took close to a hundred photos of the skull, a few of which escaped destruction in the war. They've been preserved in the Leningrad University library reference collection. Here, photographs like this."

She handed me the book and pointed to a black-and-white reproduction on the page. A somewhat indistinct photograph, but it did convey the general shape of the skull. It had been placed on a table covered with white cloth, next to a wristwatch for scale, a circle drawn around the middle of the forehead to indicate the position of the horn. It appeared to be of the same species as the skull the old man had given me. I glanced over at the skull atop the TV. The T-shirt covering made it look like a sleeping cat. Should I tell her? Nah, a secret's a secret because you don't let people in on it.

"Do you think the skull really was lost in the War?" I asked her.

"I suppose," she said, teasing her bangs around her little finger. "If you believe the book, the city of Leningrad was practically steamrollered, and seeing how the University district was the hardest hit, it's probably safe to say that the skull was obliterated along with everything else. Of course, Professor Petrov could well have whisked it away somewhere before the fighting started. Or it could have been among the spoils carted off by the German troops. . . . Whatever happened to it, nobody has spoken of seeing the skull since."

I studied the photograph and slammed the book shut. Could the skull in my possession be the very same Voltafil-Leningrad specimen? Or was it yet another unicorn skull excavated at a different place and time? The simplest thing would be to ask the old man. Like, where did you get that skull? And why did you give it to me? Well, I was supposed to see the old prankster when I handed over the shuffled data. I'd ask him then. Meanwhile, not to be worrying.

I stared absently at the ceiling, with her head on my chest, her body snug against my side. I put my arm around her. I felt relieved, in a way, about the unicorn skull, but the state of my prowess was unchanged. No matter. Erection or not, she kept on drawing dreamy patterns on my stomach.

10

The Wall

ON an overcast afternoon I make my way down to the Gatehouse and find my shadow working with the Gatekeeper. They have rolled a wagon into the clearing, replacing the old floorboards and sideboards. The Gatekeeper planes the planks and my shadow hammers them in place. The shadow appears altogether unchanged from when we parted. He is still physically well, but his movements seem wrong. Ill-humored folds brew about his eyes.

As I draw near, they pause in their labors to look up.

"Well now, what brings you here?" asks the Gatekeeper.

"I must talk to you about something," I say.

"Wait till our next break," says the Gatekeeper, readdressing himself to the half-shaved board. My shadow glances in my direction, then resumes working. He is furious with me, I can tell.

I go into the Gatehouse and sit down at the table to wait
for the Gatekeeper. The table is cluttered. Does the Gatekeeper clean only when he hones his blades? Today the table
is an accumulation of dirty cups, coffee grounds, wood shavings, and pipe ash. Yet, in the racks on the wall, his knives
are ordered in what approaches an aesthetic ideal.

The Gatekeeper keeps me waiting. I gaze at the ceiling,
with arms thrown over the back of the chair. What do people
do with so much time in this Town?

Outside, the sounds of planing and hammering are unceas-
ing.

When finally the door does open, in steps not the Gatekeeper but my shadow.

"I can't talk long," whispers my shadow as he hurries
past. "I came to get some nails from the storeroom."

He opens a door on the far side of the room, goes into the
right storeroom, and emerges with a box of nails.

"I'll come straight to the point," says my shadow under
his breath as he sorts through the nails. "First, you need to
make a map of the Town. Don't do it by asking anyone else.
Every detail of the map must be seen with your own eyes.
Everything you see gets written down, no matter how small."

"How soon do you need it?" I say.

"By autumn," speaks the shadow at a fast clip. "Also, I
want a verbal report. Particularly about the Wall. The lay of
it, how it goes along the Eastern Woods, where the River
enters and where it exits. Got it?"

And without even looking my way, my shadow disappears
out the door. I repeat everything he has told me. Lay of the
Wall, Eastern Woods, River entrance and River exit. Making
a map is not a bad idea. It will show me the Town and use
my time well.

Soon the Gatekeeper enters. He wipes the sweat and grime
off his face, and drops his bulk in the chair across from me.

"Well, what is it?"

"May I see my shadow?" I ask.

The Gatekeeper nods a few times. He tamps tobacco into his pipe and lights up.

"Not yet," he says. "It is too soon. The shadow is too strong. Wait till the days get shorter. Just so there is no trouble."

He breaks his matchstick in half and flips it onto the table.

"For your own sake, wait," he continues. "Getting too close to your shadow makes trouble. Seen it happen before."

I say nothing. He is not sympathetic. Still, I have spoken with my shadow. Surely the Gatekeeper will let down his guard again.

The Gatekeeper rises. He goes to the sink, and sloshes down cup after cup of water.

"How is the work?"

"Slow, but I am learning," I say.

"Good," says the Gatekeeper. "Do a good job. A body who works bad thinks bad, I always say."

I listen to my shadow nailing steadily.

"How about a walk?" proposes the Gatekeeper. "I want to show you something."

I follow him outside. As we enter the clearing, I see my shadow. He is standing on the wagon, putting the last sideboard in place.

The Gatekeeper strides across the clearing toward the Watchtower. The afternoon is humid and gray. Dark clouds sweep low over the Wall from the west, threatening to burst at any second. The sweat-soaked shirt of the Gatekeeper clings to his massive trunk and gives off a sour stink.

"This is the Wall," says the Gatekeeper, slapping the broad side of the battlements. "Seven yards tall, circles the whole Town. Only birds can clear the Wall. No entrance or exit except this Gate. Long ago there was the East Gate, but they walled it up. You see these bricks? Nothing can dent them, not even a cannon."

The Gatekeeper picks up a scrap of wood and expertly pares it down to a tiny sliver.

"Watch this," he says. He runs the sliver of wood between the bricks. It hardly penetrates a fraction of an inch. He tosses the wood away, and draws the tip of his knife over the bricks. This produces an awful sound, but leaves not a mark. He examines his knife, then puts it away.

"This Wall has no mortar," the Gatekeeper states. "There is no need. The bricks fit perfect; not a hair-space between them. Nobody can put a dent in the Wall. And nobody can climb it. Because this Wall is perfect. So forget any ideas you have. Nobody leaves here."

The Gatekeeper lays a giant hand on my back.

"You have to endure. If you endure, everything will be fine. No worry, no suffering. It all disappears. Forget about the shadow. This is the End of the World. This is where the world ends. Nowhere further to go."

On my way back to my room, I stop in the middle of the Old Bridge and look at the River. I think about what the Gatekeeper has said.

The End of the World.

Why did I cast off my past to come here to the End of the World? What possible event or meaning or purpose could there have been? Why can I not remember?

Something has summoned me here. Something intractable. And for this, I have forfeited my shadow and my memory.

The River murmurs at my feet. There is the sandbar midstream, and on it the willows sway as they trail their long branches in the current. The water is beautifully clear. I can see fish playing among the rocks. Gazing at the River soothes me.

Steps lead down from the bridge to the sandbar. A bench waits under the willows, a few beasts lay nearby. Often have I descended to the sandbar and offered crusts of bread to the beasts. At first they hesitated, but now the old and the very young eat from my hand.

As the autumn deepens, the fathomless lakes of their eyes assume an ever more sorrowful hue. The leaves turn color, the grasses wither; the beasts sense the advance of a long, hungry season. And bowing to their vision, I too know a sadness.

11

Dressing, Watermelon, Chaos

T HE clock read half past nine when she got out of bed, picked up her clothes from the floor, and slowly, leisurely, put them on. I stayed in bed, sprawled out, one elbow bent upright, watching her every move out of the corner of my eye. One piece of clothing at a time, liltingly graceful, not a motion wasted, achingly quiet. She zipped up her skirt, did the buttons of her blouse from the top down, lastly sat down on the bed to pull on her stockings. Then she kissed me on the cheek. Many are the women who can take their clothes off seductively, but women who can charm as they dress? Now completely composed, she ran her hand through her long black hair. All at once, the room breathed new air.

"Thanks for the food," she said.

"My pleasure."

"Do you always cook like that?"

"When I'm not too busy with work," I said. "When things get hectic, it's catch-as-catch-can with leftovers. Or I eat out."

She grabbed a chair in the kitchen and lit up a cigarette. "I don't do much cooking myself. When I think about getting home after work and fixing a meal that I'm going to polish off in ten minutes anyway, it's so-o depressing."

While I got dressed, she pulled a datebook out of her handbag and scribbled something, which she tore off and handed to me.

"Here's my phone number," she said. "If you have food to spare or want to get together or whatever, give me a call. I'll be right over."

After she left, carrying off the several volumes on mammals to be returned to the library, I went over to the TV and removed the T-shirt.

I reflected upon the unicorn skull. I didn't have an iota of proof, but I couldn't help feeling that this mystery skull was the very same specimen of Voltafil-Leningrad renown. I seemed to sense, somehow, an odor of history drifting about it. True, the story was still fresh in my mind and the power of suggestion was strong. I gave the skull a light tap with the stainless-steel tongs and went into the kitchen.

I washed the dishes, then wiped off the kitchen table. It was time to start. I switched the telephone over to my answering service so I wouldn't be disturbed. I disconnected the door chimes and turned out all the lights except for the kitchen lamp. For the next few hours I needed to concentrate my energies on shuffling.

My shuffling password was "End of the World". This was the title of a profoundly personal drama by which previously laundered numerics would be reordered for computer calculation. Of course, when I say drama, I don't mean the kind they show on TV. This drama was a lot more complex and with no discernible plot. The word is only a label, for convenience sake. All the same, I was in the dark about its contents. The sole thing I knew was its title, End of the World.

The scientists at the System had induced this drama. I had undergone a full year of Calcutec training. After I passed the final exam, they put me on ice for two weeks to conduct comprehensive tests on my brainwaves, from which was extracted the epicenter of encephalographic activity, the "core" of my consciousness. The patterns were transcoded into my shuffling password, then re-input into my brain—this time in reverse. I was informed that End of the World was the title, which was to be my shuffling password. Thus was my conscious mind completely restructured. First there was the overall chaos of my conscious mind, then inside that, a distinct plum pit of condensed chaos as the center.

They refused to reveal any more than this.

"There is no need for you to know more. The unconscious goes about its business better than you'll ever be able to. After a certain age—our calculations put it at twenty-eight years—human beings rarely experience alterations in the overall configuration of their consciousness. What is commonly referred to as self-improvement or conscious change hardly even scratches the surface. Your 'End of the World' core consciousness will continue to function, unaffected, until you take your last breath. Understand this far?"

"I understand," I said.

"All efforts of reason and analysis are, in a word, like trying to slice through a watermelon with sewing needles. They may leave marks on the outer rind, but the fruity pulp will remain perpetually out of reach. Hence, we separate the rind from the pulp. Of course, there are idle souls out there who seem to enjoy just nibbling away on the rind.

"In view of all contingencies," they went on, "we must protect your password-drama, isolating it from any superficial turbulence, the tides of your outer consciousness. Suppose we were to say to you, your End of the World is inhered with such, such, and such elements. It would be like peeling away the rind of the watermelon for you. The temptation would be irresistible: you would stick your fingers into the pulp and muck it up. And in no time, the hermetic extractability of our password-drama would be forfeited. Poof! You would no longer be able to shuffle."

"That's why we're giving you back your watermelon with an extra thick rind," one scientist interjected. "You can call up the drama, because it is your own self, after all. But you can never know its contents. It transpires in a sea of chaos into which you submerge empty-handed and from which you resurface empty-handed. Do you follow?"

"I believe so," I said.

"One more point," they intoned in solemn chorus. "Properly speaking, *should any individual ever have exact, clear knowledge of his own core consciousness?*"

"I wouldn't know," I said.

"Nor would we," said the scientists. "Such questions are, as they say, *beyond* science."

"Speaking from experience, we cannot conclude otherwise," admitted one. "So in this sense, this is an extremely sensitive experiment."

"Experiment?" I recoiled.

"Yes, experiment," echoed the chorus. "We cannot tell you any more than this."

Then they instructed me on how to shuffle: Do it alone, preferably at night, on neither a full nor empty stomach. Listen to three repetitions of a sound-cue pattern, which calls up the End of the World and plunges consciousness into a sea of chaos. Therein, shuffle the numerical data.

When the shuffling was done, the End of the World call would abort automatically and my consciousness would exit from chaos. I would have no memory of anything.

Reverse shuffling was the literal reverse of this process. For reverse shuffling, I was to listen to a reverse-shuffling sound-cue pattern.

This mechanism was programmed into me. An unconscious tunnel, as it were, input right through the middle of my brain. Nothing more or less.

Understandably, whenever I shuffle, I am rendered utterly defenseless and subject to mood swings.

With laundering, it's different. Laundering is a pain, but I myself can take pride in doing it. All sorts of abilities are brought into the equation. Whereas shuffling is nothing I can pride myself on. I am merely a vessel to be used. My consciousness is borrowed and something is processed while I'm unaware. I hardly feel I can be called a Calcutec when it comes to shuffling. Nor, of course, do I have any say in choice of calc-scheme.

I am licensed in both shuffling and laundering, but can only follow the prescribed order of business. And if I don't like it, well, I can quit the profession.

I have no intention of turning in my Calcutec qualifications. Despite the meddling and the raised eyebrows at the System, I know of no line of work that allows the individual as much freedom to exercise his abilities as being a Calcutec. Plus the pay is good. If I work fifteen years, I will have made enough money to take it easy for the rest of my life.

Shuffling is not impeded by drinking. In fact, the experts indicate that moderate drinking may even help in releasing nervous tension. With me, though, it's part of my ritual that I always shuffle sober. I remain wary about the whole enterprise. Especially since they've put the freeze on shuffling for two months now.

I took a cold shower, did fifteen minutes of hard calisthenics, and drank two cups of black coffee. I opened my private safe, removed a miniature tape recorder and the typewritten paper with the converted data, and set them out on the kitchen table. Then I readied a notepad and a supply of five sharpened pencils.

I inserted the tape, put on headphones, then started the tape rolling. I let the digital tape counter run to 16, then rewound it to 9, then forwarded it to 26. Then I waited with it locked for ten seconds until the counter numbers disappeared and the signal tone began. Any other order of operation would have caused the sounds on the tape to self-erase.

Tape set, brand new notepad at my right hand, converted data at my left. All preparations completed. I switched on the red light to the security devices installed on the apartment door and on all accessible windows. No slip-ups. I reached over to push the PLAY switch on the tape recorder and as the signal tone began, gradually a warm chaos noiselessly drank me in.

<me>

       drink————gradually   chaos————>

         ɐɹ8 'uɐ8ǝq ǝuoʇ ꞁɐu8

12

A Map of the End of the World

THE day after meeting my shadow, I immediately set about making a map of the Town.

At dusk, I go to the top of the Western Hill to get a full perspective. The Hill, however, is not high enough to afford me a panorama, nor is my eyesight as it once was. Hence the effort is not wholly successful. I gain only the most general sense of the Town.

The Town is neither too big nor too small. That is to say, it is not so vast that it eclipses my powers of comprehension, but neither is it so contained that the entire picture can be easily grasped. This, then, is the sum total of what I discern from the summit of the Western Hill: the heights of the Wall encompass the Town, and the River transects it north and south. The evening sky turns the River a leaden hue. Presently the Town resounds with horn and hoof.

In order to determine the route of the Wall, I will ultimately need to follow its course on foot. Of course, as I can be outdoors only on dark, overcast days, I must be careful when venturing far from the Western Hill. A stormy sky might suddenly clear or it might let loose a downpour. Each morning, I ask the Colonel to monitor the sky for me. The Colonel's predictions are nearly always right.

"Harbor no fears about the weather," says the old officer with pride. "I know the direction of the clouds. I will not steer you wrong."

Still, there can be unexpected changes in the sky, unaccountable even to the Colonel. A walk is always a risk.

Furthermore, thickets and woods and ravines attend the Wall at many points, rendering it inaccessible. Houses are concentrated along the River as it flows through the center of the Town; a few paces beyond these areas, the paths might stop short or be swallowed in a patch of brambles. I am left with the choice either to forge past these obstacles or to return by the route I had come.

I begin my investigations along the western edge of the Town, that is, from the Gatehouse at the Gate in the west, circling clockwise around the Town. North from the Gate extend fields deep to the waist in wild grain. There are few obstructions on the paths that thread through the grasses. Birds resembling skylarks have built their nests in the fields; they fly up from the weeds to gyre the skies in search of food. Beasts, their heads and backs floating in this sea of grasses, sweep the landscape for edible green buds.

Further along the Wall, toward the south, I encounter the remains of what must once have been army barracks. Plain, unadorned two-story structures in rows of three. Beyond these is a cluster of small houses. Trees stand between the structures, and a low stone wall circumscribes the compound. Everything is deep in weeds. No one is in sight. The fields, it would seem, served as training grounds. I see trenches and a masonry flag stand.

Perhaps the same military men, now retired to the Official Residences where I have my room, were at one time quartered in these buildings. I am in a quandary as to the circumstances that warranted their transfer to the Western Hill, thus leaving the barracks to ruin.

Toward the east, the rolling fields come to an end and the Woods begin. They begin gradually, bushes rising in patches amongst intertwining tree trunks, the branches reaching to a height between my shoulders and head. Beneath, the undergrowth is dotted with tiny grassflowers. As the ground slopes, the trees increase in number, variety, and scale. If not for the random twittering of birds, all would be quiet.

As I head up a narrow brush path, the trees grow thick, the high branches coming together to form a forest roof, obscuring my view of the Wall. I take a southbound trail back into Town, cross the Old Bridge, and go home.

So it is that even with the advent of autumn, I can trace only the vaguest outline of the Town.

In the most general terms, the land is laid out east to west, abutted by the North Wood and Southern Hill. The eastern slope of the Southern Hill breaks into crags that extend along the base of the Wall. To the east of the Town spreads a forest, more dark and dense than the North Wood. Few roads penetrate this wilderness, except for a footpath along the riverbank that leads to the East Gate and adjoins sections of the Wall. The East Gate, as the Gatekeeper had said, is cemented in solidly, and none may pass through.

The River rushes down in a torrent from the Eastern Ridge, passes under the Wall, suddenly appears next to the East Gate, and flows due west through the middle of the Town under three bridges: the East Bridge, the Old Bridge, and the West Bridge. The Old Bridge is not only the most ancient but also the largest and most handsome. The West Bridge marks a turning point in the River. It shifts dramatically to the south, flowing back first slightly eastward. At the Southern Hill, the River cuts a deep Gorge.

The River does not exit under the Wall to the south. Rather it forms a Pool at the Wall and is swallowed into some vast cavity beneath the surface. According to the

Colonel, beyond the Wall lies a plain of limestone boulders, which stand vigil over countless veins of underground water.

Of course, I continue my dreamreading in the evenings. At six o'clock, I push open the door, have supper with the Librarian, then read old dreams.

In the course of an evening, I read four, perhaps five dreams. My fingers nimbly trace out the labyrinthine seams of light as I grow able to invoke the images and echoes with increasing clarity. I do not understand what dreamreading means, nor by what principle it works, but from the reactions of the Librarian I know that that my efforts are succeeding. My eyes no longer hurt from the glow of the skulls, and I do not tire so readily.

After I am through reading a skull, the Librarian places it on the counter in line with the skulls previously read that night. The next evening, the counter is empty.

"You are making progress," she says. "The work goes much faster than I expected."

"How many skulls are there?"

"A thousand, perhaps two thousand. Do you wish to see them?"

She leads me into the stacks. It is a huge schoolroom with rows of shelves, each shelf stacked with white beast skulls. It is a graveyard. A chill air of the dead hovers silently.

"How many years will it take me to read all these skulls?"

"You need not read them all," she says. "You need read only as many as you can read. Those that you do not read, the next Dreamreader will read. The old dreams will sleep."

"And you will assist the next Dreamreader?"

"No, I am here to help you. That is the rule. One assistant for one Dreamreader. When you no longer read, I too must leave the Library."

I do not fully comprehend, but this makes sense. We lean against the wall and gaze at the shelves of white skulls.

"Have you ever been to the Pool in the south?" I ask her.

"Yes, I have. A long time ago. When I was a child, my mother walked with me there. Most people would not go there, but Mother was different. Why do you ask about the Pool?"

"It intrigues me."

She shakes her head. "It is dangerous. You should stay away. Why would you want to go there?"

"I want to learn everything about this place. If you choose not to guide me, I will go alone."

She stares at me, then exhales deeply.

"Very well. If you will not listen, I must go with you. Please remember, though, I am so afraid of the Pool. There is something malign about it."

"It will be fine," I assure her, "if we are together, and if we are careful."

She shakes her head again. "You have never seen the Pool. You cannot know how frightening it is. The water is cursed. It calls out to people."

"We will not to go too close," I promise, holding her hand. "We will look at it from a distance."

On a dark November afternoon, we set out for the Pool. Dense undergrowth closes in on the road where the River has carved the Gorge in the west slope of the Western Hill. We must change our course to approach from the east, via the far side of the Southern Hill. The morning rain has left the ground covered with leaves, which dampen our every step. We pass two beasts, their golden heads swaying as they stride past us, expressionless.

"Winter is near," she explains. "Food is short, and the animals are searching for nuts and berries. Otherwise, they do not go very far from the Town."

We clear the Southern Hill, and there are no more beasts to be seen, nor any road. As we continue west through deserted fields and an abandoned settlement, the sound of the Pool reaches our ears.

It is unearthly, resembling nothing that I know. Different from the thundering of a waterfall, different from the howl of the wind, different from the rumble of a tremor. It may be described as the gasping of a gigantic throat. At times it groans, at times it whines. It breaks off, choking.

"The Pool seems to be snarling," I remark.

She turns to me, disturbed, but says nothing. She parts the overhanging branches with her gloved hands and forges on ahead.

"The path is much worse," she says. "It was not like this. Perhaps we should turn back."

"We have come this far. Let us go as far as we can."

We continue for several minutes over the thicketed moor, guided only by the eerie call of the Pool, when suddenly a vista opens up before us. The wilderness stops and a meadow spreads flat out. The River emerges from the Gorge to the right, then widens as it flows toward where we stand. From the final bend at the edge of the meadow, the water appears to slow and back up, turning a deep sapphire blue, swelling like a snake digesting a small animal. This is the Pool.

We proceed along the River toward the Pool.

"Do not go close," she warns, tugging at my arm. "The surface may seem calm, but below is a whirlpool. The Pool never gives back what it takes."

"How deep is it?"

"I do not know. I have been told the Pool only grows deeper and deeper. The whirlpool is a drill, boring away at the bottom. There was a time when they threw heretics and criminals into it."

"What happened to them?"

"They never came back. Did you hear about the caverns? Beneath the Pool, there are great halls where the lost wander forever in darkness."

The gasps of the Pool resound everywhere, rising like huge clouds of steam. They echo with anguish from the depths.

She finds a piece of wood the size of her palm and throws it into the middle of the Pool. It floats for a few seconds, then begins to tremble and is pulled below. It does not resurface.

"Do you see?"

We sit in the meadow ten yards from the Pool and eat the bread we have carried in our pockets. The scene is a picture of deceptive repose. The meadow is embroidered in autumn flowers, the trees brilliant with crimson leaves, the Pool a mirror. On its far side are white limestone cliffs, capped by the dark brick heights of the Wall. All is quiet, save for the gasping of the Pool.

"Why must you have this map?" she asks. "Even with a map, you will never leave this Town."

She brushes away the bread crumbs that have fallen on her lap and looks toward the Pool.

"Do you want to leave here?" she asks again.

I shake my head. Do I mean this as a "no", or is it only that I do not know?

"I just want to find out about the Town," I say. "The lay of the land, the history, the people, . . . I want to know who made the rules, what has sway over us. I want even to know what lies beyond."

She slowly rolls her head, then fixes upon my eyes.

"There is no beyond," she says. "Did you not know? We are at the End of the World. We are here forever."

I lie back and gaze up at the sky. Dark and overcast, the only sky I am allowed to see. The ground beneath me is cold and damp after the morning rain, but the smell of the earth is fresh.

Winter birds take wing from the brambles and fly over the Wall to the south. The clouds sweep in low. Winter readies to lay siege.

13

Frankfurt, Door, Independent Operants

As always, consciousness returned to me progressively from the edges of my field of vision. The first things to claim recognition were the bathroom door emerging from the far right and a lamp from the far left, from which my awareness gradually drifted inward like ice flowing together toward the middle of a lake. In the exact center of my visual field was the alarm clock, hands pointing to ten-twenty-six. An alarm clock I received as a memento of somebody's wedding. One of those clever designs. You had to press the red button on the left side of the clock and the black button on the right side simultaneously to stop it from ringing, which was said to preempt the reflex of killing the alarm and falling back to sleep. True, in order to press both left and right buttons simultaneously, I did have to sit upright in bed with the thing in my lap, and by then I had made a step into the waking world.

I repeat myself, I know, but the clock was a thanks-for-coming gift from a wedding. Whose, I can't remember. But back in my late twenties, there'd been a time when I had a fair number of friends. One year I attended wedding after wedding, whence came this clock. I would never buy a dumb clock like this of my own free will. I happen to be very good at waking up.

As my field of vision came together at the alarm clock, I reflexively picked it up, set it on my lap, and pushed the red and black buttons with my right and left hands. Only then did I realize that it hadn't been ringing to begin with. I hadn't been sleeping, so I hadn't set the alarm.

I put the alarm clock back down and looked around. No noticeable changes in the apartment. Red security-device light still on, empty coffee cup by the edge of the table, the librarian's cigarette lying in a saucer. Marlboro Light, no trace of lipstick. Come to think of it, she hadn't worn any makeup at all.

I ran down my checklist. Of the five pencils in front of me, two were broken, two were worn all the way down, and one was untouched. The notepad was filled with sixteen pages of tiny digits. The middle finger of my right hand tingled, slightly, as it does after a long stint of writing.

Finally, I compared the shuffled data with the laundered data to see that the number of entries under each heading matched, just like the manual recommends, after which I burned the original list in the sink. I put the notepad in a strongbox and transferred it and the tape recorder to the safe. Shuffling accomplished. Then I sat down on the couch, exhausted.

I poured myself two fingers of whiskey, closed my eyes, and drank it in two gulps. The warm feel of alcohol traveled down my throat and spread to every part of my body. I went to the bathroom and brushed my teeth, drank some water, and used the toilet. I returned to the kitchen, resharpened the pencils, and arranged them neatly in a tray. Then I placed the alarm clock by my bed and switched the telephone back to normal. The clock read eleven-fifty-seven. I had a whole day tomorrow ahead of me. I scrambled out of my clothes, dove into bed, and turned off the bedside light. Now for a good twelve-hour sleep, I told myself. Twelve solid hours. Let birds sing, let people go to work. Somewhere out there, a volcano might blow, Israeli commandos might decimate a Palestinian village. I couldn't stop it. I was going to sleep.

I replayed my usual fantasy of the joys of retirement from Calcutecdom. I'd have plenty of savings, more than enough for an easy life of cello and Greek. Stow the cello in the back of the car and head up to the mountains to practice. Maybe I'd have a mountain retreat, a pretty little cabin where I could read my books, listen to music, watch old movies on video, do some cooking, . . . And it wouldn't be half bad if my long-haired librarian were there with me. I'd cook and she'd eat.

As the menus were unfolding, sleep descended. All at once, as if the sky had fallen. Cello and cabin and cooking now dust to the wind, abandoning me, alone again, asleep like a tuna.

Somebody had drilled a hole in my head and was stuffing it full of something like string. An awfully long string apparently, because the reel kept unwinding into my head. I was flailing my arms, yanking at it, but try as I might the string kept coming in.

I sat up and ran my hands over my head. But there was no string. No holes either. A bell was ringing. Ringing, ringing, ringing. I grabbed the alarm clock, threw it on my lap, and slapped the red and black buttons with both hands. The ringing didn't stop. The telephone! The clock read four-eighteen. It was dark outside. Four-eighteen A.M.

I got out of bed and picked up the receiver. "Hello?" I said.

No sound came from the other end of the line.

"Hello!" I growled.

Still no answer. No disembodied breathing, no muffled

clicks. I fumed and hung up. I grabbed a carton of milk out of the refrigerator and drank whole white gulps before going back to bed.

The phone rang again at four-forty-six.

"Hello," I said.

"Hello," came a woman's voice. "Sorry about the time before. There's a disturbance in the sound field. Sometimes the sound goes away."

"The sound goes away?"

"Yes," she said. "The sound field's slipping. Can you hear me?"

"Loud and clear," I said. It was the granddaughter of that kooky old scientist who'd given me the unicorn skull. The girl in the pink suit.

"Grandfather hasn't come back up. And now, the sound field's starting to break up. Something's gone wrong. No one answers when I call the laboratory. Those INKlings have gotten Grandfather, I just know it."

"Are you sure? Maybe he's gotten all wrapped up in one of his experiments and forgotten to come home. He let you go a whole week sound-removed without noticing, didn't he?"

"It's not like that. Not this time. I can tell. Something's happened to Grandfather. Something is wrong. Anyway, the sound barrier's broken, and the underground sound field's erratic."

"The what's what?"

"The sound barrier, the special audio-signal equipment to keep the INKlings away. They've forced their way through, and we're losing sound. They've got Grandfather for sure!"

"How do you know?"

"They've had their beady little eyes on Grandfather's studies. INKlings. Semiotics. *Them*. They've been dying to get their hands on his research. They even offered him a deal, but that just made him mad. Please, come quick. You've got to help, please."

I imagined what it would be like coming face to face with

an INKling down there. Those creepy subterranean passage-ways were enough to make my hair stand on end.

"I know you're going to think I'm terrible, but tabulations are my job. Nothing else is in my contract. I've got plenty to worry about as it is. I'd like to help, honest, but fighting INKlings and rescuing your grandfather is a little out of my line. Why don't you call the police or the authorities at the System? They've been trained for this sort of thing."

"I can't call the police. I'd have to tell them everything. If Grandfather's research got out now, it'd be the end of the world."

"The end of the world?"

"Please," she begged. "I need your help. I'm afraid that we'll never get him back. And next they're going to go after you."

"Me? You maybe, but me? I don't know the first thing about your grandfather's research."

"You're the key. Without you the door won't open,"

"I have absolutely no idea what you're talking about," I said.

"I can't explain over the phone. Just believe me. This is important. More than anything you've ever done. *Really!* For your own sake, act while you still can. Before it's too late."

I couldn't believe this was happening to me. "Okay," I gave in, "but while you're at it, you'd better get out of there. It could be dangerous."

"Where should I go?"

I gave her directions to an all-night supermarket in Aoyama. "Wait for me at the snack bar. I'll be there by five-thirty."

"I'm scared. Somehow it—"

The sound just died. I shouted into the phone, but there was no reply. Silence floated up from the receiver like smoke from the mouth of a gun. Was the rupture in the sound field spreading? I hung up, stepped into my trousers, threw on a sweatshirt. I did a quick once-over with the shaver, splashed water on my face, combed my hair. My puss was puffy like cheap cheesecake. I wanted sleep. Was that too much to ask? First unicorns, now INKlings—why me?

I threw on a windbreaker, and pocketed my wallet, knife, and loose change. Then, after a moment's thought, I wrapped the unicorn skull in two bath towels, gathered up the fire tongs and the strongbox with the shuffled data, and tossed everything into a Nike sports bag. The apartment was definitely not secure. A pro could break into the place and crack the safe in less time than it takes to wash a sock.

I slipped into my tennis shoes, one of them still dirty, then headed out the door with the bag. There wasn't a soul in the hallway. I decided against the elevator and sidestepped down the stairs. There wasn't a soul in the parking garage either.

It was quiet, too quiet. If they were really after my skull, you'd think they'd have at least one guy staked out. It was almost as if they'd forgotten about me.

I got in the car, set the bag next to me, and started the engine. The time, a little before five. I looked around warily as I pulled out of the garage and headed toward Aoyama. The streets were deserted, except for taxis and the occasional night-transport truck. I checked the rearview mirror every hundred meters; no sign of anyone tailing me.

Strange how well everything was going. I'd seen every Semiotec trick in the book, and if they were up to something, they weren't subtle about it. They wouldn't hire some bungling gas inspector, they wouldn't forget a lookout. They chose the fastest, most surefire methods, and executed them without mercy. A couple of years ago, they captured five Calcutecs and trimmed off the tops of their crania with one buzz of a power saw. Five Calcutec bodies were found floating in Tokyo Bay minus their skullcaps. When the Semiotecs meant business, they did business. Something didn't make sense here.

I pulled into the Aoyama supermarket parking garage at five-twenty-eight. The sky to the east was getting light. I entered the store carrying my bag. Almost no one was in the place. A young clerk in a striped uniform sat reading a magazine; a woman of indeterminate age was buying a cartload of cans and instant food. I turned past the liquor display and went straight to the snack bar.

There were a dozen stools, and she wasn't on any of them. I took a seat on one end and ordered a sandwich and a glass of milk. The milk was so cold I could hardly taste it, the sandwich a soggy ready-made wrapped in plastic. I chewed the sandwich slowly, measuring my sips to make the milk last.

I eyed a poster of Frankfurt on the wall. The season was autumn, the trees along the river blazing with color. An old man in a pointed cap was feeding the swans. A great old stone bridge was on one side, and in the background, the spire of a cathedral. People sat on benches, everyone wore coats, the women had scarves on their heads. A pretty post-card picture. But it gave me the chills. Not because of the cold autumn scene. I always get the chills when I see tall, sharp spires.

I turned my gaze to the poster on the opposite wall. A shiny-faced young man holding a filter-tip was staring obliquely into the distance. Uncanny how models in cigarette ads always have that not-watching-anything, not-thinking-anything look in their eyes.

At six o'clock, the chubby girl still hadn't shown. Unaccountable, especially since this was supposed to be so urgent. I was here; where was she?

I ordered a coffee. I drank it black, slowly.

The supermarket customers gradually increased. Housewives buying the breakfast bread and milk, university students hungry after a long night out, a young woman squeezing a roll of toilet paper, a businessman snapping up three different newspapers, two middle-aged men lugging their golf clubs in to purchase a bottle of whiskey. I love supermarkets.

I waited until half past six. I went out to the car and drove to Shinjuku Station. I walked to the baggage-check counter and asked to leave my Nike sports bag. Fragile, I told the

clerk. He attached a red HANDLE WITH CARE tag with a cock-
tail glass printed on it. I watched as he placed the bag on the
shelf. He handed me the claim ticket.

I went to a station kiosk. For two hundred sixty yen, I
bought an envelope and stamps. I put the claim ticket into
the envelope, sealed it, stamped it, and addressed it to a p.o.
box I'd been keeping under a fictitious company name. I
scribbled EXPRESS on it and dropped the goods into the post.

Then I got in the car and went home. I showered and tum-
bled into bed.

At eleven o'clock, I had visitors. Considering the sequence
of events, it was about time. Still, you'd think they could
have rung the bell before trying to break the door down. No,
they had to come in like an iron wrecking ball, making the
floor shake. They could have saved themselves the trouble
and wrangled the key out of the superintendent. They could
also have saved me a mean repair bill.

While my visitors were rearranging the door, I got dressed
and slipped my knife into my pocket. Then, to be on the prudent side, I opened the safe and pushed the ERASE button on
the tape recorder. Next, I got potato salad and a beer from
the refrigerator for lunch. I thought about escaping via the
emergency rope ladder on the balcony, but why bother? Running away wouldn't solve anything. Solve what? I didn't even
know what the problem was. I needed a reality check.

Nothing but question marks. I finished my potato salad, I
finished my beer, and just as I was about to burp, the steel
door blew wide open and banged flat down.

Enter one mountain of a man, wearing a loud aloha shirt,
khaki army-surplus pants stained with grease, and white tennis shoes the size of scuba-diving flippers. Skinhead, pug
snout, a neck as thick as my waist. His eyelids formed gun-
metal shells over eyes that bulged molten white. False eyes, I
thought immediately, until a flicker of the pupils made them
seem human. He must have stood two meters tall, with
shoulders so broad that the buttons on his aloha shirt were

practically flying off his chest.

The hulk glanced at the wasted door as casually as he might a popped wine cork, then turned his attentions toward me. No complex feelings here. He looked at me like I was another fixture. Would that I were.

He stepped to one side, and behind him there appeared a rather tiny guy. This guy came in at under a meter and a half, a slim, trim figure. He had on a light blue Lacoste shirt, beige chinos, and brown loafers. Had he bought the whole outfit at a nouveau riche children's haberdashery? A gold Rolex gleamed on his wrist, a normal adult model—guess they didn't make kiddie Rolexes—so it looked disproportionately big, like a communicator from *Star Trek*. I figured him for his late thirties, early forties.

The hulk didn't bother removing his shoes before trudging into the kitchen and swinging around to pull out the chair opposite me. Junior followed presently and quietly took the seat. Big Boy parked his weight on the edge of the sink. He crossed his arms, as thick as normal human thighs, his eyes trained on a point just above my kidneys. I should have escaped while I could have.

Junior barely acknowledged me. He pulled out a pack of cigarettes and a lighter, and placed them on the table. Benson & Hedges and a gold Dupont. If Junior's accoutrements were any indication, the trade imbalance had to have been fabricated by foreign governments. He twirled the lighter between his fingers. Never a dull moment.

I looked around for the Budweiser ashtray I'd gotten from the liquor store, wiped it with my fingers, and set it out in front of the guy. He lit up with a clipped flick, narrowed his eyes, and released a puff of smoke.

Junior didn't say a word, choosing instead to contemplate the lit end of his cigarette. This was where the Jean-Luc Godard scene would have been titled *Il regardait le feu de son tabac*. My luck that Godard films were no longer fashionable. When the tip of Junior's cigarette had transformed into a goodly increment of ash, he gave it a measured tap, and the ash fell on the table. For him, an ashtray was extraneous.

"About the door," began Junior, in a high, piercing voice. "It was necessary to break it. That's why we broke it. We could have opened it more gentleman-like if we wanted to. But it wasn't necessary. I hope you don't think bad of us."

"There's nothing in the apartment," I said. "Search it, you'll see."

"Search?" pipped the little man. "Search?" Cigarette at his lips, he scratched his palm. "And what might we be searching for?"

"Well, I don't know, but you must've come here looking for something. Breaking the door down and all."

"Can't say I *capisce*," he spoke, measuredly. "Surely you must be mistaken. We don't want nothing. We just came for a little chat. That's all. Not looking and not taking. However, if you would care to offer me a Coca-Cola, I'd be happy to oblige."

I fished two cans of Coke from the refrigerator, which I set out on the table along with a couple of glasses.

"I don't suppose he'd drink something, too?" I said, pointing to the hulk behind me.

Junior curled his index finger and Big Boy tiptoed forward to claim a can of Coke. He was amazingly agile for his frame.

"After you're finished drinking, give him your free demonstration," Junior said to Big Boy. "It's a little side show," he said to me.

I turned around to watch the hulk chug the entire can in one go. Then, after upending it to show that it was empty, he pressed the can between his palms. Not the slightest change came over his face as the familiar red can was crushed into a pathetic scrap of metal.

"A little trick, anybody could do," said Junior.

Next, Big Boy held the flattened aluminum toy up with his fingertips. Effortlessly, though a faint shadow now twitched on his lip, he tore the metal into shreds. Some trick.

"He can bend hundred-yen coins, too. Not so many

humans alive can do that," said Junior with authority.

I nodded in agreement.

"Ears, he rips 'em right off."

I nodded in agreement.

"Up until three years ago, he was a pro wrestler," Junior explained. "Wasn't a bad wrestler. He was young and fast. Championship material. But you know what he did? He went and injured his knee. And in pro wrestling, you gotta be able to move fast."

I nodded a third agreement.

"Since his untimely injury, I've been looking after him. He's my cousin, you know."

"Average body types don't run in your family?" I queried.

"Care to say that again?" said Junior, glaring at me.

"Just chatting," I said.

Junior collected his thoughts for the next few moments. Then he flicked his cigarette to the floor and ground it out under his shoe. I decided no comment.

"You really oughta relax more. Open up, take things easy. If you don't relax, how're we have gonna have our nice heart-to-heart?" said Junior. "You're still too tense."

"May I get a beer?"

"Certainly. Of course. It's your beer—in your refrigerator—in your apartment. Isn't it?"

"It was my door, too," I added.

"Forget about the door. You keep thinking so much, no wonder you're tense. It was a tacky cheapo door anyway. You make good money, you oughta move someplace with classier doors."

I got my beer.

Junior poured Coke in his glass and waited for the foam to go down before drinking. Then he spoke. "Forgive the complications. But I wanna explain some things first. We've come to help you."

"By breaking down my door?"

The little man's face turned instantly red. His nostrils flared.

"There you go with that door again. Didn't I tell you to drop it?" he bit his words. Then he turned to Big Boy and repeated the question. "Didn't I?"

The hulk nodded his agreement.

"We're here on a goodwill mission," Junior went on. "You're lost, so we came to give you moral guidance. Well, perhaps lost is not such a nice thing to say. How about confused? Is that better?"

"Lost? Confused?" I said. "I don't have a clue. No idea, no door."

Junior grabbed his gold lighter and threw it hard against the refrigerator, making a dent. Big Boy picked the lighter off the floor and returned it to its owner. Everything was back to where we were before, except for the dent. Junior drank the rest of his Coke to calm down.

"What's one, two lousy doors? Consider the gravity of the situation. We could service this apartment in no time flat. Let's not hear another word about that door."

My door. It didn't matter how cheap it was. That wasn't the issue. The door stood for something.

"All right, forget about the door," I said. "This commotion could get me thrown out of the building."

"If anyone says anything to you, just give me a call. We got an outreach program that'll make believers out of them. Relax."

I shut up and drank my beer.

"And a free piece of advice," Junior offered. "Anybody over thirty-five really oughta kick the beer habit. Beer's for college students or people doing physical labor. Gives you a paunch. No class at all."

Great advice. I drank my beer.

"But who am I to tell you what to do?" Junior went on. "Everybody has his weak points. With me, it's smoking and sweets. Especially sweets. Bad for the teeth, leads to diabetes."

He lit another cigarette, and glanced at the dial of his Rolex.

"Well then," Junior cleared his throat. "There's not much time, so let's cut the socializing out. Relaxed a bit?"

"A bit," I said.

"Good. On to the subject at hand," said Junior. "Like I was saying, our purpose in coming here was to help you unravel your confusion. Anything you don't know? Go ahead and ask." Junior made a c'mon-anything-at-all gesture with his hand.

"Okay, just who are you guys?" I had to open my big mouth. "Why are you here? What do you know about what's going on?"

"Smart questions," Junior said, looking over to Big Boy for a show of agreement. "You're pretty sharp. You don't waste words, you get right to the point."

Junior tapped his cigarette into the ashtray. Kind of him.

"Think about it this way. We're here to help you. For the time being, what do you care which organization we belong to. We know lots. We know about the Professor, about the skull, about the shuffled data, about almost everything. We know things you don't know too. Next question?"

"Fine. Did you pay off a gas inspector to steal the skull?"

"Didn't I just tell you?" said the little man. "We don't want the skull, we don't want nothing."

"Well, who did? Who bought off the gas inspector?"

"That's one of the things we don't know," said Junior. "Why don't you tell us?"

"You think I know?" I said. "All I know is I don't need the grief."

"We figured that. You don't know nothing. You're being used."

"So why come here?"

"Like I said, a goodwill courtesy call," said Junior, banging his lighter on the table. "Thought we'd introduce ourselves. Maybe get together, share a few ideas. Your turn now. What do *you* think's going on?"

"You want me to speculate?"

"Go right ahead. Let yourself go, free as a bird, vast as the sea. Nobody's gonna stop you."

"All right, I think you guys aren't from either the System or the Factory. You've got a different angle on things. I think you're independent operants, looking to expand your turf. Eyeing Factory territory."

"See?" Junior remarked to his giant cousin. "Didn't I tell you? The man's sharp."

Big Boy nodded.

"Amazingly sharp for someone living in a dump like this. Amazingly sharp for someone whose wife ran out on him."

It had been ages since anyone praised me so highly. I blushed.

"You speculate good," Junior said. "We're going to get our hands on the Professor's research and make a name for us. We got these infowars all figured out. We done our home-work. We got the backing. We're ready to move in. We just need a few bits and pieces. That's the nice thing about infowars. Very democratic. Track record counts for nothing. It's survival of the sharpest. Survival in a big way. I mean, who's to say *we* can't cut the pie? Is Japan a total monopoly state or what? The System monopolizes everything under the info sun, the Factory monopolizes everything in the shadows. They don't know the meaning of competition. What ever happened to free enterprise? Is this unfair or what? All we need is the Professor's research, and you."

"Why me?" I said. "I'm just a terminal worker ant. I don't think about anything but my own work. So if you're thinking of enlisting me—"

"You don't seem to get the picture," said Junior, with a click of his tongue. "We don't wanna enlist you. We just wanna get our hands on you. Next question?"

"Oh, I see," I said. "How about telling me something about the INKlings then."

"INKlings? A sharp guy like you don't know about INKlings? A.k.a. Infra-Nocturnal Kappa. You thought *kappa* were folktales? They live underground. They hole up in the subways and sewers, eat the city's garbage, and drink gray-

water. They don't bother with human beings. Except for a
few subway workmen who disappear, that is, heh heh."

"Doesn't the government know about them?"

"Sure, the government knows. The state's not that dumb."

"Then why don't they warn people? Or else drive the
INKlings away?"

"First of all," he said, "it'd upset too many people.
Wouldn't want that to happen, would you? INKlings swarm-
ing right under their feet, people wouldn't like that. Second,
forget about exterminating them. What are you gonna do?
Send the whole Japanese Self-Defense Force down into the
sewers of Tokyo? The swamp down there in the dark is their
stomping grounds. It wouldn't be a pretty picture.

"Another thing, the INKlings have set up shop not too far
from the Imperial Palace. It's a strategic move, you understand. Any trouble and they crawl up at night and drag people under. Japan would be upside-down, heh. Am I right?
That's why the government doesn't mind INKlings and
INKlings doesn't mind the government."

"But I thought the Semiotecs had made friends with the
INKlings," I broke in.

"A rumor. And even if it was true, it'd only mean one
group of INKlings got sweet on the Semiotecs. A temporary
engagement, not a lasting marriage. Nothing to worry
about."

"But haven't the INKlings kidnapped the Professor?"

"We heard that too. But we don't know for sure. Could be
the Professor staged it."

"Why would the Professor do that?"

"The Professor answers to nobody," Junior said, sizing up
his lighter from various angles. "He's the best and he knows
it. The Semiotecs know it, the Calcutecs know it. He just
plays the in-betweens. That way he can push on, doing what
he pleases with his research. One of these days he's gonna
break through. That's where you fit in."

"Why would he need me? I don't have any special skills.
I'm a perfectly ordinary guy."

"We're trying to figure that one out for ourselves," Junior admitted, flipping the lighter around in his hands. "We got some ideas. Nothing definite. Anyway, he's been studying all about you. He's been preparing something for a long time now."

"Oh yeah? So you're waiting for him to put the last piece in place, and then you'll have me and the research."

"On the money," said Junior. "We got some strange weather blowing up. The Factory has sniffed something in the wind and made a move. So we gotta make moves, too."

"What about the System?"

"No, they're slow on the take. But give 'em time. They know the Professor real well."

"What do you mean?"

"The Professor used to work for the System."

"The System?"

"Right, the Professor is an ex-colleague of yours. Of course, he wasn't doing your kind of work. He was in Central Research."

"Central Research?" This was getting too complicated to follow. I was standing in the middle of it all, only I couldn't see a thing.

"This System of yours is big, too big. The right hand never knows what the left hand is doing. Too much information, more than you can keep track of. And the Semiotecs are just as bad. That's why the Professor quit the organization and went out on his own. He's a brain man. He's into psychology and all kinds of other stuff about the head. He's what you call a Renaissance Man. What does he need the System for?"

And I had explained laundering and shuffling to this man? He'd invented the tech! What a joke I was.

"Most of the Calcutec compu-systems around are his design. That's no exaggeration. You're like a worker bee stuffed full of the old man's honey," pronounced the little man. "Not a very nice metaphor, maybe."

"Don't mind me," I said.

"The minute the Professor quit, who should come knocking on his door but scouts from the Factory. But the Professor said no go. He said he had his own windows to wash, which lost him a lotta admirers. He knew too much for the Calcutecs, and the Semiotecs had him pegged for a round hole. Anyone who's not for you is against you, right? So when he built his laboratory underground next to the INKlings, it was the Professor against everybody. You been there, I believe?"

I nodded.

"Real nuts but brilliant. Nobody can get near that laboratory. The whole place is crawling with INKlings. The Professor comes and goes. He puts out sound waves to scare the INKlings. Perfect defense. That girl of his and you are the only people who's ever been inside. Goes to show how important you are. So we figure, the Professor's about to throw you in the box and tie things up."

I grunted. This was getting weird. Even if I believed him, I wouldn't believe it.

"Are you telling me that all the experiment data I processed for the Professor was just so he could lure me in?"

"No-o, not at all," said the little man. He cast another quick glance at his watch. "The data was a program. A time bomb. Time comes and—*booom!* Of course, this is just our guess. Only your Professor knows for sure. Well, I see time's running out, so I think we cut short our little chit-chat. We got ourselves a little appointment after this."

"Wait a second, what's happened to the Professor's granddaughter?"

"Something happened to the kid?" Junior asked innocently. "We don't know nothing about it. Can't watch out for everybody, you know. Had something for the little sweetheart, did you?"

"No," I said. Well, probably not.

Junior stood up from his chair without taking his eyes off me, swept up his lighter and cigarettes from the table and slipped them into his pocket. "I believe it was nice getting to know you. But let me back up and tell you a secret. Right now, we're one step ahead of the Semiotecs. Still, we're small, so if they decide to get their tails in gear, we get crushed. We need to keep them occupied. *Capisce?*"

"I suppose," I said.

"Now if you were in our position, what do you think'd keep them nice and occupied?"

"The System?" was my guess.

"See?" Junior again remarked to Big Boy. "Sharp and to the point. Didn't I tell you?" Then he looked back at me. "But for that, *we* need bait. No bait, no bite."

"I don't really feel up to that sort of thing," I said quickly.

"We're not asking you how you feel," he said. "We're in a bit of a hurry. So now it's our turn for one little question. In this apartment, what things do you value the most?"

"There's nothing here," I said. "Nothing of any value. It's all cheap stuff."

"We know that. But there's gotta be something, some trinket you don't wanna see destroyed. Cheap or not, it's your life here, eh?"

"Destroyed?" I said. "What do you mean, destroyed?"

"Destroyed, you know . . . destroyed. Like with the door," said the little man, pointing to the thing lying blown off its twisted hinges. "Destruction."

"What for?"

"Destruction for the sake of destruction. You want an explanation? Why don't you just tell us what you don't want to see destroyed. We want to show them the proper respect."

"Well, the videodeck," I said, giving in. "And the TV. They're kind of expensive and I just bought them. Then there's my collection of whiskeys."

"Anything else?"

"My new suit and my leather jacket. It's a U.S. Air Force bomber jacket with a fur collar."

"Anything else?"

"That's all," I said.

The little man nodded. The big man nodded.

Immediately, Big Boy went around opening all the cupboards and closets. He found the Bullworker I sometimes use for exercising, and swung it around behind him to do a full back-press. Very impressive.

He then gripped the shaft like a baseball bat. I leaned forward to see what he was up to. He went over to the TV, raised the Bullworker, and took a full swing at the picture tube. *Krrblam!* Glass shattered everywhere, accompanied by a hundred short sputtering flashes.

"Hey! . . ." I shouted, clamoring to my feet before Junior slapped his palm flat on the table to silence me.

Next Big Boy lifted the videodeck and pounded it over and over again on a corner of the former TV. Switches went flying, the cord shorted, and a cloud of white smoke rose up into the air like a saved soul. Once the videodeck was good and destroyed, Big Boy tossed the carcass to the floor and pulled a switchblade from his pocket. The blade sprang open. Now he was going through my wardrobe and retailoring close to two-hundred-thousand-yen worth of bomber jacket and Brooks Brothers suit.

"But you said you were going to leave my valuables alone," I cried.

"I never said that. I said we were gonna show them the proper respect. We always start with the best. Our little policy."

Big Boy was bringing new meaning to the word destruction in my cozy, tasteful apartment. I pulled another can of beer out of the refrigerator and sat back to watch the fireworks.

14

Woods

IN due time, autumn too vanishes. One morning I awake, and from a glance at the sky I know winter is near. Gone are the high, sprightly autumn clouds; in their place a heavy cloud bank glowers over the Northern Ridge, like a messenger bearing ill tidings. Autumn had been welcomed as a cheerful and comely visitor; its stay was too brief, its departure too abrupt.

The passing of autumn leaves a temporary blank, an empty hole in the year that is not of a season at all. The beasts begin to lose the sheen from their coats, lose their golden hue, bleaching slowly white. It is an announcement that winter draws near. All living things in the Town hang their heads, their bodies braced for the freezing season. Signs of winter shroud the Town like an invisible skin. The sound of the wind, the swaying of the grasses, the clack of heels on the cobblestones in the still of night, all grow remote under an ominous weight. Even the waters of the River, once so pleasant as they lapped at the sandbars, no longer soothe me. There is an instinctive withdrawal for the sake of preservation, a closure that assumes the order of completion. Winter is a season unto itself. The short cries of the birds grow thin and shrill; at times only the flapping of their wings disturbs the void.

"This winter promises to be especially harsh," observes the Colonel. "You can tell from the look of the clouds. Here, see for yourself how dark they are."

The old officer leads me to the window and points toward the thick clouds astride the hills.

"Each year at this time, the first wave of winter clouds stations itself along the Northern Ridge. They are the emissaries of the onslaught to come. Light, flat clouds mean mild temperatures. Thicker clouds, colder weather. Most fearsome of all are the clouds that spread their wings, like birds of prey. When they appear, a bitter winter is on its way. For example, that cloud there."

Squinting, I scan the sky above the Northern Ridge. Faint though it is, I do recognize the cloud the old officer has described. Massive as a mountain, it stretches the entire length of the ridge, an evil roc ready to swoop down from the heights.

"Once every fifty or sixty years, there comes a killing winter," says the Colonel. "You have no coat, do you?"

"No, I do not," I say. I have only the light cotton jacket I was given when I first came to Town.

The old officer opens his wardrobe and brings out a dark blue military coat. He hands it to me. The coat is heavy as stone, its wool rough to the touch.

"A little large, but it will serve you well. I procured it for you a short while ago. How is the size?"

I slip into the coat. The shoulders are too wide and the form somehow not right, but it will do. As the old officer has said, it will serve me well.

"Are you still drawing your map?" the Colonel asks.

"I am," I say. "There are some areas I do not know, but I am determined to finish it."

"I will not discourage you from your maps. That is your own concern, and it bothers no one. No, I will not say it is wrong, although after winter is here, you must stop all excursion into the Woods. Venturing far from inhabited areas is not wise, especially this winter. The Town, as you know, is not extensive, but you can lose your way. It would be better to leave your mapmaking for spring."

"I understand," I say. "When does winter begin?"

"With the snow. The first flakes of snow signal the beginning of winter. When the snow melts from the sandbars in the River, winter is at its end."

We gaze at the clouds on the Northern Ridge, drinking our morning coffee.

"One more important thing," the Colonel resumes. "Keep your distance from the Wall and from the Woods. In winter, they take on an awesome power."

"What is this about the Woods? What is it that they have?"

"Nothing at all," says the old military man after a moment of reflection. "Nothing at all. At least, it is nothing we need. For us, the Woods are an unnecessary terrain."

"Does no one live in the woods?"

The old officer lifts the trap on the stove and sweeps out the ash. He then lays in a few twigs of kindling and some coal. "We may need to light the stoves beginning tonight," he says. "Our firewood and coal are from the Woods. Yes, and mushrooms and tea and other provisions as well. So in that sense, the Woods are of use to us. But that is all. Other than that, nothing is there."

"Then there are persons in the Woods who make their living by shovelling the coal and gathering firewood and mushrooms?"

"Yes, a few do live there. They bring their coal and firewood and mushrooms to Town, and in return we give them grain and clothing. There is a place where these exchanges

146

take place weekly, but it is carried out only by specified individuals. No other contact with the Woodsfolk is to be had. They do not come near the Town; we do not go near the Woods. Their existence is wholly different from our own."

"How so?"

"In every sense," says the old officer, "they are different from us. But it is not wise to take an interest in them. They are dangerous. They can exert an influence over you. You are not yet formed as a person here. And until such time as various aspects of you are determined, I advise you to protect yourself from such danger. The Woods are but woods. You need merely write 'Woods' on your map. Is that understood?"

"Understood."

"Then, there is the Wall. The winter Wall is the height of danger. In winter, particularly, the Wall shuts the Town in. It is impenetrable and it encloses us irrevocably. The Wall sees everything that transpires within. Be careful to do nothing that takes you near the Wall. I must repeat: you are as yet unformed. You have doubts, you have contradictions, you have regrets, you are weak. Winter is the most dangerous season for you."

All the same, before winter sets in, I must venture forth into the Woods. It will soon be time to deliver the map, as promised, to my shadow. He has expressly asked that I investigate the Woods. After I have done that, the map will be ready.

The cloud on the Northern Ridge poses, lifting its wings, leaning forward as if to sail out over the Town. The sun is setting. The sky is overcast, a pallid cover through which the light filters and settles. To my eyes that are less than eyes, this is a season of relief. Gone, the days of brazen clear skies. There will be no headstrong breezes to sweep away the clouds.

I enter the Woods from the riverside road, intending to walk straight into the interior, keeping parallel to the Wall so I do not to lose my way. Thus will I also sketch the outline of the Wall around the Woods.

This does not prove easy. Mid-route there are deep hollows where the ground drops away. I step carefully, yet find myself plunged into thick blackberry brambles. Marshy ground thwarts passage; elsewhere spiders hang their webs to net my face and hands. An awning of enormous branches tinges the Woods in sea-bottom gloom. Roots crawl through the forest floor like a virulent skin disease.

At times I imagine I hear movement in the dense undergrowth.

Yet once I turn from the Wall and set foot in the forest interior, there unfolds a mysteriously peaceful world. Infused with the life breath one senses in the wild, the Woods give me release. How can this be the minefield of dangers the old Colonel has warned me against? Here the trees and plants and tiny living things partake of a seamless living fabric; in every stone, in every clod of earth, one senses an immutable order.

The farther I venture from the Wall and proceed into the forest interior, the stronger these impressions become. All shades of misfortune soon dissipate, while the very shapes of the trees and colors of the foliage grow somehow more restive, the bird songs longer and more leisurely. In the tiny glades, in the breezes that wend through the inner woodlands, there is none of the darkness and tension I have felt nearer the Wall. Why should these surroundings make so marked a difference? Is it the power of the Wall that disturbs the air? Is it the land itself?

No matter how pleasant this walk deeper into the Woods may be, I dare not relinquish sight of the Wall. For should I stray deep into the Woods, I will have lost all direction. There are no paths, no landmarks to guide me. I moderate my steps.

I do not meet any forest dwellers. I see not a footprint,

not an artifact shaped by human hands. I walk, afraid, expectant. Perhaps I have not traveled far enough into the interior. Perhaps they are skillfully avoiding me.

On the third or fourth day of these explorations, coming to a point where the eastern Wall takes a sharp turn to the south, I discover a small glade. It is open space, which fans briefly outward from a tuck in the bend of the Wall. Inexplicably, it is untouched by the surrounding growth of dense forest. This one clearing is permeated with a repose that seems uncharacteristic so close to the Wall, a tranquillity such as I have known only in the inner Woods. A lush carpet of grass spreads over the ground, while overhead a puzzle-piece of sky cuts through the treetops.

At one extreme of the glade stands a raised masonry foundation that once supported a building. The foundation suggests that the walls of this edifice had been laid out with meticulous precision. Tracing the floorplan, I find three separate rooms in addition to what I imagine were a kitchen, bath, and hallway. I struggle to understand why a home had been built so deep in the Woods, why it has been so completely abandoned.

Behind the kitchen are the remains of a stone well. It is overgrown with grass. Would the occupants themselves have filled it in?

I sit down, leaning against the well and gazing up at the sky. A wind blowing in off the Northern Ridge rustles the branches of the trees around me. A cloud, heavy with moisture, edges across the sky. I turn up my collar and watch it move slowly past.

The Wall looms behind the ruins of the house. Never in the Woods have I been this close to the Wall. It is literally breathtaking. Here in this tiny clearing in the Eastern Woods, resting by this old well, listening to the sound of the wind, looking up at the Wall, I fully understand the words of the Gatekeeper: *This Wall is perfect.* A perfect creation.

It rises as it has risen from the beginning. Like the clouds above, like the River etched into the earth.

The Wall is far too grand to capture on a map. It is not static. Its pulse is too intense, its curves too sublime. Its face changes dramatically with each new angle. An accurate rendering on paper cannot be possible. I feel a futility in my attempt to do so in my sketchbook.

I shut my eyes to doze. The wind swirls at an incessant pitch, but the trees and the Wall offer protection from the chill. I think about my shadow. I think of the map he has asked for. There is not much time left.

My map is lacking in precision and detail. The inner reaches of the Woods are a near blank. But winter is almost here. There will be less and less opportunity to explore further. In the sketchbook I have drawn a general outline of the Town, including the location of landmarks and buildings. I have made annotations of facts I have learned.

It is not certain that the Gatekeeper will allow me near my shadow, even as he has promised to let us meet once the days are shorter and my shadow is weaker. Now that winter is near, these conditions would seem surely to be fulfilled.

My eyes still closed, I think about the Librarian. I am filled with sadness, although I cannot locate the source of these feelings.

I have been seeing the Librarian daily, but the void in me remains. I have read the old dreams in the Library. She has sat beside me. We have supped together. I have walked her home. We have talked of many things. Unreasonably, my sorrow only seems to grow, to deepen. Whatever is the loss becomes greater each time we meet. It is a well that will never be filled. It is dark, unbearably so.

I suppose these feelings are linked to forgotten memories. I have sought for some connection in her. I learn nothing in myself. The mystery does not yield. My own existence seems weak, uncertain.

I shake these convoluted thoughts from my head and seek out sleep.

I awake to find that the day is nearly over, that the temperature has dropped sharply. I am shivering. I pull my coat tight around me. As I stand and brush off the grass, flakes of snow touch my cheek. I look up. The clouds are low, a forbidding gloom builds. There is a flurry of large snowflakes drifting gently down. Winter is come.

Before I begin my way back, I steal one more glance at the Wall. Beneath the snow-swept heavens, it rears up more stately, more perfect than ever. As I gaze up at it, I feel *them* peering at me. *What are you doing here?* they seem to say. *What are you looking for?*

Questions I cannot answer. The short sleep in the cold has consumed all warmth in me, leaving my head swimming with abstract shapes. Do I occupy the body of another? Everything is so ponderously heavy, so vague.

I race through the Woods, toward the East Gate, determined now not to look at the Wall. It is a long distance I must travel. The darkness gathers moment by moment. My balance degenerates. I stop again and again to stir up the strength to persevere, to press the numbness from my nerves. I feel the visit of night. I may hear the sounding of the horn in the Woods. It passes through my awareness without trace.

At last I emerge from the Woods onto the bank of the River. The ground is clothed in blankness. No moon, no stars, all has been subdued by the flurries of snow. I hear the chill sound of the water, the wind taunting through the trees behind me. How much further to the Library? I cannot remember. All I recall is a road along the River, leading on and on. The willows sway in the shadows, the wind whips overhead. I walk and walk, but there is no end in sight.

She sits me in front of the stove and places her hand on

my forehead. Her hand is as ice. My reflex is to push it away, but I cannot raise my hand. For when I do, I feel a sudden nausea.

"You are fevered," she says. "Where on the earth have you gone?"

I find it impossible to answer. I am without words. I cannot even comprehend what it is she asks.

She brings several blankets and wraps me in them. I lie by the stove. Her hair touches my cheek. I do not want her to go away. I cannot tell if the thought is mine or if it has floated loose from some fragment of memory. I have lost so many things. I am so tired. I feel myself drifting, away, a little by little. I am overcome by the sensation that I am crumbling, parts of my being drifting, away. Which part of me is thinking this?

She holds my hand.

"Sleep well," I hear her say, from beyond a dark distance.

15

Whiskey, Torture, Turgenev

IG BOY didn't leave one bottle unbroken. Not one lousy bottle of my collection of whiskeys. I had a standing relationship with the neighborhood liquor dealer who would bring over any bargains in imported whiskey, so it had gotten to be quite a respectable stash. Not any more.

The hulk started with two bottles of Wild Turkey, moving next to one Cutty Sark and three I. W. Harpers, then demolished two Jack Daniels, the Four Roses, the Haig, saving the half dozen bottles of Chivas Regal for last. The racket was intense, but the smell was worse.

"I'm getting drunk just sitting here," Junior said with admiration.

There wasn't much for me to do but plant my elbows on the table and watch the mound of broken glass pile up in the sink. Big Boy whistled through it all. I couldn't recognize the tune, supposing there was one. First high and shrill, then low and harsh, it sounded more like a scraping violin bow. The screech of it was insanity itself.

Big Boy was methodical with the meaningless destruction. Maybe it made sense to them, not to me. He overturned the bed, slit the mattress, rifled through my wardrobe, dumped my desk drawers onto the floor, ripped the air-conditioner panel off the wall. He knocked over the trash, then plowed through the bedding closet, breaking whatever happened to be in the way. Swift and efficient.

Then it was on to the kitchen: dishes, glasses, coffeepot, the works.

Junior and I moved our seats to the living room. We righted the toppled sofa, which by a freak stroke of fortune was otherwise unscathed, and sat on opposite armrests. Now this was a truly comfortable sofa, a top-of-the-line model I'd bought cheap off a cameraman friend who'd blown his fuse in the middle of a thriving commercial career and split for the back country of Nagano. Too bad about the fuse, not so bad about the sofa I'd acquired as a result. And there was a chance that the sofa would be salvageable still.

For all the noise that Big Boy was making, not one other resident of the apartment building came to investigate. True, almost everyone on my floor was single and at work during the day—a fact apparently not lost upon my visitors. These guys were thugs, but they weren't dumb.

The little man eyed his Rolex from time to time as if to check the progress of the operation, while Big Boy continued his tour of destructive duty with never a wasted motion. He was so thorough, I couldn't have hidden away a pencil if I had wanted to. Yet, like Junior had announced at the beginning, they weren't really looking for anything. They were simply making a point.

For what?

To convince a third party of their attention to detail?

And who might that third party be?

I drank the rest of my beer and set the empty can on the coffee table. Big Boy had gotten to the food: salt, flour, and rice went flying everywhere; a dozen frozen shrimp, a beef filet, natural ice cream, premium butter, a thirty-centimeter length of salmon roe, my homemade tomato sauce on the linoleum floor like meteorites nosediving into asphalt.

Next, Big Boy picked up the refrigerator and flipped it door-side down to the floor. The wiring shorted and let loose with a shower of sparks. What electrician was going to believe this? My head hurt.

Then, as suddenly as it had begun, the destruction stopped. No ifs, ands, or buts—the demolition came to an instant halt, Big Boy standing in the doorway between the kitchen and living room, very nonchalant.

How long had it taken him to total my apartment so exquisitely? Fifteen minutes, thirty minutes? Something like that. Too long for fifteen, too short for thirty. But however long it took, the way that Junior was proudly eyeing his Rolex suggested that Big Boy had made good time. As with marathon runs and lengths of toilet paper, there had to be standards to measure up to.

"Seems like you're gonna be busy cleaning up," Junior said to me.

"And paying for it too," I added.

"Money's no object here. This is war. Nobody would win a war if they stopped to calculate the cost."

"It's not my war."

"Whose war don't matter. Whose money don't matter either. That's what war is."

Junior coughed into a white handkerchief, inspecting it before putting it back into his pocket. Never trust a man who carries a handkerchief, I always say. One of many prejudicial rules of thumb.

"Now listen," Junior got serious, "not too long after we leave, the boys from the System will be stopping by to pay their respects. You go ahead and tell them about us. Say we broke in and busted up the place hunting for something.

Tell them we asked you where the skull was, but you didn't know nothing about no skull. Got it? You can't squeal about something you don't know and you can't fork over something you don't have. Even under torture. That's why we're gonna leave empty-handed as when we came."

"Torture?" I choked.

"Nobody's gonna doubt you. They don't even know you paid a visit to the Professor. For the time being, we're the only ones who know that. So no harm's gonna come to you. A Calcutec like yourself with a Record of Excellence? Hell, they got no choice but to trust you. They're gonna think we're Factory. And they're gonna wanna do something about it. We got it all worked out."

"Torture?" I choked again. "What do you mean, torture?"

"You'll find out soon enough," said the little man.

"What if I spilled the whole works to the folks at Headquarters?" Just thought I'd ask.

"Don't be dumb. You'd get rubbed out by your own fellas. That's not an exaggeration. Think about it. You went to the Professor's place on a job, you didn't tell the System. You broke the freeze on shuffling. And worse, you let the Professor use you in his experiments. They gonna like that? You're doing a very dangerous balancing act, pal."

Our faces met from either end of the sofa.

"I have a question," I said. "How do I stand to benefit from cooperating with you and lying to the System? I know zero about you guys. What's in it for me?"

"That's easy," Junior chirped. "We got the lowdown on what's in store for you, but we're letting you live. Your organization doesn't know nothing about the situation you're in. But if they did, they might decide to eliminate you. I figure your odds are way better with us."

"Sooner or later, the System is going to find out about this situation, as you call it. I don't know what this situation is, but the System's not so stupid."

"Maybe so," said Junior. "But that's later. This is now. If

all goes according to schedule, you and us, we're gonna have our problems solved in the meantime. That's your choice, if you're looking for one. Let me put it another way: it's like chess. You get checked, you beat a retreat. And while you're scrambling around, maybe your opponent will screw up. Everybody screws up, even the smartest players."

Junior checked his watch again, then turned to Big Boy and snapped his fingers. Whereupon the hulk blinked to life, a robot with the juice switched on. He lifted his jaw and hunkered over to the sofa, positioning himself like a room divider. No, not a room divider, more like a drive-in movie screen. His body blocked the ceiling light, throwing me into a pale shadow, like when I was in elementary school and all the kids held up a pane of glass smoked with candle soot to view a solar eclipse. A quarter of a century ago that was. Look where that quarter of a century had gotten me.

"And now," he resumed, "I'm afraid we're gonna have to make things a little unpleasant. Well, maybe you're gonna think it's more than a little unpleasant. But just remember, we're doing it for you. It's not like we wanna do it. We're doing it because we got no choice. Take off your pants."

I did as I was told. As if I had any choice.

"Kneel down."

I kneeled down. I felt funny doing it in my sweatshirt and jockey shorts, but there wasn't much time for meditation as Big Boy swooped in behind me and pinned my wrists to the small of my back. Then he locked my ankles firmly between his legs. His movements were very fluid. I didn't particularly feel tied down, but when I tried to budge, a sharp pain shot through me. I was immobilized, like a duck sitting in a shooting gallery.

Meanwhile, Junior found Big Boy's knife. He flicked the seven-centimeter blade open, then ran the blade through the flame of his lighter. This compact knife didn't look like a lethal weapon, but it was obviously no dime-store toy. It was sharp enough to slice a person to pieces. The human fruit is always ripe for peeling.

After sterilizing the blade, Junior let it cool slightly. Then he yanked down the waistband of my jockey shorts and exposed my penis.

"Now this is going to hurt a little," he said.

A tennis-ball-sized lump of air bounced up from my stomach and lodged in my throat. Sweat beaded up on my nose. I was shaking. At this rate, I'd never be able to get an erection.

But no, the guy didn't do anything to my cock. He simply gripped it to death, while he took the still-warm blade and glided it across my stomach. Straight as a ruler, a six-centimeter horizontal gash, two centimeters below my navel.

I tried to suck in my gut, but between Big Boy's clamp on my back and Junior's grip on my cock, I couldn't move a hair. Cold sweat gushed from every pore of my body. Then, a moment after the surgery was over, I was wracked with searing pain.

Junior wiped the blood off the knife with a kleenex and folded the blade away. Big Boy let me drop. My white jockey shorts were turning red. Big Boy fetched a towel from the bathroom, and I pressed it to the wound.

"Seven stitches and you'll be like new," Junior diagnosed. "It'll leave a scar, but nobody's gonna see it. Sorry we had to do it, but you'll live."

I pulled back the towel and looked at the wound. The cut wasn't very deep, but deep enough to see pink.

"We're gonna go now. When your System boys show up, let 'em see this little example of wanton violence. Tell 'em when you wouldn't tell us where the skull was, we went nuts. But next time, our aims won't be so high, and we might have to go for your nuts, heh heh. You can tell 'em we said that. Anyway, you didn't know nothing, so you didn't tell us nothing. That's why we decided to take a rain check. Got it? We can do a real nice job if we want to.

Maybe one day soon, if we have the time, we'll give you another demonstration."

I crouched there with the towel pressed against my gut. Don't ask me why, but I got the feeling I'd be better off playing their game.

"So you did set up that poor gas inspector," I sputtered. "You had him blow the act on purpose so I would go hide the stuff."

"Clever, clever," said the little man. "Keep that head of yours working and maybe you'll survive."

On that note, my two visitors left. There was no need to see them out. The mangled frame of my steel door was now open for all the world.

I stripped off my blood-stained underwear and threw it in the trash, then I moistened some gauze and wiped the blood from the wound. The gash throbbed pain with every move. The sleeves of my sweatshirt were also bloody, so I tossed it too. Then from the clothes scattered on the floor, I found a dark T-shirt which wouldn't show the blood too much, a pair of jockeys, and some loose trousers.

Thirty minutes later, right on schedule, three men from Headquarters arrived. One of whom was the smart-ass young liaison who always came around to pick up data, outfitted in the usual business suit, white shirt, and bank clerk's tie. The other two were dressed like movers. Even so, they didn't look a thing like a bank clerk and movers; they looked like they were trying to look like a bank clerk and movers. Their eyes shifted all over the place; every motion was tense.

They didn't knock before walking into the apartment, shoes and all, either. The two movers began immediately to check the apartment while the bank clerk proceeded to debrief me. He scribbled the facts down with a mechanical pencil in a black notebook. As I explained to him, a two-man unit had broken in, wanting a skull. I didn't know anything about a skull; they got violent and slashed my stomach. I pulled my briefs down. The clerk examined the wound momentarily, but made no comment about it.

"Skull? What the hell were they talking about?"

"I have no idea," I said. "I'd like to know myself."

"You really don't know?" the bank clerk probed further, his voice uninflected. "This is critical, so think carefully. You won't be able to alter your statement later. Semiotecs don't make a move if they have nothing to go on. If they came to your apartment looking for a skull, they must have had a reason for thinking you had a skull in your apartment. They don't dream things up. Furthermore, that skull must have been valuable enough to come looking for. Given these obvious facts, it's hard to believe you don't know anything about it."

"If you're so smart, why don't you tell me what this skull business is supposed to be about," I said.

"There will be an investigation," the bank clerk said, tapping his mechanical pencil on his notebook. "A thorough investigation, and you know how thorough the System can be. If you're discovered to be hiding something, you will be dealt with commensurately. You are aware of this?"

I was aware of this, I told him. I didn't know how this was going to turn out, but neither did they. Nobody can outguess the future.

"We had a hunch the Semiotecs were up to something. They're mobilizing. But we don't know what they're after, and we don't know how you fit into it. We don't know what to make of this skull either. But as more clues come in, you can be sure we'll get to the heart of the matter. We always do."

"So what am I supposed to do?"

"Be very careful. Cancel any jobs you have. Pay attention to anything unusual. If anything comes up, contact me immediately. Is the telephone still in service?"

I lifted the receiver and got a dial tone. Obviously, the

two thugs had chosen to leave the telephone alone.

"The line's okay."

"Good," he said. "Remember, if anything happens, no matter how trivial, get in touch with me right away. Don't even think about trying to solve things yourself. Don't think about hiding anything. Those guys aren't playing softball. Next time you won't get off with a scratch."

"Scratch? You call that a scratch?"

The movers reported back after completing their survey of the premises.

"We've conducted a full search," said the older mover. "They didn't overlook a thing, went about it very smoothly. Professional job. Semiotecs."

The liaison nodded, and the two operants exited. It was now the liaison and me.

"If all they were looking for was a skull," I wondered out loud, "why would they rip up my clothes? How was I supposed to hide a skull there? If there *was* a skull, I mean."

"They were professionals. Professionals think of every contingency. You might have put the skull in a coin locker and they were looking for the key. A key can be hidden any-where."

"True," I said. Quite true.

"By the way, did these Factory henchmen make you a proposition?"

"A proposition?"

"Yeah, a propostion. That you go to work for them, for example. An offer of money, a position."

"If they did, I sure didn't hear it. They just demanded their skull."

"Very well," said the liaison. "If anyone makes you an offer, you are to forget it. You are not to play along. If the System ever discovers you played ball with them, we will find you, wherever you are, and we will terminate you. This is not a threat; this is a promise. The System is the state. There is *nothing* we cannot do."

"I'll keep that in mind," I said.

When I was alone again, I went over the story piece by piece. No matter how I stacked the essential details, they didn't lead anywhere. At the heart of the mystery was the Professor and whatever he was up to. If I didn't know that, I couldn't know anything. And I didn't have the vaguest notion what was whirling around in that old head of his.

The only thing I knew for certain was that I had let myself betray the System. If they found that out—and soon enough they would—that'd be the end, exactly as my smart-ass bank-clerk liaison had been kind enough to point out. Even if I had been coerced into lying like I did. The System wasn't known for making exceptions on any account.

As I was assessing these circumstances, my wound began to throb. Better go to the hospital. I rang up for a taxi. Then I stepped into my shoes. Bending over to tie my laces, I was in such pain I thought my body was going to shear in two.

I left the apartment wide open—as if I had any other option—and took the elevator down. I waited for the cab behind the hedge by the entranceway. It was one-thirty by my watch. Two and a half hours since the demolition derby had begun. A very long two-and-a-half hours ago.

Housewives filed past, leek and *daikon* radish tops sticking up from supermarket bags. I found myself envying them. They hadn't had their refrigerators raped or their bellies slashed. Leeks and *daikon* and the kids' grades—all was right with the world. No unicorn skulls or secret codes or consciousness transfers. This was normal, everyday life.

I thought, of all things, about the frozen shrimp and beef and tomato sauce on the kitchen floor. Probably should eat the stuff before the day was out. Waste not, want not. Trouble was, I didn't want.

The mailman scooted up on a red Supercub and distributed the mail to the boxes at the entrance of the building. Some boxes received tons of mail, others hardly anything at all. The mailman didn't touch my box. He didn't even look at it.

Beside the mailboxes was a potted rubber plant, the ceramic container littered with popsicle sticks and cigarette butts. The rubber plant looked as worn out as I felt. Seemed like every passerby had heaped abuse on the poor thing. I didn't know how long it'd been sitting there. I must have walked by it every day, but until I got knifed in the gut, I never noticed it was there.

When the doctor saw my wound, the first thing he asked was how I managed to get a cut like that.

"A little argument—over a woman," I said. It was the only story I could come up with.

"In that case, I have to inform the police," the doctor said.

"Police? No, it was me who was in the wrong, and luckily the wound isn't too deep. Could we leave the police out of it, please?"

The doctor muttered and fussed, but eventually he gave in. He disinfected the wound, gave me a couple of shots, then brought out the needle and thread. The nurse glared suspiciously at me as she plastered a thick layer of gauze over the stitches, then wrapped a rubber belt of sorts around my waist to hold it in place. I felt ridiculous.

"Avoid vigorous activity," cautioned the doctor. "No sex or belly-laughing. Take it easy, read a book, and come back tomorrow."

I said my thanks, paid the bill, and went home. With great pain and difficulty, I propped the door up in place, then, as per doctor's orders, I climbed into what there was of my bed with Turgenev's *Rudin*. Actually, I'd wanted to read *Spring Torrents*, but I would never have found it in my shambles of an apartment. And besides, if you really think about it, *Spring Torrents* isn't that much better a novel than *Rudin*.

I got up and went to the kitchen, where I poked around in the mess of broken bottles in the sink. There under spears of glass, I found the bottom of a bottle of Chivas that was fairly intact, holding maybe a jigger of precious amber liquid. I held the bottle-bottom up to the light, and seeing no glass bits, I took my chances on the lukewarm whiskey for a bedtime nurse.

I'd read *Rudin* before, but that was fifteen years ago in university. Rereading it now, lying all bandaged up, sipping my whiskey in bed in the afternoon, I felt new sympathy for the protagonist Rudin. I almost never identify with anybody in Dostoyevsky, but the characters in Turgenev's old-fashioned novels are such victims of circumstance, I jump right in. I have a thing about losers. Flaws in oneself open you up to others with flaws. Not that Dostoyevsky's characters don't generate pathos, but they're flawed in ways that don't come across as faults. And while I'm on the subject, Tolstoy's characters' faults are so epic and out of scale, they're as static as backdrops.

I finished *Rudin* and tossed the paperback on top of what had been a bookcase, then I returned to the glass pile in the sink in search of another hidden pocket of whiskey. Near the bottom of the heap I spied a scant shot of Jack Daniels, which I coaxed out and took back to bed, together with Stendhal's *The Red and the Black*. What can I say? I seemed to be in the mood for passé literature. In this day and age, how many young people read *The Red and the Black?*

I didn't care. I also happened to identify with Julien Sorel. Sorel's basic character flaws had all cemented by the age of fifteen, a fact which further elicited my sympathy. To have all the building blocks of your life in place by that age was, by any standard, a tragedy. It was as good as sealing yourself into a dungeon. Walled in, with nowhere to go but your own doom.

Walls.

A world completely surrounded by walls.

I shut the book and bid the last thimbleful of Jack Daniels farewell, turning over in my mind the image of a world within walls. I could picture it, with no effort at all. A very high wall, a very large gate. Dead quiet. Me inside. Beyond that, the scene was hazy. Details of the world seemed to be distinct enough, yet at the same time everything around me was dark and blurred. And from some great obscure distance, a voice was calling.

It was like a scene from a movie, a historical blockbuster. But which? Not *El Cid*, not *Ben Hur*, not *Spartacus*. No, the image had to be something my subconscious dreamed up.

I shook my head to drive the image from my mind. I was so tired.

Certainly, the walls represented the limitations hemming in my life. The silence, residue of my encounter with sound-removal. The blurred vision of my surroundings, an indication that my imagination faced imminent crisis. The beckoning voice, the everything-pink girl, probably.

Having subjected the hallucination to this quick-and-dirty analysis, I reopened my book. But I was no longer able to concentrate. My life is nothing, I thought. Zero. Zilch. A blank. What have I done with my life? Not a damned thing. I had no home. I had no family. I had no friends. Not a door to my name. Not an erection either. Pretty soon, not even a job.

That peaceful fantasy of Greek and cello was vaporizing as I lay there. If I lost my job, I could forget about taking life easy. And if the System was going to chase me to the ends of the earth, when would I find the time to memorize irregular Greek verbs?

I shut my eyes and let out a deep sigh, then rejoined *The Red and the Black*. What was lost was lost. There was no retrieving it, however you schemed, no returning to how things were, no going back.

I wouldn't have noticed that the day was over were it not for the Turgenevo-Stendhalian gloom that had crept in around me.

By my keeping off my feet, the pain in my stomach had subsided. Dull bass beats throbbed occasionally from the wound, but I just rode them out. Awareness of the pain was passing.

The clock read seven-twenty, but I felt no hunger. You'd think I might have wanted to eat something after the day I'd had, but I cringed at the very thought of food. I was short of sleep, my gut was slashed, and my apartment was gutted. There was no room for appetite.

Looking at the assortment of debris around me, I was reminded of a near-future world turned wasteland buried deep in its own garbage. A science fiction novel I'd read. Well, my apartment looked like that. Shredded suit, broken videodeck and TV, pieces of a flowerpot, a floor lamp bent out of shape, trampled records, tomato sauce, ripped-out speaker wires, . . . Joseph Conrad and Thomas Hardy novels spattered with dirty vase water, cut gladioli lying in memorium on a fallen cashmere sweater with a blob of Pelikan ink on the sleeve, . . . All of it, useless garbage.

When microorganisms die, they make oil; when huge timbers fall, they make coal. But everything here was pure, unadulterated rubbish that didn't make anything. Where does a busted videodeck get you?

I went back to the kitchen to try to salvage a few more sips of whiskey, but the proverbial last drop was not to be found. Gone down the drain, to the world of the INKlings.

As I rummaged through the sink, I cut a finger on a sliver of glass. I studied my finger as the blood fell drop by drop onto a whiskey label. After a real wound, what's a little cut? Nobody ever died from a cut on his finger.

I let the blood run and drip. The bleeding showed no sign of stopping, so I finally staunched it with kleenex.

Several empty beer cans were lying around like shell cas-
ings after a mortar barrage. I stooped to pick one up; the
metal was warm. Better warm drops of beer than none, I
thought. So I ferried the empties back to bed and continued
reading *The Red and the Black* while extracting the last few
milliliters out of each can. I needed something to release the
tensions and let me rest. Was that too much to ask? I
wanted to nod out for as long as it took the earth to spin
one Michael Jackson turnaround.

Sleep came over me in my wasteland of a home a little
before nine o'clock. I tossed *The Red and the Black* to the
floor, switched off the light, and curled up to sleep. Embry-
onic amid devastation.

But only for a couple of hours. At eleven, the chubby girl
in her pink suit was shaking me by the shoulders.

"Wake up, please. Please!" she cried. "This is no time to
be sleeping!" She pounded on me with her fists. "Please. If
you don't get up, the world is going to end!"

16

The Coming of Winter

I WAKE amidst reassuringly familiar smells. I am in my bed, my room. But the impression of everything is slightly altered. The scene seems recreated from memory. The stains on the ceiling, the marks on the plaster walls, small details.

It is raining outside. I hear it, ice cold, striking the roof, pouring into the ground. The sounds could be coming from my bedside, or from a mile away.

I see the Colonel sitting at the window, back as straight as ever, unmoving as he gazes out at the rain. What can there be to watch so intently in the rain?

I try to raise my hand, but my arm refuses to move. I try to speak but no voice will issue; I cannot force the air out of my lungs. My body is unbearably heavy, drained. It is all I can do to direct my eyes to the old officer by the window.

What has happened to me? When I try to remember, my head throbs with pain.

"Winter," says the Colonel, tapping his finger on the windowpane. "Winter is upon us. Now you understand why winter inspires such fear."

I nod vaguely.

Yes, it was winter that hurt me. I was running, from the Woods, toward the Library.

"The Librarian brought you here. With the help of the Gatekeeper. You were groaning with a high fever, sweating profusely. The day before yesterday."

"The day before yesterday . . . ?"

"Yes, you have slept two full days," says the old officer. "We worried you would never awaken. Did I not warn you about going into the Woods?"

"Forgive me."

The Colonel ladles a bowl of soup from a pot simmering on the stove. Then he props me up in bed and wedges a backrest in place. The backrest is stiff and creaks under my weight.

"First you eat," he says. "Apologize later if you must. Do you have an appetite?"

"No," I say. It is difficult even trying to inhale.

"Just this, then. You must eat this. Three mouthfuls and no more. Please."

The herbal stew is horribly bitter, but I manage to swallow the three mouthfuls. I can feel the strain melt from my body.

"Much better," says the Colonel, returning the spoon to the bowl. "It is not pleasant to taste, but the soup will force the poisons from your body. Go back to sleep. When you awaken, you will feel much better."

When I reawaken, it is already dark outside. A strong wind is pelting rain against the windowpanes. The old officer sits at my bedside.

"How do you feel? Some better?"

"Much better than before, yes," I say. "What time is it?"

"Eight in the evening."

I move to get out of bed, but am still dizzy.

"Where are you going?" asks the Colonel.

"To the Library. I have dreamreading to do."

"Just try walking that body of yours five yards, young fool!" he scolds.

"But I must work."

The Colonel shakes his head. "Old dreams can wait. The Librarian knows you must rest. The Library will not be open."

The old officer goes to the stove, pours himself a cup of tea, and returns to my bedside. The wind rattles the window.

"From what I can see, you seem to have taken a fancy to the Librarian," volunteers the Colonel. "I do not mean to pry, but you called out to her in your fever dream. It is nothing to be ashamed of. All young people fall in love."

I neither affirm nor deny.

"She is very worried about you," he says, sipping his tea. "I must tell you, however, that such love may not be prudent. I would rather not have to say this, but it is my duty."

"Why would it not be prudent?"

"Because she cannot requite your feelings. This is no fault of anyone. Not yours, not hers. It is nothing you can change, any more than you can turn back the River."

I rub my cheeks with both hands.

"Is it the mind you are speaking of?"

The old officer nods.

"I have a mind and she does not. Love her as I might, the vessel will remain empty. Is that right?"

"That is correct," says the Colonel. "Your mind may no longer be what it once was, but she has nothing of the sort. Nor do I. Nor does anyone here."

"But are you not being extremely kind to me? Seeing to my needs, attending my sickbed without sleep? Are these not signs of a caring mind?"

"No. Kindness and a caring mind are two separate qualities. Kindness is manners. It is superficial custom, an acquired practice. Not so the mind. The mind is deeper, stronger, and, I believe, it is far more inconstant."

I close my eyes and try to collect my scattered thoughts.

"From what I gather," I begin, "the mind is lost when the shadow dies. Is that not true?"

"It is."

"If her shadow is dead, as she tells me, does this mean that she can never regain her mind?"

The Colonel nods. "I have seen her records in the Town Hall. There has been no mistake. Her shadow died when she was seventeen. It was buried in the Apple Grove, as dictated. She may remember. Nonetheless, the girl was stripped of her shadow before she attained an awareness of the world, so she does not know what it is to have a mind. This is different from someone like me, who lost his shadow late in life. That is why I can account for the movements of your mind, while she cannot."

"But she remembers her mother. And her mother had a mind. Does that have no significance?"

He stirs the tea in his cup, then slowly drinks.

"No," says the Colonel. "The Wall leaves nothing to chance. The Wall has its way with all who possess a mind, absorbing them or driving them out. That seems to have been the fate of her mother."

"Is love then a thing of mind?"

"I do not want to see you disappointed. The Town is powerful and you are weak. This much you should have learned by now."

The old officer stares into his empty cup.

"In time your mind will not matter. It will go, and with it goes all sense of loss, all sorrow. Nor will love matter. Only liv-ing will remain. Undisturbed, peaceful living. You are fond of the girl and I believe she is fond of you. Expect no more."

"It is so strange," I say. "I still have a mind, but there are times I lose sight of it. Or no, the times I lose sight of it are few. Yet I have confidence that it will return, and that conviction sustains me."

The sun does not show its face for a long time thereafter.

When the fever subsides, I get out of bed and open the window to breathe the outside air. I can rise to my feet, but my strength eludes me for two days more. I cannot even turn the doorknob. Each evening the Colonel brings more of the bitter herbal soup, along with a gruel. And he tells me stories, memories of old wars. He does not mention the girl or the Wall again, nor do I dare to ask.

On the third day, I borrow the Colonel's walking stick and take a long constitutional about the Official Residences. As I walk, my body feels light and unmanageable. Perhaps the fever has burnt off, but that cannot be all. Winter has given everything around me a mysterious weight; I alone seem an outsider to that ponderous world.

From the slope of the Hill where stand the Official Residences, one looks out over the western half of the Town: the River, the Clocktower, the Wall, and far in the distance, the Gate in the west. My weak eyes behind black glasses cannot distinguish greater detail, although I have the impression that the winter air must give the Town a clarity.

I remember the map I must deliver to my shadow. It is now finished, but being bedridden has caused me to miss our appointed day by nearly a week. My shadow is surely worrying about me. Or he may have abandoned hope for me entirely. The thought depresses me.

I beg a pair of work boots from the Colonel. "My shadow wears only thin summer shoes," I say. "He will need these as winter gets colder."

I remove the inner sole of one, conceal the map, and replace the sole. I approach the Colonel again. "The Gatekeeper is not someone I can trust. Will you see that my shadow receives these?"

"Certainly," he says.

Before evening, he returns, stating that he has handed the boots to my shadow personally. "Your shadow expressed concern about you."

"How does he look?" I ask.

"The cold is beginning to diminish him. But he is in good spirits."

On the evening of the tenth day after my fever, I am able to descend to the base of the Western Hill and go to the Library.

As I push open the Library door, the air in the building hangs still and musty, more so than I recall. It is unlit and only my footfalls echo in the gloom. The fire in the stove is extinguished, the coffeepot cold. The ceiling is higher than it was. The counter lies under dust. She is not to be found. There is no human presence.

I sit on a wooden bench for lack of anything to do. I wait for her to come. If the door is unlocked, as it was, then she will. I keep my vigil, but there is no sign of her. All time outside the Library has ceased. I am here, alone, at the end of the world. I reach out and touch nothing.

The room is heavy with winter, its every item nailed fast. My limbs lose their weight. My head expands and contracts of its own will.

I rise from the bench and turn on the light. Then I scoop coal from the bucket to fuel the stove, strike a match to it, and sit back down. Somehow the light makes the room even gloomier, the fire in the stove turns it cold.

Perhaps I plumb too deep. Or perhaps a lingering numbness in the core of my body has lured me into a brief sleep. When I look up again, she is standing before me. A yellow powder of light diffuses in a halo behind her, veiling her silhouette. She wears her blue coat, her hair gathered round inside her collar. The scent of the winter wind is on her.

"I thought you would not come," I say. "I have been waiting for you."

She rinses out the coffeepot and puts fresh water on to heat. Then she frees her hair from inside her collar and removes her coat.

"Did you not think I would come?" she asks.

"I do not know," I say. "It was just a feeling."

"I will come as long as you need me."

Surely I do need her. Even as my sense of loss deepens each time we meet, I will need her.

"I want you to tell me about your shadow," I say. "I may have met her in my old world."

"Yes, that may be so. I remember the time you said we might have met before."

She sits in front of the stove and gazes into the fire.

"I was four when my shadow was taken away and sent outside the Wall. She lived in the world beyond, and I lived here. I do not know who she was there, just as she lost touch of me. When I turned seventeen, my shadow returned to the Town to die. Shadows always return to die. The Gatekeeper buried her in the Apple Grove."

"That is when you became a citizen of the Town?"

"Yes. The last of my mind was buried in the name of my shadow. You said that the mind is like the wind, but perhaps it is we who are like the wind. Knowing nothing, simply blowing through. Never aging, never dying."

"Did you meet with your shadow before she died?"

She shakes her head. "No, I did not see her. There was no reason for us to meet. She had become something apart from me."

The pot on the stove begins to murmur, sounding to my ears like the wind in the distance.

17

End of the World, Charlie Parker, Time Bomb

P LEASE," cried the chubby girl. "If you don't get up, the world is going to end!"

"Let it end," I said, groaning. The wound in my gut hurt too much for me to care.

"Why are you saying that? What's wrong? What's happened here?"

I grabbed a T-shirt and wiped the sweat off my face. "A couple of guys busted in and gave my stomach a six-centimeter gash," I spat out.

"With a knife?"

"Like a piggy bank."

"But why?"

"I've been trying to figure that one out myself," I said. "It occurred to me that the two guys with the knife might be friends of yours."

The chubby girl stared at me. "How could you think such a thing?" she cried.

"Oh, I don't know. I just wanted to blame somebody. Makes me feel better."

"But that doesn't solve anything."

"It doesn't solve anything," I seconded. "But so what. This had nothing to do with me. Your grandfather waved his hands, and suddenly I wind up in the middle of it."

Another boxcar of pain rolled in. I shut my mouth and waited at the crossing.

"Take today, for example. First, you call at who-knows-what hour of the morning. You tell me your grandfather's disappeared and you want me to help. I go to meet you; you don't show. I come back home to sleep; the Dynamic Duo busts into my apartment and knifes me in the gut. Next the guys from the System arrive and interrogate me. Now you're here. Seems like you all have things scheduled. Great little team you got." I took a breath. "All right, you're going to tell me everything you know about what's going on."

"I swear, I don't know any more than you do. I helped with Grandfather's research, but I only did what I was told. Errands. Do this, do that, go there, come here, make a phone call, write a letter, things like that. I don't really know anything else."

"But you did help with the research."

"I helped, but I just processed data. Technical stuff. I don't have the academic background, so I never understood anything more."

I tried to regroup my thoughts. I needed to figure things out before the situation dragged me under.

"Okay, just now, you were saying the world was going to end. What was that all about?"

"I don't know. It's something Grandfather said. 'If I had this in me, it'd be the end of the world.' Grandfather doesn't joke about things like that. If he said the world is going to end, then honest, the world is going to end."

"I don't get it," I said. "What's it supposed to mean, this end-of-the-world talk? What exactly did he say? Are you sure he didn't say, 'The world is going to be obliterated' or 'The world is going to be destroyed'?"

"No, he said, 'The world is going to end'."

More mental regrouping.

"So then, this . . . uh . . . 'end of the world' has something to do with me?"

"I guess so. Grandfather said you were the key. He started researching all about you a couple of years ago."

"A couple of years ago!" I couldn't believe what I was hearing. "What else? Anything about a time bomb?"

"A time bomb?"

"That's what the guy who knifed me said. That the data I processed for your grandfather was like a time bomb waiting to explode. Know anything about that?"

"Only hunches," said the chubby girl. "Grandfather has been studying human consciousness for a long time. And I don't believe shuffling is all there was to it. At least up until the time he came out with shuffling, Grandfather would tell me all kinds of things about his research. Like I said, I had practically no background, but Grandfather kept things simple, and it was really interesting. I used to love those little talks of ours."

"But then, once he finalized his system for shuffling, he clammed up?"

"That's right. Grandfather shut himself up in his underground laboratory and never told me anything more. Whenever I'd ask him about his research, he'd change the subject."

"Didn't that strike you as odd?"

"Well, it did make me unhappy. And very lonely." Then, looking me in the face, she asked, "Do you think I could I get under the covers with you? It's awfully cold in here."

"As long as you don't touch my wound or move around too much," I said.

She circled over to the opposite side of the bed and

slipped under the covers, pink suit and all. I handed her a pillow. She fluffed it up a bit before placing it under her head. Her neckline exuded the same melon scent. I struggled to shift my body to face her. So here we were, lying face to face in the same bed.

"This is the first time I've ever been so close to a man," said the chubby girl.

Uh-oh.

"I've hardly ever even been out in town. That's why I couldn't find my way to that Aoyama supermarket this morning. I was going to ask you for better directions, but the sound went dead."

"You could have told any cab driver to take you there."

"I hardly had any money. I ran out of the building so quickly, I forgot to take more with me. So I had to walk."

"Don't you have any other family?" I asked, not quite believing her.

"When I was six, my parents and brother were killed in an accident. A truck plowed into our car from behind and the gas tank exploded. They were burned to death."

"And you were the only who survived?"

"I was in the hospital at the time. They were coming to visit me."

"Ah, yes," I said.

"Ever since then, Grandfather watched over me. I didn't even go to school, hardly ever went out, didn't have any friends . . ."

"Why didn't you go to school?"

"Grandfather said it wasn't necessary," she answered matter-of-factly. "He taught me all the subjects—English and Russian and anatomy, everything. Stuff like cooking and sewing, I learned from Auntie."

"Your aunt?"

"Well, not my real aunt. She was the live-in lady who did the cleaning and chores. A really wonderful person. She died from cancer three years ago. Since Auntie died, it's been just Grandfather and me."

"So you didn't go to school after you were six years old?"

"That's right, but what difference does that make? I mean, I can do all sorts of things. I can speak four foreign languages, I can play piano and alto sax, I can assemble a wireless, I've studied navigation and tightrope walking, I've read tons of books. And my sandwiches were good, weren't they?"

"Very good," I admitted.

"Grandfather always said school's a place where they take sixteen years to wear down your brain. Grandfather hardly went to school either."

"Incredible," I said. "But didn't you feel deprived not having friends your own age?"

"Well, I can't really say. I was so busy, I never had time to think about it. And besides, I don't know what I could have said to people my own age."

"Hmm."

"On the other hand," she perked up, "you fascinate me."

"Huh?"

"I mean, here you are so exhausted, and yet your exhaustion seems to give you a kind of vitality. It's tremendous," she chirped. "I bet you'd be good at sax!"

"Excuse me?"

"Do you have any Charlie Parker records?"

"I believe so. But I'm in no condition to look for them in this disaster zone. The stereo's broken, so you couldn't listen anyway."

"Can you play an instrument?"

"Nope."

"May I touch you?"

"No!" I laid down the law. "I'm in too much pain besides."

"When the wound heals, can I touch?"

"When the wound heals, if the world hasn't come to an end . . . Let's just go back to what we were talking about.

You said your grandfather clammed up after he invented his system of shuffling."

"Oh yes, that's right. From that point on, Grandfather seemed to change radically. He would hardly talk to me. He was irritable, always muttering to himself."

"Do you remember if he said anything else about shuffling?"

The chubby girl fingered one gold earring. "Well, I remember him saying shuffling was a door to a new world. He said that although he'd developed it as a method for scrambling computer data, with a little doing a person might scramble the world. Kind of like nuclear physics."

"But if shuffling is the door to a new world, why am I supposed to hold the key?"

"I don't know."

I longed for a big glass of whiskey on the rocks. Lots of luck around my place.

"Let's try this again. Was it your grandfather's purpose to end the world?"

"No. Nothing like that. Grandfather may be moody and a bit presumptuous and he may not like people in general, but deep down he really is a good person. Like me and you."

"Thanks." No one ever said that about me before.

"He was also afraid his research would fall into the wrong hands. He quit the System because he knew if he stayed on, the System would use his findings for anything they felt like. That's when he opened up his own laboratory."

"But the System does good," I said. "It keeps the Semiotecs from robbing data banks and selling on the black market, thereby upholding the rightful ownership of information."

The chubby girl shrugged her shoulders. "Grandfather didn't seem too concerned about good or bad. Or at least, he said, it had nothing to do with claims of ownership."

"Well, maybe not," I said, backing off.

"Grandfather never trusted any form of authority. He did temporarily belong to the System, but that was only so he could get free use of data and experimental resources and a mainframe simulator."

"That so? Tell me, when your grandfather quit the System, did he, by any chance, take my personal file from the data bank with him?"

"I don't know," she said. "But if it did occur to him to do it, who would have stopped him? I mean, he was the head of Central Research. He had full clearance to do as he pleased with the data."

So that was the deal. The Professor had walked out with the data on me. He'd applied it to some private research project of his, with me as the sample on which to advance the principle of shuffling generations beyond anyone else. And now, as my friend Junior had suggested, the Professor was ready for me. His primary sample was to become his guinea pig. He'd probably given me bogus data to shuffle, planting it with a code that would react in my consciousness.

If that was in fact the case, then the reaction had already begun. *A time bomb.* What if Junior was right? I did a quick mental calculation. It was last night when I came to after the shuffling. Since then nearly twenty-four hours had passed. Twenty-four hours. I had no idea when the time bomb was set to go off, but I'd already lost a whole day.

"One more question. You did say it was 'the world is going to end', didn't you?"

"Yes, that's right. That's what Grandfather said."

"Would your grandfather have started this end-of-the-world talk before he got to researching my data? Or only after?"

"After," she said. "At least I think so. I mean, Grandfather just started saying 'the world is going to end' quite recently. Why is it important? What's this got to do with anything?"

"I'm not sure. But I've got a feeling there's a hook in it

somewhere. My shuffling password is 'End of the World'. Now I can't believe that's pure coincidence."

"What's your 'End of the World' story about?"

"I wasn't told. It's part of my consciousness, but it's inaccessible to me. The only thing I know about it is the code name, 'End of the World'."

"Couldn't you retrieve it? Reverse the process or something?"

"Impossible," I said. "The process is safeguarded by System Central. A whole army division couldn't pry the information loose. Security is unbelievable."

"And Grandfather pulled the file?"

"Probably. But I'm only guessing. We'd have to ask your grandfather himself."

"Then you'll help save Grandfather from the INKlings?"

Pressing my gut wound in, I got out of bed. My head lit up with pain like a busy switchboard.

"I don't have much choice, it seems," I said. "I don't know what your grandfather's end-of-the-world scenario means, but from the look of things, I don't think I can afford to ignore it."

"Either way, we have to help Grandfather."

"Because all three of us are good people?"

"Of course," said the chubby girl.

18

Dreamreading

UNABLE to know my own mind, I return to the task of dreamreading. As winter deepens, I concentrate on this effort, and the sense of loss that haunts me is forgotten, albeit temporarily.

On the other hand, the more old dreams I read, the more I apprehend my own helplessness. I cannot divine the message of the dreams. I read them without any understanding of them. They are as indecipherable texts passing before my eyes night after night. I could as well be gazing at the waters of the River.

My dreamreading has improved. I have become proficient at the technique and can manage quantities of old dreams. But to what avail?

"What does dreamreading mean?" I ask the Librarain. "My job, as you have said, is to read the old dreams out of these skulls. But the dreams go through me, for no reason. I feel tired more and more."

"Even so, you read the dreams as if possessed. Is that not so?"

"I don't know," I answer. There is also the fact that I concentrate as I do to fill my emptiness. As she has said, though, there is something in dreamreading that has me possessed.

"Perhaps the problem is in you," she says.

"A problem in me?"

"I wonder if you need to unclose your mind. I do not understand things of the mind very well, but perhaps yours is too firmly sealed. The old dreams need to be read by you and you need to seek the old dreams."

"What makes you think so?"

"That is dreamreading. As the birds leave south or north in their season, the Dreamreader has dreams to read."

Then she reaches out across the table and places her hand on mine. She smiles. A smile that promises spring.

"Unclose your mind. You are not a prisoner. You are a bird in flight, searching the skies for dreams."

In time I take up each old dream, and conscientiously give myself over to it. I select a skull from the long shelves and carry it to the table. She helps me, first, to wipe off the dust with a dampened cloth. With meticulous care, she then polishes it with a dry cloth until the skull becomes like sleet.

I gently place both hands upon the skull and stare, waiting for a warm glow to emanate. When it reaches a certain temperature—like a patch of sun in winter—the white-polished skull offers up its old dreams. I strain my eyes and breathe deeply, using my fingertips to trace the intricate lines of the tale it commences to tell. The voice of the light remains ever so faint; images quiet as ancient constellations float across the dome of my dawning mind. They are indistinct fragments that never merge into a sensate picture.

There would be a landscape I have not seen before, unfamiliar melodic echoes, whisperings in a chaos of tongues. They drift up fitfully and as suddenly sink into darkness. Between one fragment and the next there is nothing in common. I experiment with ways to concentrate my energies into my fingertips, but the outcome never varies. For while I recognize that the old dreams relate to something in me, I am lost.

Perhaps I am inadequate as a dreamreader. Perhaps the light has dimmed, the language eroded over untold years. Or again, are these dimensions of a different order? Does there exist an intractable chasm between my waking time and the dream time of the skulls?

I watch the disparate fragments float up and disappear, without comment. To be sure, the skulls also show me scenes well within my ken. Grasses moving in the breeze, white clouds traveling across the sky, sunlight reflecting on a stream—pure unpretentious visions. In my mind, however, these simple scenes summon forth a sadness that I can find no words for. Like a ship sailing past a window, they appear only to disappear without a trace.

I read and the old dream slowly loses its warmth, like a tide receding, claimed back into the cold white skull it was. The old dream returns to its ageless sleep. And all the water of vision slips through the fingers and spills to the ground. My dreamreading is an endless repetition of this.

When the old dreams are spent, I hand the skull to the Librarian and she lines it on the counter. In the pause I rest, both hands on the table, and unravel my powers. I have found that at most I can read six skulls in a night. More than that and my concentration fails; the dreams garble into noise. By eleven o'clock, I can scarcely stand from fatigue.

At the end of each session, she serves coffee. Occasionally we share biscuits or fruitbread she bakes at home. We do not speak as we eat.

"Am I hindering your dreamreading?" she asks me. "Perhaps your mind is hard shut because I cannot respond to you?"

As always, we sit on the narrow steps that lead from the Old Bridge down to the sandbar. A pale silver moon trembles on the face of the water. A wooden boat lashed to a post modulates the sound of the current. Sitting with her, I feel her warm against my arm.

"It's not that way at all," I say. "It is something in me. My mind is turning away from me. I'm confused."

"Is the mind beyond you?"

"I don't know," I say. "There are times when the understanding does not come until later, when it no longer matters. Other times I do what I must do, not knowing my own mind, and I am led astray."

"How can the mind be so imperfect?" she says with a smile.

I look at my hands. Bathed in the moonlight, they seem like statues, proportioned to no purpose.

"It may well be imperfect," I say, "but it leaves traces. And we can follow those traces, like footsteps in the snow."

"Where do they lead?"

"To oneself," I answer. "That's what the mind is. Without the mind, nothing leads anywhere."

I look up. The winter moon is brilliant, over the Town, above the Wall.

"Not one thing is your fault," I comfort her.

19

Hamburgers, Skyline, Deadline

W E decided to get something to eat before venturing off. I wasn't really hungry myself, but who knew when we'd have a chance to sit down to a meal later. Anyway, the girl said she'd only had enough money for a chocolate bar for lunch and was starving.

I maneuvered my legs into jeans, trying not to aggravate the wound, pulled on a shirt over my T-shirt and a light sweater over that, then a nylon windbreaker over that. Her pink suit wasn't quite right for a spelunking expedition, but there was little in what was left of my wardrobe to fit her. I was ten centimeters taller than her; she was ten kilos heavier than me. I supposed we should get her a more appropriate outfit, but no stores were going to be open at this hour, so I got her to squeeze into my old GI-surplus flight jacket. Her high heels presented a problem, but she said she had jogging shoes and galoshes at the office.

"Pink jogging shoes and pink galoshes."

"You seem to like pink," I said.

"Grandfather likes it. He says I look pretty in pink."

"You do," I said. And she did. Chubby girls in pink tend to conjure up images of big strawberry shortcakes waltzing on a dance floor, but in her case the color suited her.

I dragged my knapsack out from under a pile of bedding, and after checking that it too hadn't been slashed, I packed it with a small flashlight, a magnet, gloves, towels, a large knife, a cigarette lighter, rope, and solid fuel. Next I went into the kitchen and scavenged bread and cans of corned beef, peaches, vienna sausage, and grapefruit from the holocaust on the floor. I filled my canteen with water, then stuffed all the cash I had in the apartment into my pocket.

"This reminds me of a picnic," said the girl.

"You bet."

I stopped to take a last look at my scrap heap of an apartment. Once again, life had a lesson to teach me: It takes years to build up, it takes moments to destroy. Sure, I'd gotten tired of this tiny space, but I'd had a good home here. In the time it takes to swill two cans of beer, all had sublimed like morning mist. My job, my whiskey, my peace and quiet, my solitude, my Somerset Maugham and John Ford collections—all of it trashed and worthless.

The splendor of the fields, the glory of the flowers, I recited under my breath. Then I reached up and pulled the breaker switch to cut the electricity.

I was in too much pain, physically, to reflect more deeply on closing this chapter in my life. I hurt too much and I was too tired. Better not to think at all than to think halfway.

We got into the elevator, went down to the basement garage, and put our things on the back seat of the car. I didn't even bother to look for hidden pursuers. They could be waiting in a stakeout, they could be tailing us, what did it matter now? And anyway, who the hell would they have been? Semiotecs? The boys from the System? That friendly tag team? Was it to be fun and games with all three? I love surprises. If they had a job to do, they could damn well do it.

I didn't want to drive the car, the way I was hurting, but the girl didn't know how.

"Sorry. But I can ride a horse," she said.

"That's okay. You may need to ride a horse yet," I said.

The fuel gauge read almost full. I nosed the car out. Winding our way out of the residential backstreets, we got to the main drag. It was surprisingly busy for this hour, mostly taxis. Why were so many people out racing around in the middle of the night? Why couldn't they just leave work at six o'clock, go home, and lights-out by ten?

But that, as they say, was none of my business. OPEC would go on drilling for oil, regardless of anyone's opinion, conglomerates would make electricity and gasoline from that oil, people would be running around town late at night using up that gasoline. At the moment, however, I had my own problems to deal with.

I sat there at a red light, both hands on the wheel, and yawned.

To the right of us was a white Skyline. In it sat a young man and woman, on their way to or back from a night on the town, looking vaguely bored. Duran Duran blared from the car stereo. The woman, two silver bracelets on the hand she dangled out the window, cast a glance in my direction. I could have been a Denny's restaurant sign or a traffic signal, it would have been no different. She was your regular sort of beautiful young woman, I guess. In a TV drama, she'd be the female lead's best friend, the face that appears once in a café scene to say, "What's the matter? You haven't been yourself lately."

The light turned green, and in the time it took the truck ahead to gear up, the white Skyline zoomed off with a flamboyant show of exhaust.

"Watch the cars behind us, will you?" I told the chubby girl. "Tell me if you think anybody's following us."

The girl nodded and turned around. "Do you think we're in for a chase?"

"No idea," I said. "Just curious. How about a hamburger? It'd be quick."

"Fine."

I pulled the car into the first drive-in burger place I saw. A waitress in a red micro-miniskirt fastened trays to our windows, then asked for our orders.

"A double cheeseburger with french fries and a hot chocolate," said the chubby girl.

"A regular burger and a beer," I said.

"I'm sorry, but we don't serve beer," said the waitress.

"A regular burger and a Coke," I corrected myself. What was I thinking?

While we waited for the food to come, no cars entered the drive-in. Of course, if anyone were really tailing us, the last thing they'd do is drive into the same parking lot with us. They'd be somewhere out of sight, sitting tight, waiting for our next move. I turned my attention to the food that had arrived, and mechanically shovelled hamburger with its expressway-ticket-sized leaf of lettuce down the hatch. Miss Pink, on the other hand, relished each bite of her cheeseburger, while daintily picking at her fries and slurping her hot chocolate.

"Care for some french fries?" she asked me.

"No thanks," I said.

The girl polished off everything on her tray. She savored the last sip of hot chocolate, licked the ketchup and mustard from her fingers, then wiped her hands and mouth with the napkin.

"Now, then, about your grandfather," I said, "we probably ought to go to his underground laboratory first."

"Yes. There might be something to give us a lead."

"But do you think we'll be able to get by the INKlings? The ultrasonic repel system is broken, isn't it?"

"It is, but there's a small device for emergencies. It's not very powerful, but if we carry it with us, the INKlings will stay away."

"Good," I said, relieved.

"The battery only lasts for thirty minutes, though," she added. "After that, it has to be recharged."

"How long to recharge?"

"Fifteen minutes. But for just going back and forth between the office and the lab, we should have time to spare."

Okay, better than nothing. We left the drive-in, and stopped at an all-night supermarket for a couple cans of beer and a flask of whiskey. Whereupon I immediately drank both cans of beer and a fourth of the whiskey. There, that took the edge off things. I recapped the whiskey and passed it to the girl, who packed it in the knapsack.

"Why do you drink so much?" she wanted to know.

"It makes me feel brave," I said.

"I'm scared too, but you don't see me drinking."

"Your 'scared' and my 'scared' are two different things."

"What's that supposed to mean?" she asked.

"As you get older, you don't recover from things so easy."

"And as you get older, you also get tired?"

"Yeah," I said, "you get tired."

She turned toward me, reached out her hand, and touched my earlobe.

"It's all right. Don't worry. I'll be by your side," she said.

"Thanks."

I parked the car in the lot of her grandfather's office building. Shouldering the knapsack, I felt the wound throb sharply. Like rain, the pain would pass, I told myself, and loped after the girl.

At the entrance to the building was a muscular young watchman who asked for her resident's ID. She produced a plastic card, which the watchman then inserted into a table-top computer slot. After confirming her name and room number in the monitor, he flipped a switch to open the door.

"This is an extraordinary building," the girl explained to me as we cut across the large, open floor. "Everyone in the building has some secret that needs protecting. Important research or business dealings, stuff like that. That's why all this security. They check you at the door, then they watch you with TV cameras to make sure you reach your room. So even if someone had been following us, they wouldn't be able to get to us inside."

"Do they know that your grandfather dug a shaft through the building?"

"Probably not. Grandfather had the office specifically designed to connect directly to the sub-basement at the time the building went up. Only the owner of the building and the architect know about it. The construction crew was told it was a 'media well,' a communications cortex that would house fiber-optic networks later. I think the blueprints are fudged also."

"I bet it must have cost."

"I'm sure it did. But Grandfather's got oodles of money," said the girl. "Me, too. I'm very well-off. I multiplied my inheritance and the life-insurance money I got on the stock market."

She took a key out of her pocket and opened the elevator door. Back into that overgrown vacu-pac elevator.

"Stock market?"

"Sure, Grandfather taught me the tricks. He taught me how to choose among all the information, how to read the market, how to dodge taxes, how to transfer funds to banks overseas, stuff like that. Stocks are a lot of fun. Ever tried?"

"Afraid not," I said. I'd never opened a fixed-term com-pounded-interest account.

The elevator moved at its requisite impossible ascending-or-descending speed.

"Grandfather says that schools are too inefficient to pro-duce top material. What do you think?" she asked.

"Well, probably so," I answered. "I went to school for many years and I don't believe it made that much difference in my life. I can't speak any languages, can't play any instruments, can't play the stock market, can't ride a horse."

"So why didn't you quit school? You could have quit any time you wanted, couldn't you?"

"I guess so," I said. "I could have quit, but I didn't want to. I guess it didn't occur to me to do anything like that. Unlike you, I had a perfectly average, ordinary upbringing. I never had what it takes to make a first-rate anything."

"That's wrong," she declared. "Everyone must have one thing that they can excel at. It's just a matter of drawing it out, isn't it? But school doesn't know how to draw it out. It crushes the gift. It's no wonder most people never get to be what they want to be. They just get ground down."

"Like me," I said.

"No, you're different. I can tell there's something special about you. The emotional shell around you is so hard, everything inside has got to be still intact."

"Emotional shell?"

"That's right," she said. "That's why it's not too late. After all this is over, why don't we live together? It's not like we'd have to get married or anything. We could move to Greece or Finland or somewhere easy-going like that and pass the time riding horses and singing songs. We'd have plenty of money, and meanwhile you could be reborn as a first-rate human being."

"Hmm." Not a bad offer.

The elevator came to a stop. She stepped out and I followed. She walked at a fast pace, as she had the first time we met, the click of her high heels echoing down the long corridor. Before my eyes, her pleasing wiggle, her flashing gold earrings.

"But suppose I took you up on the offer," I spoke to her back, "you'd be doing all the giving and I'd be doing all the taking. That doesn't strike me as fair."

She slowed her pace to walk beside me.

"There's bound to be something you can give me," she said.

"For instance?"

"For instance, your emotional shell. That's something I really want to find out about. I want to know what it's made up of and how it functions and stuff like that.

"It's nothing to get excited about," I said. "Everybody has more or less of an emotional shell—if that's what you want to call it. You've never been out in the world. You don't know how the mind of the ordinary person works."

"You act as if you're worthless!" exclaimed the chubby girl. "You can shuffle, can't you?"

"Of course I can. But that's just a matter of practice. Not so different from using an abacus or playing the piano."

"That is *not* all there is to it," she said. "Everyone thought that way at first. That with the necessary training, anyone—anyone who passed the tests, that is—could shuffle. Even Grandfather thought so. Well, twenty-six people happened to have the same surgery and training, and all of them got the ability to shuffle. In the beginning, there weren't any problems—"

"Hey, I never heard about any problems at all. I heard everything went according to plan."

"Officially, yes," she spoke with authority. "But the truth is, out of these twenty-six, twenty-five died within a year and a half after training. Only one of them is still alive."

"What? You mean—"

"You. You're the only survivor after three years. You've gone on with your shuffling, and you've had no problems or breakdowns. Do you still think you're so ordinary? You are a most important person!"

I thrust both hands in my pockets and continued down the corridor. It was getting to be too much, the way the scale of this thing kept expanding.

"Why did the others die?" I asked the girl.

"I don't think they know. There was no visible cause of death. Some brain malfunction, nothing clear."

"They must have some idea."

"Well, Grandfather put it like this. Really ordinary persons probably can't tolerate irradiation of their brain, which was done to catalyze the core consciousness. The brain cells try to produce antibodies and react with overkill. I'm sure it's more complicated than that, but that's a simple explanation."

"Then what's the reason I'm alive?"

"Perhaps you had natural antibodies. Your 'emotional shell'. For some reason you already had a safeguard factor in your brain that allowed you to survive. Grandfather tried to simulate this shell, but it didn't hold up."

I thought this over. "This antibody factor or guard or whatever, is it an innate faculty? Or is it something I acquired?"

"Part inborn and part learned, I seem to remember. But beyond that, Grandfather wouldn't say. Knowing too much could have put me in jeopardy. Although, according to his hypothesis, people with your natural antibodies are about one in a million to a million and a half. And even then, short of actually endowing them with shuffling, there's no way to single these people out."

"Which means, if your grandfather's hypothesis is correct, that my happening to be among those twenty-six was an incredible fluke."

"That's why you're so valuable as a sample. That's why you're the key."

"What did your grandfather have planned for me? The data he gave me to shuffle, that unicorn skull—what was that all about?"

"If I knew that, I could save you right here and now," said the girl.

"Me and the world."

*   *   *

The office had been ransacked, not to the same degree as my apartment, but someone had done a number on the place. Papers were strewn everywhere, the desk overturned, the safe pried open, the cabinet drawers flung across the room, the Professor's and the girl's change of clothes pulled out of their lockers and tossed like salad over a bed of shredded sofa. The girl's clothes were, verifiably, all pink. An orchestration of pink in every gradation from light rose to deep fuchsia.

"Unforgivable!" she cried. "They must have come up from below."

"INKlings?"

"No, not them. INKlings wouldn't come up this far above ground. And if they had, you could tell by the smell."

"What smell?"

"A fishy kind of—swampy kind of—horrible smell. INKlings didn't do this. I bet they were the people who trashed your apartment."

I looked around the room. In front of the overturned desk, a whole box of scattered paperclips glinted in the fluorescent light. There was something about them, I didn't know what. I picked one up from the floor and slipped it into my pocket.

"Was anything of importance kept here?" I asked.

"No," she said. "Practically everything here is expendable. Just account ledgers and receipts and general research stuff. Nothing was irreplaceable."

"How about the INKling-repel device? Is that still in one piece?"

She rooted through the debris in front of the lockers, throwing aside a flashlight and radio-cassette player and alarm clock and a can of cough drops to find a small black box with something like a VU-meter, which she tested several times.

"It's all right, it works fine. They probably thought it was a useless contraption. Lucky for us, because the mechanism's so simple, one little whack could have broken it."

Then the chubby girl went over to a corner of the room and crouched down to undo the cover of an electrical outlet. Pushing a tiny switch inside, she stood up, gently pressed her palms flat against a section of the adjacent wall, and a panel the size of a telephone directory popped open, revealing a safe within.

"Not bad, eh? Bet nobody would think of looking here, eh?" she congratulated herself. Then she dialed the combination and opened the safe.

Holding back the pain, I helped her right the desk and set out the contents of the safe. There was a thick rubber-banded bundle of bank books, a stack of stock certificates, a cloth bag holding something solid, a black leather notebook, and a brown envelope. She poured out the contents of the envelope: a gold ring and a discolored old Omega watch, its crystal crazed.

"A memento of my father," said the girl. "The ring was my mother's. Everything else got burned."

She slipped the ring and watch back into the envelope. Next, from the cloth bag, she removed an object in an old shirt; unwrapped, it turned out to be a small automatic pistol. It bore no resemblance to a toy. This was a real gun that shot real bullets. I'm no expert, but my years of moviegoing told me it was either a Browning or a Beretta. With the gun was a spare cartridge and a box of bullets.

"I guess you Calcutecs are all good shots," said the girl.

"You've got to be kidding. I've never even held a gun before."

"Really? Shooting's another thing I learned by not going to school. I like it as a sport. Anyway, seeing as how you don't have any experience with a gun, I'll hold on to it."

"By all means. Just don't shoot me by mistake. I don't think I could stand any more damage to my body."

"Don't worry. I'm very careful," she said, slipping the automatic into her pocket.

She then opened the black leather notebook to a middle

page and studied it under the light. The page was scribbled entirely in an unintelligible rune of numbers and letters.

"This is Grandfather's notebook," she explained. "It's written in a code that only he and I know. Plans, events of the day, he writes it all down here. So then—what's this now?—September 28th, you're down as having finished laundering the data."

"That's right."

"There's a (1) written there. Probably the first step. Then, he has you finishing the shuffling on the 29th or the 30th. Or is that wrong?"

"Not at all."

"That's (2). The second step. Next, there's . . . uh, let's see . . . noon, the 2nd, which is (3). 'Cancel Program'."

"I was supposed to meet your grandfather on the 2nd at noon. My guess is that he was going to disarm whatever program he'd set inside me. So that the world wouldn't end. But a lot has changed. And something's happened to him. He's been dragged off somewhere."

"Hold on," she said, still reading the notebook. "The code gets pretty involved."

While she read, I organized the knapsack, making sure to include her pink jogging shoes. Slickers and boots were scattered about, but thankfully they weren't slashed or anything like that. Going under the waterfall without rain gear would mean getting soaked and chilled to the bone; it would also mean wonders for my wound. My watch read a little before midnight.

"The notebook is full of complicated calculations. Electrical charge and decay rates, resistance factors and offsets, stuff like that. I don't understand any of it."

"Skip it. We don't have much time," I said. "Just decode what you can make out."

"There's no need to decode."

"Why not?"

She handed me the notebook and pointed to the spot.

There was no code, only a huge scrawl:

"Do you suppose this marks the deadline?" she asked.

"Either that, or it's (4). Meaning, if the program is cancelled at (3), X won't happen. But if for some reason it doesn't get cancelled and the program keeps on reading, then I think we get to X."

"So that means we have to get to Grandfather by noon of the 2nd."

"If my guess is correct."

"How much time is left? Before the big bang . . ."

"Thirty-six hours," I said. I didn't need to look at my watch. The time it takes the earth to complete one and a half rotations. Two morning papers and one evening edition would be delivered. Alarm clocks would ring twice, men would shave twice. Fortunate souls would have sex two or three times. Thirty-six hours and no more. One over seventeen-thousand thirty-three of a life expectancy of seventy years. Then, after those thirty-six hours, the world was supposed to come to an end.

"What do we do now?" asked the girl.

I located some painkillers in the first-aid kit lying on the floor and swallowed them with a gulp of water from the canteen. Then I hiked the knapsack up on my shoulders.

"There's nothing to do but go underground," I said.

20

The Death of the Beasts

*T*HE beasts have already lost several of their number. The first ice-bound morning, a few of the old beasts succumbed, their winter-whitened bodies lying under two inches of snow. The morning sun tore through the clouds, setting the frozen landscape agleam, the frosty breath of more than a thousand beasts dancing whitely in the air.

I awake before dawn to find the Town blanketed in snow. It is a wondrous scene in the somber light. The Clocktower soars black above the whitened world, the dark band of the River flows below. I put on my coat and gloves and descend to the empty streets. There is not yet a footprint in the snow. When I gather the snow in my hands, it crumbles. The edges of the River are frozen, with a dusting of snow.

There is no wind, no birds, no movement in the Town. I hear nothing but the crunching of snow under my feet.

I walk to the Gate and see the Gatekeeper out by the Shadow Grounds. The Gatekeeper is under the wagon that he and my shadow repaired. He is lubricating the axles. The wagon is loaded with ceramic crocks of the kind used to hold rapeseed oil, all roped fast to the sideboards. I wonder why the Gatekeeper would have need for so much oil.

The Gatekeeper emerges from under the wagon and raises his hand to greet me. He seems in a good mood.

"Up early, eh? What wind blows you this way?"

"I have come out to see the snow," I say. "It was so beautiful from up on the Hill."

The Gatekeeper scoffs and throws a big arm around me as he has done before. He wears no gloves.

"You are a strange one. Winter here is nothing but snow, and you come down from your Hill just to see it."

Then he belches, a locomotive cloud of steam, and looks toward the Gate. "But I will say, you came at the right time," he smiles. "Want to climb the Watchtower? Something you ought to see from there. A winter treat, ha ha. In a little while I will blow the horn, so keep your eyes open."

"A treat?"

"You will see."

I climb the Watchtower beside the Gate, not knowing what to expect. I look at the world beyond the Wall. Snow is deep in the Apple Grove, as if a storm cloud had specifically sought it out. The Northern and Eastern Ridges are powdered white, with a few dark-limned crags to mar their complexion.

Immediately below the Watchtower are the beasts, sleeping as they usually do at this hour. Legs folded under them, they huddle low to the ground, their horns thrust forward, each seeking sleep. All peacefully unaware of the thick coat of snow that has fallen upon them.

The clouds disperse and the sun begins to illuminate the earth. Beams of sun slant across the land. My eyes strain in the brightness to see the promised "treat".

Presently, the Gatekeeper pushes open the Gate and sounds the horn. One long note, then three short notes. The beasts awaken at the first tone and lift their heads in the direction of the call. White breaths charge the air anew, heralding the start of the new day.

The last note of the horn fades, and the beasts are risen to their feet. They prow their horns at the sky, then shake off the snow as if they had not previously noticed it. Finally they walk toward the Gate.

As the beasts amble by, some hang their heads low, some paw their hooves quietly. Only after they have filed inside do I understand what the Gatekeeper has wanted me to see. A few beasts have frozen to death in their posture of sleep. Yet they appear not dead so much as deep in meditation. No breath issues from them. Their bodies unmoving, their awareness swallowed in darkness. After all the other beasts have gone through the Gate, these dead remain like growths on the face of the earth. Their horns angle up into space, almost alive.

I gaze at their hushed forms as the morning sun rises and the shadow of the Wall withdraws, the brilliance melting the snow from the ground. Will the morning sun thaw away even their death? At any moment, will these apparently lifeless forms stand and go about their usual morning routine?

They do not rise. The sun but glistens on their wet fur. My eyes behind black glasses begin to hurt.

Descending the Watchtower, I cross the River and go back to my quarters on the Western Hill. I discover that the morning sun has done harm to my eyes, severely. When I close my eyes, the tears do not stop. I hear each drop fall to my lap. I darken the room and stare for hours at the weirdly shaped patterns that drift and recede in a space of no perspective.

At ten o'clock the Colonel, bringing coffee, knocks on my door and finds me face down on the bed, rubbing my eyes with a cold towel. There is a pain in the back of my head, but at least the tears have subsided.

"What has happened to you?" he asks. "The morning sun is stronger than you think. Especially on snowy mornings. You knew that a Dreamreader cannot tolerate strong light. Why did you want to go outdoors?"

"I went to see the beasts," I say. "Many died. Eight, nine head. No, more."

"And many more will die with each snowfall."

"Why do they die so easily?" I ask the old officer, removing the towel from my face to look at him.

"They are weak. From the cold and from hunger. It has always been this way."

"Do they never die out?"

The old officer shakes his head. "The creatures have lived here for many millenia, and so will they continue. Many will die over the winter, but in spring the survivors will foal. New life pushes old out of the way. The number of beasts that can live in this Town is limited."

"Why don't they move to another place? There are trees in the Woods. If they went south, they would escape the snow. Why do they need to stay?"

"Why, I cannot tell you," he says. "But the beasts cannot leave. They belong to the Town; they are captured by it. Just as you and I are. By their own instincts, they know this."

"What happens to the bodies?"

"They are burned," replies the Colonel, warming his great parched hands on his coffee cup. "For the next few weeks, that will be the main work of the Gatekeeper. First he cuts off their heads, scrapes out their brains and eyes, then boils them until the skulls are clean. The remains are doused with oil and set on fire."

"Then old dreams are put into those skulls for the Library, is that it?" I ask the Colonel. "Why?"

The old officer does not answer. All I hear is the creaking of the floorboards as he walks away from me, toward the window.

"You will learn that when you see what old dreams are," he says. "I cannot tell you. You are the Dreamreader. You must find the answer for yourself."

I wipe away the tears with the towel, then open my eyes. The Colonel stands, a blur by the window.

"Many things will become clear for you over the course of the winter," he continues. "Whether or not you like what you learn, it will all come to pass. The snow will fall, the beasts will die. No one can stop this. In the afternoon, gray smoke will rise from the burning beasts. All winter long, every day. White snow and gray smoke."

21

Bracelets, Ben Johnson, Devil

B EYOND the closet opened the same dark inner sanctum
as before, but now that I knew about the INKlings, it
seemed a deep, chill horror show.

She went down the ladder ahead of me. With the INKling-
repel device stuffed in a large pocket of her slicker and her
large flashlight slung diagonally across her body, she swiftly
descended alone. Then, flashlight thrust in my pocket, I
started down the slick rungs of the ladder. It was a bigger
drop than I remembered. All the way down, I kept thinking
about that young couple in the Skyline, Duran Duran on
stereo. Oblivious to everything.

I wished *I* could have been a little more oblivious. I put
myself in the driver's seat, woman sitting next to me, cruising the late night streets to an innocuous pop beat. Did the
woman take off her bracelets during sex? Nice if she didn't.

Even if she was naked, those two bracelets needed to be there.

Probably she did take them off. Women tend to remove their jewelry before they shower. Which meant, therefore, sex before showering. Or getting her to keep her bracelets on. Now, which was the better option?

Anyway, I'm in bed with her, *with* her bracelets. Her face is a blank, so I darken the lights. Off go her silky undergarments. The bracelets are all she has on. They glint slightly, a pleasant muffled clinking on the sheets. I have a hard-on.

Which, halfway down the ladder, is what I noticed. Just great. Why now? Why didn't I get an erection when I needed one? And why was I getting so excited over two lousy bracelets? Especially under this slicker, with the world about to end.

She was shining her light around when I reached bottom. "There are INKlings about. Listen," she said. "Those sounds."

"Sounds?"

"Fins flapping. Listen carefully. You can feel them."

I strained, but didn't detect anything of the kind.

"Once you know what to listen for, you can even detect their voices. It's not really speech; it's closer to sound waves. They're like bats. Humans can only hear a portion of their vocal range."

"So then how did the Semiotecs make contact with them? If they couldn't communicate verbally?"

"A translation device isn't so hard to make. Grandfather could have, easy. But he decided not to."

"Why not?"

"Because he didn't want to talk to them. They're disgusting creatures and they speak a disgusting language. Whatever they eat or drink has got to be almost putrified."

"They don't consume anything fresh?"

"No. If they catch you, they immerse you in water for days. When your body starts to rot, they eat it."

Lovely. I was ready to turn back, but we forged on. She knew every step of the way and scampered ahead. When I trained my light on her from behind, her gold earrings flashed.

"Tell me, do you take off your earrings when you take a shower?" I spoke up.

"I leave them on," she slowed down to answer. "Only my earrings. Sexy?"

"I guess." Why did I have to go and bring up the subject?

"What else do you think is sexy? I'm not very experienced, as I said. Nobody teaches you these things."

"Nobody will. It's something you have to find out for yourself," I said.

I made a conscious effort to sweep all images of sex from my head.

"Umm," I changed the subject, "you say this device of yours emits ultrasonic waves that put off the INKlings?"

"As long as the device is sending out signals, they won't come within fifteen meters of us. So you should try to stay close to me. Otherwise, they'll nab you and pickle you for a snack. In your condition, your stomach would be the first thing to rot. And their teeth and claws are razor sharp."

I scooted up right behind her.

"Does your stomach wound still hurt?" she asked.

"Only when I move," I replied. "But thanks to the painkillers, it's not so bad."

"If we find Grandfather, he'll be able to remove the pain."

"Your grandfather? How's he going to help?"

"Simple. He's done it for me lots of times. Like when I have a terrible headache, he uses an impulse to cancel out my awareness of pain. Really, though, pain is an important signal from the body, so you shouldn't do it too much. In this case, it's an emergency. I'm sure he'll help."

"Thanks," I said.

"Don't thank me. Thank Grandfather. If we find him," she reminded.

Panning her powerful light left and right, she continued upstream along the subterranean river. Moisture seeped out from between the rocks, running in rivulets past our feet. Slimy layers of moss coated wherever this groundwater trickled through. The moss appeared unnaturally green, inexplicable for these depths beyond the reach of photosynthesis.

"Say, do you suppose the INKlings know we're walking around down here now?"

"Of course, they do," she said, without emotion. "This is their world. They're all around, watching us. I've been hearing noises the whole time we've been down here."

I swung my flashlight beam to the side, but all I saw were rocks and moss.

"They're in the cracks and boreholes, where the light doesn't reach," she said. "Or else they're creeping up on us from behind."

"How many minutes has it been since you switched on the device?" I asked.

"Ten minutes," she said, looking at her watch. "Ten minutes, twelve seconds. Another five minutes to the waterfall. We're doing fine."

Exactly five minutes later we arrived at the waterfall. Again the roar of the waterfall had been selectively suppressed; apparently the sound-removal equipment was still functioning.

"Odd," she remarked, ducking under the noiseless cascade. "This sound removal means the laboratory wasn't broken into. If the INKlings had attacked, they would have torn the whole place apart. They hate this laboratory."

Sure enough, the laboratory door was still locked. She inserted the electronic key; the door swung open. The laboratory interior was dark and cold and smelled of coffee. She anxiously shut the door behind us, tested the lock, and only then switched on the lights.

It was true that the laboratory was basically a repeat of the upheaval in the office above: papers everywhere, furniture overturned, cups and plates smashed, the carpet an abstract expressionist composition of what must have been a bucket of coffee grounds. But there was a pattern to the destruction. The demolition crew had clearly distinguished between what was and was not to be destroyed. The former had been shown no mercy, but the computer, telecommunications console, sound-removal equipment, and electric generator were untouched.

The next room was like that as well. A hopeless mess, but the destruction was carefully calculated. The shelves of skulls had been left perfectly intact, instruments necessary for experimental calibrations set aside with care. Less critical, inexpensive equipment and replaceable research materials had been dashed to pieces.

The girl went to the safe to check its contents. The safe door wasn't locked. She scooped out two handfuls of white ash.

"The emergency auto-incinerator did its stuff," she said. "They didn't get any papers."

"Who do you think did it?" I asked.

"Humans, first of all. The Semiotecs or whoever may have had INKling help to get in here, but only they came inside. They even locked the door to keep the INKlings from finishing the job."

"Doesn't look like they took anything valuable."

"No."

"But they did get your grandfather, the most valuable property of all," I said. "That leaves me stuck with whatever he planted inside me. Now I'm really screwed."

"Not so fast," said the chubby girl. "Grandfather wasn't abducted at all. There's a secret escape route from here. I'm sure he got away, using the other INKling-repel device."

"How can you be so sure?"

"Grandfather's not the type to let himself get caught. If he heard someone breaking in, he'd get himself out of here."

"So he's safe above ground?"

"Above ground, no," she corrected. "The escape route is like a maze. At the very fastest, it'd take five hours to get through, and the INKling-repel device only lasts thirty minutes. He's still in the maze."

"Or else he's been caught by the INKlings."

"I don't think so. Grandfather prepared an extra-safe shelter for himself, exactly for times like these. It's the one place underground no INKling will go near. I bet he's there, waiting for us to show up."

"Where is that?"

"Grandfather explained the way once, but there should be a shorthand map in the notebook. It shows all the danger points to look out for."

"What kind of danger points?"

"The kind that you're probably better off not knowing. You seem to get nervous when you hear too much."

"Sure, kid." I didn't want to argue. "How long does it take to reach that shelter?"

"About a half hour to the approach. And from there, another hour or hour and a half to Grandfather. Once we make the approach we'll be okay; it's the first half hour that's the problem. Unless we really hurry, the INKling-repel device's battery will run out."

"What happens if our porta-pack dies midway?"

"Wish us luck. We'd have to keep swinging our flashlights like crazy."

"Then we'd better get moving," I said. "The INKlings wouldn't waste any time telling the Semiotecs we're here. They'll be back any minute."

She peeled off her rain gear and got into the GI jacket and jogging shoes I'd packed. Meanwhile I stripped off my slicker and pulled on my nylon windbreaker. Then I traded my sneakers for rain boots and shouldered the knapsack again. My watch read almost twelve-thirty.

The girl went to the closet in the far room and threw the hangers onto the floor. As she rotated the clothes rod, there was the sound of gears turning, and a square panel in the lower right closet wall creaked open. In blew cold, moldy air.

"Your grandfather must be some kind of cabinet fetishist," I remarked.

"No way," she defended. "A fetishist's someone who's got a fixation on one thing only. Of course, Grandfather's good at cabinetry. He's good at everything. Genius doesn't specialize; genius is reason in itself."

"Forget genius. It doesn't do much for innocent by-standers. Especially if everyone's going to want a piece of the action. That's why this whole mess happened in the first place. Genius or fool, you don't live in the world alone. You can hide underground or you can build a wall around your-self, but somebody's going to come along and screw up the works. Your grandfather is no exception. Thanks to him, I got my gut slashed, and now the world's going to end."

"Once we find Grandfather, it'll be all right," she said, drawing near to plant a little peck by my ear. "You can't go back now."

The girl kept her eye on the INKling-repel device while it recharged. Then, when it was done, she took the lead and I followed, same as before. Once through the hole, she cranked a handle to seal the opening. With each crank, the patch of light grew smaller and smaller, becoming a slit, then disappearing.

"What made your grandfather choose this for an escape route?"

"Because it links directly to the center of the INKling lair," she said, without hesitation. "They themselves can't go near it. It's their sanctuary."

"Sanctuary?"

"I've never actually seen it myself, but that's what

Grandfather called it. They worship a fish. A huge fish with no eyes," she told me, then flashed her light ahead. "Let's get going. We haven't got much time."

The cave ceiling was low; we had to crouch as we walked, banging our heads on stalactites. I thought I was in good shape, but now, bent low like this, each pitch of my hips stabbed an ice pick into my gut. Still, the pain had to be a hell of a lot better than wandering around here alone if I ever let her out of my sight.

The further we traveled in the darkness, the more I began to feel estranged from my body. I couldn't see it, and after a while, you start to think the body is nothing but a hypothetical construct. Sure, I could feel my wound and the ground beneath the soles of my feet. But these were just kinesthesis and touch, primitive notions stemming from the premise of a body. These sensations could continue even after the body is gone. Like an amputee getting itchy toes.

Thoughts on the run, literally, as I chased after the chubby girl. Her pink skirt poked out from under the olive drab GI jacket. Her earrings sparkled, a pair of fireflies flitting about her. She never checked to see if I was following; she simply forged ahead, with girl scout intensity. She stopped only when she came to a fork in the path, where she pulled out the map and held it under the light. That was when I managed to catch up with her.

"Okay up there? We're on the right path?" I asked.

"For the time being at least," she replied.

"How can you tell?"

"I can tell we're on course because we are," she said authoritatively, shining her light at our feet. "See? Take a look."

I looked at the illuminated circle of ground. The pitted rock surface was gleaming with tiny bits of silver. I picked one up—a paperclip.

"See?" she said, snidely. "Grandfather passed this way. He knew we'd be following, so he left those as trail markers."

"Got it," I said, put in my place.

"Fifteen minutes gone. Let's hurry," she pressed.

There were more forks in the path ahead. But each time, scattered paperclips showed us the way. There were also boreholes in the passage floor. These had been marked on the map, spots where we had to walk with care, with flashlights trained on the ground.

The path wormed left and right but kept going further and further down. There were no steep inclines, only a steady, even descent. Five minutes later, we came to a large chamber. We knew this from the change in the air and the sound of our footsteps.

She took out the map to check our location. I shone my light all around. The room was circular in shape; the ceiling formed a dome. The curved walls were smooth and slick, clearly the work of . . . human hands? In the very center of the floor was a shallow cavity one meter in diameter, filled with an unidentifiable slime. A tincture of something was in the air, not overpowering, but it left a disagreeable acid gumminess in your mouth.

"This seems to be the approach to the sanctuary," she said. "That means we're safe from INKlings. For the time being."

"Great, but how do we get out of here?"

"Leave that up to Grandfather. He'll have a way."

On either side of the sanctuary entrance was an intricate relief. Two fishes in a circle, each with the other's tail in its mouth. Their heads swelled into aeroplane cowlings, and where their eyes should have been, two long tendril-like feelers sprouted out. Their mouths were much too large for the rest of their bodies, slit back almost to the gills, beneath which were fleshy organs resembling severed animal limbs. On each of these appendages were three claws. Claws? The dorsal fins were shaped like tongues of flames, the scales rasped out like thorns.

"Mythical creatures? Do you suppose they actually exist?" I asked her.

"Who knows?" she said, picking up some paperclips. "Quick, let's go in."

I ran my light over the carving one more time before following her through the entrance. It was nothing short of amazing that the INKlings could render such detail in absolute darkness. Okay, they could see in the dark, but this vision of theirs was otherworldly. And now they were probably watching our every move.

The approach to the sanctuary sloped gradually upward, the ceiling at the same time rising progressively higher until finally it soared out of the flashlight's illumination.

"From here on, we climb the mountain," she said. "Not a real mountain, anyway. More like a hill. But to them, it's a mountain. That's what Grandfather said. It's the only documented subterranean mountain, a sacred mountain."

"Then we're defiling it."

"Not at all. The reverse. The mountain was filthy from the beginning. This place is a Pandora's box sealed over by the earth's crust. Filth was concentrated here. And we're going to pass right through the center of it."

"You make it sound like hell."

"You said it."

"I don't think I'm ready for this."

"Oh come on, you've got to believe," said my pink cheerleader. "Think of nice things, people you loved, your childhood, your dreams, music, stuff like that. Don't worry, be happy."

"Is Ben Johnson happy enough?" I asked.

"Ben Johnson?"

"He played in those great old John Ford movies, riding the most beautiful horses."

"You really are one of a kind," she laughed. "I really like you."

"Thanks," I said, "but I can't play any musical instruments."

*   *   *

As she had forecast, the path began to get steeper, until finally we were scaling a rock face. But my thoughts were on my happy-time hero. Ben Johnson on horseback. Ben Johnson in *Fort Defiance* and *She Wore a Yellow Ribbon* and *Wagonmaster* and *Rio Grande*. Ben Johnson on the prairie, sun burning down, blue sky streaked with clouds. Ben Johnson and a herd of buffalo in a canyon, womenfolk wiping hands on gingham aprons as they lean out the door. Ben Johnson by the river, light shimmering in the dry heat, cowboys singing. The camera dollies, and there's Ben Johnson, riding across the landscape, swift as an arrow, our hero forever in frame.

As I gripped the rocks and tested for foothold, it was Ben Johnson on his horse that sustained me. The pain in my gut all but subsided. Maybe *he* was the signal to put physical pain out of mind.

We continued scaling the mountain in the dark. You couldn't hold your flashlight and still use your hands to climb, so I stuffed my flashlight in my jeans, she strapped hers up across her back. Which meant we saw nothing. Her flashlight beam bounced on her hip, veering off uselessly into space. And all I saw by mine were mute rock surfaces going up, up, up.

From time to time she called out to make sure I kept pace. "You okay?" she'd say. "Just a little more."

Then, a while later, it was "Why don't we sing something?"

"Sing what?" I wanted to know.

"Anything, anything at all."

"I don't sing in dark places."

"Aw, c'mon."

Okay, then, what the hell. So I sang the Russian folksong I learned in elementary school:

Snow is falling all night long—
  Hey-ey! Pechka, ho!
Fire is burning very strong—
  Hey-ey! Pechka, ho!
Old dreams bursting into song—
  Hey-ey! Pechka, ho!

I didn't know any more of the lyrics, so I made some up: Everyone's gathered around the fire—the *pechka*—when a knock comes at the door and Father goes to inquire, and there's a reindeer standing on wounded feet, saying, "I'm hungry, give me something to eat"; so they feed it canned peaches. In the end everyone's sitting around the stove, singing along.

"Wonderful. You sing just fine," she said. "Sorry I can't applaud, but I've got my hands full."

We cleared the bluff and reached a flat area. Catching our breath, we panned our flashlights around. The plateau was vast; the tabletop-slick surface spread in all directions. She crouched and picked up another half dozen paperclips.

"How far can your grandfather have gone?" I asked.

"Not much farther. He's mentioned this plateau many times."

"You mean to say your grandfather's come here out of choice?"

"Of course. Grandfather had to cover this terrain in order to draw up his subterranean map. He knows everything about this place."

"He surveyed it all by himself?"

"Certainly," she said. "Grandfather likes to operate alone. It's not that he doesn't like people or can't trust them; it's just that nobody can keep up with him."

"I can believe it," I said. "But tell me, what's the low-down on this plateau?"

"This mountain is where the INKlings first lived. They dug holes into the rock face and lived together inside. The area we're standing on now is where religious ceremonies were held. It's supposed to be the dwelling place of their gods, where they made living sacrifices to them."

"You mean those gruesome clawed fish?"

"According to Grandfather, the fish are supposed to have led the INKlings' ancestors here." She trained her light at our feet and showed me a shallow trough carved into the ground. The trough led straight off into the darkness. "If you follow this trough, you get to the ancient altar. It's the holiest spot in this sanctuary. No INKling would go near it. That's probably where Grandfather is, safe and sound- removed."

We followed the trough. It soon got deeper, the path descending steadily, the walls to either side rising higher and higher. The walls seemed ready to close in and crush us flat any second, but nothing moved. Only the queer squishing rhythm of our rubber boots echoed between the walls. I looked up time and again as I walked.

It was the urge to look up at the sky. But of course there was no sun nor moon nor stars overhead. Darkness hung heavy over me. Each breath I took, each wet footstep, everything wanted to slide like mud to the ground.

I lifted my left hand and pressed on the light of my digi- tal wristwatch. Two-twenty-one. It was midnight when we headed underground, so only a little over two hours had passed. We continued walking down, down the narrow trench, mouths clamped tight.

I could no longer tell if my eyes were open or shut. The only thing impinging on my senses at this point was the echo of footsteps. The freakish terrain and air and darkness distorted what reached my ears. I tried to impose a verbal meaning on the sounds, but they would not conform to any words I knew. It was an unfamiliar language, a string of tones and inflections that could not be accommodated within the range of Japanese syllables. In French or Ger- man—or English perhaps—it might approximate this:

Even—through—be—shopped—degreed—well

Still, when I actually pronounced the words, they were far from the sounds of those footsteps. A more accurate transcription would have been:

Efgvén—gthôuv—bge—shpèvg—égvele—wgevl

Finnish? Yet another gap in my linguistic abilities. If pressed to give a meaning, I might have said something like, "A Farmer met the agéd Devil on the road." Just my impression, of course.

I kept trying to puzzle together various words and phrases as I walked. I pictured her pink jogging shoes, right heel onto ground, center of gravity shifting to tiptoe, then just before lifting away, left heel onto ground. An endless repetition. Time was getting slower, the clock spring running down, the hands hardly advancing.

Efgvén—gthôuv—bge—shpèvg—égvele—wgevl

Efgvén—gthôuv—bge—shpèvg—égvele—wgevl

Efgvén—gthôuv—bge—

The aged Devil sat on a rock by the side of a Finnish country road. The Devil was ten thousand, maybe twenty thousand years old, and very tired. He was covered in dust. His whiskers were wilting. *Whither be ye gang in sich 'aste?* the Devil called out to a Farmer. *Done broke me ploughshare and must to fixe it,* the Farmer replied. *Not to hurrie,* said the Devil, *the sunne still playes o'erhead on highe, wherefore be ye scurrying? Sit ye doun and 'eare m' tale.* The Farmer knew no good could come of passing time with the Devil, but seeing him so utterly haggard, the Farmer—

Something struck my cheek. Something flat, fleshy, not too hard. But what? I tried to think, and it struck my cheek again. I raised my hand to brush it away, to no avail. An unpleasant glare was swimming in my face. I opened my eyes, which until then I hadn't even noticed were closed. It was her flashlight on me, her hand slapping me.

"Stop it," I shouted. "It's too bright. It hurts."

"You can't fall asleep here like this! Get up! Get up!" she screamed back.

"Get up? What are you talking about?"

I switched on my flashlight and shone it around me. I was on the ground, back against a wall, dripping wet. I had dozed off without knowing it.

I slowly raised myself to my feet.

"What happened? One minute I'm keeping pace, the next I'm asleep. I have no recollection of sitting down or going to sleep."

"That's the trap," she said. "They'll do anything to make us fall asleep."

"They?"

"Whoever or whatever it is that lives in this mountain. Gods, evil spirits, I don't know—*them*. They set up interference."

I shook my head.

"Everything got so hazy. Your shoes were making those sounds and . . ."

"My shoes?"

I told her about her Finnish footsteps. The old Devil. The Farmer—

"That was all a trick," she broke in. "Hypnosis. If I hadn't looked back, you probably would have slept there for . . . for ages."

"Ages?"

"Yes, that's right. You'd have been a goner," she intoned. Too far gone for what, she didn't say. "You have rope in the knapsack, don't you?"

"Uh-huh, about five meters."

"Out with it."

I unstrapped the knapsack from my back, reached inside among the cans, whiskey, and canteen, and pulled it out. She tied one end of the rope to my belt, winding the other end around her waist.

"There. That ought to do," she said. "This way we won't get separated."

"Unless we both fall asleep," I said.

"Don't add to our problems. Let's get going."

And so off we went, tied together. I tried hard not to hear her footsteps. I maintained flashlight contact with the back of her GI jacket. I bought that jacket in 1971, I was pretty sure. The Vietnam War was still going on, Nixon and his ugly mug were still in the White House. Everybody and his brother had long hair, wore dirty sandals and army-surplus jackets with peace signs on the back, tripped out to psychedelic music, thought they were Peter Fonda, screaming down the road on a Chopped Hog to a full-blast charge of *Born to Be Wild*, blurring into *I Heard It through the Grapevine*. Similar intros—different movie?

"What are you thinking about?" asked the chubby girl.

"Oh nothing," I said.

"Shall we sing something?"

"Do we have to?"

"Well, then, think of something else."

"Let's have a conversation."

"About what?"

"How about rain?"

"Sure."

"What do you associate with rain?"

"It rained the night my folks died."

"How about something more cheerful?"

"That's okay. I don't mind talking about it," she said. "Unless you don't want to hear it."

"If you want to talk about it, you should talk about it," I replied.

"It wasn't really raining. The sky was overcast, and I was in the hospital. There was a camphor tree by the window. I lay in bed and memorized every branch. A lot of birds came. Sparrows and shrikes and starlings, and other more beautiful birds. But when it was about to rain, the birds wouldn't be there. Then they'd be back, chirping thanks for the clear weather. I don't know why. Maybe because when rain stops, bugs come out of the ground."

"Were you in the hospital a long time?"

"About one month. I had a heart operation. Funny, isn't it? I was the only one sick, now I'm the only one alive. The day they died was a busy day for the birds. They had the heat turned up in the hospital, so the window was steamed up and I had to get up out of bed to wipe the window. I wasn't supposed to get out of bed, but I had to see the tree and birds and rain. There were these couple of birds with black heads and red wings. That's when I thought, how strange the world is. I mean, there must be millions of camphor trees in the world—of course, they didn't all have to be camphor trees—but on that one day, when it rained and stopped and rained and stopped, how many birds must have been flying back and forth? It made me really sad."

"It made you sad?"

"Because, like I said, there's got to be millions of trees in the world and millions of birds and millions of rainfalls. But I couldn't even figure one out, and I'd probably die that way. I just cried and cried, I felt so lonely. And that was the night my whole family got killed. Though they didn't tell me until much later."

"That must have been horrible."

"Well, it was the end of the world for me. Everything got so dark and lonely and miserable. Do you know what that feels like?"

"I can imagine," I said.

Her thoughts on rain occupied my thoughts. So much so I didn't notice that she'd stopped and I bumped into her, again.

"Sorry," I said.

"Shh!" She grabbed hold of my arm. "I hear something. Listen!"

We stood absolutely still and strained our ears. At first, faint, almost imperceptible. A deep rumbling, like a tremor. The sound got louder. The air began to tremble. Everything told us something was about to happen.

"An earthquake?" I asked.

"No," the girl shuddered. "It's much worse than that."

22

Gray Smoke

As the Colonel forewarned, one sees smoke almost every day. Gray smoke that rises from the vicinity of the Apple Grove and ascends into the clouds. If one watches long enough, the Apple Grove will seem itself to create these clouds. The first signs of smoke are visible at exactly three in the afternoon, and the burning goes on according to the number of dead. The day after a blizzard or a freezing night, a thick column of smoke will continue for hours.

Why is there not a scheme to prevent the beasts from dying?

"Could not a shelter be built for them?" I ask the Colonel while we play chess. "Should they not be protected from the snow and wind and cold? A simple roofed enclosure would save many of them."

"It would do no good," is all he responds, never lifting

his eyes from the chessboard. "They would never take to the shelter. They would continue to sleep on the ground as always. They would sleep out in the elements, even if it means they die."

The Colonel threatens, placing his High Priest directly before my King. To either side, two Horns are positioned in fire line. I wait for them to initiate the attack.

"It almost seems the beasts wish to suffer and die," I say.

"In a way, yes. That is natural to them. Cold and discomfort. That might even be their salvation."

The Colonel falls silent, allowing me to entrench my Ape beside his Wall. Perhaps I can lure the Wall into moving. The Colonel reaches to take the bait, only to pull back one of his Knights and fortify his defenses.

"Getting your wiles, are you now?" says the military man with a laugh.

"Nowhere near you, of course." I also laugh. "What do you mean by 'their salvation'?"

"Odd to say, dying might be what saves them. They die and are reborn in the spring. As new young, that is."

"But then those newborn young grow to suffer and die all the same. Why must they suffer so?"

"Because it is ordained," he pronounces. "Your turn. You cannot win unless you eliminate my High Priest."

After three days of snow appears a sudden sky of clarity. Rays of sun spill a blinding glare upon the frozen white Town. I hear snow falling from branches everywhere. I stay indoors and draw the curtains against the light, but I cannot escape. The ice-encrusted Town refracts like a huge, many-faceted jewel, sending knives of light to stab my eyes.

I pass the afternoons face down on my bed. I strain to hear the songs of the birds that visit the windowsills for breadcrumbs the old men leave. I can hear the old men themselves sitting in front of the house, talking in the sun. I alone shun the warm bounty of sunshine.

When the sun sets, I get out of bed and bathe my sore eyes in cold water. I put on my black glasses and descend the snowbanked slope to the Library. I cannot read as much as usual. After only one skull, the glowing of the old dreams pricks needles of pain into my eyeballs. The vague hollows behind my vision grow heavy, my fingertips lose their sensitivity.

At these times, the Librarian brings me a cool towel compress for my eyes and some light broth or warm milk to drink. They are gritty on my tongue, wholly lacking in flavor. I grow accustomed to this, but I still do not find the taste agreeable.

"You are gradually adjusting to the Town," she says. "The food here is different than elsewhere. We use only a few basic ingredients. What resembles meat is not. What resembles eggs is not. What resembles coffee only resembles coffee. Everything is made in the image of something. The soup is good for you. It warms you."

"Yes, it does," I say.

My head is not so heavy, my body not as cold. I thank her and close my eyes to rest.

"Is there something else you require?" she asks.

"What makes you say that?"

"Surely there is something that would help to unclose your winter shell."

"What I want is the sun," I say. Whereupon I remove my black glasses and wipe the lenses with a rag. "But it's impossible. My eyes can't tolerate light."

"Something more true than sunlight. Something perhaps from your former world that gave you comfort."

I chase up the pieces of memory left to me, but none completes the puzzle.

"It's no good. I cannot remember a thing. I've lost it all."

"Something small, anything, the first thing that comes to you. Let me help you."

My memory is solid rock. It does not budge. My head hurts. Losing my shadow, I have lost much. What is left is sealed over in the winter cold.

She puts her hand on my temple.

"We can think about this later. Perhaps you will remember."

"Let me read one last old dream," I insist.

"You are tired. Should you not wait until tomorrow? There is no need to strain yourself. The old dreams will keep."

"No, I would rather read dreams than do nothing. At least then, I don't have to think about anything."

She stands, and disappears into the stacks. I sit there, eyes shut, plunging into darkness. How long will this winter last? *A killing winter,* the Colonel has said. And it has only begun. Will my shadow survive? No, the question is, will I survive, uncertain as I am?

She places a skull on the table and wipes it with a dampened cloth, as usual, followed by a dry cloth. I sit there, head resting on my hand, and watch her fingers at work.

"Is there nothing else I can do for you?" she says, looking up unexpectedly.

"You do so much for me already," I say.

She stays her hand and sits facing me. "I mean something else. Perhaps you wish to sleep with me."

I shake my head.

"I do not understand," she implores. "You said you needed me."

"I do. But now it is not right."

She says nothing and at length returns to polishing the skull. I look at the ceiling, at the yellowed light hanging from it. No matter how hard my mind becomes, no matter how winter closes me, it is not for me to be sleeping with her. It is the Town that wants me to sleep with her. That is how they would claim my mind.

She places the polished skull before me, but I do not pick it up. I am looking at her fingers on the table. I try to read meaning from her fingers, but they tell me nothing.

"Tell me more about your mother," I say.

"My mother?"

"Yes. Anything at all."

"Well," she begins, her hands on the skull, "it seems I felt differently toward my mother than I did toward others. I cannot recall well, it was so long ago. Why that should be, I do not know."

"That's the way it is with the mind. Nothing is ever equal. Like a river, as it flows, the course changes with the terrain."

She smiles. "That seems wrong."

"That's the way it is," I say. "Do you not miss your mother?"

"I do not know."

She moves the skull to stare at it from various angles.

"Is the question too vague?"

"Yes, probably."

"Shall we talk of something else?" I suggest. "What sort of things did your mother like? Can you remember?"

"Yes, I remember very well. On warm days we took walks and watched the beasts. The Townfolk do not often take walks, unlike you."

"Yes, I enjoy walking," I say. "What else can you recall?"

"When she was alone in her room, I would hear her talking, although I do not know if it pleased her."

"What sort of things did she say?"

"I do not remember. It was not talking as one usually does. I do not know how to explain, but it seemed to have importance to Mother."

"Importance?"

"Yes, the talking had a . . . an accent to it. Mother would draw words out or she would make them short. Her voice would sound high and low, like the wind."

"That is singing," I suddenly realize.

"Can you talk like that?"

"Singing is not talking. It is song."

"Can you do it too?" she says.

I take a deep breath but find no music in my memory.

"I'm sorry. I cannot remember a single song," I say.

"Is it impossible to bring the songs back?"

"A musical instrument might help. If I could play a few notes, perhaps a song would come to me."

"What does a musical instrument look like?"

"There are hundreds of musical instruments, all different shapes and sizes. Some are so large, four persons are needed to lift them; others will fit in the palm of the hand. The sounds are different as well."

Having said this, I begin to feel a string of memory slowly unravelling inside me.

"There may be a musical instrument in the Collection Room. It is not really a collection, but there are many things from the past. I have only glanced in there."

"May we look?" I ask. "It seems I can do no more dreamreading today."

We walk past the stacks of skulls to another hallway, arriving at frosted glass doors like those at the Library entrance. She enters, finds the light switch, and a dim illumination filters down over a confined space. The floor is cluttered with trunks and valises, piles of suitcases large and small. Too many to count, all are covered with dust. Among them are odd objects, either lying open or in fitted cases. Why are these things here?

I kneel to open one of these cases. A cloud of white dust flies up. Inside sits a curious machine, with rows of round keys on its slanted face. It is apparently well used, the black paint flaked in places on its iron frame.

"Do you know what this is?"

"No," she says, standing over me. "Is it a musical instrument?"

"No, this does not make music. It makes words. I think they called it a typewriter."

I close the case on the ancient mechanism, moving now

to the wicker basket next to it. I raise the lid and find a complete set of knives and forks, cups, plates, and yellowed napkins neatly packed.

A large leather portmanteau contains an old suit, shirts, neckties, socks, and undergarments. Between layers of clothing are a set of toiletries, the shaving brush caked with dirty soap, and a liquor flask devoid of odor.

Each piece of luggage I open reveals a similar tawdry inventory. Clothes and some few sundry items, all seem to have been packed for a sudden journey. Yet each wants for identifying detail, each impresses as somehow unremarkable, lacking in particularity. The clothes are neither quality tailored items, nor tatttered hand-me-downs. They show differences in period, season, and gender, varying in their cut according to age, yet nothing is especially striking. They even smell alike. It is as if someone has painstakingly removed any indication of individuality. Only person-less dregs remain.

After examining five or six suitcases, I relinquish the effort. If any musical instruments are to be found in the Town, they will not be here.

"Let's go," I say. "The dust scratches my eyes."

"Are you disappointed not to find a musical instrument?"

"We can try looking somewhere else," I say.

I bid her good-night and climb the Western Hill alone. The winter wind whips between the trees, driving at my back. I look behind me to find the moon hovering half-obscured over the Clocktower, the heavens boiling thick with cloud matter. In the less than lunar light, the River recedes black as tar.

I remember seeing a warm scarf among the clothes in the Collection Room. It has more than a few moth holes, but wrapped around several times, it will stave off the cold. I must ask whether those suitcases have owners, and whether

I might have use of the contents. Standing in the wind with no scarf, I shiver; my ears sting as if slashed.

I shall visit the Gatekeeper tomorrow. I also must see after my shadow.

I turn away to the Town, and resume my steps up the frozen incline toward the Official Residences.

23

Holes, Leeches, Tower

I T'S not an earthquake," the girl shuddered. "It's much worse than that."

"Like what?"

She didn't answer, only swallowed her breath and shook her head in distress.

"No time for explanations now. Run! That's the only thing that can save us. You might rip your stitches, but it's better than dying."

Tethered by nylon rope, we ran full speed straight ahead. The light in her hand swung violently, tracing a jagged seismographic pattern between the walls. My knapsack bounced on my back. I'd have liked to dump it, but there was no time. There was no way to slacken my pace; I was on a leash.

The rumble grew louder the farther we got. We seemed to be heading directly into its source. What started as an underground tremor was now a grating, hissing, bubbling, rasping—I don't know what else.

I cringed as we ran—my body wanted to go the other way—but she was leading and I was following. Fortunately, there were no turns or obstacles. The trough was flat as a bowling alley. No boreholes or rocks to worry about.

Then came a series of sharp creaks and cracks, like boulders scraping together with tremendous force. All was relentless noise; suddenly silence. A second of nothing at all. Then everywhere was filled with a weird hissing, as if thousands of old men were sucking air between their teeth. A reedy whistling echoing through the darkness like the humming of thousands of subterranean insects triggered by the same stimulus. The sound did not wish us well.

At the same time, I got the uncanny feeling that the sound was beckoning us, a beast lying in wait for its prey. Whatever horror was out there, *it* knew we were coming. Whatever it was, I had no idea. We'd left my imagination a long way back.

We kept running—for how long? My sense of time was paralyzed. I ran and ran but felt no fatigue, my gut wound allocated to a far corner of my consciousness. My elbows felt stiff, but that was my only body sensation. I was hardly aware I was running. My legs flew and bounded. A dense mass of air was pushing me from behind.

I was poetry in motion when she screamed out a warning, which I didn't hear. I smashed into her, knocking her to the ground. I continued my forward motion, falling in an arc over her. I didn't even hear myself hit. An instant after my head slammed into the hard rock slab, the thought occurred to me: it was as if I were sound-removed. Or was evolution creeping up on me?

Next—or more accurately, overlapping with this—I was blinded with pain in my frontal lobe. The darkness exploded before my eyes. I was sure I had a concussion. Had I fractured my skull? Maybe I was brain-dead, and this was a vestigial lizard-tail of pain firing away in my cortex.

That all passed in an instant. I was alive. I was alive and breathing. And breathing, I felt pain. I felt tears on my cheeks, streaming into the corner of my mouth and down onto the rock slab.

I thought I would pass out, but I fastened the pain to the darkness. I'd been doing something. Yes, I was running. I was running from something. I fell. In the cut ends of my memory, I labored to get to my knees.

As awareness spliced together, I noted the nylon rope. I was a piece of laundry blown off the line by gale winds. I had developed a habit of transposing my circumstances into all sorts of convenient analogues.

The next thing I realized was that my body was missing from the waist down. I reassessed the situation. My lower half was there, just unable to feel anything. I shut my eyes and concentrated. Trying to resurrect sensations below the belt reminded me of trying to get an erection. The effort of forcing energy into a vacuum.

So here I was, thinking about my friendly librarian with the gastric dilation and the whole bedroom fiasco. That's where everything began going wrong, it now struck me. Still, getting a penis to erect itself is not the sole purpose of life. That much I understood when I read Stendhal's *Charterhouse of Parma* years ago.

My lower half seemed to be stuck in some halfway strait. Or cantilevered out over empty space or . . . dangling off the edge of the rock slab. It was only my upper half that prevented me from falling. That's why my hands were clinging to the rope so desperately.

I opened my eyes into bright light. The chubby girl was shining her flashlight in my face. I gripped the rope and struggled to drag my lower half up onto solid rock.

"Hurry up!" yelled the girl, "or we'll both be killed!"

My body was dead heavy, the ground slippery with blood. My wound had probably split open. I dropped the rope and arm-pressed myself up, agonizing. My belt caught on the edge of the rock slab, while the nylon rope wanted to pull me forward.

"Don't yank!" I shouted at the approaching light. "I'll manage myself. Don't touch the rope."

"Are you all right?"

"All right enough."

Belt still caught on the rock edge, I squeezed out all of my strength to throw one foot up.

"Sorry I couldn't help you," she said. "I was trying to hold on to the rocks so the two of us wouldn't fall over the edge."

"That I don't mind," I said. "But why didn't you tell me about this hole?"

"There wasn't time. That's why I yelled for you to stop."

"I couldn't hear."

"Let's not argue. We're almost there. We've got to get out of here. If we don't, we'll get the blood sucked out of us."

"Blood?"

She shined her flashlight into the hole. It was perfectly round, about a meter in diameter. Then she panned the light, revealing rows of identical holes as far as the eye could see. We were walking on a honeycomb.

Except that the ground appeared to be like shifting sand. I thought my eyes were playing tricks on me after the blow to my head. But my hands, when held under the light, showed no particular sign of trembling. Which meant the ground really was moving.

"Leeches!" she squealed. "Zillions of leeches are crawling up from the holes. If we hang around here, they'll suck us dry."

"Uggh." I felt sick. "Is this what's supposed to be worse than an earthquake?"

"No. The leeches are only the beginning. The real incredible part comes later."

Still leashed together, we ventured out onto the viscous

surface, squashing leeches with every step. It made me squirm involuntarily.

"Don't slip. If you fall into a hole, that'll be the end of you."

She clung to my elbow. I held onto the tail of her jacket. For anyone not accustomed to this sort of thing, stepping on thirty-centimeter wide sections of slick rock crawling with leeches in the dark is an experience likely to be memorable. The squashed leeches made a thick layer of sticky, gelatinous mush.

Leeches must have gotten on me when I stumbled. I could feel a couple sucking on my neck and ears. I tried not to make too much of this because I couldn't stand the thought of it. Also, my hands were occupied. To be exact, I had a flashlight in my left hand and her in my right. I couldn't just stop to yank the damn things off.

Each time I shined my flashlight on the ground, I saw a sickening ooze of leeches. They just kept coming.

"I'll bet the INKlings used to throw their sacrificial victims into these holes."

"You're very smart," she said.

"Aren't I, though," I answered.

"The leeches, Grandfather says, are acolytes of those fish. So the INKlings make offerings to the leeches too. Fresh meat, warm blood, humans dragged under from the surface world."

Gasping noises seemed to be rushing up from the dark holes. Twisting whips of air, like feelers from below, completely enveloped us in a bristling night forest.

"The water is almost here," she announced. "The leeches were only the beginning. Once they disappear, we get the water. It gushes up from the holes. We've got to reach the altar before the water rises."

"You knew all this? Why the hell didn't you tell me?"

"Because I didn't know, okay? It's not like the water rises every day. It only happens once or twice a month. How was I to know today would be one of those days?"

There was no end to the holes. My shoes were so sticky with leech innards, I couldn't walk straight. Funny thing.

"Just a little more," she assured me. "Just a little more and we'll be safe."

It was too much trouble to speak. I nodded instead, which was less than meaningless in total darkness.

"Can you hear me? You okay?" she called out.

"I feel like puking, but I'm fine."

I'm not such a wimp usually, but a sundae of leeches, all squashed and sticky on top of darkness and fatigue and lack of sleep was testing the limits of my cool. Gastric juices backed up, acid sweet, into my throat.

I didn't dare look at my watch. Thoughts of the sky intruded. Morning, trees, hot coffee, newspaper, . . . I wanted light, any light, real light.

"Once we get out of this spot, you can throw up all you want. Hang in there." She gripped my elbow.

"Not me. You won't see me throwing up. I only feel like it," I gurgled inside my mouth.

"It happens to everyone. I know it's horrible, but it's got to end sometime. Trust me," she said with irrepressible optimism.

No, these holes *could* go on forever. And I would never get to read that morning edition. The fresh ink coming off on your fingers. Thick with all the advertising inserts. The Prime Minister's wake-up time, stock market reports, whole family suicides, *chawan-mushi* recipes, the length of skirts, record album reviews, real estate, . . .

The only thing was, I didn't subscribe to a newspaper. I'd given up on newspapers three years ago. Why? I felt disconnected. Converting numbers in my brain was my only connection to the world. Most of my free time I chose to spend alone, reading old novels, watching old Hollywood movies on video, drinking. I had no need for a newspaper.

Even so, deprived of light in this netherworld, I found myself longing for the morning edition. To sit down in a sunny spot and lap it up like a cat at its dish of milk, first page to last, to read every word of print.

"There's the altar," she said abruptly. "Another ten meters."

At that moment, as if to underscore her words, the air wheezing out of the holes stopped, cut off by a single giant razor stroke. No forewarning, no aftertones, all that noise pressure, gone. And with it the entire aural space, and my equilibrium.

Total silence. Once the sound was severed, that was it. Both she and I froze in position, straining our ears for . . . what? I swallowed, but it sounded as raucous as a needle striking the edge of a turntable.

"The water's receded?" I asked hopefully.

"The water's about to spew," she said. "All that noise was the air being forced out of the water table. It's all out now. The action comes after this."

She took my hand as we crossed the last few holes. At last we were over the worst part. The leeches seemed to have fled in the opposite direction. Even if we drowned now, it beat a slow slimy death in a leech pit.

I reached up to peel the sucker off my neck, but she stopped me.

"Don't! You'll tear your skin. A few leeches never hurt anyone," she said. "Anyway, we have to climb the tower quick. Didn't they ever teach you about leeches in school?"

"No," I admitted. That's me, dumb as the anchor under a buoy.

A little farther on, she shined her light up at the the "tower" that rose before us. It was a smooth, featureless cylinder that loomed like a lighthouse, seeming to narrow from base to top. I couldn't tell its height, but it was very tall. Without a word, she started up the "steps". I, of course, had to be pulled along.

Seen from a slight distance in limited light, this tower had appeared to be a noble monument constructed over centuries, but close up, you realized it was a natural rock formation. And a rather crude stalagmite at that. Even the winding steps chiseled into this deceptive pylon were not quite stairs. Uneven and irregular, barely wide enough for one foot, sometimes missing entire footholds. We scrambled and fell and plastered ourselves against the rock face.

After thirty-six steps—I'm a habitual step counter—we were met by the sound of a loud slap, as if a huge cut of roast beef had been flung against a stone wall. Followed by a tentative half beat of quiet. The something was coming.

It came. Torrents of water, gushing up from those hundreds of leech-infested holes. Tons of water, sluicing through darkness. In the next instant, I am a child in a movie theater, watching a newsreel of the inauguration of a dam. The floodgates are open, a massive column of water leaps from the screen. The governor, wearing a helmet, has done the honors and pushed the button. Billowing clouds of spray, a deafening roar.

"What are you doing down there?" she barked.

"How high do you think the water will rise?" I blinked awake and shouted up.

"High," was her pointed reply. "The only sure thing is the water won't reach the top."

"How many more steps?"

"Lots." Another nice answer.

We kept climbing. Her flashlight swung about wildly by its shoulder strap. I gave up counting the steps after two hundred. The sound of the angry torrent slowed to a hungry maelstrom to a racy gurgle. No doubt about it, the water level was rising. At any moment now, the water would be licking my heels.

"Couldn't we swim?" I asked her. "We could float up. It's got to be easier than this."

"No," she ruled. "There's a whirlpool under the surface. If you get caught in the undertow, you're not going to do a whole lot of swimming."

Which meant this way was the only way. Plodding up

these miserable steps, not knowing when the water was going to get to us. I was sick of it.

Back to the newsreel, arcs of water shooting across the screen, spillway emptying into the big bowl below. Dozens of camera angles: up, down, head on, this side, that side, long, medium, zoom in close-up on the tumbling waters. An enormous shadow of the arching water is cast against the concrete expanse. I stare, and the shadow gradually becomes *my* shadow. I sit there, transfixed. I know it's my shadow flickering on the curve of the dam, but I don't know how to react as a member of the audience. I'm a ten-year-old boy, wide-eyed and afraid to act. Should I get my shadow back from the screen? Should I rush into the projection room and steal the film? I do nothing.

My shadow stays on screen, a figure in the distance, unsteady through the shimmering heat. The shadow cannot speak, knows no sign language, is helpless, like me. The shadow knows I am sitting here, watching. The shadow is trying to tell me something.

No one in the audience realizes that the shadow is really my shadow. My older brother, sitting next to me, doesn't notice either. If he had, he wouldn't miss the opportunity to box my ears. He's that kind of brother.

Nor do I let on that it's my shadow. No one would believe me anyway.

Instantly the dam segment ends and the news changes to the coronation of a king. A team of horses with fancy headgear is pulling a fairy-tale carriage across a flagstone plaza. I search for my shadow in the procession, but all I see are shadows of the horses and carriage.

There ended the memory. Though I couldn't be sure any of it had really happened to me. I had no recollection. Perhaps this was a hallucination induced by the sounds of the water in the darkness, a daydream dredged up in the face of extreme circumstances. But the image was too vivid. It had the smell of memory, real memory. This *had* happened to me, it came to me with a jolt.

Until this moment the memory, it seemed, had been sealed off from the sludge of my consciousness by an intervening force.

An intervening force?

Or an operation, like the one done on my brain to give me shuffling faculty. They had shoved memories out of my conscious awareness. They had stolen my memories from me!

Nobody had that right. Nobody! My memories *belonged* to me. Stealing memories was stealing time. I got so mad, I lost all fear. I didn't care what happened. *I want to live!* I told myself. I *will* live. I will get out of this insane netherworld and get back my stolen memories back and live. Forget the end of the world, I was ready to reclaim my whole self.

"A rope!" she yelled out of nowhere.

"Rope?"

"Quick, get on up here. There's a rope hanging down."

I hurried up the next three or four steps to where she stood and felt along the rock surface with my hand. Most definitely, there was a rope, a length of mountaineering line, the end of which reached chest-high on me. I pulled at it to test its strength. It seemed to be secured at the other end.

"It's got to be Grandfather's doing," she exclaimed. "Grandfather's dropped a line for us."

"To give us a better start, let's go around once more."

Exasperating as it was to keep checking each step, especially in my tennis shoes, we ascended one more circle around the tower and found the rope hanging in the same position. There were knots for footing every thirty centimeters or so. Let's hope they went up all the way to the top.

"It's Grandfather all right. Only he would think of such details."

"I'll say," I said. "Can you climb rope?"

"Of course," she retorted. "I've been a climber since I was a little girl. Didn't I tell you?"

"Well then, you first," I said. "When you get to the top

flash me a signal with your light. Then I'll start my climb."

"But by then the water will have reached here. We'd better climb together."

"No, one rope, one person. That's a mountaineering rule. There's the strength of the rope to consider, plus it takes more time for two people to climb the same rope. And even if the water does rise this high, as long as I hold onto the rope I'll be safe."

"You're braver than you look," she said.

She was up the rope without so much as another word. I clung with both hands to the rocks and stared up at her swinging, like the assumption of a drunken soul.

I craved a swig of whiskey, but it was in the knapsack on my back and the idea of twisting around to extract the bottle did not seem altogether wise. Nix on that. So I *thought* about having a drink instead. A quiet bar, MJQ's *Vendome* playing low, a bowl of nuts, a double whiskey on the rocks. The glass is sitting on the counter, untouched for a moment, just looked at. Whiskey, like a beautiful woman, demands appreciation. You gaze first, then it's time to drink.

This scene set up, it came to me I didn't have the right clothes. The two thugs had taken care of that. What to do? Get some new clothes. A dark blue tweed suit. Three buttons, natural shoulder, no taper, old-fashioned cut. A George Peppard number from the early sixties. The shirt, a lighter shade of blue, Oxford broadcloth, regular collar. The necktie, a two-color stripe, a subdued red with a might-be-blue-might-be-green storm-swept seafoam shade. The drink, Scotland's finest.

Bringing the glass to my lips, I noticed that the sound of the water had stopped. Did this mean that the water had stopped gushing up from the holes? Or merely that the water level had risen to where it drowned out the sound?

I no longer cared. The water could rise all it wanted. I was set to survive. To get back my memories. I would be manipulated no more. I'd shout it out loud. I'm mad as hell! Nobody's pushing me around any more! Do you hear!

Not that it would do much good to shout it out while clinging to a rock in subterranean darkness. I decided to forgo the proclamations and craned my neck to look up again. The chubby girl had climbed a good three or four flights' worth of department store steps. Up in the women's wear or kimono department. How tall was this mountain anyway? Why couldn't her grandfather be waiting for us in a saner, less baroque place?

Finally, she signaled with her light that she'd made it to the top. I signaled back, then shined the light downward to see how far the water had risen. I couldn't make out a thing.

My watch read four-twelve in the morning. Not yet dawn. The morning papers still not delivered, trains not yet running, citizens of the surface world fast asleep, oblivious to all this. I pulled the rope taut with both hands, took a deep breath, then slowly began my climb.

24

Shadow Grounds

THREE days of clear weather have come to an end. I
know it as soon as I awaken. I open my eyes with
no discomfort.

The sun is stripped of light and warmth, the sky is
cloaked in heavy clouds. Trees send up crooked, leafless
branches into the chill gray, like cracks in the firmament.
Surely snow will fall through, yet the air is still.

"It will not snow today," the Colonel informs me. "Such
clouds do not bring snow."

I open the window to look out, but cannot know what
the Colonel understands.

The Gatekeeper sits before his iron stove, shoes
removed, warming his feet. The stove is like the one in the

Library. It has a flat heating surface for a kettle and a drawer at the bottom for the ash. The front opens with a large metal pull, which the Gatekeeper uses as his footrest. The Gatehouse is stuffy from kettle steam and cheap pipe tobacco, or more probably some surrogate. The Gatekeeper's feet also smell.

"I need a scarf," I begin. "I get chills in my head."

"I can see that," snorts the Gatekeeper. "Does not surprise me at all."

"There are old clothes in the Collection Room at the back of the Library. I was wondering if I might borrow a few."

"Oh, those things," says the Gatekeeper. "You can help yourself to any of them. Take a muffler, take a coat, take whatever you like."

"And the owners?"

"Forget about the owners. Even if the owners are around, they have forgotten about those things. But say, I heard you were looking for a musical instrument?"

He knows everything.

"Officially, the Town has no musical instruments," he says. "But that does not rule out the possibility. You do serious work, so what could be wrong if you had yourself an instrument. Go to the Power Station and ask the Caretaker. He might find you something."

"Power Station?" I ask, surprised.

"We use power, you know," he says, pointing to the light overhead. "You think power grows on apple trees?" The Gatekeeper laughs as he draws a map. "You take the road along the south bank of the River, going upstream. Then after thirty minutes, you see an old granary on your right-hand side. The shed with the roof caved in and no door. You make a right turn there, and follow the road until you see a hill. Beyond the hill is the Woods. Go five hundred yards into the Woods, and there is the Power Station. Understand?"

"I believe so," I say. "But it is dangerous to go into the Woods in winter. Everyone tells me so. I fell ill the last time."

"Ah, yes, I nearly forgot. I had to carry you up the Hill," says the Gatekeeper. "Are you better now?"

"Much better, thank you."

"A little less foolish?"

"Yes, I hope so."

The Gatekeeper grins broadly and shifts his feet on the stove handle. "You got to know your limits. Once is enough, but you got to learn. A little caution never hurt anyone. A good woodsman has only one scar on him. No more, no less. You get my meaning?"

I nod appropriately.

"No need to worry about the Power Station. It sits right at the entrance to the Woods. Only one path, you cannot get lost. No Woodsfolk around there. The real danger is deep in the Woods, and near the Wall. If you stay away from them, everything will be fine. Keep to the path, do not go past the Power Station."

"Is the Caretaker one of the Woodsfolk?"

"Not him. Not Woodsfolk and not Townfolk. We call him nobody. He stays at the edge of the Woods, never comes to Town. Harmless, got no guts."

"What are Woodsfolk like?"

The Gatekeeper turns his head and pauses before saying, "Like I believe I told you the very first time, you can ask whatever questions you please, but I can answer or not answer as I see fit."

I open my mouth, a question on my lips.

"Forget it. Today, no answers," says the Gatekeeper. "But say, you wanted to see your shadow? Time you saw it, no? The shadow is down in strength since winter come along. No reason for you not to see it."

"Is he sick?"

"No, not sick. Healthy as can be. It has a couple of hours exercise every day. Healthy appetite, ha ha. Just that when winter days get short and cold, any shadow is bound to lose a little something. No fault of mine. Just the way things go. Well, let it speak for itself."

The Gatekeeper retrieves a ring of keys from the wall and puts them in his pocket. He yawns as he laces up his leather boots. They look heavy and sturdy, with iron cleats for walking in snow.

My shadow lives between the Town and the outside. As I cannot leave to go to the world beyond the Wall, my shadow cannot come into Town. So the one place we can meet is the Shadow Grounds, a close behind the Gatehouse. It is small and fenced in.

The Gatekeeper takes the keys out of his pocket and opens the iron gate to the enclosure. We enter the Shadow Grounds. It is a perfect square, one side backed up almost against the Wall. In the center is an old elm tree, underneath which is a bench. The tree is blanched with age; I do not know if it is alive or dead.

In a corner stands a lean-to of bricks and building scraps. No glass in the window; only a rude wooden panel that swings up for a door. I see no chimney, so there must be no heat.

"That is where your shadow sleeps," says the Gate-keeper. "Not as bad as it looks. Even got water and a toilet. Not quite a hotel, but it is shelter. Care to go in?"

"No, I'll meet him here," I say, still dizzy from the stale air in the Gatehouse. Cold or not, it is better to be out in the fresh air.

"Fine by me, let me bring it outside." The Gatekeeper storms into the lean-to by himself.

I turn up my collar and sit down on the bench, scraping at the ground with the heel of my shoe. The ground is hard, with lingering patches of snow where shaded by the Wall.

Presently, the Gatekeeper emerges and strides across the Grounds, my shadow following slowly after. My shadow is not the picture of health the Gatekeeper has led me to believe. His face is haggard, all eyes and beard.

"I imagine you two want to be alone, ha ha," says the Gatekeeper. "Probably got heaps to talk about. Well, have yourselves a nice, long talk. But not too long, if you know what I mean."

I know what he means. My shadow and I watch the Gatekeeper lock the enclosure gate and withdraw to the Gatehouse. His cleats rasp into the frozen distance. We hear the heavy wooden door shutting behind him. Not until he is gone from sight does the shadow approach and sit next to me. He wears a bulky rough-knit sweater, work pants, and the boots I got for him.

"How are you holding up?" I ask.

"How do you expect?" says my shadow. "It's freezing and the food's terrible."

"But he said you exercise every day."

"Exercise?" says my shadow. "Every day the Gatekeeper drags me out and makes me burn dead beasts with him. Some exercise."

"Is that so bad?"

"It's not fun and games. We load up the cart with carcasses, haul them out to the Apple Grove, douse them with oil, and torch them. But before that, the Gatekeeper lops off the heads with a hackblade. You've seen his magnificent tool collection, haven't you? The guy's not right in his head. He'd hack the whole world to bits if he had his way."

"Is the Gatekeeper what they call Townfolk?"

"No, I don't think he's from here. The guy takes pleasure in dead things. The Townpeople don't pay him any mind. As if they could. We've already gotten rid of loads of beasts. This morning there were thirteen dead, which we have to burn after this."

The shadow digs his heels into the frozen ground.

"I found the map," says my shadow. "Drawn much better than I expected. Thoughtful notes, too. But it was just a little late."

"I got sick," I say.

"So I heard. Still, winter was too late. I needed it earlier.

I could have formulated a plan with time to spare."

"A plan?"

"A plan of escape. What else? You didn't think I wanted a map for my amusement, did you?"

I shake my head. "I thought you would explain to me what's what in this Town. After all, you ended up with almost all our memories."

"Big deal," says my shadow. "I got most of our memories, but what am I supposed to do with them? In order to make sense, we'd have to be put back together, which is not going to happen. If we try anything, they'd keep us apart forever. We'd never pull it off. That's why I thought things out for myself. About the way things work in this Town."

"And did you figure anything out?"

"Some things I did. But nothing I can tell you yet. Without more details to back it all up, it would hardly be convincing. Give me more time, I think I'll have it. But by then it might already be too late. Since winter came on, I am definitely getting weaker. I might draw up an escape plan, but would I even have the strength to carry it out? That's why I needed the map sooner."

I look up at the elm tree overhead. A mosaic of winter sky shows between the branches.

"But there is no escape from here," I say. "You looked over the map, didn't you? There is no exit. This is the End of the World."

"It may be the End of the World, but it has to have a way out. I know that for certain. Look at the sky. Where do those birds go when they fly over the Wall? To another world. If there was nothing out there, why surround the place with a Wall? It has to let out somewhere."

"Or maybe—"

"Leave it to me, I'll find it," he cuts me short. "We'll get out of here. I don't want to die in this miserable hole."

He digs his heel into the ground again. "I repeat what I said at the very beginning: this place is wrong. I know it. More than ever. The problem is, the Town is *perfectly* wrong. Every last thing is skewed, so that the total distortion is seamless. It's a whole. Like this—"

My shadow draws a circle on the ground with his boot.

"The Town is sealed," he states, "like this. That's why the longer you stay in here, the more you get to thinking that things are normal. You begin to doubt your judgment. You get what I'm saying?"

"Yes, I've felt that myself. I get so confused. Sometimes it seems I'm the cause of a lot of trouble."

"It's not that way at all," says my shadow, scratching a meandering pattern next to the circle. "We're the ones who are right. They're the ones who are wrong, absolutely. You have to believe that, while you still have the strength to believe. Or else the Town will swallow you, mind and all."

"But how can we be absolutely right? What could their being absolutely wrong mean? And without memory to measure things against, how could I ever know?"

My shadow shakes his head. "Look at it this way. The Town seems to contain everything it needs to sustain itself in perpetual peace and security. The order of things remains perfectly constant, no matter what happens. But a world of perpetual motion is theoretically impossible. There has to be a trick. The system must take in and let out somewhere."

"And have you discovered where that is?"

"No, not yet. As I said, I'm still working on it. I need more details."

"Can you tell me anything? Perhaps I can help."

My shadow takes his hands out of his pockets, warms them in his breath, then rubs them on his lap.

"No, it's too much to expect of you. Physically I'm a mess, but your mind is in no shape either. The first thing you have to do is recover. Otherwise, we're both stuck. I'll think these things out by myself, and you do what you need to do to save yourself."

"My confidence is going, it's true," I say, dropping my eyes to the circle on the ground. "How can I be strong when I do not know my own mind? I am lost."

"That's not true," corrects my shadow. "You are not lost. It's just that your own thoughts are being kept from you, or hidden away. But the mind is strong. It survives, even without thought. Even with everything taken away, it holds a seed—your self. You must believe in your own powers."

"I will try," I say.

My shadow gazes up at the sky and closes his eyes.

"Look at the birds," he says. "Nothing can hold them. Not the Wall, nor the Gate, nor the sounding of the horn. It does good to watch the birds."

I hear the Gatekeeper calling. I am to curtail my visit.

"Don't come see me for a while," my shadow whispers as I turn to go. "When it comes time, I'll arrange to see you. The Gatekeeper will get suspicious if we meet, which will only make my work harder. Pretend we didn't get along."

"All right," I say.

"How did it go?" asks the Gatekeeper, upon my return to the Gatehouse. "Good to visit after all this time, eh?"

"I don't really know," I say, with a shake of the head.

"That's how it is," says the Gatekeeper, satisfied.

25

Meal, Elephant Factory, Trap

CLIMBING the rope was easier than climbing the steps. There was a strong knot every thirty centimeters. Rope in both hands, I swung suspended, bounding off the tower. A regular scene from *The Big Top*. Although, of course, in the film the rope wouldn't be knotted; the audience wouldn't go for that.

I looked up from time to time. She was shining her light down at me, but I could get no clear sense of distance. I just kept climbing, and my gut wound kept throbbing. The bump on my head wasn't doing bad either.

As I neared the top, the light she held became bright enough for me to see my whole body and surroundings. But by then I'd gotten so used to climbing in the dark that actually seeing what I was doing slowed me down and I nearly slipped a couple of times. I couldn't gauge distance. Lighted surfaces jumped out at me and shadowed parts inverted into negative.

Sixty or seventy knots up, I reached the summit. I grabbed the rock overhang with both hands and pushed up like a competition swimmer at poolside. My arms ached from the long climb, so it was a struggle. She grabbed my belt and helped pull me up.

"That was close," she said. "A few more minutes and we'd have been goners."

"Great," I said, stretching out on the level and taking a few deep breaths, "just great. How far up did the water come?"

She set her light down and pulled up the rope, hand over hand. At the thirtieth knot she stopped and passed the rope over to me. It was dripping wet.

"Did you find your grandfather?"

"Why of course," she beamed. "He's back there at the altar. But he's sprained his foot. He got it caught in a hole."

"And he made it all the way here with a sprained foot?"

"Yes, sure. Grandfather's in very good shape."

"I'd imagine so," I said.

"Let's go. Grandfather's waiting inside. There's lots he wants to talk to you about."

"Likewise here," I said.

I picked up the knapsack and followed her toward the altar. This turned out to be nothing more than a round opening cut into a rock face. It led into a large room illuminated by the dim amber glow of a propane lamp set in a niche, the walls textured with myriad shadows from the grain of the rock. The Professor sat next to the lamp, wrapped in a blanket. His face was half in shadow. His eyes looked sunken in the half-light, but in fact he was chipper as could be.

"Seems we almost lost you," the Professor greeted me ever so gladly. "I knew the water was goin' t'rise, but I thought you'd get here a bit sooner."

"I got lost in the city, Grandfather," said his chubby granddaughter. "It was almost a whole day before I finally met up with him."

"*Tosh,*" said the Professor. "But we're here now and 'sall the same."

"Excuse me, but what exactly is 'sall the same?" I asked.

"Now, now, hold your horses. I'll get t'all that. Just take yourself a seat. First thing, let's just remove that leech from your neck."

I sat down near the Professor. His granddaughter sat beside me. She lit a match and held it to the giant sucker feasting on my neck. It was big as a wine cork. The flame hissed as it touched the engorged parasite. The leech fell to the ground, wriggling in spasms, until she put it out of its misery.

My neck felt seared. If I turned my head too far, I thought the skin would slip off like the peel of a rotten tomato. A week of this life-style and I'd be a regular scar tissue showcase, like one of those full-color photos of athlete's foot posted in the windows of pharmacies. Gut wound, lump on the head, leech welt—throw in penile dysfunction for comic relief.

"Y' wouldn't by any chance have brought along anything to eat, would you?" the Professor asked me. "Left in such a hurry, I didn't pack."

I opened the knapsack and removed several cans, squashed bread, and the canteen, which I handed to him. The Professor took a long drink of water, then examined each can as if inspecting vintage wines. He decided on corned beef and peaches.

"Care t'join me?" offered the Professor.

I declined. We watched the Professor tear off some bread and top it with a chunk of corned beef, then dig into it with real zest. Next he had at the peaches and even brought the can up to his lips to drink the syrup. I contented myself with whiskey, for medicinal purposes. It helped numb my various aches and pains. Not that the alcohol actually reduced the pain; it just gave the pain a life of its own, apart from mine.

"Yessir, that hit the spot," the Professor thanked me. "I usually keep two or three days' emergency rations here, but this time it so happened I hadn't replenished supplies. Unforgivable. Get accustomed to carefree days and you drop your guard. You know the old saying: *When the sun leaks through again, patch the roof for rain.* Ho-ho-ho."

"Now that you've finished your meal," I began, "there's a few things we need to talk about. Let's take things in order, starting from the top. Like, what is it you were trying to do? What did you do? What was the result? And where does that leave me?"

"I believe you'll find it all rather technical," the Professor said evasively.

"Okay, then break it down. Make it less technical."

"That may take some time."

"Fine. You know exactly how much time I've got."

"Well, uh, t'begin with," the Professor owned up, "I must apologize. Research is research, but I tricked you and used you and I put your life in danger. Set a scientist down in front of a vein of knowledge and he's goin' t'dig. It's this pure focus, exclusive of all view to loss or gain, that's seen science achieve such uninterrupted advances . . . You've read your Aristotle."

"Almost not at all," I said. "I grant you your pure scientific motives. Please get to the point."

"Forgive me, I only wanted t'say that the purity of science often hurts many people, just like pure natural phenomena do. Volcanic eruptions bury whole towns, floods wash bridges away, earthquakes knock buildings flat—"

"Grandfather!" interrupted his chubby granddaughter. "Do we really have the time for that? Won't you hurry up a bit with what you have to say?"

"Right you are, child, right you are," said the Professor,

taking up his granddaughter's hand and patting it. "Well, then, uh, what is it y' want t'know? I'm terrible at explanations. Where should I begin?"

"You gave me some numbers to shuffle. What were they all about?"

"T'explain that, we have t'go back three years. I was working at System Central Research. Not as a formal employee researcher, but as a special outside expert. I had four or five staffers under me and the benefit of magnificent facilities. I had all the money I could use. I don't put much by money, mind you, and I do have something of an allergy t'servin' under others. But even so, the resources the System put at my disposal and the prospect of puttin' my research findings into practice was certainly attractive.

"The System was at a critical point just then. That's t'say, virtually every method of data-scramblin' they devised t' protect information had been found out by the Semiotecs. That's when I was invited t'head up their R&D.

"I was then—and still am, of course—the most able and the most ambitious scientist in the field of neurophysiology. This the System knew and they sought me out. What they were after wasn't further complexification or sophistication of existing methods, but unprecedented technology. Wasn't the kind of thinkin' you get from workaday university lab scholars, publish-or-perishin' and countin' their pay. The truly original scientist is a free individual."

"But on entering the System, you surrendered that freedom," I countered.

"Exactly right," said the Professor. "I did my share of soul-searchin' on that one. Don't mean t'excuse myself, but I was eagerer than anythin' t'put my theories into practice. Back then, I already had a fully developed theory, but no way t'verify it. That's one of the drawbacks of neurophysiology; you can't experiment on animals like you can in other branches of physiology. No monkey's got functions complex enough t'stand in for human subconscious psychology and memory."

"So you used us as your monkeys."

"Now, now, let's not jump to conclusions. First, let me give you a quick rundown on my theories. There's one given about codes, and that is there's no such thing as a code that can't be cracked. The reason bein' that codes are composed accordin' to certain basic principles. And these principles, it doesn't matter how complicated or how exactin', ultimately come down to commonalities intelligible to more than one person. Understand the principle and you can crack the code. Even the most reliable book-to-book codes, where two people exchange messages denotin' words by page and line number in two copies of the same edition of the same book—even then, if someone discovers the right book, the game is up.

"That got me t'thinkin'. There's only one true crackproof method: you pass information through a 'black box' t'scramble it and then you pass the processed information back through the same black box t'unscramble it. Not even the agent holdin' the black box would know its contents or principle. An agent could use it, but he'd have no understanding of how it worked. If that agent didn't know how it worked, no one could steal the information. Perfect."

"So the black box is the subconscious."

"Yes, that's correct. Each individual behaves on the basis of his individual mnemonic makeup. No two human beings are alike; it's a question of identity. And what is identity? The cognitive system arisin' from the aggregate memories of that individual's past experiences. The layman's word for this is the mind. Not two human beings have the same mind. At the same time, human beings have almost no grasp of their own cognitive systems. I don't, you don't, nobody does. All we know—or think we know—is but a fraction of the whole cake. A mere tip of the icing.

"Now let me ask you a simple question: are you bold, or are you timid?"

"Huh?" I had to think. "Sometimes I get bold and sometimes I'm timid. I can't really say."

"Well, there's your cognitive system for y'. You just can't say all at once. Accordin' t'what you're up against, almost instantaneously, you elect some point between the extremes. That's the precision programming you've got built in. You yourself don't know a thing about the inner shenanigans of that program. 'Tisn't any need for you t'know. Even without you knowin', you function as yourself. That's your black box. In other words, we all carry around this great unexplored 'elephant graveyard' inside us. Outer space aside, this is truly humanity's last terra incognita.

"No, an 'elephant graveyard' isn't exactly right. 'Tisn't a burial ground for collected dead memories. An 'elephant factory' is more like it. There's where you sort through countless memories and bits of knowledge, arrange the sorted chips into complex lines, combine these lines into even more complex bundles, and finally make up a cognitive system. A veritable production line, with you as the boss. Unfortunately, though, the factory floor is off-limits. Like *Alice in Wonderland,* you need a special drug t'shrink you in."

"So our behavioral patterns run according to commands issued by this elephant factory?"

"Exactly as you say," said the old man. "In other words—"

"Just a second. I have a question."

"Certainly, certainly."

"I get the gist. But the thing is, those behavioral patterns do not dictate actual surface-level behavior. Say I get up in the morning and decide whether I want to drink milk or coffee or tea with my toast. That depends on my mood, right?"

"Exactly so," said the Professor with a nod. "Another complication's that the subconscious mind is always changin'. Like an encyclopedia that keeps puttin' out a whole new edition every day. In order t'stabilize human consciousness, you have to clear up two trouble spots."

"Trouble spots?" I asked. "Why would there be any

trouble spots? We're talking about perfectly normal human actions."

"Now, now," said the Professor. "Pursue this much further and we enter into theological issues. The bottom line here, if you want t'call it that, is whether human actions are plotted out in advance by the Divine, or self-initiated beginnin' to end. Of course, ever since the modern age, science has stressed the physiological spontaneity of the human organism. But soon's we start askin' just what this spontaneity is, nobody can come up with a decent answer. Nobody's got the keys t'the elephant factory inside us. Freud and Jung and all the rest of them published their theories, but all they did was t'invent a lot of jargon t'get people talkin'. Gave mental phenomena a little scholastic color."

Whereupon the Professor launched into another round of guffaws. Oh-ho-ho. The girl and I could only wait for him to stop laughing.

"Me, I'm of a more practical bent," continued the Professor. "*Render unto Caesar what is Caesar's* and leave the rest alone. Metaphysics is never more than semantic pleasantries anyway. There's loads t'be done right here before you go drainin' the reality out of everything. Take our black box. You can set it aside without so much as ever touchin' it, or you can use its bein' a black box t'your advantage. Only—" paused the Professor, one finger raised theatrically, "only—you have t'solve two problems. The first is random chance on the surface level of action. And the other is changes in the black box due t'new experiences. Neither is very easy t'resolve. Because, like you said, both are perfectly normal for humans. As long as an individual's alive, he will undergo experience in some form or other, and those experiences are stored up instant by instant. To stop experiencin' is to die.

"This prompted me t'hypothesize. What would happen if you fixed a person's black box at one point in time? If afterwards it were t'change, well, let it change. But that black box of that one instant would remain, and you could call it up in just the state it was. Flash-frozen, as it were."

"Wait a minute. That would mean two different cognitive systems coexisted in the same person."

"You catch on quick," said the old man. "It confirms what I saw in you. Yes, Cognitive System A would be on permanent hold, while the other would go on changin' . . . A′, A″, A‴, . . . without a moment's pause. You'd have a stopped watch in your right pocket and a tickin' watch in your left. You can take out whichever you want, whenever you want.

"We can address the other problem by the same principle: cut off all options open to Cognitive System A at surface level. Do you follow?"

No, I didn't.

"In other words, we scrape off the surface just like the dentist scrapes off plaque, leaving the core consciousness. No more margin of error. We just strip the cognitive system of its outer layers, freeze it, and plunk it in a secret compartment. That's the original scheme of shuffling. This much I'd worked out in theory for myself before I joined the System."

"In order to conduct brain surgery?"

"Yes, but only as necessary," the Professor allowed. "No doubt, if I'd proceeded with my research, I would have bypassed the need for surgery. Sensory-deprivation parahypnotics or some such external procedure t'create similar conditions. But for now, there's only electrostimulation. That is, artificial alteration of currents flowin' through the brain circuitry. Nothin' fancy. 'Tisn't anythin' more than a slight modification of normal procedures in current use on psychotics or epileptics. Cancel out electrical impulses emitted by the aberration in the . . . I take it I should dispense with the more technical details?"

"If you don't mind," I said.

"Well, the main thing is, we set up a junction box t' channel brain waves. A fork, as it were. Then we implant electrodes along with a tiny battery so that, at a given signal, the junction box switches over, click-click."

"You put electrodes and a battery inside my head?"

"Of course."

"Great," I said, "just great."

"No need for alarm. Isn't anythin' so frightenin'. The implant is only the size of an *azuki* bean, and besides, there's plenty of people walkin' around with similar units and pacemakers in other parts of their body.

"Now the original cognitive system—the stopped-watch circuit—is a blind circuit. Once you enter that circuit, you don't perceive a thing in your own flow of thought; you have absolutely no awareness of what you think or do. If we didn't arrange it that way, you'd be in there foolin' with the cognitive system yourself."

"But there's got to be problems with irradiating the core consciousness after it's stripped. That's what one of your staff told me after the operation."

"All very correct. But we still hadn't established that at the time. We were workin' on supposition. Well, we'd done a *few* human experiments. Didn't want t'expose valuable human resources such as you Calcutecs t'any dangers right off the bat, y'know. The System selected ten people for us. We operated on them and watched for results."

"What sort of people?"

"The System wouldn't tell us. They were ten healthy males, with no history of mental irregularities. IQ 120 or above. Those were the only conditions. The results were moderately encouragin'. In seven out of the ten, the junction box functioned without a hitch. In the other three, the junction box didn't work; they couldn't switch cognitive system or they confused them or they got both."

"What happened to the confused ones?"

"We fixed them back the way they were, disconnected the junction box. No harm done. Meanwhile, we continued trainin' the seven, until a number of problems became apparent: one was a technical problem, others had t'do with the subjects themselves. First of all, the call sign for switchin' the junction box was too codependent. We started off with a five-digit number, but for some reason a few of them switched junctions at the smell of grape juice. Found that out one lunchtime."

The chubby girl giggled next to me, but for me it was no laughing matter. Soon after my shuffling actualization, I'd been by disturbed by all sorts of different smells. For example, I could swear the girl's melon *eau de cologne* made me hear things. If your cognitive system turned over each time you smelled a different odor, it could be disaster.

"We solved that by dispersin' special sound waves between the numbers. Call signs that caused reactions very similar t'the reactions t'certain smells. Another problem, depending on the individual, was that the junction box would kick over, but the stored cognitive system wouldn't operate. We found out, after investigatin' all sorts of possibilities, that the problem lay with the subjects' cognitive system from the very beginnin'. The subjects' core consciousness was unstable or too rarefied. Oh, they were healthy and sharp enough, but pyschologically they hadn't established an identity. Or rather, they had identity enough, but had put things in order accordin' t'that identity, so you couldn't do a thing with them. Just because you got the operation didn't mean you could do shuffling. As clear as could be, there was a screenin' factor at work here.

"Well, that left three of them. And in all three, the junction box kicked over at the prescribed call sign and the frozen cognitive system functioned stably and effectively. So we did additional experiments with them for one more month, and at that point we were given the go-ahead."

"And then, I gather, you proceeded with shuffling actualization?"

"Exactly so. The next phase was t'conduct tests and interviews with close to five hundred Calcutecs. We selected twenty-six healthy males with no history of mental disorders, who exhibited strong psychological independence, and who could control their own behavior and emotions. This all took quite some doin'. Seein' as tests and interviews leave a lot in the dark, I had the System draw up detailed files on each and every one of you. Your family background, upbringin', school records, sex life, drinkin', . . . anyway, everythin'."

"Just one thing I don't understand," I spoke up. "From what I've heard, our core consciousness, our black boxes, are stored in the System vault. How is that possible?"

"We did thorough tracings of your cognitive systems. Then we made up simulations for storage in a main computer bank. We did it as a kind of insurance; you'd be stuck if anything happened t'you."

"A total simulation?"

"No, not total, of course, but functionally quite close t' total, since the effective strippin' away of surface layers made tracin' that much easier. More exactly, each simulation was made up of three sets of planar coordinates and holographs. With previous computers that wasn't possible, but these new-generation computers incorporate a good many elephant factory-like functions in themselves, so they can handle complex mental constructs. You see, it's a question of fixed structural mappin'. It's rather involved, but t'put it simple for the layman, the tracin' system works like this: first, we input the electrical pattern given off by your conscious mind. This pattern varies slightly with each readin'. That's because your chips keep gettin' rearranged into different lines, and the lines into bundles. Some of these rearrangements are quantifiably meaningful; others not so much. The computer distinguishes among them, rejects the meaningless ones, and the rest get mapped as a basic pattern. This is repeated and repeated and repeated hundreds of thousands of unit-times. Like overlayin' plastic film cells. Then, after verifyin' that the composite won't stand out in greater relief, we keep that pattern as your black box."

"You're saying you reproduced our minds?"

"No, not at all. The mind's beyond reproducin'. All I did was fix your cognitive system on the phenomenological level. Even so, it has temporal limits—a time frame. We have t'throw up our hands when it comes to the brain's flexibility. But that's not all we did. We successfully rendered a computer visualization from your black box."

Saying this, the Professor looked first at me, then at his chubby granddaughter.

"A video of your core consciousness. Something nobody'd ever done. Because it wasn't possible. I made it possible. How do you think I did it?"

"Haven't a clue."

"We showed our subjects some object, analyzed the electromagnetic reactions in their brains, converted that into numerics, then plotted these as dots. Very primitive designs in the early stages, but over many many repetitions, revisin' and fillin' in details, we could regenerate what the subjects had seen on a computer screen. Not nearly so easy as I've described it, but simply put, that's what we did. So that after goin' over and over these steps how many times, the computer had its patterns down so well it could autosimulate images from the brain's electromagnetic activity. The computer's really cute at that.

"Next thing I did was t'read your black box into the computer pre-programmed with those patterns, and out came an amazin' graphic renderin' of what went on in your core consciousness. Naturally, the images were jumbled and fragmentary and didn't mean much in themselves. They needed editin'. Cuttin' and pastin', tossin' out some parts, resequencin', exactly like film editin'. Rearrangin' everything into a story."

"A story?"

"That shouldn't be so strange," said the Professor. "The best musicians transpose consciousness into sound; painters do the same for color and shape. Mental phenomena are the stuff writers make into novels. It's the same basic logic.

Of course, as encephalodigital conversion, it doesn't represent an accurate mappin', but viewin' an accurate, random succession of images didn't much help us either. Anyway, this 'visual edition' proved quite convenient for graspin' the whole picture. True, the System didn't have it on its agenda. This visualization was all me, dabblin'."

"Dabbling?"

"I used t'—before the War, that is—work as an assistant editor in the movies. That's how I got so good at this line of work. Bestowin' order upon chaos. I did the editin' alone in my laboratory, without assistance from any other staff. Nobody had any idea what I had holed myself up doin'. So of course, I could walk off with those visualizations without anybody the worse for knowin'. They were my treasures."

"Did you render all twenty-six visualizations?"

"Sure did. Did them all, for what it's worth. Gave each one a title, and that title became the title of the black box. Yours is 'End of the World', isn't it?"

"You know it is. 'The End of the World'. It's a rather unusual title, wouldn't you say?"

"We'll go into that later," said the Professor. "The fact is, nobody knew I'd succeeded in visualizin' twenty-six consciousnesses. I never told anyone. I wanted t'take the research beyond anythin' related to the System. I'd completed the project I was commissioned t'do, and I'd taken care of the human experiments I needed for my research. I didn't want t'hang around there any longer. I told the System I wanted t'quit. They didn't want me t'quit; I knew too much. If I were t'run over to the Semiotecs at this stage, the whole shuffling plan would come to nothin', or so they thought. Wait three months, they told me. Continue with whatever research I felt like in their laboratory. They'd pay me a special bonus. In three months' time, their top-secret protection system would be perfected, so if I was goin' t'leave, hang around until then.

"Now, I'm a free-born individual and such restrictions don't sit well with me, but, well, this wasn't such a bad deal. So I decided t'hang around. Still, takin' things easy doesn't lead to much good. With all this time and these subjects on my hands, I hit upon the idea of installin' another separate circuit to the junction boxes in your brains. Make it a three-way cognitive circuitry. And into this third circuit, I'd load my edited version of your core consciousness."

"Why would you want to do that?"

"For one thing, just t'see what effect it'd have on the subjects. I wanted t'find out how an edited consciousness put in order by someone else would function in the original subjects themselves. No such precedent in all of human history. And for another thing—an incidental motivation, granted—if the System really was tellin' me t'do whatever I liked, well then, by darn, I was goin' t'take them at their word and do what I liked. I thought I'd go ahead and concoct one more function they'd never suspect."

"And for that reason, you screwed around in our heads, laying down those electric train tracks of yours?"

"Well, a scientist isn't one for controlling his curiosity. Of course, I deplore how those scientists cooperated with the Nazis conductin' vivisection in the concentration camps. That was wrong. At the same time, I find myself thinkin', if you're goin' t'do live experiments, you might as well do something a little spiffier and more productive. Given the opportunity, scientists all feel the same way at the bottom of their heart. I was only addin' a third widget where there already was two, slightly alterin' the current of circuits already in the brain. What could be the harm of usin' the same alphabet flashcards t'spell an extra word?"

"But the truth is, aside from myself, all the others who underwent shuffling actualization have died. Now why is that?"

"That's somethin' . . . even I don't know why," admitted the Professor. "Exactly as y' say, twenty-five of the twenty-six Calcutecs who underwent shuffling actualization have died. All died the same way, as if their fates were sealed. They went to bed one night; come morning they were dead."

"Well, then, what about me?" I said. "Come tomorrow, I might be dead."

"Now hold your horses, son," held forth the Professor from inside his blanket. "All twenty-five of them died within a half-year of each other. Anywhere from one year and two months to one year and eight months after the actualization. And here you are, three years and three months later, still shuffling with no problems. This leads us t'believe that you possess some special oomph that the others didn't."

"Special? In what sense, special?"

"Now, now. Just a minute, please. Let me ask you this: since your actualization, you haven't suffered any strange symptoms, have you? No hearin' things or hallucinatin' or faintin' or anythin' like that?"

"No," I said. "Haven't seen or heard things. Except, as I said, I have become sensitive to fruit smells."

"That was common t'everyone. Even so, that hasn't resulted in any auditory or visual hallucinations, has it? No sudden loss of consciousness?"

"No."

"Hmm," the Professor trailed off. "Anythin' else?"

"Well, yes, as a matter of fact. Something I'd totally forgotten as ever having happened to me just came back to me as a memory. Up until now, I've recalled only fragments of memories, so they didn't seem to call for attention. But as we were making our way here, I experienced one long, vivid continuity, triggered by the sound of the water. It was no hallucination. It was a substantial memory. I know that beyond a doubt."

"No, it wasn't," the Professor contradicted me flatly. "You may have experienced it as a memory, but that was an artificial bridge of your own makin'. You see, quite naturally there are going t'be gaps between your own identity and my edited input consciousness. So you, in order t'justify your own existence, have laid down bridges across those gaps."

"I don't follow. Not once has anything like that ever happened to me before. Why suddenly now does it choose to spring up?"

"'That's because I switched the junction to the third circuit," said the Professor. "But, well, let's just take things in order. Make things difficult if we don't, and it'd be even harder for you t'follow."

I took a gulp of whiskey. This was turning into a nightmare.

"When the first eight men died one after another, I got a call from System Central. Ascertain the cause of death, they said. Frankly, I didn't want t'have any more t'do with them, but since it was my technology, not t'mention a matter of life and death, I couldn't very well ignore them. Anyway, I went t'have a look. They briefed me on the circumstances of the deaths and showed me the brain autopsy findings. Like I told y', all eight had died of unknown causes in the same way. There was no apparent damage to brain or body; all had quietly stopped breathing in their sleep."

"You didn't discover the cause of death?"

"Never found out. Naturally, I came up with a few hypotheses. If for any reason the junction boxes we implanted in their brains burnt out or just went down, mightn't the cognitive systems muddle together and overload brain functions? Or say it wasn't a junction problem, supposing there was something fundamentally wrong with liberatin' the core consciousness even for short periods of time, maybe it was simply too much for the human brain?" The Professor then paused to pull the blanket up to his chin.

"The brain autopsies didn't clear anything up?"

"The brain is not a toaster, and it isn't a washing machine either. Codes and switches are pretty much imperceptible to the eye. All we're talkin' about is redirectin' the flow of invisible electrical charges, so takin' out the junction box for testin' after the subject's dead won't tell you anything. We can detect irregularities in a living brain, but not in a dead brain. Of course, if there's hemorrhagin' or tumors, we can tell, but there wasn't any. These brains were clean.

"Next thing we did was t'call in ten of the surviving subjects to the lab and check them all over again. Did brain scans, switched over cognitive systems t'see that the junctions were working right. Conducted detailed interviews, asked them whether they had any physical disorders, any auditory or visual hallucinations. But none of them had any problems t'speak of. All were healthy and kept up a perfectly unremarkable career of shuffling jobs. We could only conclude that the ones who died had had some a priori glitch in their brain that rendered them unsuitable for shuffling. We didn't have any idea what that glitch might be. That was something for further investigation, something t'be solved before attemptin' a second round of shuffling actualization.

"But as it turned out, we were wrong. Within one month, another five died, three of which had undergone our thorough recheck. Persons we had deemed fit on the basis of our recheck had up and died soon after without battin' an eyelash. Needless t'say, this came as quite a shock to us. Half of our twenty-six subjects were dead, and we were powerless t'know why. This was no longer a question of fit versus unfit; this was a basic program design error. The idea of switchin' between two different cognitive systems was untenable from the very beginning as far as the brain was concerned. At that point I proposed that the System freeze the project. Take the junction boxes out of the survivors' heads, cancel all further shuffling jobs. If we didn't, we'd lose everyone. Out of the question, the System informed me. They overruled me."

"They what?"

"They overruled me. The shuffling system itself was extremely successful, and it was unrealistic t'expect the System t'return to square one. And besides, we weren't sure the rest would die. If any survived, they'd serve as ideal research samples toward the next generation. That's when I stepped down."

"And only I survived."

"Correct."

I leaned my head back against the rock wall and stroked my growth of beard. When was the last time I shaved?

"So why didn't I die?"

"This is also only a hypothesis," resumed the Professor. "A hypothesis built on hypotheses. Still I can't be too far off the mark. It seems you were operatin' under multiple cognitive systems t'begin with. Not even you knew you were dividin' your time between two identities. Our paradigm of one watch in one pocket, another watch in another pocket. You probably had your own junction box that gave you a kind of mental immunity."

"Got any evidence?"

"'Deed I do. Two or three months ago, I went back and replayed all twenty-six visualizations. And something struck me. Yours was the least random, most coherent. Well-plotted, even perfect. It could have passed for a novel or a movie. The other twenty-five were different. They were all confused, murky, ramblin', a mess. No matter how I tried t'edit them, they didn't pull together. Strings of nonsequential dream images. They were like children's finger paintings.

"I thought and thought, now why should that be? And I came to one conclusion: this was somethin' you yourself made. You gave structure to your images. It's as if you descended to the elephant factory floor beneath your consciousness and built an elephant with your own hands. Without you even knowin'!"

"I find that *very* hard to believe," I said.

"I can think of many possible causes," the Professor assured me. "Childhood trauma, misguided upbringin', over-objectified ego, guilt, . . . Whatever it was made you extremely self-protective, made you harden your shell."

"Well, okay. What if it's so, where does that lead?"

"Nowhere special. If left alone, you'd probably live a good, long life," said the Professor. "But unfortunately, that's not goin' t'happen. Like or not, you're the key to the outcome of these whole idiotic infowars. It won't be long before the System starts up a second-generation project with you as their model. They'll tweak and probe and buzz every part of you there is t'test. I don't know how far they'll go, but I can assure you it won't be pleasant. I wanted t' save you from all that."

"Wonderful," I groaned. "You're to going to save me by boycotting the project, is that it?"

"No, but you've got to trust me."

"Trust you? After you've been deceiving me all this time? Lying to me, making me do those phony tabulations . . ."

"I wanted t'get to you before either the System or Semiotecs did, so I could test my hypothesis. If I could come up with positive proof, they wouldn't have t'put you through the wringer. Embedded in the data I gave you was a call sequence. After you switched over to your second cognitive system, you switched one more click to the third cognitive system."

"The one you visualized and edited."

"Exactly," said the Professor, nodding.

"How *exactly* is that going to prove your hypothesis?"

"It's a question of gaps," answered the Professor. "You've got an innate grasp on your core consciousness. So you have absolutely no problem as far as your second cognitive system. But this third circuit, being something I edited, will be part foreign, and the difference should call up some kind of reaction on your part. From measuring that, I should have been able t'obtain a complete electropictographic registration of your subconscious mind."

"*Should* have been able?"

"Yes, should have been able. That was before the Semiotecs teamed up with the INKlings and destroyed my laboratory. They walked off with all my research materials, everything that mattered."

"Are you sure? We thought they left critical things alone."

"No, I went back to the lab and checked. There's not one thing of importance left. There's not a chance I could make meaningful measurements with what's left."

"So how does all this have anything to do with the world ending?" An innocent question.

"Accurately speaking, it isn't *this* world. It's the world in your mind that's going to end."

"You've lost me," I said.

"It's your core consciousness. The vision displayed in your consciousness is the End of the World. Why you have the likes of that tucked away in there, I can't say. But for whatever reason, it's there. Meanwhile, this world in your mind here is coming to an end. Or t'put it another way, your mind will be living there, in the place called the End of the World.

"Everythin' that's in this world here and now is missin' from that world. There's no time, no life, no death. No values in any strict sense. No self. In that world of yours, people's selves are externalized into beasts."

"Beasts?"

"Unicorns," said the Professor. "You've got unicorns, herded in a town, surrounded by a wall."

"Does this have something to do with the unicorn skull you gave me?"

"That was a replica. I made it. Pretty realistic, eh? Modelled it after a visualized image of yours. It took quite some doin'. No particular significance to it. Just thought I'd make it up on a phrenological whim, ho ho. My little gift to you."

"Now just a minute, please," I said. "I'm willing to swallow that such a world exists in the depths of my consciousness. I'll buy that you edited it into a clearer form and input it into a third circuit in my head. Next, you've sent in call signs to direct my consciousness over there to do shuffling. Correct so far?"

"Correct."

"Then, what's this about the world ending? Once the shuffling is over, isn't the third circuit going to break and my consciousness automatically return to circuit one?"

"No. That's the problem," corrected the Professor. "If it went like that, things'd be easy, but it doesn't. The third circuit doesn't have an override function."

"You mean to tell me my third circuit's permanently engaged?"

"Well, yes, that's the size of it."

"But right now I'm thinking and acting according to my first circuit."

"That's because your second circuit's plugged up. If we diagram it, the arrangement looks like this," said the Professor. He sketched a diagram on a memo pad and handed it to me.

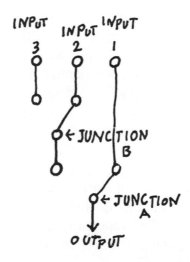

"This here's your normal state. Junction A connected to Input 1, Junction B to Input 2. Whereas now," continued the Professor, drawing another diagram on another sheet, "it's like this."

"Get the picture? Junction B's linked up with the third circuit, while Junction A is auto-switched t'your first circuit. This being the case, it's possible for you t'think and act in the first circuit mode. However, this is only temporary. We have t'switch Junction B back t'circuit two, but soon. The third circuit, strictly speaking, isn't something of your own. If we just let it go, the differential energy is goin' t'melt the junction box, with you permanently linked into circuit three, the electric discharge drawing Junction A over to Point 2 and fusin' it there in place. It was my intention t' measure the differential energy and return you back to normal before that happened."

"Intention!"

"Yes, my intention, but I'm afraid that hand's been played out for me. Like I said before, the fools destroyed my lab and stole my most important materials."

"You mean I'm going to be stuck inside this third circuit with no hope of return?"

"Well, uh, yes. You'll be livin' in the End of the World. I'm terribly, terribly sorry."

"Terribly sorry?" The words veered out abstractly. "Terribly sorry? Easy for you to say, but what the hell's going to become of me? This is no game! This is my life!"

"I never dreamed anythin' like this would happen. I never dreamed the Semiotecs and INKlings would form a pact. And now System Central's probably thinkin' we've got somethin' goin' on our own. That is, the Semiotecs, they've had their sights on you, too. They as good as informed the System of that. And as far as the System's concerned, we betrayed them, so even if it meant settin' back the whole of shuffling, they'd just as soon eliminate us. And that's exactly what the Semiotecs have in mind. They'd be delighted if our own Calcutecs did us in—that would mean the end of the System's edge on Phase Two Shuffling. Or they'd be happy if we went runnin' t'them—what could be better? Either way, they have nothin' t'lose."

"Great," I said, "just great." Then those two guys who came and wasted my apartment and slit my stomach had been Semiotecs after all. They'd put on that song and dance of a story to divert System attention. Which meant I'd fallen right into their trap. "So it's all a foregone conclusion. I'm screwed. Both sides are after me, and if I stand still my existence is annulled."

"No, not annulled. Your existence isn't over. You'll enter another world."

"Interesting distinction," I grumbled. "Listen. I may not be much, but I'm all I've got. Maybe you need a magnifying glass to find my face in my high school graduation photo. Maybe I haven't got any family or friends. Yes, yes, I know all that. But, strange as it might seem, I'm not entirely dissatisfied with this life. It could be because this split personality of mine has made a stand-up comedy routine of it all. I wouldn't know, would I? But whatever the reason, I feel pretty much at home with what I am. I don't want to go anywhere. I don't want any unicorns behind fences."

"Not fences," corrected the Professor. "A wall."

"Whatever you say. A wall, fences, I don't need any of it," I fumed. "Will you permit me to get a little mad?"

"Well, under the circumstances, I guess it can't be

helped," said the Professor, scratching his ear.

"As far as I can see, the responsibility for all this is one hundred percent yours. You started it, you developed it, you dragged me into it. Wiring quack circuitry into people's heads, faking request forms to get me to do your phony shuffling job, making me cross the System, putting the Semiotecs on my tail, luring me down into this hell hole, and now you're snuffing my world! This is worse than a horror movie! Who the fuck do you think you are? I don't care what you think. Get me back the way I was."

The Professor grunted.

"I think he's right, Grandfather," interjected the chubby girl. "You sometimes get so wrapped up in what you're doing, you don't even think about the trouble you make for others. Remember that ankle-fin experiment? You've got to do something to help him."

"I thought I was doin' good, honest. Except circumstances kept turnin' worse and worse," the old man moaned. "Things're completely out of my hands. There's nothing I can do about it any more. There's nothin' you can do about it either."

"Just wonderful," I said.

"'Tis a small comfort, I know," the Professor said meekly, "but all's not lost. Once you're there in that world, you can reclaim everything from this world, everything you're goin' t'have t'give up."

"Give up?"

"That's right," said the Professor. "You'll be losin' everything from here, but it'll all be there."

26

Power Station

WHEN I tell the Librarian of my intention to go to the Power Station, she is visibly distraught.

"The Power Station is in the Woods," she objects, dousing red coals in the bucket of sand.

"At the entrance to the Woods," I tell her. "The Gatekeeper himself said there should be no problem."

"I do not understand the Gatekeeper. Perhaps the Power Station is not far, still the Woods are dangerous."

"I don't care. I will go. I must find a musical instrument."

Having removed all the coals, she empties ash from the stove into the bucket. She shakes her head.

"I will go with you," she says.

"Why? You dislike the woods. I do not wish to put you in danger."

"I will not let you go alone. The Woods are cruel; you still do not understand."

We set out under cloudy skies, walking due east along the River. The morning is a pleasant precursor of spring warmth. There is no breeze, the River sounds gentle. After a quarter of an hour, I take off my gloves and scarf.

"Spring weather," I say.

"Perhaps. But this is only for a day. Winter will soon be upon us again," she says.

We leave the last houses along the south bank, and now only fields appear on the right side of the road. Meanwhile, the cobblestone road gives way to a dirt path. Furrows are crested with icy chips of snow. To our left the willows along the River drape branches into the flowing mirror. Tiny birds perch awkwardly on the bobbing limbs, shifting again and again before flying off. Her left hand is in my coat pocket, holding my hand. In my other hand I carry a valise containing our lunch and a few small gifts for the Caretaker.

So many things will be easier in spring, I think as I feel her warmth. If my mind holds out over the winter, and if my shadow survives, I will be closer to my former self.

We walk at an easy pace, hardly speaking, not for lack of things to say but because there is no need. We view the scenery: snowy contours hollowed into the land, birds with beaks full of red berries, plantings thick with winter vegetables, small crystal-clear pools in the river course, the distant snowcapped ridges. Each sight bursts upon us.

We encounter beasts scavenging for food in the withered grasses. Their pale gold tinged with white, strands of fur grown longer than in autumn, their coats thicker. Yet their hunger is plain; they are lean and pitiful. Their shoulder blades underscore the skin of their backs like the armature of old furniture, their spindly legs knock on swollen joints. The corners of their mouths hang sallow and tired, their eyes lack life.

Beasts in groups of three or four stalk the fields, but few

berries or clumps of grass are to be found. Branches of tall trees retain perhaps some edible nuts, but far out of reach; the beasts linger by the trees and gaze up sadly at the birds that peck at even this meager offering.

"What keeps the beasts from eating the crops in the field?" I ask.

"I myself do not know," she says. "That is the way of things. The beasts stay away from food that is for the Town. Although they do eat what we feed them, they will not eat anything else."

Several beasts crouch down on the riverbank, legs folded under them, to drink from a pool. We pass, but they do not look up. Their white horns reflect in the water like bones sunken to the river bottom.

As the Gatekeeper has instructed, a half hour along the River past the East Bridge brings one to a turning point, to the right, a narrow footpath one might ordinarily miss. The fields are now engulfed by tall weeds on either side of the path, a grassy belt that extends between the cultivated areas and the Eastern Woods.

The land rises slightly through this underbrush, the grass thinning to patches as the path angles to a rocky outcropping on its north face. None so steep, with steps cut into the rock. It is a soft sandstone and the edges of the steps are rounded with wear. After walking a few more minutes, we arrive at the summit, which is slightly lower than the Western Hill where I live. Thereon, the south face of the rock descends in a gentle grassy incline, and beyond that is the dark oceanic expanse of the Woods.

We pause on the rock and gaze around us. The Town from the east presents a vista far different from my accustomed perspective. The River is surprisingly straight, without a single sandbar, seeming more a manmade channel. On the far side of the River, one sees the great Northern Swamp, its easterly spread invaded by isolated patches of woodlands; on this, the southern side of the River, one sees the fields through which we walked. There are no houses; even the Eastern Bridge looks deserted and forlorn. The Workers' Quarter and Clocktower are as insubstantial as mirages.

We are rested now and begin our descent toward the Woods. At the edge of the trees lies a shallow pond, its icy, murky bottom giving issue to the parched form of a giant skeletal stump. On it perch two white birds, fixedly observing our approach. The snow is hard and our boots leave no tracks. We proceed and find ourselves amidst massive oaks that tap the unfrozen depths of the earth to reach toward the cloud-dark sky.

As we enter the Woods, a strange sound meets our ears. Monotonous, influctuant in pitch, the murmur grows more distinct as the path leads in. Is winter breathing through the trees? Yet there is no sign of moving air. The Librarian cannot place the sound any more than can I; it is her first time in these Woods.

The path stops at a clearing. At the far end stands a structure like a warehouse. No particular sign betrays the building's identity. There are no unusual contraptions, no lines leading out, nothing save the queer droning that seems to emanate from within. The front entrance has double doors of solid iron; a few small openings ride high on the brick wall.

"This seems to be the Power Station," I say.

The front doors, however, are locked. Our combined strength fails to budge them.

We decide to walk around the building. The Power Station is slightly longer than wide, its side wall similarly dotted with clerestory vents, but it has no other door. One recognizes in the featureless brick walls something of the Wall that surrounds the Town, though on closer inspection these bricks prove much more coarse. They are rough to the touch and broken in places.

To the rear of the building, we find a smaller house of the

same brick construction. It has an ordinary door and windows hung with grain sacks for curtains. A soot-blackened chimney juts from the roof. Here at least, one senses human presence. I knock three times on the door, but there is no answer. This door is also locked.

"Over there is a way in," she says, taking my hand.

I look in the direction she points. There, in the rear wall of the Power Station is a low portal with an iron-plate door ajar. I stand at the opening and remove my black glasses before entering. She stands back, not wanting to go in. The building interior is dark. There is no illumination in the Power Station—how curious that it does not power a single light of its own—and what scant light that does stray in reveals only empty space.

My eyes are nocturnal creatures. I soon discern a figure in the middle of the darkness. A man, slight of build, faces what appears to be an enormous column. Apart from this central shaft of perhaps three yards width, extending from floor to ceiling, there is no generator. No geared machinery block, no whirring drive shafts. The building could well be an indoor riding stable. Or a gigantic kiln, the floor laid with the same brick as the walls.

I am halfway to the column, before the man finally notices me. Unmoving, he turns his head to watch my approach. He is young, his years numbering perhaps fewer than my own. His appearance and manner are antithetical to the Gatekeeper in every way. Lanky and pale of complexion, he has smooth skin, with hardly a trace of beard. His hair recedes to the top of his broad forehead; his clothes are neat and well pressed.

"Good-day," I raise my voice over the noise.

He looks at me, lips tight, then gives a perfunctory nod.

"Am I bothering you?" I shout again.

The man shakes his head, then points to a panel bolted fast to the column that has occupied his attention. I look through a glass peephole in the panel and see a huge fan mounted parallel to the ground, the blades driven by some great force. What fury is tamed here to generate power for the Town?

"Wind power?" I can barely hear myself ask.

The man nods, then takes me by the arm and conducts me back toward the portal. We walk shoulder to shoulder, he a half-head shorter than I. We find the Librarian standing outside, anxiously awaiting my re-emergence. The Caretaker greets her with the same perfunctory nod.

"Good-day," she says.

"Good-day," the man answers quietly.

He leads us both to where the noise is less intense, behind the small house, to a cleared acre in the Woods. There we seat ourselves on crop stubble scythed close to the ground.

"Excuse me. I cannot speak loud," apologizes the young Caretaker. "You are from Town, I suppose?"

"That is right," I tell him.

"The Town is lighted by wind," he says. "There is a powerful cry in the earth here. We harness it to turn the works."

The man looks to the wintering ground at his feet.

"It wails up once every three days. There are great underground deposits of emptiness here. On days with no wind, I tighten the bolts on the fan, grease the shaft, see that the valves and switches do not freeze. And I send the power generated here to Town, again by underground."

The Caretaker shifts his gaze about the clearing. We are walled in by tall, dark forest. The soil is black and tilled, but there is no sign of plantings.

"I like to do things with my hands. When I have time, I clear back the Woods. I am alone in this, so I cannot do large things. I work around the tall trees and choose less angering places. In spring, I grow vegetables. That is, . . . Have you both have to come here to observe?"

"Yes, something like that," I say.

"Townfolk almost never come here," says the Caretaker. "No one comes into the Woods. Only the delivery man. Once a week he brings me food and necessities."

"So you live here alone?" I ask.

"Why, yes. For some time now. I can tell the mood of the works just by its sound. I am talking with the apparatus every day. That is reasonable, I have been here so long. If the works are in good condition, then I am at ease. . . I also know the sounds of the Woods. I hear many voices."

"Isn't it hard, living alone in the Woods?"

"Is living alone hard?" the Caretaker says. "I mind the Station. That is, I live here, in the Woods but not *in* the Woods. I do not know much further in."

"Are there others like you here?" asks the Librarian.

The Caretaker considers the question, then nods.

"A few. Much further in, I believe there are more. They dig coal, they clear trees. I rarely meet them, I have hardly spoken to them. They do not accept me. They live in the Woods, but I live here. That is, . . . I go no deeper in and they almost never come out."

"Have you ever seen a woman around here?" she asks. "An older woman, perhaps, who looks like me?"

The Caretaker shakes his head. "No, not one woman. Only men."

I look at the Librarian, but she says nothing more.

27

Encyclopedia Wand, Immortality, Paperclips

J UST great," I said. "So I'm screwed. How far gone are these circumstances of yours?"

"You mean the circumstances in your head?" asked the Professor.

"What else?" I snapped. "How far have you wiped out the insides of my head?"

"Well, according to my estimates, maybe six hours ago, Junction B suffered a meltdown. Of course, I say meltdown for convenience sake; it's not as if any part of your brain actually melted. You see—"

"The third circuit is set and the second circuit is dead, correct?"

"That's correct. So, as I was sayin', you've already started bridging. In other words, you've begun t'produce memories. Or t'fall back on our metaphor, as your subconscious elephant factory changes, you're makin' adjustments via a channel to surface consciousness."

"Which I gather means that Junction A isn't fully functional? That information is leaking through from my subconscious?"

"Strictly speakin', no," said the Professor. "The channel was already in existence. Whatever we do t'your cognitive circuits, we must never sever that channel. The reason bein' that your surface consciousness—your first circuit—developed on nurture from your subconsious—that is, from your second circuit. That channel's the roots of your tree. Without it, your brain wouldn't function. But the question here is that with the electrical discharge from the meltdown of Junction B, the channel's been dealt an abnormal shock. And your brain's so surprised, it's started up emergency adjustment procedures."

"Meaning, I'll keep producing more and more new memories?"

"'Fraid so. Or more simply, déjà vus of sorts. Don't differ all that much in principle. That'll go on for a while. Till finally you reassemble a world out of these new memories."

"Reassemble a world?"

"You heard correct. This very moment you're preparin' t'move to another world. So the world you see right now is changin' bit by bit t'match up. Changin' one percept at a time. The world here and now does exist. But on the phenomenological level, this world is only one out of countless possibilities. We're talkin' about whether you put your right foot or your left foot out—changes on that order. It's not so strange that when your memories change, the world changes."

"Pretty academic if you ask me," I said. "Too conceptual. You're disregarding the time factor. You're reversing the order of things."

"No, the time paradox here's in your mind," said the Professor. "As you create memories, you're creatin' a parallel world."

"So I'm pulling away from the world as I originally knew it?"

"I'm just sayin' it's not out of the realm of possibility. Mind you, I'm not talkin' about any out-of-this-world science-fiction type parallel universe. It's all a matter of cognition. The world as perceived. And that's what's changin' in your brain, is what I think."

"Then after these changes, Junction A switches over, a completely different world appears, and I go on living there. There's no avoiding that turnover—I just sit and wait for it to happen?"

"'Fraid so."

"And for how long does that world go on?"

"Forever," said the Professor.

"I don't get it," I said. "What do you mean 'forever'? The physical body has its limits. The body dies, the brain dies. Brain dies, mind ceases. Isn't that the way it goes?"

"No, it isn't. There's no time to tautologies. That's the difference between tautologies and dreams. Tautologies are instantaneous, everything is revealed at once. Eternity can actually be experienced. Once you set up a closed circuit, you just keep spinnin' 'round and 'round in there. That's the nature of tautologies. No interruptions like with dreams. It's like the encyclopedia wand."

"The encyclopedia wand?" I was evolving into an echo.

"The encyclopedia wand's a theoretical puzzle, like Zeno's paradox. The idea is t'engrave the entire encyclopedia onto a single toothpick. Know how you do it?"

"You tell me."

"You take your information, your encyclopedia text, and you transpose it into numerics. You assign everything a two-digit number, periods and commas included. 00 is a blank, A is 01, B is 02, and so on. Then after you've lined them all up, you put a decimal point before the whole lot. So now you've got a very long sub-decimal fraction. 0.173000631. . . Next, you engrave a mark at exactly that point along the toothpick. If 0.50000's your exact middle on the toothpick, then 0.3333's got t'be a third of the way from the tip. You follow?"

"Sure."

"That's how you can fit data of any length in a single point on a toothpick. Only theoretically, of course. No existin' technology can actually engrave so fine a point. But this should give you a perspective on what tautologies are like. Say time's the length of your toothpick. The amount of information you can pack into it doesn't have anything t'do with the length. Make the fraction as long as you want. It'll be finite, but pretty near eternal. Though if you make it a repeatin' decimal, why, then it *is* eternal. You understand what that means? The problem's the software, no relation to the hardware. It could be a toothpick or a two-hundred-meter timber or the equator—doesn't matter. Your body dies, your consciousness passes away, but your thought is caught in the one tautological point an instant before, sub-dividin' for an eternity. Think about the koan: *An arrow is stopped in flight.* Well, the death of the body is the flight of the arrow. It's makin' a straight line for the brain. No dodgin' it, not for anyone. People have t'die, the body has t'fall. Time is hurlin' that arrow forward. And yet, like I was sayin', thought goes on subdividin' that time for ever and ever. The paradox becomes real. The arrow never hits."

"In other words," I said, "immortality."

"There you are. Humans are immortal in their thought. Though strictly speakin', not immortal, but endlessly, asymptotically close to immortal. That's eternal life."

"And that was the real goal of your research?"

"Not at all, not at all," said the Professor. "It's something that struck me only recently. I was just seein' where my research would take me and I ran smack into this one. That expandin' human time doesn't make you immortal; it's subdividin' time that does the trick."

"And so you decided to abandon me in immortality, is that it?"

"No, no, no. That's completely by accident, too. Never intended that at all. Believe me. It's the truth. I never meant t'do anything of the kind. But if you act now, you can choose, if choice is what you want. There's one last hand you can play."

"And what might that be?"

"You can die right now," said the Professor, very business-like. "Before Junction A links up, just check out. That leaves nothing."

A profound silence fell over us. The Professor coughed, the chubby girl sighed, I took a slug of whiskey. No one said a word.

"That . . . uh, world . . . what is it like?" I brought myself to voice the question. "That immortal world?"

"Like I told you before," said the Professor. "It's a peaceful world. Your own world, a world of your own makin'. You can be your self there. You've got everythin' there. And at the same time, there is nothin'. Can you picture a world like that?"

"Not really."

"Still, it's your consciousness that's created it. Not somethin' just anyone could do. Others could be wanderin' around forever in who-knows-what contradictory chaos of a world. You're different. You seem t'be the immortal type."

"When's the turnover into that world going to take place?" asked the chubby girl.

The Professor looked at his watch. I looked at my watch. Six-twenty-five. Well past daybreak. Morning papers delivered.

"Accordin' t'my estimates, in another twenty-nine hours and thirty-five minutes," said the Professor. "Plus or minus forty-five minutes. I set it at twelve noon for easy reference. Noon tomorrow."

I shook my head. For easy reference? I took another slug of whiskey. The alcohol didn't register. I didn't even taste it. My stomach had petrified.

"What do you plan to do now?" asked the chubby girl,

laying her hand on my lap.

"Hell, beats me," I said. "But whatever, I want to get above ground. I can't see waiting it out down here for things to take their course. I'm going up where the sun is out. Then I'll think about what comes next."

"Was my explanation enough for you?" inquired the Professor.

"It'll do, thanks," I replied.

"S'ppose you're still mad?"

"Sure," I said. "Though I guess anger won't do much for me now, will it? Besides, I'm so blitzed, I still haven't swallowed the reality of it. Later on, when it hits me, I might get furious. But by then, of course, I'll be dead to this world."

"Really, I hadn't intended to go into so much detail," said the Professor. "If I hadn't warned you, it'd have all been over and done with before you even knew it. Probably would've been less stressful, too. Still, it's not like you're goin' t'die. It's just your conscious mind what's goin' t'disappear forever."

"Same difference," I said. "But either way, I'd have wanted to know. At least where my life's concerned. I don't want some switch like that tripping on me without my knowing about it. I like to take care of my own affairs as much as I can. Now, which way to the exit, please?"

"Exit?"

"The way out of here, to above ground."

"It takes some time, takes you right past an INKling lair."

"I don't mind. At this point, there's not much that can spook me."

"Very well," said the Professor. "You go down the mountain to the water, which is perfectly still by now, so it's easy t'swim. You swim to the south-southwest. I'll shine a light that way as a beacon. Swim straight in that direction, and on the far shore, a little ways up, there's a small openin'. Through that you get to the sewer. Head straight along the sewer and you come to subway tracks."

"Subway?"

"Yessir, the Ginza Line. Exactly midway between Gaien-mae and Aoyama Itchome."

"How did this all get hooked up with the subway?"

"Those INKlings got control of the subway tracks. Maybe not durin' the daytime, but at night they're all over the stations like they own the place. Tokyo subway system construction dramatically expanded the sphere of INKling activity. Just made more passages for them. Every once in a while they'll attack a track worker and eat him."

"Why don't the authorities own up to that fact?"

"'Cause then who'd work for the subway? Who'd ride the subway? Of course, when they first found out, they tried brickin' over holes, brightenin' the lightin', steppin' up security, but none of that's goin' t'hold back your INKling. In the space of one night, they can break through walls and chew up electrical cables."

"If it exits between Gaienmae and Aoyama Itchome, that would put us where right now?"

"Somewhere under Meiji Shrine, toward Omotesando. Never pinpointed the exact spot. Anyway, there's only one route, you can't go wrong. It's narrow, meanders a lot. From here you'll be headin' in the direction of Sendagaya, toward the INKling lair, a little this side of the National Sports Arena. Then the tunnel takes a turn to the right, in the direction of the Jingu Baseball Stadium, then on past the Art Forum to Aoyama Boulevard to the Ginza Line. Probably take you 'bout two hours t'reach the exit. Got it?"

"Loud and clear."

"Get yourself past the INKling lair as quickly as possible. Nothin' good can come of dallyin' 'round there. Mind when you get to the subway. There's high-tension lines and subway cars. Be a pity t'make it that far and get yourself hit by a subway car."

"I'll remember that," I said. "But what are you going to do?"

"I'll stay down here for a while. I sprained my foot. Anyway, if I surfaced now, I'd only be chased by the System or

Semiotecs. Nobody's goin' t'come after me here. Fortunately, thanks to you, I've got provisions. This all should keep me alive for three or four days," said the Professor calmly. "You go on ahead. No need t'worry 'bout me."

"What about the INKling-repel devices? It'll take both of them to reach the exit, which will leave you without a single porta-pack."

"Take my granddaughter along with you," said the Professor. "The child can see you off, then return t'fetch me."

"Fine by me," she said.

"But suppose something were to happen to her? What if she were caught or—"

"I won't get caught," she stated firmly.

"Not to be worryin'," said the Professor. "The child's really quite dependable for her age. I trust her. And it's not like I'm without special emergency measures. Fact is, if I have a battery and water and pieces of metal, I can throw together some makeshift INKling repellent. Quite simple, really, though short of the full effect of a porta-pack. All along the way here, didn't y' notice? Those bits of metal I scattered? Keeps the INKlings away for maybe fifteen or twenty minutes."

"You mean the paperclips?" I asked.

"Yessir, paperclips are ideal. Cheap, don't rust, magnetize in a jiff, loop them t'hang 'round your neck. All things said, I'll take paperclips."

I reached into my windbreaker pocket, pulled out a handful of paperclips, and handed them to the Professor. "Will these be enough?"

"My, oh my," exclaimed the Professor with surprise. "Just what the doctor ordered. I was actually a bit concerned. I scattered a few too many on the way here and I was thinkin' I might not have enough. You really are a sharp one."

"We'd better be going, Grandfather," said the girl. "He doesn't have all that much time."

"Take care now. Step light," said the Professor, "and

don't let the INKlings bite. Ho-ho-ho."

"I'll be back for you soon," said the granddaughter, planting a peck on his forehead.

"I'm truly sorry 'bout the way things turned out," the Professor apologized one last time. "I'd change places with you if could. I've already enjoyed a full life. I'd've no regrets. But you, there's all that time you had comin'. There's a lot of things you'll leave behind in this world."

A loss greater than I would ever know, right? I said nothing.

"Still, it's nothing t'fear," the Professor philosophized. "It's not death. It's eternal life. And you get t'be yourself. Compared to that, this world isn't but a momentary fantasy. Please don't forget that."

"Let's get going," said the girl, taking my arm.

"Yes, until the beginning of autumn. Toward winter, they will not come near the Woods. In warm weather, they come here in groups and I play with them and I share my rations . . . But winter, no. They know I will give them food, and still they do not come. All winter I am alone."

"Will you join us for lunch?" the Librarian offers. "We have brought sandwiches and fruit, too much for two."

"That is kind of you," says the Caretaker. "I have not eaten the food of another in a long time . . . Oh yes, there are forest mushrooms I picked, if you care to try."

"Yes, very much," I say.

We share her sandwiches and his mushrooms, and later have fruit and more tea. We hardly speak a word. In the absence of talk, the cry of the empty earth pours into the room and fills our silence.

"You never leave the Woods?" I ask the Caretaker.

"Never," he replies, with a shake of his head. "That is decided. I am to stay here always and man the Power Station. . . . Always, until someone comes to replace me. When, I do not know. Only then can I leave the Woods and return to Town. . . . But now is always, and I cannot. I must wait for the wind that comes every three days."

I drink the last of my tea. How long has it been since the wind-cry started? Listening to its droning wail, one is pulled in that direction. It must be lonely to pass the winter here in the Woods.

"But you have come here to look at the Power Station?" the young Caretaker remembers.

"We have come looking for musical instruments," I say. "I was told you would know where to find them."

He regards the knife and fork crossed on his plate.

"Yes, I have musical instruments here. They are old, I cannot say whether they will play . . . That is, you are welcome to them. I myself cannot play. My pleasure is to look at their shapes. Will you see them?"

"Please," I say.

He rises from his chair and we follow.

28

Musical Instruments

THE young Caretaker of the Power Station invites us into his modest quarters. He checks the fire in the stove, then takes the boiling kettle into the kitchen to make tea. It is good to drink the hot infusion; we are cold from our day in the Woods. The wind-cry does not subside.

"I pick this herb in the Woods," the Caretaker tells us. "I dry it in the shade all summer, and in winter I have it for tea. It stimulates and warms the body."

The drink is fragrant, with an unassuming sweetness.

"What is the plant called?" I ask.

"The name? I have no idea," he says. "It grows in the Woods, it smells good, so I make tea with it. It has green stalks about yea high, blooms midsummer, I pick the young leaves . . . The beasts like to eat the flowers."

"The beasts come here?"

"This way. I have them in my room," he says.

"I will stay here and clean up," she says.

The Caretaker opens a door, turns on the light, and invites me in. "Over here," he says.

Arranged along the wall are various musical instruments. All are old. Most of them are string instruments, the strings hopelessly rusted, broken or missing. Some I am sure I once knew, but do not remember the names; others are totally unknown to me. A wooden instrument resembling a washboard that sprouts a row of metallic prongs. I try to play it, but can make no song. Another, a set of small drums, even has its own sticks, yet this clearly will not yield a melody. There is a large tubular instrument, one obviously meant to be blown from the end, but how do I give breath to it?

The Caretaker sits on the edge of his cot, its coverlet neatly tucked, and watches me examine the instruments.

"Are any of these of use to you?" he speaks up.

"I don't know," I hesitate. "They're all so old."

He walks over to shut the door, then returns. There is no window, so with the door closed, the wind-cry is less intrusive.

"Do you want to know why I collected these things?" the Caretaker asks. "No one in the Town takes any interest in them. No one in the Town has the least interest. Everyone has the things they need for living. Pots and pans, shirts and coats, yes . . . It is enough that their needs are met. No one wants for anything more. Not me, however. I am very interested in these things. I do not know why. I feel drawn to them. Their forms, their beauty."

He rests one hand on the pillow and puts his other hand in his pocket.

"If you wish to know the truth, I like this Power Station," he continues. "I like the fan, the meters, the transformer. Perhaps I liked these things before, so they sent me here. But it was so long ago. I have forgotten the before . . . Sometimes I think I will never be allowed to return to Town. They would never accept me as I am now."

I reach for a wooden instrument. It is hollow and sand-glass-shaped, with only two strings remaining. I pluck them. A dry twang issues.

"Where did you find these instruments?" I ask.

"From all over," he says. "The man who delivers my provisions brings them to me. In the Town, old musical instruments sometimes lie buried in closets and sheds. Often they were burned for firewood. It is a pity. . . . That is, musical instruments are wonderful things. I do not know how to use them, I may not want to use them, I enjoy their beauty. It is enough for me. Is that strange?"

"Musical instruments are very beautiful," I answer. "There is nothing strange about that."

My eyes light upon a box hinged with leather folds lying among the instruments. The bellows is stiff and cracked in a few places, but it holds air. The box has buttons for the fingers.

"May I try it?" I ask.

"Please, go ahead," the young Caretaker says.

I slip my hands into the straps on either end and compress. It is difficult to pump, but I can learn. I finger the buttons in ascending order, forcing the bellows in and out. Some buttons yield only faint tones, but there is a progression. I work the buttons again, this time descending.

"What sounds!" smiles the fascinated Caretaker. "As if they change colors!"

"It seems each button makes a note," I explain. "Each one is different. Some sounds belong together and some do not."

"What do you mean?"

I press several buttons at once. The intervals are awry, but the combined effect is not unpleasing. Yet I can recall no songs, only chords.

"Those sounds belong together?"

"Yes."

"I do not understand," he says. "It seems I am hearing something for the first time. It is different from the sound of the wind and different from the voices of the birds."

He rests his hands on his lap, as he looks back and forth between my face and the bellows box.

"I will give you the instrument. Please have any others you want. They belong with someone who can use them," he says, then turns his ear attentively to the wind. "I must check the machinery now. I must see that the fan and the transformer are working. Please wait for me in the other room."

The young Caretaker hurries away, and I return to where the Librarian waits.

"Is that a musical instrument?" she asks.

"One kind of musical instrument," I say.

"May I touch it?"

"Of course," I say, handing her the bellows box. She receives it with both hands, as if cradling a baby animal. I look on in anticipation.

"What a funny thing!" she exclaims with an uneasy smile. "Do you feel better that you have it?"

"It was worth coming here."

"The Caretaker, they did not rid him of his shadow well. He still has a part of a shadow left," she whispers to me. "That is why he is here, in the Woods. I feel sorry for him."

"Sorry?"

"Perhaps he is not strong enough to go deeper into the Woods, but he cannot return to Town."

"Do you think your mother is in the Woods?"

"I do not really know," she says. "The thought occurred to me."

The Caretaker comes not long thereafter. I open the take out the gifts we have brought for him. A and a cigarette lighter found in a trunk in the oom.

cept these. They are a token of my gratitud ment," I say.

The young Caretaker refuses at first, but eventually gives in. He studies the objects.

"You know how to use them?" I ask.

"No, but there is no need. I will be fine," He says. "They are beautiful in themselves. In time, I may find a use for them. I have too much time."

At that, I tell him we will be leaving.

"Are you in a hurry?" he asks sadly.

"I must return to town before sundown, then go to work," I say.

"I understand. I wish I could accompany you to the entrance to the Woods, but I cannot leave the Power Station."

We part outside the small house.

"Please come back. Let me hear you play the instrument," he says.

"Thank you."

Gradually, the wail of the wind weakens as we walk farther from the Power Station. At the entrance to the Woods, we do not hear it at all.

29

Lake, Masatomi Kondo, Panty Hose

THE girl and I wrapped up our belongings in spare shirts, and I balanced the bundles on our heads. We looked funny, but we had no time to laugh. We left behind the rations and whiskey, so our loads were not too bulky.

"Take care," said the Professor. In the scant light, he looked much older than when I first met him. His skin sagging, his hair going to seed like a scraggly shrub, his face blotched with liver spots. He looked like a tired old man. Genius scientist or not, everyone grows old, everyone dies.

"Good-bye," I said.

We descended by rope to the water's surface. I went down first, signaled with my light when I reached bottom, then she followed. Plunging into water in total darkness was bound to be therapeutic. Not that I had a choice. The water was cold catharthis. It was plain, ordinary water, the usual aqueous specific gravity. Everything was still. Not air, not water, not darkness moved a quiver. Only our own splashing echoed back. Once in the water, it struck me that I'd forgotten to ask the Professor to treat my wound.

"Don't tell me those clawed fish are swimming around in here," I called back in her general direction.

"Don't be silly. They're just a myth," she said. "I think."

Some reassurance. I imagined some giant fish suddenly surfacing and biting off a leg or two. Well, let 'em come.

We swam a slow one-handed breaststroke, roped together, bundles on our head. We aimed for where the Professor trained his light like a beacon on the surface of the water. I swam in the lead. Our arms thrashed the water alternately. I stopped from time to time to check our progress and realign our course.

"Make sure your bundle stays dry," she shouted this way. "The repel device won't be worth a thing if it gets wet."

"No problem," I said. But in fact, it was a great struggle.

I was swimming. Orpheus ferried across the Styx to the Land of the Dead. All the varieties of religious experience in the world, yet when it comes to death, it all boils down to the same thing. At least Orpheus didn't have to balance laundry on his head. The ancient Greeks had style.

"You aren't really mad at Grandfather, are you?" asked the girl. An echo in the dark, it was hard to tell where the question was coming from.

"I don't know, but does it matter?" I said, shouting, my voice coming back from an impossible direction. "The more I listened to your grandfather, the less I cared."

"How can you say that?"

"Wasn't much of a life anyway. Wasn't much of a brain."

"But didn't you say you were satisfied with your life?"

"Word games," I dismissed. "Every army needs a flag."

She didn't respond. We swam on in silence.

Where *were* those fish? Those claws were no figment of even a nonhuman imagination. I worried, after all, that they were cruising our way. I expected a slimy, clawed fin to be grabbing hold of my ankle any second. Okay, I may have been destined to disintegrate in the very near future, but I wasn't prepared to be pâté for some creature from the black lagoon. I wanted to die under the sun.

"But you're such a nice guy," she said, sounding like she'd just stepped fresh out of a bath. "At least I think so."

"You're one of the very few," I said.

"Well, I do."

I looked back over my shoulder as I swam. I saw the Professor's light retreating into the distance, but my hand had yet to touch solid rock. How could it be so far? Decent of him to keep us guessing.

"I'm not trying to defend Grandfather," the girl started in again, "but he's not evil. He gets so wrapped up in his work, he can't see anything else. He had the best of intentions. He wanted to save you before the System got to you. In his own way, Grandfather is ashamed of what he's done."

Saying it was wrong did a hell of a lot of good.

"So forgive Grandfather," she said.

"What's forgiveness going to do?" I answered. "If he really felt responsible, he wouldn't create a monster and run off when it got ugly. He doesn't like working for big organizations, fine, but he's got lives hanging on his line of research."

"Grandfather simply couldn't trust the System," she pleaded. "The Calcutecs and Semiotecs are two sides of the same coin."

"Tech-wise, maybe, but like I said before, one protects information while the other steals."

"But what if the System and Factory were both run by the same person?" she said. "What if the left hand stole and the right hand protected?"

Hard to believe, but not inconceivable. The whole time I worked for the System, I never heard anything about what went on inside System Central. We received directives; we carried them out. We terminal devices never got access to the CPU.

"True, it'd be one hell of a lucrative business," I agreed. "One side pitted against the other; you can raise your stakes as high as you like. No bottom dropping out of the market either."

"That's what struck Grandfather while he was in the System. After all, the System is really just private enterprise that enlisted state interests. And private enterprise is always after profit. Grandfather realized that if he went ahead with his research, he'd only make things worse."

So the System hangs out a sign: In Business to Protect Information. But it's all a front. If the old man hands over technologies to reconfigure the brain, he seals the fate of humanity. To save the world, he steps down. Too bad about the defunct Calcutecs—and me, who gets stuck in the End of the World.

"Were you in on this all along?" I asked her.

"Well, yes, I knew," she confessed after slight hesitation.

"Then why didn't you tell me? What was the point? You could have saved me blood and time."

"I wanted you to see things through Grandfather's eyes," she answered. "You wouldn't have believed me anyway."

"I suppose not," I said. Third circuit, immortality— who'd believe that straight out, cold?

The next few breaststrokes brought my hand in contact with a stone wall. Somehow we'd managed to swim across this subterranean lake.

"We've made it," I announced.

She pulled up next to me. We looked back to the tiny light in the distance and adjusted our position ten meters to the right.

"Should be about here," she said. "An opening just above the waterline."

I carefully undid the bundle on my head and removed the pocket-sized flashlight, then shined it up the wall.

"I don't see a hole," I said.

"Try a little more to the right," she suggested.

I swept the flashlight beam over the wall, but still no hole.

"To the right? Are you sure?"

"A little further right."

I inched to the right, my whole body shaking. Feeling my way along the wall, my hand touched a shield-like surface. It was the size of an LP record, with carvings. I shined my light on it.

"A relief," she said.

Maybe so, but it was the same two evil-clawed fishes. The sculpted disk was a third submerged in the water.

"This is the way out," she said with authority. "The INKlings must have placed these as markers at all exits. Look up."

Shining my flashlight higher, I could barely make out a shadowy recession. I handed her the light and went to investigate. I couldn't really see the hole, but I felt a damp, mildewy air.

"I found it," I shouted down.

"Thank goodness!" she exclaimed.

I pulled her up. We paused there at the mouth of the passage, drenched and shivering. Undoing our bundles, we changed into dry tops. I gave her my sweater and threw away my wet shirt and jacket. This left me still sopping wet from the waist down, but I didn't have a change of slacks.

While she checked the INKling repel device, I flashed a signal to the Professor that we'd arrived safely. The yellow point of light blinked two times, three times, then went out. All was pitch black again.

"Let's go," she prompted. I looked at my watch. Seven-eighteen. Above ground, morning news on every TV channel. People eating breakfast, cramming their half-asleep heads with the weather, headache remedies, car export trade problems with America. Who'd know that I'd spent the whole night in the colon of the world? Did they care that I'd been swimming in stinking water and had leeches feeding on my neck, that I'd nearly keeled over from the pain in my gut? Did it matter to anybody that my reality would end in another twenty-eight hours and forty-two minutes? It'd never make the news.

The passage was smaller than anything we had come through this far. We had to crawl on all fours. It led us through intestinal twists and turns, sometimes angling up near vertically, dropping back straight down or looping over like a roller coaster. Progress was hard. This was nothing the INKlings had bored out. Nobody, not even INKlings, would make a passage this convoluted.

After thirty minutes, we exchanged INKling-repel porta-packs, then another ten minutes later the narrow passage suddenly opened up into a place with a high ceiling. Dead silent, it was dark and musty. The path split left and right, air was blowing from right to left. She trained her light on the divide. Each way led straight off into blackness.

"Which way?" I asked.

"To the right," she said. "Grandfather's instructions put us at Sendagaya, so a right turn should take us toward Jingu Stadium."

I pictured the world above ground. We were directly under the Kawade Bookshop, the Victor Recording Studio, and those two landmark *ramen* shops—Hope-ken and Copain.

"We're close to my barber shop, too," I said.

"Oh?" she said without much interest.

I thought about getting a haircut before the end of the world. It wasn't, after all, like I had lots of better things to do with twenty-four hours left. Taking a bath, getting dressed, and going to the barber shop were about all I could hope for.

"Careful now," she warned. "We're getting close to the INKling nest. There's their voices and that awful stench. Stay with me."

I sniffed the air. I couldn't smell anything. I couldn't hear anything either.

We shortened the rope linking us to fifteen centimeters.

"Watch out, the wall's missing here," she spoke sharply, shining her light to the left. She was right: no wall, only a dark expanse. The beam shot off like an arrow and disappeared into thick black space, which seemed almost to be breathing, quivering, a disgustingly gelatinous consistency.

"Hear that?" she asked.

"Yeah, I can hear them," I said.

INKling voices. More like a ringing in my ears, actually. Cutting through like drill bits of high-pitched sound, like the humming of insects gone wild, the sound careened off the walls and screwed into my eardrums.

"Keep moving!" she yelled in my ear. I hadn't noticed I wasn't.

She yanked on the rope. "We can't stop here. If we stop, we'll be dragged off and liquefied."

I couldn't move. I was glued to the ground. Time was flowing backwards toward primeval swamps.

Her hand came out of the dark and slapped me across the face. The sound was deafening.

"To the right!" she barked. "To the right! You hear? Right foot forward! Right, you lamebrain!"

My right leg creaked ahead.

"Left!" she screamed.

I moved my left foot.

"That's it. Slow and steady, one step at a time."

They were after us for sure, piping fear into our ears, conniving to freeze our footsteps, then lay their slimy hands on us.

"Shine your light at your feet!" she commanded. "Back against the wall! Walk sideways, one step at a time. Got it?"

"Got it," I said.

"Do not raise your light, under any condition."

"Why not?"

"Because there are INKlings. Right there," she lowered her voice. "But you must never, ever, look at an INKling. If you set eyes on an INKling, you'll never look away."

We proceeded sideways, one step at a time, light at our feet. Cool air licked our faces, leaving the rank odor of dead fish. I wanted to puke. It was like we were in the worm-ridden guts of a giant fish carcass. The INKlings whined, frenzied, disorientingly shrill. My eardrums turned to stone. Gulps of bile backed up my throat.

My feet kept edging along by sheer reflex. Occasionally, she called out to me, but I could no longer hear what she was saying. The blue light of her INKling-repel device was still on, so I guessed we were still safe. But for how long?

I noticed a change in the air. The stink grew less putrid; the pressure on my ears evaporated. Sounds resonated in a different way. The worst was over. We let out sighs of relief and wiped off a cold sweat.

For the longest time, she didn't speak. Droplets of water echoed through the void.

"Why were they so mad?" I asked.

"We intruded on their sanctuary. They hate the world of light and all who live there."

"Hard to believe the Semiotecs would work with them, no matter what the benefits."

Her only response was to squeeze my wrist.

Then after a bit: "Know what I'm thinking?"

"No idea," I said.

"I'm thinking it would be wonderful if I could follow you into that world where you're going."

"And leave this world behind?"

"That's right," she said. "It's a boring old world anyway. I'm sure it'd be much more fun living in your consciousness."

I shook my head. Hell, *I* didn't want to live in my own consciousness.

"Well, let's keep going," she said. "We've got to find the exit through the sewer. What time is it?"

"Eight-twenty."

"Time to switch porta-packs," she said, turning on the other unit, then wedging the expended one clumsily into her waistband.

It was exactly one hour since we entered the tunnel. According to the Professor's instructions, there ought to be a turn to the left under the tree-lined avenue toward the Art Forum. This was early autumn, I seemed to remember. The leaves would still be green. Sunshine, the smell of the grass, an early autumn breeze played through my head. Ah, to lie back and look at the sky. I'd go to the barber, get a shave, stroll over to Gaien Park, lie down and gaze up at the blue. Maybe sip an ice-cold beer. Just the thing, while waiting for the end of the world.

"You suppose it's good weather out?"

"Beats me. How should I know?" she retorted.

Were the stars out when I left the house last evening? All I could remember was the couple in the Skyline listening to Duran Duran. Stars? Who remembers stars? Come to think of it, had I even looked up at the sky recently? Had the stars been wiped out of the sky three months ago, I wouldn't have known. The only things I noticed were silver bracelets on women's wrists and popsicle sticks in potted rubber plants. There had to be something wrong with my life. I should have been born a Yugoslavian shepherd who looked up at the Big Dipper every night. No car, no car stereo, no silver bracelets, no shuffling, no dark blue tweed suits.

My world foreshortened, flattening into a credit card. Seen head on, things seemed merely skewed, but from the side the view was virtually meaningless—a one-dimensional wafer. Everything about me may have been crammed in there, but it was only plastic. Indecipherable except to some machine.

My first circuit must have been wearing thin. My real memories were receding into planar projection, the screen of consciousness losing all identity.

The couple in the Skyline came to mind. Why did I have this fixation on them? Well, what else did I have to think about? By now, the two of them might be snoozing away in bed, or maybe pushing into commuter trains. They could be flat character sketches for a TV treatment: Japanese woman marries Frenchman while studying abroad; husband has traffic accident and becomes paraplegic. Woman tires of life in Paris, leaves husband, and returns to Tokyo, where she works in Belgian or Swiss embassy. Silver bracelets, a memento from her husband. *Cut* to beach scene in Nice: woman with the bracelets on left wrist. Woman takes bath, makes love, silver bracelets always on left wrist. *Cut*: enter Japanese man, veteran of student occupation of Yasuda Hall, wearing tinted glasses like lead in *Ashes and Diamonds*. A top TV director, he is haunted by dreams of tear gas, by memories of his wife who slit her wrist five years earlier. *Cut* (for what it's worth, this script has a lot of jump cuts): he sees the bracelets on woman's left wrist, flashes back to wife's bloodied wrist. So he asks woman: could she switch bracelets to her right wrist?

"I refuse," she says. "I wear my bracelets on my left wrist."

Cut: enter piano player, like in *Casablanca*. Alcoholic, always keeps shot glass of gin, straight with twist of lemon, on top of piano. A jazz musician of some talent until his career went on the rocks, he befriends both man and woman, knows their secrets, . . .

Par for TV, totally ridiculous underground. Some imagination. Or was this supposed to be reality? I hadn't even seen the stars in months.

"I can't stand it any more," I spoke up.

"Can't stand what?" she asked.

"The darkness, the moldy stink, the INKlings, you name it. These wet slacks, the wound in my gut. I can't even imagine the world outside."

"Not much longer," she said. "We'll be out of here soon."

"My head's out of it already," I said. "Ideas are warping off in weird directions. I can't think straight."

"What were you thinking about?"

"Movie people. Masatomi Kondo and Ryoko Nakano and Tsutomu Yamazaki."

"Stop. Don't think about anything," she said. "We're almost there."

I tried not to think and my mind lowered to the clammy slacks clinging to my legs. When was the last time I took a leak?

At the very least, I hadn't pissed since going underground. Before that? I was driving, ate a hamburger, saw the couple in the Skyline. And before that? I was asleep. Then the chubby girl came and woke me. We'd headed out soon after. So before that? Probably I'd used the toilet at the hospital, when they sewed me up. But if I'd gone then, the pain would have been something to remember; the fact that I didn't remember meant I hadn't relieved myself—for how long?

Everything wheeled around closer and farther, closer and farther, like a merry-go-round. When was it those two had come and done their dirty work on my belly? It had to have been before I was sitting at the supermarket snack bar—or no? When had I last pissed? Why did I care?

"Here it is," she proclaimed, tugging my elbow. "The sewer. The exit."

I swept all thought of urination from my head and directed my eyes toward that one section of wall illuminated by her flashlight beam. I could make out the squared mouth of a dust chute, just big enough for one person to squeeze through.

"That's not a sewer pipe," I observed.

"The sewer's beyond. This is a side vent. Just smell."

I stuck my head in and took a whiff. A drainpipe smell, to be sure. After wandering in this stinking underground maze, even the smell of sewage was comforting. A definite wind was blowing from up ahead.

Presently there came slight ground vibrations, accompanied by the far-off sound of subway cars. The sound kept up for ten, maybe fifteen seconds, then passed, like a tap turning off. Yes, this was the exit.

"We made it," she said, planting a peck on my neck. "How do you feel?"

"You had to ask," I said. "I don't know myself."

She crawled head first into the opening. Once her cushiony tail had disappeared into the hole, I followed suit. The narrow conduit led straight for a while. All my flashlight revealed was the wiggling of her bulbous behind. It reminded me of a head of Chinese cabbage in a wet skirt, tight over her thighs.

"Are you back there?" she yelled out.

"Right behind you," I shouted.

"There's a shoe lying there."

"What kind of shoe?"

"A man's black lace-up."

It was an old shoe, the kind salarymen wear. Worn-out heel, mud caked on the toe.

"Do you suppose the INKlings . . . ?" I wondered out loud.

"What do you think," she answered.

There was nothing else for me to look at, so I kept my eye on the hem of her skirt. It would rise way up on her thighs, revealing unmuddied white flesh. Up where women used to affix their stockings, up in that band of exposed skin between their stockings and their girdles. This, of course, was before the appearance of panty hose.

One thing led to another, and soon my thoughts were wandering down memory lane. Back to the days of Jimi

Hendrix and Cream and the Beatles and Otis Redding. I
started whistling the beginning riff to Peter and Gordon's *I
Go to Pieces*. Nice song, a hell of lot better than Duran
Duran. Which probably meant I was getting old. I mean,
the song was popular twenty years ago. And who twenty
years ago could have predicted the advent of panty hose?

"Why are you whistling?" she shouted.

"I don't know. I felt like it," I answered.

"What's the song?"

"Something you probably never heard of."

"You're right."

"It was a hit before you were born."

"What's the song about?"

"It's about coming apart at the seams," I said simply.

"Why'd you want to whistle a song like that?"

I couldn't come up with any cogent reason. It'd just
popped into my head. "Beats me," I said.

Before I could think up another tune, we arrived at the
sewer. A concrete pipe, really. Maybe a meter and a half in
diameter, with effluent running at the bottom, about twenty
centimeters deep. The edge was covered with mossy slime.
The sound of several passing subway cars came from up
ahead. Quite loud, actually. I could even see a brief glimmer
of yellow lights.

"What's a sewer doing connected to the subway tracks?"

"It's not really a sewer," she said. "It channels groundwater into the track gutters. It's full of seeping wastes.
Okay, only a little further. But we can't let down our guard
yet. The INKlings' power extends all the way into the stations. You saw that shoe, didn't you?"

"Sure did," I said.

We followed the stream down the pipe, our shoes splashing in the liquid, dubbed over by the rumble of the trains.
Never in my whole life had I been so happy to hear the subway. People boarding trains, reading papers and magazines,
bound for work and pleasure. I thought about the color
advertisements hanging over the aisles and the subway sys-

tem maps over the doors. The Ginza Line is always yellow. Why yellow, I don't know, but yellow it is. When I think Ginza Line, I see yellow.

It didn't take very long to reach the mouth of the pipe. There was an iron grill over the opening, with a hole torn just big enough for a person to pass. The concrete was gouged where an iron bar had been ripped out. INKling handiwork, happily for once. If the grill weren't broken, we'd be stuck here with the outside world dangling before our eyes.

Beyond the hole was a box for signal lanterns and other equipment. On the blackened row of oar-shaped columns between the tracks were lamps, the ones that always looked so faint when seen from the station platform but which now glared inordinately bright.

"We'll wait here until our eyes adjust to the light," she instructed. "About ten minutes. Then we'll go a little bit further and pause until we get used to stronger light. Otherwise we'll be blinded. If the subway passes, do not look at it, not yet."

She sat me down on a dry patch of concrete, then took her place next to me.

When we heard a train approaching, we looked down and shut our eyes. A flashing yellow light streaked across my eyelids. My eyes began to water. I wiped away the tears with my shirt sleeve.

"It's okay. You'll get used to it," she said, tears trailing down her cheeks as well. "We'll just let the next three or four trains pass. Then our eyes will be ready for the station. Once we get there, we can forget about INKlings."

"I seem to remember this happening to me before," I said.

"Waiting in a subway tunnel?"

"No, the light, the glare, my eyes tearing up."

"That happens to everyone."

"No, this was special light, special vision. My eyes had

been altered. They couldn't tolerate light."

"Can you remember anything else?"

"No, that's it. My recall is gone."

"Your memory is running backward," she said.

She leaned against me. I was cold to my bones, sitting in my wet slacks. The only warmth on my body was where the bulge of her breasts touched my arm.

"Now that we're going above ground, I suppose you have plans. Places to see, things to do, maybe some person you want to see?" she urged, looking over at my watch. "You've got twenty-five hours and fifty minutes left."

"I want to go home and take a bath, then go to the barber shop," I said.

"You'll still have plenty of time left."

"I haven't thought that far ahead," I said.

"May I go to your place with you?" she asked. "I'd like to take a bath, too."

"Sure, why not."

A second train was passing from the direction of Aoyama Itchome. We lowered our gaze and closed our eyes again.

"You don't need a haircut," she said, shining her light on my head. "In fact, you'd probably look better with longer hair."

"I'm tired of long hair."

"Okay, but you still don't need to go to the barber. When was the last time you had a haircut?"

"I don't remember," I said. I really couldn't remember. I couldn't even remember if I'd taken a leak yesterday; what happened a few weeks ago was ancient history.

"Do you have any clothes I could fit into?"

"Don't think so."

"Oh well, I'll think of something," she said. "Are you going to use your bed?"

"Use my bed?"

"You know, call a girl over for sex?"

"I hadn't exactly planned on it," I said.

"Well, can I sleep there? I'd like to rest before going back for Grandfather."

"Fine by me, but the Semiotecs and System boys might barge in at any moment. I'm still quite popular, you know. And I don't have a door."

"I don't mind," she said.

A third train approached from the direction of Shibuya. I closed my eyes and counted slowly. I'd reached fourteen by the time the last car went by. My eyes were hardly affected at all.

She released my arm and stood up. "Let's get going."

I rose to my feet and followed her down to the tracks toward Aoyama Itchome.

30

Hole

*T*HE following morning the events in the Woods seem like a dream. Yet there on the table lies the old bellows box, curled up like a hurt animal. Everything *was* real: the fan turning in the underground wind, the sad face of the young Caretaker, his collection of musical instruments.

I hear a distinct, alien sound in my head. It is as if something has pushed its way into my skull. Some flat intrusion, ceaselessly tapping. Other than that, my head feels fine. The sensation is simply not real.

I look around the room from my bed. Nothing out of the ordinary. Ceiling, walls, warped floorboards, curtains in the window. Coat and scarf hanging on the wall, gloves peeking out of the coat pocket. There is the table and there, the musical instrument on the table.

I test each joint and muscle of my body. Every articulation is as it should be. There is no pain in my eyes; not a thing is wrong.

In spite of which, the flat sound persists. Irregularly, compositely, a weave of varying tones. Where can the sound be coming from? Listen as I might, the source eludes me.

I get out of bed and check the weather. Immediately below my window, three old men are digging a large hole, the points of their shovels scooping into the frozen earth. The air is so cold that the sound glances off, to the bewilderment of my ears.

The clock reads close to ten. Never have I slept so late. Where is the Colonel? Save for those days when I was feverish, he has always awakened me at nine o'clock without fail, bearing a breakfast tray.

I wait for half an hour. When still the Colonel does not appear, I go down to the kitchen myself. After so many breakfasts with the Colonel, today I am without appetite. I eat half my bread and set aside the rest for the beasts. Then I return to my bed, wrap my coat about me, and wait for the stove to heat the room.

What warmth we enjoyed yesterday has disappeared overnight. The Town is immersed in cold; the entire landscape has reverted to the depths of winter. From the Northern Ridge to the Southern Plain, the sky hangs unbearably low with snow-laden clouds.

Below the window, the four old men are still digging in the open ground.

Four men?

Before there were three. The Official Residences, however, are populated with innumerable old men. Each stands silently in place as he digs the earth at his feet. Occasional gusts of wind flap through their thin jackets, but the old men show little sign of discomfort as they thrust their shovels relentlessly into the frozen earth. They are sweating, faces flushed. One of their number has even removed his jacket, draping it over a tree branch like molted skin.

The room is now warm. I sit at the table with the musical instrument in hand, slowly working the bellows. The leather folds are stiff, but not unmanageable; the keys are discolored. When was the last time anyone touched it? By what route had the heirloom traveled, through how many hands? It is a mystery to me.

I inspect the bellows box with care. It is a jewel. There is such precision in it. So very small, it compresses to fit into a pocket, yet seems to sacrifice no mechanical details.

The shellac on the wooden boards at either end has not flaked. They bear a filligreed decoration, the intricate green arabesques well preserved. I wipe the dust with my fingers and read the letters A-C-C-O-R-D- . . .

This is an accordion!

I work it, in and out, over and over again, learning the feel of it. The buttons vie for space on the miniature instrument. More suited to a child's or woman's hand, the accordion is exceedingly difficult for a grown man to finger. And then one is supposed to work the bellows in rhythm!

I try pressing the buttons in order with my right hand, while holding down the chord keys with my left. I go once through all the notes, then pause.

The sound of the digging continues. The wind rattles at the windowpane now and again. Do the old men even hear my accordion?

I persist with this effort for one or two hours, until I am able to render a few simple chords without error. No melody comes. Still, I press on, hoping to strike some semblance of song, but the progressions of notes lead nowhere. An accidental configuration of tones may seem almost melodic, but in the next moment all vanishes into the air.

Perhaps it is the sound of the shovelling outdoors that keeps the notes from forming into a melody. I cannot concentrate for the noise. A rasping, uneven rhythm, the shovels plunging into the soil, how clear it reaches inside here! The sound grows so sharp, the men are digging in my head. They are hollowing out my skull.

The wind picks up before noon, intermingled with flurries of snow. White pellets strike the windowpane with a dry patter, tumbling in disarray along the sash, soon to blow away. It is a matter of time before the snowflakes swell with moisture. Soon the earth will be covered in white again.

I give up my struggle for song, leave the accordion on the table, and go over to the window. The old men keep digging, heedless of the snow. They do not acknowledge the white specks falling on them. No one looks at the sky, no one stays his hand, no one speaks. The forsaken jacket clings to the branch, fluttering in the wind.

There are now six old men; the hole is waist deep. One old man is in the hole, wielding a pick at the hard bottom with astounding efficiency. The four men with shovels toss out the dirt, and the last member of the team carts the dirt downhill with a wheelbarrow. I cannot discern a leader among them. All work equally hard, no one gives orders, no one assigns tasks.

Something about the hole begins to disturb me. It is far too large for waste disposal. And why dig now, in the gathering blizzard? They apparently dig for some purpose, even though the hole will be completely filled with snow by tomorrow morning.

I return to my chair and gaze absently at the glowing coals. I have an instrument. Will I never be able to recall a tune? Is the accordion on the table to remain beautiful but useless? I shut my eyes and listen to the shovelling as the snow softly hits the windowpane.

It is time for lunch. The old men finally set down their work and go indoors, leaving pick and shovels on the ground.

There is a knock on my door. The Colonel enters, wearing his usual heavy coat and a visored cap pulled down low onto his forehead. Coat and cap are both dusted in snow.

"Shall we have lunch?" he asks.

"That would be wonderful," I say.

A few minutes later, he returns and puts a pot on the stove. Only then does he shed his coat and cap and gloves. Last he takes a seat, rubbing his tousled frosted-white scalp.

"I was not able to be here for breakfast," says the old officer. "I had tasks to attend to this morning. I had no time to eat."

"Were you digging the hole?"

"The hole? No, that is nothing I do," answers the Colonel, with a hesitant laugh. "I had business in Town."

The pot is now hot. He ladles out two bowls and sets them on the table. A hearty vegetable chowder with noodles. He blows to cool it before taking a sip.

"Tell me, what is that hole for?" I ask the Colonel.

"Nothing at all," he says, guiding a spoonful of soup to his mouth. "They dig for the sake of digging. So in that sense, it is a very pure hole."

"I don't understand."

"It is simple enough. They dig their hole because they want to dig. Nothing more or less."

I think about the pure hole and all it might mean.

"They dig holes from time to time," the Colonel explains. "It is probably for them what chess is for me. It has no special meaning, does not transport them anywhere. All of us dig at our own pure holes. We have nothing to achieve by our activities, nowhere to get to. Is there not something marvelous about this? We hurt no one and no one gets hurt. No victory, no defeat."

"I think I understand."

The old officer finishes one last spoonful of soup.

"Perhaps you do not understand. But our way is proper to us. It is proper, peaceful, and pure. Soon enough, it will begin to make sense to you.

"For many years, I led the life of a soldier. I do not regret that; it was a fine life. The smell of gunsmoke and blood, the flash of sabers, the call of the bugle. I sometimes still think about the drama. Yet I cannot recall what it was that sent us charging into the fray. Honor? Patriotism? A thirst for combat? Hatred? I can only guess.

"You are fearful now of losing your mind, as I once feared myself. Let me say, however, that to relinquish your self carries no shame," the Colonel breaks off and searches the air for words. "Lay down your mind and peace will come. A peace deeper than anything you have known."

I nod quietly.

"I hear talk in Town about your shadow," says the Colonel. "Your shadow is not well. He cannot hold down food, he has been sick in bed for three days, he may not have long. Will you see him one last time? If you have nothing against it, that is. I am sure he wants to see you."

"Of course, I will see him," I say. "But will the Gatekeeper let me?"

"Your shadow is on the verge of death. A person has the right to see his own shadow under these circumstances. There are rules about this. The Town observes the passing of a shadow as a solemn event, and the Gatekeeper does not interfere. There is no reason for him to interfere."

"I'll go over right away," I say, with only the slightest pause.

"Good. I knew you would," says the old soldier, drawing near to pat me on the shoulder. "Best to hurry before evening, before the snow gets too thick. A shadow is the closest thing a person has. Take a long look and leave no remorse. See that your shadow dies well. It is for your own sake."

"Yes," I say. I don my coat, wrapping my scarf around my neck.

31

Fares, Police, Detergent

T HE distance to Aoyama Itchome was not great. We walked along the tracks, hiding behind columns whenever a train passed. We could see all the passengers clearly, but none of them even looked outside. They read newspapers or stared blankly. Few in number, practically all had seats. The rush-hour peak had passed; still I seemed to remember the ten-o'clock Ginza Line being more crowded.

"What day is it today?" I asked the girl.

"I couldn't tell you," she said.

"Not many passengers for a weekday. Do you think it could be Sunday?"

"And if it is Sunday?"

"Oh, nothing. It'd just be Sunday."

The subway tracks were wide with no obstructions, a dream to walk. The fluorescent light on the walls gave off more than adequate illumination, and thanks to the ventilation system, there was plenty of fresh air. At least compared to the dead air below.

We let one Ginza-bound shuttle go past, then another heading in the opposite direction toward Shibuya. By then we were near enough to Aoyama Itchome to watch the station platform from the shadows. What a nuisance it'd be to get caught on the tracks by a station attendant. A steel ladder led up onto the end of the platform, after which we only had to climb over a short barrier.

We looked on as another Ginza-bound shuttle pulled to a stop at the platform, let passengers out, then took on new passengers. The conductor saw that all was in order and gave the signal to depart. The station attendants disappeared once the train was out of sight.

"Let's go," I said. "Don't run, just walk normal."

"Check."

Stepping out from behind a pillar, we mounted the ladder at the end of the platform, nonchalant and disinterested, as if we did this sort of thing every day. We stepped around the railing. Several people looked our way, visibly alarmed. We were covered with mud, clothes drenched, hair matted, eyes squinting at the ordinary light—I guess we didn't look like subway employees. Who the hell were we?

Before they'd reached any conclusions, we'd sauntered past and were already at the wicket. That's when it occurred to me, we didn't have tickets.

"We'll say we lost them and pay the fare," she said.

So that's what I told the young attendant at the gate.

"Did you look carefully?" he asked. "You have lots of pockets. Could you please check again?"

We stood there dripping and filthy and searched our clothes for tickets that had never been there, while the attendant eyed us incredulously.

No, it seemed we'd really lost them, I said.

"Where did you get on?"

"Shibuya."

"How much did you pay?"

"A hundred twenty, hundred forty yen, something like that."

"You don't remember?"

"I was thinking about other things."

"Honestly, you got on at Shibuya?"

"The line starts from Shibuya, doesn't it? How could we cheat on the fare?"

"You could have come through the underpass from the opposite platform. The Ginza Line's pretty long. For all I know, you could have caught the Tozai Line all the way from Tsudanuma and transferred at Nihonbashi."

"Tsudanuma?"

"Strictly hypothetical," said the station attendant.

"So how much is it from Tsudanuma? I'll pay that. Will that make you happy?"

"Did you come from Tsudanuma?"

"No," I said. "Never been to Tsudanuma in my life."

"Then why pay the fare?"

"I'm just doing what you said."

"I said that was strictly hypothetical."

By now, the next train had arrived. Twelve passengers got off and passed through the wicket. We watched them. Not one of them had lost a ticket. Whereupon we resumed negotiations with the attendant.

"Okay, tell me from where do I have to pay?" I said.

"From where you got on," he insisted.

"Shibuya, like I've been trying to tell you."

"But you don't remember the fare."

"Who remembers fares? Do you remember how much coffee costs at McDonald's?"

"I don't drink McDonald's coffee," said the station attendant. "It's a waste of money."

"Purely hypothetical," I said. "But you forget details like that."

"That may be, but people who say they've lost tickets always plead cheaper fares. They all come over to this platform and say they got on in Shibuya."

"I already said I'd pay whatever fare you want, didn't I? Just tell me how much."

"How should I know?"

I threw down a thousand-yen bill and we marched out. The attendant yelled at us, but we pretended not to hear. Who's going to argue over subway tickets when the world's about to end. And we hadn't even taken the subway.

Above ground, fine needles of rain were coming down. On my last, precious day. It could rain for a whole month like in a J. G. Ballard novel, but let it wait until I was out of the picture. Today was my day to lie in the sun, listen to music, drink a cold beer.

The rain, however, showed no sign of letting up. I thought of buying a morning edition and reading the weather forecast, but the nearest newsstand was back down in the subway station. Scratch the paper. It was going to be a gray day, whatever day it was.

Everyone was walking with open umbrellas. Everyone except us. We ducked under the portico of a building and gazed out at the drizzly intersection streaming with cars of different colors.

"Thank goodness, it's raining," said the girl.

"How's that?"

"Easy on the eyes."

"Great."

"What do we do now?"

"First we get something hot to drink, then head home for a bath."

We went into a supermarket with the ubiquitous sandwich stand. The checker jumped when she saw us all covered in mud, but quickly recovered to take our orders.

"That's two cream of corn soups and one ham and egg-salad sandwich, is that right, sir?" she confirmed.

"Right," I said. "Say there, what day is it today?"

"Sunday."

"What did I tell you?" I said to the chubby girl.

"How come?" asked the girl.

"Me, I only pick up rockers. Clean, dirty, makes no difference. Music's my poison. You guys into the Police?"

"Sure." I told him what he wanted to hear.

"In a company, they don't letcha play this shit. They say, play *kayokyoku*. No way, man. I mean, really. Matchi? Seiko? I can't hack sugar pop. But the Police, they're *baad*. Twenty-four hours, nonstop. And reggae's happenin', too. How're you guys for reggae?"

"I can get into it," I said.

After the Police tape, the driver popped in *Bob Marley Live*. The dashboard was crammed with tapes.

I was tired and cold and sleepy. I was coming apart at the seams and in no good condition. I couldn't handle the vibes, but at least we got a ride. I sat back and watched the driver's shoulders bounce to the reggae beat.

The taxi pulled up in front of my apartment. I got out and handed the driver an extra thousand yen as a tip. "Buy yourself a tape," I told him.

"Get down," he said. "You can ride with me anytime."

"Sure thing," I said.

"In ten, fifteen years, it's gonna be rock taxis all over, eh? World's going to be *baaad*."

"Yeah," I said, "real bad."

As if I really believed that. It'd been fifteen years since Jim Morrison died, and never once had I come across a Doors taxi. There are things that change in this world and things that don't. Department stores haven't stopped piping in Raimond Lefebvre Orchestra muzak, beer halls still play to polkas, shopping arcades play Ventures' Christmas carols from mid-November.

We went up in the elevator to find the apartment door propped up against the door frame. Why had anyone bothered? I pushed open the steel door like Cro-Magnon Man rolling the boulder from the mouth of his cave. I let the girl in first, slid the door back in place so that no one could see in, then fastened the door chain as a pretense of security.

I picked up a copy of *Sports Nippon* from the adjacen
stool. Not much to gain from a tabloid, but what the hell
The paper was dated Sunday, October 2. No weather forecast, but the racing page went into track conditions in some
detail. Rain made it tough racing for quarterhorses. At Jingu Stadium, Yakult lost to Chunichi, 6–2. And no one the
wiser that there was a huge hive of INKlings right under
them.

The girl claimed the back pages. Some seedy article
which addressed the question "Is Swallowing Semen Good
for the Complexion?"

"Do you like having your semen swallowed?" the girl
wanted to know.

"It's okay," I answered.

"Listen to what it says here: 'The typical man enjoys it
when a woman swallows his semen. This is a sign of total
obeisance toward the man on the part of the woman. It is at
once a ceremony and an affirmation.'"

"I don't get it," I said.

"Anyone ever swallow yours?"

"Uh, I can't remember."

"Hmph," she pouted and dove back into her article. I
read the batting averages for the Central and Pacific
Leagues.

Our order arrived. Anything would have tasted good.

We left the place and caught a taxi. It was ages before we
got one to stop, we were so dirty. The driver was a young
guy with long hair, a huge stereoblaster on the seat next to
him. I shouted our destination over the blare of the Police,
then sank into the backrest.

"Hey, where you guys been?" asked the driver.

"We had a knock-down drag-out fight in the rain,"
answered the girl.

"Wow, *baad*," said the driver. "Oughta see yourselves.
You look wild. Got a great bruise there upside your neck."

"I know," I said.

"Like I dig it," said the driver.

The room was neat and clean. For a second I thought I was in the wrong apartment. The furniture had been righted, the food cleaned from the floor, the broken bottles and dishes had disappeared. Books and records were back on the shelf, clothes were hanging in the wardrobe. The kitchen and bathroom and bedroom were spotless.

More thorough inspection, however, revealed the aftermath of destruction. The imploded TV tube gaped like a short-circuited time tunnel. The refrigerator was dead and empty. Only a few plates and glasses remained in the cupboard. The wall clock had stopped, and none of the electrical appliances worked. The slashed clothes were gone, leaving barely enough to fill one small suitcase. Someone had thrown out just about everything that was beyond hope, leaving the place with a generic, no-frills look. My apartment had never seemed so spacious.

I went to the bathroom, lit the gas heater, and after seeing that it functioned properly, ran the bathwater. I still had an adequate lineup of toiletries: soap, razor, toothbrush, towel, shampoo. My bathrobe was in one piece.

While the tub filled, I looked around the apartment. The girl sat in a corner, reading Balzac's *Chouans*.

"Say, were there really otters in France?" she asked.

"I suppose."

"Even today?"

"Who knows?"

I took a seat in the kitchen and tried to think who it was that might have cleaned up the apartment. Might have been those two Semiotecs, might have been someone from the System. Even if it was one of them, I couldn't help feeling grateful.

I suggested that the chubby girl bathe first. While she was in in the tub, I changed into some salvaged clothes and plopped down on what had been my bed. It was nearly eleven-thirty. I had to come up with a plan of action. For the last twenty-four hours of my life.

Outside, it was raining in a fine mist. If not for the

droplets along the eaves, I wouldn't have been able to tell. Drowsiness was creeping up on me, but this was no time to sleep. I didn't want to lose even a minute.

Well, I didn't want to stay here in the apartment. What was there to gain from that?

A person with twenty-four hours left to live ought to have countless things to do, but I couldn't think of a single one. I thought of the Frankfurt travel poster on the supermarket wall. Wouldn't be so bad to end my life in Frankfurt, though it probably was impossible to get there in twenty-four hours. Even if I could, I'd have to spend ten hours strapped into an airplane seat eating those yummy in-flight snacks. Besides, posters have a way of looking better than the real thing: the reality never lived up to the expectation. I didn't want to end my life disappointed.

That left one option: a fine meal for two. Nothing else I particularly wanted to do.

I dialed the Library.

"Hello," answered my reference librarian.

"Thanks for the unicorn books," I said.

"Thanks for the wonderful meal," said she.

"Care to join me for dinner again tonight?"

"*Din-ner?*" she sang back to me. "Tonight's my study group."

"Study group?"

"My water pollution study group. You know, detergents getting into the streams and rivers, killing fish. Everyone's got a research topic, and tonight we present our findings."

"Very civic, I'm sure."

"Yes, very. Couldn't we make it tomorow night? The library's closed on Monday, so we could have more time together."

"I won't be around from tomorrow afternoon. I can't really explain over the phone, but I'm going far away."

"Far away? You mean travel?"

"Kind of," I said.

"Just a sec, can you hold on?" She broke off to answer a

"With this weather, it'll be tomorrow morning before your clothes dry."

"Then what am I supposed to do?"

"Ever heard of clothes driers? There's a laundromat near here."

"But I don't have any other clothes to wear out."

I racked my brains, but failed to come up with any spark of wisdom. Which left me to take her things to the laundromat. I went to the bathroom and threw her wet clothes into a Lufthansa bag.

So it was that part of my last precious hours were spent sitting on a folding chair in a laundromat.

32

Shadow in the Throes of Death

I OPEN the door to the Gatehouse and find the Gatekeeper at the back door splitting firewood.

"Big snow on the way. I can feel it in the air," says
the Gatekeeper, axe in hand. "Four beasts dead in this
morning alone. Many more will die by tomorrow. This winter the cold is something fierce."

I take off my gloves and warm my fingers at the stove.
The Gatekeeper ties the splits into a bundle and tosses it
onto a stack in the woodshed, then shuts the door behind
him and props his axe up against the wall. Finally, he comes
over and warms his fingers, too.

"From now on, looks like I burn the beasts alone. Made
my life easier having the help, but everything has to end
sometime. Anyway, it was my job to begin with."

"Is my shadow so ill as that?"

"The thing is not well," answers the Gatekeeper, rolling

his head on his shoulders. "Not well at all. Been looking after it as best I can, but only so much a person can do."

"Can I see him?"

"Sure, I give you a half hour. I have to go burn dead beasts after that."

The Gatekeeper takes his key ring off the hook and unlocks the iron gate to the Shadow Grounds. He walks quickly across the enclosure ahead of me, and shows me into the lean-to. It is as cold as an icehouse.

"Not my fault," the Gatekeeper says. "Not my idea to throw your shadow in here. No thrill for me. We got regulations, and shadows have to be put in here. I just follow the rules. Your shadow even has it better than some. Bad times, there are two or three shadows crammed in here together."

Objection is by now beside the point. I nod and say nothing. I should never have left my shadow in a place like this.

"Your shadow is down below," he says. "Down below is a little warmer, if you can stand the smell."

The Gatekeeper goes over to a corner and lifts a damp wooden trapdoor to reveal not a staircase but a ladder. The Gatekeeper descends the first few rungs, then motions for me to follow. I brush the snow from my coat and follow him.

Down below, the stale smell of shit and piss assaults the senses. Without a window, the air cannot escape. It is a cellar the size of a small trunkroom. A bed occupies a third of the floor. Beneath the bed is a crockery chamber pot. A candle, the sole source of light and heat, flickers on a tottering old table. The floor is earthen, and the dampness in the room chilling. My shadow lies in bed, unmoving, with a blanket pulled up to his ears. He stares at me with lifeless eyes. As the old Colonel has said, my shadow does not seem to have much time left.

"I need fresh air," says the Gatekeeper, overcome by the stench. "You two talk all you want. This shadow no longer has the strength to stick to you."

The Gatekeeper leaves. My shadow hesitates a moment, cautiously looking about the room, then beckons me over to his bedside.

"Go up and check that the Gatekeeper isn't listening," whispers the shadow.

I steal up the ladder, crack open the trapdoor, see that no one is about.

"He's gone," I say.

"We have things to talk about," declares my shadow. "I'm not as weak as I appear. It's all an act to fool the Gatekeeper. I am weak, that's true, but my vomiting and staying bedridden is pretend. I can still get up and walk."

"To escape?"

"What else? If I wasn't making to get out of here, why would I go to all the trouble? I've gained myself three days doing this. But three days is probably my limit. After that, I won't be able to stand. This stinking cellar air is killing me. And the cold—it pierces to the bone. What's the weather like outside?"

"It's cold and snowing hard," I say, hands in my coat pockets. "It's even worse at night. The temperature really drops."

"The more it snows, the more beasts die," says the Shadow. "More dead beasts mean more work for the Gatekeeper. We'll slip out when he's occupied, while he's burning the carcasses in the Apple Grove. You'll lift his keys, unlock the enclosure, and we escape, the two of us."

"By the Gate?"

"No, the Gate's no good. He'd be on top of us in no time. The Wall's no good either. Only birds can make it over the Wall."

"So how do we escape?"

"Leave it to me. I've got it worked out from the information I've pieced together. I pored over your map enough to wear holes in it, plus I learned all sorts of things from the Gatekeeper himself. The ox took it into his head that I wasn't a problem anymore, so he was willing to talk about the Town. The Gatekeeper is right that I don't have the strength to stick to you. Not now anyway. But once we get out and I recover, we can be back together. I won't have to die here like this; you'll regain your memory and become your former self."

I stare into the candle flame and say nothing.

"What's the matter? Out with it."

"Just what was this former self of mine?"

"What's this now? Don't tell me you're having doubts," jeers my shadow.

"Yes, I have doubts," I say. "To begin with, I can't even recall my former self. How can I be sure that self is worth returning to? Or that world?"

The shadow is about to say something, but I raise my hand to cut him short. "Wait, please. Just let me finish what I have to say. It is not only that I may have forgotten how things used to be. I am beginning to feel an attachment to this Town. I enjoy watching the beasts. I have grown fond of the Colonel and the girl at the Library. No one hurts each other here, no one fights. Life is uneventful, but full enough in its way. Everyone is equal. No one speaks ill of anyone else, no one steals. They work, but they enjoy their work. It's work purely for the sake of work, not forced labor. No one is jealous of anyone. There are no complaints, no worries."

"You've forgotten no money or property or rank either. And no internal conflicts," says the shadow. "More important, there's no growing old, no death, no fear of death."

"Tell me, then—what possible reason would I have for leaving this Town?"

"It all makes sense, what you say," he allows, extending a shadowy hand from under his blanket to touch his parched lips, "on the face of it. The world you describe would truly be a utopia. I cannot fault you that. You have every right to be taken with it, and if that's the case, then I will accept your choice and I will die. Still, you are overlooking things, some very important things."

The shadow breaks into a cough. I wait for him to resume.

"Just now, you spoke of the Town's perfection. Sure, the people here—the Gatekeeper aside—don't hurt anyone. No one hurts each other, no one has wants. All are contented and at peace. Why is that? It's because they have no mind."

"That much I know too well," I say.

"It is by relinquishing their mind that the Townfolk lose time; their awareness becomes a clean slate of eternity. As I said, no one grows old or dies. All that's required is that you strip away the shadow that is the grounding of the self and watch it die. Once your shadow dies, you haven't a problem in the world. You need only to skim off the discharges of mind that rise each day."

"Skim off?"

"I'll come back to that later. First, about the mind. You tell me there is no fighting or hatred or desire in the Town. That is a beautiful dream, and I do want your happiness. But the absence of fighting or hatred or desire also means the opposites do not exist either. No joy, no communion, no love. Only where there is disillusionment and depression and sorrow does happiness arise; without the despair of loss, there is no hope.

"Then, of course, there's love. Which surely makes a difference with this Library girl of yours. Love is a state of mind, but she has no mind for it. People without a mind are phantoms. What would be the meaning of loving someone like that? Do you seek eternal life? Do you too wish to become a phantom? If you let me die, you'll be one of the Townfolk. You'll be trapped here forever."

A stifling silence envelops the cellar. The shadow coughs again.

"I cannot leave her here," I brave to say. "No matter what she is, I love her and want her. I cannot lie to *my* own mind. If I run out now, I will always regret it."

"This is just great," my shadow says, sitting up in bed

and leaning against the wall. "You're an old, old friend. I know how stubborn you can be. You *had* to make an issue at the last minute, didn't you? *What is it you want?* It is impossible for you and me and the girl to escape, the three of us. People without a shadow cannot live outside of here."

"I know this too," I say. "I wonder, why don't you escape alone? I will help you."

"You still don't understand, do you?" says my shadow, wearily resting his head. "If I run away and leave you behind, your life here would be sheer misery. That much the Gatekeeper's told me. Shadows, all shadows, die here. Banished shadows all come back to die. Shadows that don't die here can only leave behind incomplete deaths. You'd live out all eternity in the embrace of what's left of your mind. In the Woods. Those with undead shadows are driven out of Town to wander through the Woods forever and ever, possessed by their thoughts. You're acquainted with the Woods?"

He knows I am.

"Nor would you be able to take her to the Woods," my shadow continues. "Because she is perfect, she has no mind, no conflict in herself. Perfect half-persons live in Town, not in the Woods. You'll be alone, I promise you."

"But then, where do people's minds go?"

"You're the Dreamreader, aren't you?" retorts my shadow. "I don't know how you haven't managed to figure that one out!"

"I'm sorry. I haven't . . ."

"Fine, let me tell you. People's minds are transported outside the Wall by the beasts. That is what I meant by skimming off. The beasts wander around absorbing traces of mind, then ferry them to the outside world. When winter comes, they die with a residue of self inside them. What kills them is not the cold and not the lack of food; what kills them is the weight of self forced upon them by the Town. In spring, new young are born—exactly the same number as the beasts that died—and it happens all over again. This is the price of your perfection. A perfection that forces everything upon the weak and powerless."

I cannot say a thing. I look down at my shoes.

"When the beasts die, the Gatekeeper cuts off their heads," my shadow goes on, unrelenting. "By then, their skulls are indelibly etched with self. These skulls are scraped and buried for a full year in the ground to leech away their energy, then taken to the Library stacks, where they sit until the Dreamreader's hands release the last glimmers of mind into the air. That's what 'old dreams' are. Dreamreading is a task for newcomers to the Town—people whose shadows have not yet died. The Dreamreader reads each spark of self into the air, where it diffuses and dissipates. You are a lightning rod; your task is to ground. Do you see?"

"I believe I do."

"When the Dreamreader's shadow dies, he ceases to be Dreamreader and becomes one with the Town. This is how it's possible for the Town to maintain its perfection. All imperfections are forced upon the imperfect, so the 'perfect' can live content and oblivious. Is that the way it should be? Did you ever think to look at things from the viewpoint of the beasts and shadows and Woodsfolk?"

I have been staring at the candle flame for so long, my head hurts. I remove my black glasses and rub my watering eyes.

"I will be here tomorrow at three," I vow. "All is as you say. This is no place for me."

33

Rainy-Day Laundry, Car Rental, Bob Dylan

O N a rainy Sunday, the four driers at the laundromat were bound to be occupied. So it came as no surprise to find four different-colored plastic shopping bags hanging on the door handles. There were three women in the place: one, a late-thirtyish housewife; the other two, coeds from the nearby girls' dorm. The housewife was sitting in a folding chair, staring blankly at her clothes going around and around. It could have been a TV. The coeds were pouring over a copy of *JJ*. All three of them glanced up at me the moment I entered, but quickly found their wash and their magazine more interesting.

I took a seat to wait my turn, Lufthansa bag on my knee. It looked like I was next in line. Great. A guy can only watch somebody else's clothes revolve for so long. Especially on his last day.

I sprawled out in the chair and gazed off into space. The

laundromat had that particular detergent and clothes-drying smell. Contrary to my expectations, none of the driers opened up. There are unwritten rules about laundromats and "The watched drier never stops" is one of them. From where I sat, the clothes looked perfectly dry, but the drums didn't know when to quit.

I longed to close my eyes and sleep, but I didn't want to miss my turn. I wished I'd brought something to read. It would keep me awake and make the time go faster. But then again, did I really want to make the time go faster? Better I should make the time go slow—but in a laundromat?

Thinking about time was torment. Time is too conceptual. Not that it stops us from filling it in. So much so, we can't even tell whether our experiences belong to time or to the world of physical things.

But what to do after leaving the laundromat? First, buy some clothes. Proper clothes. No time for alterations, so forget the tweed suit. Make do with chinos, a blazer, shirt, and tie. Add a light coat. Perfectly acceptable attire for any restaurant. That's an hour and a half. Which put me at three o'clock. I'd have three hours until I was supposed to pick her up.

Hmm. What to do for three hours? Mind impeded by sleepiness and fatigue, mind blocked.

The drier on the right ground to a halt. The housewife and college girls glanced at the machine, but none made a move. The drier was mine. In keeping with the unwritten rules of laundromats, I removed the warm mass of clothes and stuffed them into the bag hanging on the handle. After which I dumped in my Lufthansa bagful of wet clothes, fed the machine some coins, and returned to my chair. Twelve-fifty by the clock.

The housewife and college girls stared at me. Then they stared at the laundry in the drier. Then they stared at me again. So I stared at the laundry in the drier myself. That was when I noticed my small load dancing in plain view for all to see—all of it the girl's things, all of it pink. Better get out of here, find something else to do for twenty minutes.

The fine rain of the morning didn't let up, a subtle message to the world. I opened my umbrella and walked. Through the quiet residential area to a street lined with shops. Barber, bakery, surf shop—a surf shop in Setagaya?—tobacconist, *patisserie*, video shop, cleaners. Which had a sign outside, "All Clothes 10% Off on Rainy Days." Interesting logic. Inside the shop the bald, dour-looking proprietor was pressing a shirt. Electrical cables dangled from the ceiling, a thick growth of vines running to the presses and irons. An honest-to-goodness, neighborhood cleaners, where all work was done on premises. Good to know about. I bet they didn't staple number tags—which I hate—to your shirttails. I never send my shirts to the cleaners for that very reason.

On the front stoop of the cleaners sat a few potted plants. I knew I knew what they were, but I couldn't identify a single one. Rain dripped from the eaves into the dark potting soil on which a lonely snail rolled along singlemindedly. I felt useless. I'd lived thirty-five years in this world and couldn't come up with the name of one lousy ornamental. There was a lot I could learn from a local cleaners.

I returned to the tobacconists and bought a pack of Lark Extra Longs. I'd quit smoking five years before, but one pack of cigarettes on the last day of my life wasn't going to kill me. I lit up. The cigarette felt foreign. I slowly drew in the smoke and slowly exhaled.

I moved on to the *patisserie,* where I bought four *gateaux*. They had such difficult French names that once they were in the box, I forgot what I'd selected. I'd taken French in university, but apparently it had gone down the tubes. The girl behind the counter was prim, but bad at tying ribbons. Inexcusable.

The video shop next door was one I'd patronized a few times. Something called *Hard Times* was on the twenty-seven-inch monitor at the entrance. Charles Bronson was a bare-knuckle boxer, James Coburn his manager. I stepped inside and asked to see the fight scene again.

The woman behind the counter looked bored. I offered her one of the *gateaux* while Bronson battered a bald-headed opponent. The ringside crowd expected the brute to win, but they didn't know that Bronson never loses. I got up to leave.

"Why don't you stick around and watch the whole thing?" invited Mrs. Video Shop.

I'd really have liked to, I told her, if it weren't for the things I had in the drier. I cast an eye at my watch. One-twenty-five. The drier had already stopped.

She made one last pitch. "Three classic Hitchcock pictures coming in next week."

I retraced my steps to the laundromat. Which, I was pleased to find, was empty. Just the wash awaiting my return at the bottom of the drier. I stuffed the wash into my bag and headed home.

The chubby girl didn't hear me come in and was fast asleep on the bed. I placed her clothes by the pillow and the cake box on the night stand. The thought of crawling into bed was appealing, but it was not to be.

I went into the kitchen. Faucet, gas water heater, ventilator fan, gas oven, various assorted pots and pans, refrigerator and toaster and cupboard and knife rack, a big Brooke Bond tea cannister, rice cooker, and everything else that goes into the single word "kitchen". Such order composed this world.

I was married when I first moved in to the apartment. Eight years ago, but even then I often sat at this table alone, reading in the middle of the night. My wife was such a sound sleeper, I sometimes worried if she was still alive. And in my own imperfect way, I loved her.

That meant I'd lived for eight years in this dump. Three

of us had moved in together: me and my wife and the cat. My wife was the first to move out, next was the cat. Now it was my turn. I grabbed a saucer for an ashtray and lit a cigarette. I drank a glass of water. Eight years. I could hardly believe it.

Well, it didn't matter. Everything would be over soon enough. Eternal life would set in. Immortality.

I was bound for the world of immortality. That's what the Professor said. The End of the World was not death but a transposition. I would be myself. I would be reunited with what I had already lost and was now losing.

Well, maybe so. No, probably so. The old man had to know what he was talking about. If he said it was an undying world, then undying it was. Yet, none of the Professor's words had the ring of reality. They were abstractions, vague shadows of contingency. I mean, I already was myself, wasn't I? And how would someone who's immortal perceive his immortality? What was this about unicorns and a high wall? *The Wizard of Oz* had to be more plausible.

So what had I lost? I'd lost many things. Maybe a whole college chapbook full, all noted down in tiny script. Things that hadn't seemed so important when I let go of them. Things that brought me sorrow later, although the opposite was also true. People and places and feelings kept slipping away from me.

Even if I had my life to live over again, I couldn't imagine not doing things the same. After all, everything—this life I was losing—was me. And I couldn't be any other self but my self. Could I?

Once, when I was younger, I thought I could be someone else. I'd move to Casablanca, open a bar, and I'd meet Ingrid Bergman. Or more realistically—whether actually more realistic or not—I'd tune in on a better life, something more suited to my true self. Toward that end, I had to undergo training. I read *The Greening of America*, and I saw *Easy Rider* three times. But like a boat with a twisted rudder, I kept coming back to the same place. I wasn't going anywhere. I was myself, waiting on the shore for me to return.

Was that so depressing?

Who knows? Maybe that was "despair". What Turgenev called "disillusionment". Or Dostoyevsky, "hell". Or Somerset Maugham, "reality". Whatever the label, I figured it was me.

A world of immortality? I might actually create a new self. I could become happy, or at least less miserable. And dare I say it, I could become a better person. But that had nothing to do with me now. That would be another self. For now, *I* was an immutable, historical fact.

All the same, I had little choice but to proceed on the hypothesis of my life ending in another twenty-two hours. So I was going to die—I told myself for convenience sake. That was more like me, if I did say so myself. Which, I supposed, was some comfort.

I put out my cigarette and went to the bedroom. I looked at the chubby girl's sleeping face. I went through my pockets to check that I had everything I needed for this farewell scene. What did I really need? Almost nothing any more. Wallet and credit cards and . . . was there anything else? The apartment key was of no use, neither were my car keys, nor my Calcutec ID. Didn't need my address book, didn't need a knife. Not even for laughs.

I took the subway to Ginza and bought a new set of clothes at Paul Stuart, paying the bill with American Express. I looked at myself in the mirror. Not bad. The combination of the navy blazer with burnt orange shirt did smack of yuppie ad exec, but better that than troglodyte.

It was still raining, but I was tired of looking at clothes, so I passed on the coat and instead went to a beer hall. It was almost empty. They were playing a Bruckner symphony. I couldn't tell which number, but who can? I ordered a draft and some oysters on the half shell.

I squeezed lemon over the oysters and ate them in clockwise order, the Bruckner romantic in the background. The giant wall-clock read five before three, the dial supporting two lions which spun around the mainspring. Bruckner came to an end, and the music shifted into Ravel's *Bolero*.

I ordered a second draft, when I was hit by the long overdue urge to relieve myself. And piss I did. How could one bladder hold so much? I was in no particular hurry, so I kept going for a whole two minutes—with *Bolero* building to its enormous crescendo. It made me feel as if I could piss forever.

Afterwards I could have sworn I'd been reborn.

I washed my hands, looked at my face in the warped mirror, then returned to my beer at the table and lit up a cigarette.

Time seemed to stand still, although in fact the lions had gone around one hundred eighty degrees and it was now ten after three. I leaned one elbow on the table and considered the clock. Watching the hands of a clock advance is a meaningless way to spend time, but I couldn't think of anything better to do. Most human activities are predicated on the assumption that life goes on. If you take that premise away, what is there left?

The hands of the clock reached half past three, so I paid up and left. The rain had virtually stopped during this beer interlude, so I left my umbrella behind too. Things weren't looking so bad. The weather had brightened up, so why not me?

With the umbrella gone, I felt lighter. I felt like moving on. Preferably to somewhere with a lot of people. I went to the Sony Building, where I jostled with Arab tourists ogling the lineup of state-of-the-art TV monitors, then went underground to the Marunouchi Line and headed for Shinjuku. I apparently fell asleep the instant I took a seat, because the next thing I knew I was there.

Exiting through the wicket, I suddenly remembered the skull and shuffled data I'd stashed at the station baggage-check a couple days before. The skull made no difference now and I didn't have my claim stub, but I had nothing better to do, so I found myself at the counter, pleading with the clerk to let me have my bag.

"Did you look for your ticket carefully?" asked the clerk.

I had, I told him.

"What's your bag look like?"

"A blue Nike sports bag," I said.

"What's the Nike trademark look like?"

I asked for a piece of paper and a pencil, drew a squashed boomerang and wrote Nike above it. The clerk looked at it dubiously and wandered off down the aisles of shelves. Presently he returned with my bag.

"This it?"

"That's right," I said.

"Got any ID?"

My prize retrieved, it suddenly struck me, you don't go to out to dinner lugging gym gear. Instead of carrying it around, I decided to rent a car and throw the bag nonchalantly in the back seat. Make that a smart European car. Not that I was such a fan of European cars, but it seemed to me that this very important day of my life merited riding around in a nice car.

I checked the yellow pages and jotted down the numbers of four car-rental dealerships in the Shinjuku area. None had any European cars. Sundays were high-demand days and they never had foreign cars to begin with. The last dealership had a Toyota Carina 1800 GT Twin-Cam Turbo and a Toyota Mark II. Both new, both with car stereos. I said I'd take the Carina. I didn't have a crease of an idea what either car looked like.

Having done that, I went to a record shop and bought a few cassettes. *Johnny Mathis's Greatest Hits*, Zubin Mehta conducting Schönberg's *Verklärte Nacht*, Kenny Burrell's *Stormy Sunday*, *Popular Ellington*, Trevor Pinnock on the harpsichord playing the *Brandenburg Concertos*, and a Bob

Dylan tape with *Like A Rolling Stone*. Mix'n'match. I wanted to cover the bases—how was I to know what kind of music would go with a Carina 1800 GT Twin-Cam Turbo?

I bagged the tapes and headed for the car rental lot. The driver's seat of the Carina 1800 GT seemed like the cabin of a space shuttle compared to my regular tin toy. I popped the Bob Dylan tape in the deck, and *Watching the River Flow* came on while I tested each switch on the dashboard control panel.

The nice lady who'd served me came out of the office and came over to the car to ask if anything was wrong. She smiled a clean, fresh TV-commercial smile.

No problems, I told her, I was just checking everything before hitting the road.

"Very good," she said. Her smile reminded me of a girl I'd known in high school. Neat and clear-headed, she married a Kakumaru radical, had two children, then disappeared. Who would have guessed a sweet seventeen-year-old, J. D. Salinger- and George Harrison-fan of a girl would go through such changes.

"I only wish all drivers were as careful as you. It would make our job a lot easier," she said. "These computerized panels in the latest models are pretty complicated."

"Which button do I push to find the square root of 185?" I asked.

"I'm afraid you'll have to wait until the next model," she laughed. "Say, isn't that Bob Dylan you have on?"

"Right," I said. *Positively 4th Street*.

"I can tell Bob Dylan in an instant," she said.

"Because his harmonica's worse than Stevie Wonder?"

She laughed again. Nice to know I could still make someone laugh.

"No, I really like his voice," she said. "It's like a kid standing at the window watching the rain."

After all the volumes that have been written about Dylan, I had yet to come across such a perfect description.

She blushed when I told her that.

"Oh, I don't know. That's just what he sounds like to me."

"I never expected someone as young as you to know Bob Dylan."

"I like old music. Bob Dylan, the Beatles, the Doors, Jimi Hendrix—you know."

"We should get together sometime," I told her.

She smiled, cocking her head slightly. Girls who are on top of things must have three hundred ways of responding to tired thirty-five-year-old divorced men. I thanked her and started the car. *Stuck Inside of Mobile with the Memphis Blues Again.* I felt better for having met her.

The digital dashboard clock read four-forty-two. The sunless city sky was edging toward dusk as I headed home, crawling through the congested streets. This was not your usual rainy Sunday congestion; a green sports compact had slammed into an eight-ton truck carrying a load of concrete blocks. Traffic was at a standstill. The sportscar looked like a cardboard box someone sat on. Several raincoated cops stood around as the wrecker crew cleaned up the debris.

It took forever to get by the accident site, but there was still plenty of time before the appointed hour, so I smoked and kept listening to Dylan. *Like A Rolling Stone.* I began to hum along.

We were all getting old. That much was as plain as the falling rain.

34

Skulls

I SEE birds flying. They strafe the white frozen slope of the Western Hill and vanish from my field of vision. I warm my feet and hands at the stove and drink the hot tea the Colonel has brought me.

"Are you going to read dreams tonight? The snow will be deep. It will be dangerous walking on the Hill. Perhaps you might rest a day," he suggests.

"I cannot lose a day," I tell him.

The Colonel shakes his head, goes out, and returns with a pair of snow boots.

"Here, wear these. At least you not will slip."

I try them on. They fit well, a good sign.

It is time to go. I wrap my scarf around my neck, pull on my gloves, borrow a cap from the Colonel. Then I slip the folded accordion into my pocket. I refuse to be without it.

"Take care," bids the old officer.

As I had envisioned, the hole is filling with drifts of snow. Gone are the old men; gone too are their tools. If the snow continues like this, the hole will be brimming by tomorrow morning. I watch the bold white gusts, then begin down the Hill.

Snow is falling thick and fierce. It is difficult to see more than a few yards ahead. I remove my glasses and pull my scarf to beneath my eyes. I hear birds crying overhead, above the squeak and crack of these boots. What do birds feel about snow? And the beasts, what do they think about this blizzard?

I arrive at the Library a full hour early and find her waiting for the stove to heat the room. She brushes the snow from my coat and dislodges the snow caked between the spikes of the boots.

Although I was here only yesterday, I am overcome with feelings of nostalgia at the yellow light through the frosted glass, the warm intimacy of the stove, the smell of coffee steaming out of the pot.

"Would you care to eat now? Or perhaps a little later?"

"I don't want to eat. I'm not hungry," I say.

"Would you like coffee?"

"Yes, please."

I pull off my gloves and hang them on the stove to dry. Then I thaw my fingers in front of the fire, while she pours two cups of coffee. She hands me a cup, then she sits down at the table to drink.

"Bad snow outside. I could hardly before me," I say.

"Yes. It will keep falling for the next few days. Until those clouds dead in the sky drop all their snow."

I drink half my coffee, then without a word, take a seat opposite her. Looking at her, I feel myself overcome with sadness again.

"By the time it stops, there will be more snow on the ground than you have probably ever seen," she says.

"I may not be able to see it."

She raises her eyes from her cup to look at me.

"What do you mean? Anyone can see snow."

"I will not be dreamreading today. Let's just talk, the two of us," I say. "There are many things I want to tell you and many things I want you to tell me. Is that all right?"

She folds her hands on the table and looks at me blankly.

"My shadow is dying," I begin. "He cannot last out the winter. It's only a matter of time. If my shadow dies, I lose my mind forever. That is why I must decide many things now. Things about myself, things that concern you. There is little time left to think about these things, but even if I could think as long as I liked, I'm sure I would reach the same conclusion. That is, I must leave here."

I take a sip of coffee and assure myself that my conclusion is not wrong. To be sure, either way I will be losing a part of me.

"I will leave the Town tomorrow," I speak again. "Exactly how and from where I don't know. My shadow will tell me. He and I will leave together and go back to our world. I will drag my shadow after me as I once did. I will worry and suffer, grow old and die. I doubt you can understand, but I belong in that world, where I will be led around, even led astray, by my own mind."

She stares at me. No, she stares into the space I occupy.

"Do you not like the Town?"

"In the beginning, you said that if it was quiet I wanted, I would like it here. Yes, I am taken with the peace and tranquillity of the Town. I also know that if I stay on at the expense of my mind, that peace and tranquillity will become total. Very likely, I will regret leaving this Town for the rest of my life. Yet I cannot stay. My mind cannot forgive my gain at the sacrifice of my shadow and the beasts. Even as my mind dwindles this very instant, I cannot lie to it. That is totally beside the point. What I lose would be eternal. Do you understand?"

She looks down at her hands for a long time. The steam has long since vanished from her coffee cup; not a thing in the room moves.

"Will you never come back here?"

I shake my head. "Once I leave here, I can never come back. That is clear. And should I return, the Gate would never open for me."

"And does that not matter to you?"

"Losing you is most difficult for me, but the nature of my love for you is what matters. If it distorts into half-truth, then perhaps it is better not to love you. I must keep my mind but lose you."

The room is silent again, except for the crackling of the coals. Hanging by the stove are my coat and scarf and hat and gloves—items given to me here by the Town.

"I considered helping my shadow escape alone, then staying behind myself," I say. "Yet I would be driven into the Woods, sure never to see you again either. You cannot live in the Woods. Only those whose shadows have not been completely exterminated, who still bear traces of mind in them, can live in the Woods. I still have a mind. Not you. And for that reason, you can never need me."

She shakes her head.

"No, I do not have this thing you call mind. Mother had mind, but I do not. And because Mother kept her mind, she was driven into the Woods. I never told you, but I remember very well when Mother was sent to the Woods. I still think about her from time to time. That if I had mind, too, I could be with Mother. And that if I had mind, I could want you as you want me."

"Even if it meant exile in the Woods? You would have a mind at such cost?"

She meditates on her hands folded on the table before her, then unclasps them.

"I remember Mother told me that if one has mind, nothing is ever lost, regardless where one goes. Is that true?"

"I don't know," I tell her. "But true or not, that is what your mother believed. The question is whether you believe it."

"I think I can," she says, gazing into my eyes.

"You can?" I ask, startled. "You think you can believe that?"

"Probably," she says.

"No. Think it over carefully. This is very important," I say, "because to believe something, whatever it might be, is the doing of the mind. Do you follow? When you say you believe, you allow the possibility of disappointment. And from disappointment or betrayal, there may come despair. Such is the way of the mind. Do you know these things?"

She shakes her head. "I cannot tell. I was merely thinking about Mother. Nothing more than that. I think that I can believe."

"Something in you must still be in touch with your mind! Although it is locked tightly in and cannot get out."

"When you say I still have mind in me, do you mean that they did not really kill my shadow, the same as with Mother?"

"No, your shadow is dead and buried in the Apple Grove. But perhaps there are echoes of mind inside the memories of your mother, if you could only retrace them."

All is hushed, as if the swirling snow outside has swallowed all sound from the room, as the Wall holds its breath, straining to listen in.

"Let's talk about old dreams," I change the subject. "Is it true that the beasts absorb what mind we give off each day? That this becomes old dreams?"

"Why yes, of course. When our shadows die, the beasts breathe in mind."

"That means I should be able to read out your mind from the old dreams."

"No, it is impossible. Our minds are not taken in whole.

My mind is scattered, in different pieces among different beasts, all mixed with pieces from others. They cannot be untangled."

She is right. I have been dreamreading day after day and I have yet to understand even a fragment of one. And now, if I am to save my shadow, there are only twenty-one hours left. Twenty-one hours to gather the pieces of her mind. How can it be, here in this timeless Town, I have so little time? I close my eyes and breathe deeply. I must find the thread that pulls my concentration together, yet unravels the fabric.

"We must go to the stacks," I say.

"The stacks?"

"We must think while we look at the skulls. We may discover something."

I take her by the hand, and we step behind the counter to the door to the stacks. She turns on the dim light and the shelves of countless skulls float up through the gloom. Pallid shapes, covered thick with dust, jaws sprung at the same angle, eye sockets glaring vacuously, their silence hangs over the stacks like a ghostly mist. A chill creeps over my flesh again.

"Do you really think you can read out my mind?" she asks me, face to face.

"I think so," I say, wishing to convince myself. "There has to be a way."

"It is like looking for lost drops of rain in a river."

"You're wrong. The mind is not like raindrops. It does not fall from the skies, it does not lose itself among other things. If you believe in me at all, then believe this: I promise you I will find it. Everything depends on this."

"I believe you," she whispers after a moment. "Please find my mind."

35

Nail Clippers, Butter Sauce, Iron Vase

I T was five-twenty-five when I pulled up in front of the library. Still early for our date, so I got out of the car and took a stroll down the misty streets. In a coffee shop I watched a golf match on television, then I went to an entertainment center and played a video game. The object of the game was to wipe out tanks invading from across the river. I was winning at first, but as the game went on, the enemy tanks bred like lemmings, crushing me by sheer number and destroying my base. An on-screen nuclear blast took care of everything, followed by the message GAME OVER—INSERT COIN.

I slipped another hundred-yen coin into the slot. My base reappeared, completely unscathed, accompanied by a flourish of trumpets. Talk about a downhill struggle. I *had* to lose. If I didn't, the game would go on forever. Not to worry. I was soon wiped out again, followed by the same nuclear blast, followed by the same GAME OVER—INSERT COIN.

Next door was a hardware store, with a vast assortment of tools in the window. Wrench-and-screwdriver sets, power tack-guns, and drills, as well as a cased precision tool kit made in West Germany. Next to that was a set of some thirty woodcarving knives and gouges.

I walked in to the store. After the buzzing and booming of the entertainment center, the hardware store seemed as quiet as the interior of an iceberg. Next to the razor sets, I found nail clippers arrayed like entomological specimens. I picked up the most featureless of the lot and took it over to the register.

The thin-haired, middle-aged man at the counter put down the electric eggbeater that he was dismantling and instructed me on the use of the clippers.

"Okay, watch carefully." He showed me the simple three-step procedure and handed the clippers back to me. "Prime item," he confided. "They're made by Henkel, they'll last you a lifetime. Never rust, good blade. Strong enough to clip a dog's claws."

I put out two thousand eight hundred yen for the clippers. They came with a black leather case.

The man immediately returned to his eggbeater disassembly. He had sorted screws of different sizes into clean white trays. They looked so happy.

I returned to the car and listened to the *Brandenburg Concertos* while I waited. I thought about the screws and their happiness. Maybe they were glad to be free of the eggbeater, to be independent screws, to luxuriate on white trays. It did feel good to see them happy.

On toward closing time, people started filing out of the library. Mostly high school students who were toting plastic sports bags like mine, but there were older people, too. At six o'clock, a bell sounded. And for the first time since I

could remember, I was ravenous. I'd had very little to eat
since the fun and games began. I pushed back the reclining
seat and looked up at the low car ceiling as food of all
kinds floated through my head. The screws on white trays
became screws in white sauce alongside a few sprigs of
watercress.

Fifteen minutes later, my reference desk girlfriend
emerged through the front door. She was wearing a dark
blue velvet dress with a white lace collar and double-
stranded silver necklace.

"Is this your car?" she asked.

"Nope, a rental. What do you think?"

"Okay, I guess. Though it doesn't really seem to be your
style."

"I wouldn't know. It was what they had at the car
rental."

She inspected the car outside and in, opened the ashtray
and checked the glove compartment.

Then she asked, "Whose *Brandenburg* is this?"

"Trevor Pinnock."

"Are you a Pinnock fan?"

"Not especially," I said. "The tape just caught my eye.
It's not bad."

"Richter's is my favorite, but did you know Pablo Casals
also has a version?""

"Casals?"

"It's not what you'd expect the *Brandenburg* to sound
like. It's very interesting."

"I'll look for it," I said. "Where shall we eat?"

"How about Italian?"

"Great."

"I know a place that's not too far and is really good."

"Let's go. I'm so hungry I could eat screws."

"I'm hungry too," she said, ignoring the screws. "Hmm,
nice shirt."

"Thanks."

The restaurant was a fifteen-minute drive from the

library, dodging cyclists and pedestrians on winding residential streets. Midway up a hill, amid homes with tall pines and Himalayan cedars and high walls, appeared an Italian restaurant. A white woodframe Western-style house that now functioned as a trattoria. The sign was so small you could easily have missed the place if you didn't know it was there.

The restaurant was tiny—three tables and four counter seats. We were shown to the table furthest back, where a side window gave us a view of plum trees.

"Shall we have some wine?" she said.

"Why don't you choose," I said. While she discussed the selection with the waiter, I gazed out at the plum tree. A plum tree growing at an Italian restaurant seemed somehow incongruous. But perhaps not. Maybe they had plum trees in Italy. Hell, they had otters in France.

Having settled on an *aperitivo*, we opened our menus. We took our time making our selections. First, for *antipasti*, we chose *insalata di gamberetti alle fragole, ostriche al vivo, mortadella di fegato, sepie al nero, melanzane alla parmigiana*, and *wakasagi marinata*. For *primi*, she decided on a *spaghetti al pesto genovese*, and I decided on a *tagliatelle alla casa*.

"How about splitting an extra *maccheroni al sugo di pesce?*" she suggested.

"Sounds good to me," I said.

"What is the fish of the day?" she turned to ask the waiter.

"Today we have fresh *branzino*—that's *suzuki*," pronounced the waiter, "which we steam in *cartoccio* and sprinkle with almonds."

"I'll have that," she said.

"Me, too," I said. "And for *contorni, spinaci* and *risotto al funghi.*"

"*Verdure cotte* and *risotto al pomodoro* for me."

"I think you will find our *risotti* quite filling," the waiter spoke up, a bit uneasily.

"Maybe so, but I've barely eaten in days, and she's got gastric dilation," I explained.

"It's a regular black hole," she confirmed.

"Very well," said the waiter.

"For dessert, I'll have *granita di uva, crema fredda, sufflé al limone,* and *espresso,*" she added before he could get away.

"Why not—me too," I said.

After the waiter had at last finished writing down our order, she smiled at me.

"You didn't have to order so much just to keep pace with me, you know."

"No, I really am famished," I said. "It's been ages since I've been this hungry."

"Great," she said. "I never trust people with no appetite. It's like they're always holding something back on you, don't you think?"

"I wouldn't know," I said. I really wouldn't.

"'I wouldn't know' seems to be a pet expression with you," she observed.

"Maybe so."

"And 'maybe so' is another."

I didn't know what to say.

"Why are all your thoughts so uncertain?"

I wouldn't know, but maybe so, I repeated over and over in my head when the waiter arrived and with the air of the court chiropractor come to treat the crown prince's slipped disc, reverently uncorked the wine and poured it into our glasses.

"In *L' Etranger,* the protagonist had a habit of saying 'It's not my fault'. Or so I seem to recall. Umm—what was his name now?"

"Meursault," I said.

"That's right, Meursault," she repeated. "I read it in high school. But you know, today's high school kids don't read anything of the kind. We did a survey at the library not so long ago. What authors do you read?"

"Turgenev."

"Turgenev wasn't so great. He was an anachronist."

"Maybe so," I said, "but I still like him. Flaubert and Thomas Hardy, too."

"You don't read anything new?"

"Sometimes I read Somerset Maugham."

"There aren't many people who'd consider Somerset Maugham new," she said, tipping back her glass. "The same as they don't put Benny Goodman in jukeboxes these days either."

"I love Maugham. I've read *The Razor's Edge* three times. Maybe it's not a spectacular novel, but it's very readable. Better that than the other way around."

"Maybe so," she laughed. "That orange shirt suits you."

"Thank you very much," I said. "You look beautiful."

"Thank *you*," she said.

"I went home during lunch and changed. I don't live far from work so it was very convenient."

Several of the appetizers arrived, and for the next few minutes we ate in silence. The flavors were light, delicate, subtle. The shrimp were consummately fresh, the oysters kissed by the sea.

"So did you finish with the unicorn business?" she asked, as she let an oyster roll into her mouth.

"More or less," I said, wiping squid ink from my lips.

"And where were these unicorns?"

"In here," I said, tapping my temple. "The unicorns were all in my head."

"Symbolically speaking, you mean?"

"No, not at all. Do I seem like the symbolic type? They really were living in my consciousness. Someone found them out for me."

"Well, I'm glad they were found. Sounds very interesting. Tell me more."

"It's not so very interesting," I said, passing her the eggplant. She, in return, passed me the smelt.

"Still, I'd like to know more. Really I would."

"Well, it's like this. Deep in your consciousness there's this core that is imperceptible to yourself. In my case, the core is a town. A town with a river flowing through it and a high brick wall surrounding it. None of the people in the town can leave. Only unicorns can go in and out. The unicorns absorb the egos of the townpeople like blotter paper and carry them outside the wall. So the people in the town have no ego, no self. I live in the town—or so the story goes. I don't know any more than that, since I haven't actually seen any of this with my own eyes."

"Well, it's certainly original, I'll say that."

River? The old man hadn't said anything about a river.

"But it's none of my creation, at least not that I'm aware of," I said.

"It's still yours, isn't it? Nobody else made it."

"Well, I guess."

"The smelt's not bad, eh?"

"Not bad."

"All this does resemble a little that Russian unicorn story I read you, don't you think?" she said, slicing through the eggplant. "The Ukranian unicorns were supposed to have lived in a completely isolated community."

"It's similar in that way, yes."

"Maybe there's some link . . ."

"Just a second," I interrupted and reached into my blazer pocket. "I have a present for you."

I handed her the small black leather case.

"What is it?" she asked, turning over the curious metal object she removed from the case.

"I'll show you. Watch carefully."

She watched.

"Nail clippers?"

"Right! Folds back in reverse order. Like this."

"Very interesting," she said. "Tell me, though, do you often give nail clippers to women?"

"No, you're the first. Just now while I was waiting, I went into a hardware store and felt like buying something.

The woodcarving sets were too big."

"Thank you. I'll keep them in my bag and think of you every time I use them."

The appetizers were cleared away and presently the entrees were served. My hunger had hardly subsided. Six plates of appetizers hadn't even put a dent in it. I shovelled a considerable volume of *tagliatelle* into my mouth in a relatively short period of time, then devoured half the macaroni. Having put that much under my belt, I could swear I saw faint lights looming up through darkness.

After the pasta, we sipped wine until the bass came.

"By the way," she said, "about your apartment, was the destruction done by some special machine? Or was it a demolition team?"

"Maybe you could call him a machine, but it was the work of one person," I said.

"Must have had a *lot* of determination."

"You wouldn't believe."

"A friend of yours?"

"A total stranger."

"It wouldn't have had anything to do with that unicorn business?" she asked.

"It did. But nobody'd bothered to ask me what I thought from the very beginning."

"And does that have something to do with your going away tomorrow?"

"Mm . . . yeah."

"You must have gotten yourself caught in a terrible mess."

"It's so complicated, I myself don't know what's what. Well, in my case, the simplest explanation is that I'm up to here in information warfare."

The waiter appeared suddenly with our fish and rice.

"I can't follow all this," she said, flaking her *suzuki* with the edge of her fork. "Our library is full of books and everyone just comes to read. Information is free to everyone and nobody fights over it."

"I wish I'd worked in a library myself," I said.

"The fish was exquisite," she purred, after we'd finished off our entrees. "Especially the sauce."

"Good butter sauce is an art," I said. "It takes time. You stir finely minced shallots into melted butter, then heat it over a very low flame. No short cuts."

"Ah yes, you like to cook, don't you?"

"Well, I used to. You need real dedication. Fresh ingredients, a discerning palate, an eye for presentation. It's not a modern art. Good cooking has hardly evolved since the nineteenth century."

"The lemon soufflé here is wonderful," she said, as the desserts arrived. "You still have room?"

The grape ice was light, the soufflé tart, the expresso rich and heady. Once we'd finished, the chef came out to greet us.

"Magnificent meal," we told him.

"It is a joy to cook for guests who love to eat," said the chef. "Even in Italia, my family does not eat this much."

"Why, thank you." We took it as a compliment.

The chef returned to the kitchen and we ordered another *espresso* each.

"You're the first person I've met who could match my appetite," she said.

"I can still eat," I said.

"I have some frozen pizza at home, and a bottle of Chivas."

"Let's do it."

Her place was indeed near the library. A small prefab affair, but it had a real entryway and a yard, if only big enough for one person to lie down. Doubtless it got no sun, but there was an azalea bush over to one corner. There was even a second story.

"It's really too much room for one person," she explained. "We bought the house because my husband and I were planning to have kids. I paid back the loan with his life insurance."

She took the pizza out of the freezer and popped it in the oven, then brought the Chivas Regal out to the living room table. While she opened a bottle of wine for herself, I selected a few tapes—Jackie McLean and Miles Davis and Wynton Kelly—and pushed the PLAY button on the cassette deck. We settled back to *Bags' Groove,* followed by *Surrey with a Fringe on Top,* and drinks until the pizza was done.

"You like old jazz?" she asked.

"When I was in high school, I listened to jazz all the time in coffee shops."

"And nowadays?"

"A bit of everything. I hear what people play me."

"But you don't listen of your own choosing?"

"Don't need to."

"My husband was something of a jazz buff. You probably had similar tastes. He was beaten to death in a bus, with an iron vase."

"He what?"

"Some punk was using hair spray in a bus, and when my husband asked him to quit, the guy brained him with an iron vase."

I didn't know what to say. "What was the kid doing carrying an iron vase?"

"Who knows?" she answered. "It was a pitiful way to die."

The oven timer rang: the pizza was done. Sitting side by side on the sofa, we each ate half.

"Want to see a unicorn skull?" I asked.

"A real one?" she said. "You honestly have one?"

"A replica. Not the real thing."

I went out to the car. It was a tranquil early October night. Here and there a patch of sky cut through the cloud cover to reveal a near-full moon. Fair weather tomorrow.

I returned with the Nike sports bag and produced the towel-wrapped skull. She set down her wine glass and examined the skull up close.

"Extremely well made, I'll say that much."

"It was made by a skull specialist," I explained, taking a sip of whiskey.

"It's as good as real."

I stopped the cassette deck, took the fire tongs out of the bag, and tapped the skull. The skull gave off the same parched *mo-oan*.

"What's that?"

"Each skull has a unique resonance. And a skull expert can read all sorts of things from these sounds."

"Incredible!" she exclaimed. She then tried striking the skull with the tongs herself. "I can't believe this is a replica."

She set the skull on the table and reclaimed her wine glass. We scooted together, raised our glasses, and gazed at the skull.

"Put on more music," she smiled suggestively.

I chose another couple of cassettes and returned to the sofa.

"Is here okay? Or shall we go upstairs?"

"Here's perfect," I said.

Pat Boone sang softly, *I'll Be Home*. Time seemed to flow in the wrong direction, which was fine by me. Time could go whichever way it pleased.

She drew the lace curtain on the window to the yard and turned out the lights. We stripped by moonlight. She removed her necklace, removed her bracelet-watch, took off her velvet dress. I undid my watch and threw it over the back of the sofa. Then I doffed my blazer, loosened my necktie, and bottomed-up the last of my whiskey.

She rolled down her panty hose as a bluesy Ray Charles came on with *Georgia on My Mind*. I closed my eyes, put both feet up on the table and swizzled the minutes around in my head like the ice in a drink. Everything, everything, seemed once-upon-a-time. The clothes on the floor, the music, the conversation. Round and round it goes, and where it stops everyone knows. Like a dead heat on the merry-go-round. No one pulls ahead, no one gets left behind. You always get to the same spot.

"It seems so long ago," I said, my eyes still shut.

"Of course, silly," she said mysteriously, taking the glass from my hand and undoing the buttons of my shirt. Slowly, deliberately, as if stringing green beans.

"How'd you know?"

"I just know," she said. She put her lips to my bare chest. Her long hair swept over my stomach.

Eyes closed, I gave my body over to sensation. I thought about the *suzuki,* I thought about the nail clippers, I thought about the snail on the cleaners' front stoop. I opened my eyes and drew her to me, reaching around behind to undo the hook of her brassiere. There was no hook.

"Up front," she prompted.

Things do evolve after all.

We made love three times. We took a shower, then snuggled together on the sofa under a blanket while Bing Crosby crooned away. Euphoria. My erections had been perfect as the pyramids at Giza. Her hair smelled fresh and wonderful. The sofa cushions were nice and firm. Not bad, from back in the days when sofas were sofas.

I sang along with Bing:

> *Oh Danny boy, the pipes, the pipes are calling*
> *From glen to glen, and down the mountain side.*
> *The summer's gone, and all the roses falling—*
> *It's you, it's you must go, and I must bide.*
> *But come ye back when summer's in the meadow,*
> *And when the valley's hushed and white with snow.*
> *It's I'll be here in sunshine or in shadow,*
> *Oh Danny boy, oh Danny Boy, I'll miss you so!*

"A favorite of yours?" she asked.

"Yeah, I like it well enough," I said. "I won a dozen pencils in a school harmonica contest playing this tune."

She laughed. "Life's funny like that."

"A laugh a minute."

She put on Danny Boy so I could sing it again.

> *But if you fall as all the flowers're dying,*
> *And you are dead, as dead you well may be,*
> *I'll come and find the place where you are lying,*
> *And kneel and say an ave there for thee.*
> *But come ye back when summer's in—*

The second time through made me terribly sad.

"Send me letters from wherever it is you're going," she said, touching me.

"I will," I promised. "If it's the sort of place I can mail letters from."

She poured wine into both our glasses.

"What time is it?" I asked.

"Night time," she answered.

36

Accordion

"Do you truly feel you can read out my mind?" she asks.

"Yes. Your mind has been here all along, but I have not known where to seek it. And yet the way must have already been shown to me."

We sit on the floor of the stacks, backs against the wall, and look up at the rows of skulls that tell us nothing.

"Perhaps if you tried to think back. One thing at a time," she suggests.

The floor is cold. I close my eyes, and my ears resound with the silence of the skulls.

"This morning, the old men were digging a hole outside the house. A very big hole. The sound of their shovels woke me. It was as if they were digging in my head. Then the snow came and filled it."

"And before that?"

"You and I went to the Woods, to the Power Station. We met the Caretaker. He showed me the works. The wind made an amazing noise."

"Yes, I remember."

"Then I received an accordion from him. A small folding accordion, old, but still usable."

She sits, thinking and rethinking. The temperature in the room is falling, minute by minute.

"Do you have your accordion?" she asks.

"The accordion?" I question.

"Yes, it may be the key. The accordion is connected to song, song is connected to my mother, my mother is connected to my mind. Could that be right?"

"It does follow," I say, "though one important link is missing from the chain. I cannot recall a single song."

"It need not be a song."

I retrieve the accordion from the pocket of my coat and sit beside her again, instrument in hand. I slip my hands into the straps on either end of the bellows and press out several chords.

"Beautiful!" she exclaims. "Are the sounds like wind?"

"They *are* wind," I say. "I create wind that makes sounds, then put them together."

She closes her eyes and opens her ears to the harmonies.

I produce all the chords I have practiced. I move the fingers of my right hand along the buttons in order, making single notes. No melody comes, but it is enough to bring the wind in the sounds to her. I have only to give myself to the wind as the birds do.

No, I cannot relinquish my mind.

At times my mind grows heavy and dark; at other times it soars high and sees forever. By the sound of this tiny accordion, my mind is transported great distances.

I call up different images of the Town behind closed eyes. Here are the willows on the sandbar, the Watchtower by the Wall in the west, the small tilled plot behind the Power Station. The old men sitting in the patch of sun in front of my quarters, the beasts crouching in the pooled waters of the River, summer grasses bowing in the breeze on the stone steps of the canal. I remember visiting the Pool in the south with the Librarian. I view the Abandoned Barracks near the north Wall, the ruins of the house and well near the Wall in the Woods.

I think of all the people I have met here. The Colonel next door, the old men of the Official Residences, the Caretaker of the Power Station, the Gatekeeper—each now in his own room, no doubt, listening to the blizzard outside.

Each place and person I shall lose forever; each face and feature I shall remember the rest of my life. If this world is wrong, if its inhabitants have no mind, whose fault is that? I feel almost a . . . love . . . toward the Town. I cannot stay in this place, yet I do not want to lose it.

Presently, I sense within me the slightest touch. The harmony of one chord lingers in my mind. It fuses, divides, searches—but for what? I open my eyes, position the fingers of my right hand on the buttons, and play out a series of permutations.

After a time, I am able, as if by will, to locate the first four notes. They drift down from inward skies, softly, as early morning sunlight. They find *me;* these are the notes I have been seeking.

I hold down the chord key and press the individual notes over and over again. The four notes seem to desire further notes, another chord. I strain to hear the chord that follows. The first four notes lead me to the next five, then to another chord and three more notes.

It is a melody. Not a complete song, but the first phrase of one. I play the three chords and twelve notes, also, over and over again. It is a song, I realize, that I know.

Danny Boy.

The title brings back the song: chords, notes, harmonies now flow naturally from my fingertips. I play the melody again.

When have I last heard a song? My body has craved

music. I have been so long without music, I have not even known my own hunger. The resonance permeates; the strain eases within me. Music brings a warm glow to my vision, thawing mind and muscle from their endless wintering.

The whole Town lives and breathes in the music I play. The streets shift their weight with my every move. The Wall stretches and flexes as if my own flesh and skin. I repeat the song several times, then set the accordion down on the floor, lean back, and close my eyes. Everything here is a part of me—the Wall and Gate and Woods and River and Pool. It is all my self.

Long after I set down the instrument, she clings to me with both hands, eyes closed. Tears run down her cheeks. I put my arm around her shoulder and touch my lips to her eyelids. The tears give her a moist, gentle heat.

A blush of light comes over her cheeks, making her tears gleam. Clear as starlight, yet a light not from the heavens. It is the room that is aglow.

I turn out the ceiling lamp, and only then do I see the source of the glow. It is the skulls. An ancient fire that has lain dormant in them is now awakening. The phosphorescence yields pure to the eye; it soothes with memories that warm and fill my heart. I can feel my vision healing. Nothing can harm these eyes any more.

It is a wondrous sight. Quietude itself. Countless flecks of light fill the space. I pick up a skull and run my fingers over its surface. Here, I sense a glimmer, a remembrance of mind, an indication of her mind. Tiny sparks drift up into my fingertips, touching me, each particle bearing the faintest light, the merest warmth.

"There is your mind," I say.

She stares at me, eyes tearful.

"Your mind has not been lost nor scattered to the winds. It's here, and no one can take it away. To read it out, I must bring all these together. "

I kiss her again on the eyelids.

"I want you to leave me by myself," I say. "It will take

me until morning to read it all out. I cannot rest until then."

She surveys the rows of softly glowing skulls before exiting the stacks. The door closes behind her. The flecks of light dance upon the skulls. Some are old dreams that are hers, some are old dreams of my own.

My search has been a long one. It has taken me to every corner of this walled Town, but at last I have found the mind we have lost.

37

Lights, Introspection, Cleanliness

How long I slept, I don't know. Someone was rocking my shoulders. I smelled the sofa. I didn't want to be awakened. Sleep was too lovely.

Nonetheless, at the same time, something in me demanded to be roused, insisted that this was no time to sleep. A hard metal object was tapping.

"Wake up! Wake up!"

I sat up.

I was wearing an orange bathrobe. She was leaning over me in a white men's T-shirt and tiny white panties, shaking me by the shoulder. Her slender body seemed fragile, insecure, childlike, with no sign of last night's Italian excesses. Outside was not yet dawn.

"The table! Look at the table!" she exclaimed.

A small Christmas tree-like object sat on the table. But it was not a Christmas tree: it was too small and this was the beginning of October. I strained my eyes toward this object. It was the skull, exactly where I'd placed it, or she'd placed it. In either case, the glowing object was my unicorn skull.

Lights were playing over the skull. Perishing points of microscopic brilliance. Like a glimmering sky, soft and white. Hazy, as if each glowing dot were layered in a fluid electric film, which made the lights seem to hover above the surface. We sat and watched the minuscule constellations drift and whirl. She held onto my arm as I gripped my bathrobe collar. The night was deep and still.

"Is this your idea of a joke?" she said.

I shook my head. I'd never seen the skull glow before. This was no phosphorescent lichen, no human doing. No manmade energy source could produce such soft, tranquil light.

I gently disengaged her from my arm, reached out for the skull, and brought it over to my lap.

"Aren't you afraid?" she now asked under her breath.

"No." For some reason, I wasn't.

Holding my hands over the skull, I sensed the slightest ember of heat, as my fingers were enveloped in that pale membrane of light. I closed my eyes, letting the warmth penetrate my fingers, and images drifted into view like clouds on a distant horizon.

"This can't be a replica," she said. "It has to be the real thing."

The object was emitting light into my hands. It seemed somehow purposeful, to bear meaning. An attempt to convey a signal, to offer a touchstone between the world I would enter and the world I was leaving.

Opening my eyes, I looked at the twinkling nebula at my fingers. The glow was without menace or ill will. It sufficed that I take the skull up in my hands and trace the subtle veins of light with my fingertips. There was nothing to fear.

I returned the skull to the table and brought my fingers to her cheek.

"Your hands are warm," she said.

"The light is warm."

I guided her hands over the skull. She shut her eyes. A field of white light gently enveloped her fingers as well.

"I do feel something," she said. "I don't know what, but it doesn't make sense."

"I can't explain either," I said.

I stooped to pick up my watch from the floor. Four-sixteen. Another hour until dawn.

I went to the telephone and dialed my own number. It'd been a long time since I'd called home, so I had to struggle to remember the number. I let it ring fifteen times; no answer. I hung up, dialed again, and let it ring another fifteen times. Nobody.

Had the chubby girl gone back underground to get her grandfather? Or had the Semiotecs or the boys from the System paid her a courtesy call? I wasn't worried. I was sure she'd come through fine. The girl was amazing. She was half my age, and she could handle things ten times better than me. I set down the receiver with a tinge of sadness, knowing I'd never see her again. I was watching the chandeliers get carried out of a once-grand hotel, now bankrupt. One by one the windows are sealed, the curtains taken down.

I returned to where she sat on the sofa.

"Is the skull glowing in response to you?" she asked.

"It does seem so, doesn't it."

The unwaking world was as hushed as a deep forest. I looked down and lost myself in my shirt and pants and tie, which lay scattered on the carpet among her dress and slip and stockings. They were the shed skin of a life of thirty-five years, its culmination.

"What is it?" she asked.

"These clothes. Up until a little while ago, they were a part of me. But no longer. They're different clothes belonging to a different person. I don't recognize them as my own."

"It's sex that does it," she smiled. "After sex, you get introspective."

"No, that's not it," I said, picking up my empty glass. "I'm not withdrawing into self-reflection. I feel as if I'm tuning in on details, on the minute particulars of the world. Snails and the sound of the rain and hardware store displays, things like that."

"Should I straighten up?"

"No, leave the clothes as they are. They seem quite natural."

I reached for my pack of cigarettes and lit up with matches from the beer hall. Then I looked at our clothes again. Shirt sleeves stretched across stockings, velvet dress folded over at the waist, sweet nothing of a slip dropped like a limp flag. Necklace and watch tossed up on the couch, black shoulder bag on its side on a corner table. Even cast aside, clothes know a permanence that eludes their wearers.

"How'd you decide to become a librarian?" I asked.

"I've always liked libraries," she said. "They're quiet and full of books and full of knowledge. I knew I didn't want to work in a bank or a trading company, and I would have hated being a teacher. So the library it was."

I blew cigarette smoke up at the ceiling and watched it drift away.

"You want to know about me?" she asked. "Where I was born, what I was like as a girl, where I went to school, when I lost my virginity, what's my favorite color—all that?"

"No," I said. "You're fine as you are. I'll learn more as it comes."

"I'd like to get to know more about you though, little by little."

"I was born by the sea," I said. "I'd go to the beach the morning after a typhoon and find all sorts of things that the waves had tossed up. There'd be bottles and wooden *geta* and hats and cases for glasses, tables and chairs, things from nowhere near the water. I liked combing through the stuff, so I was always waiting for the next typhoon."

I put out my cigarette.

"The strange thing is, everything washed up from the sea was purified. Useless junk, but absolutely clean. There wasn't a dirty thing. The sea is special in that way. When I look back over my life so far, I see all that junk on the beach. It's how my life has always been. Gathering up the junk, sorting through it, and then casting it off somewhere else. All for no purpose, leaving it to wash away again."

"This was in your home town?"

"This is all my life. I merely go from one beach to another. Sure I remember the things that happen in between, but that's all. I never tie them together. They're so many things, clean but useless."

She touched my shoulder, then went to the kitchen. She returned with wine for her and a beer for me.

"I like the moments of darkness before dawn," she said. "Probably because it's a clean slate. Clean and unused."

She snuggled up close next to me on the sofa, pulling the blanket up to her breasts, then took a sip of wine. I poured myself some beer and looked, glass in hand, at the skull on the table, its pale fires reflecting in the bottle. She rested her head on my shoulder.

"I watched you coming back from the kitchen just now," I said.

"Did I pass?"

"You've got great legs."

"You like them?"

"A whole lot."

She put her glass down on the table and kissed me below the ear.

"Did I ever tell you?" she said. "I love compliments."

As dawn drew near, sunlight gradually diminished the cranial foxfires, returning the skull to its original, undistinguished bone-matter state. We made love on the sofa again, her warm breath moist on my shoulder, her breasts small and soft. Then, when it was over, she folded her body into mine and went to sleep.

The sun shone brightly on the roofs of the neighboring houses, birds came and went. I could hear the sounds of TV News, hear someone starting a car. How many hours had I slept? I eased her head off my shoulder and went to the kitchen. I shut the door and turned the radio on low. An FM station on low, Roger Williams playing *Autumn Leaves*, that time of year.

Her kitchen resembled mine. The appliances, the layout, the utensils, the wear, everything was normal. There were knives for various purposes, but their sharpening left something to be desired. Very few women can sharpen knives properly.

I don't know why I was poking about in another person's kitchen. I didn't mean to be nosy, but everything seemed meaningful. *Autumn in New York,* by the Frank Chacksfield Orchestra, was next on the FM. I moved on to the shelves of pots and pans and spice bottles. The kitchen was a world unto itself.

Orchestral stylings over, the FM hostess floated her silken voice over the airwaves: "Yes, it's time to get out the sweaters." I could almost smell them. Images out of an Updike novel. Woody Herman swinging into *Early Autumn.* Seven-twenty-five by the clock-timer.

Twenty-five minutes after seven A.M., Monday, the third of October.

The sky had broken, clear and deep, carved out with a

sharp knife. Not a bad day for taking leave of this life.

I put some water on to boil, took tomatoes from the refrigerator and blanched them to remove the skin. I chopped up a few vegetables and garlic, added the tomatoes, then stirred in some sausage to simmer. While that cooked down, I slivered some cabbage and peppers for a salad, dripped coffee. I sprinkled water on to a length of French bread, wrapped it in foil, and slid it into the toaster-oven. Once the meal was ready, I cleared away the empty bottles and glasses from the living room and woke her up.

"Mmm. Something smells good," she said.

"Can I get dressed now?" I asked. I have this thing about not getting dressed before the woman does. It jinxes every-thing if I do. Maybe it's just a civil gesture."

"How polite of you!" she said, stripping off her T-shirt. The new morning light breathed across her breasts and stomach, highlighting the fine hairs on her skin. She paused to look herself over.

"Not bad." Her humble evaluation.

"Not bad at all," I said. "Let's eat."

She pulled on a yellow sweatshirt and a pair of faded jeans. We sat across from each other at the kitchen table and started our breakfast.

"Compliments to the chef," she said. "It's delish," she said. "How can you cook this well if you live alone? Doesn't it bother you?"

"No, not really. I had five years of marriage, but now I can hardly remember what it was like. It seems as if I'd always lived alone."

"You never thought of remarrying?"

"Would it make any difference?"

She laughed. I looked at the clock. Half past eight.

"What are your plans for the day?" she asked.

"Let's leave here at nine," I said, "and go to a park. I want to sit in the sun. Maybe have a couple of beers. Then around ten-thirty, I'm thinking of going for a drive. I'll take off after that. What about you?"

"I'll come home, do the laundry, clean the house, lie around thinking about sex. That sound okay?"

"I envy you."

While I washed the dishes, she sang in the shower. The dishwashing liquid was one of those ecological vegetable-based soaps that hardly sudsed at all. I wiped off the dishes and set them on the table. Then I borrowed a toothbrush. Did she have anything to shave with?

"In the upper right-hand corner of the cabinet," she said. "His things should still be there."

I located a Schick razor and a can of Gillette Lemon-Lime Foamy with a dry sputter of white around the nozzle. Death leaves cans of shaving cream half-used.

"Find it?" she called out.

"Yep," I said, returning to the kitchen with her husband's effects and a towel. I heated some water and shaved. Afterwards I rinsed the razor, and some of the dead man's stubble washed away with mine.

She was still getting dressed, so I read the morning paper in the living room. There was nothing that would interest me in my last few hours.

She emerged in beige slacks and a brown checked blouse, brushing her hair. I knotted my tie and slipped on my blazer.

"What do you want to do with the unicorn skull?" she asked.

"It's a present for you," I said. "Put it out somewhere, as a conversation piece."

"Think it'll glow again?"

"I'm sure it will," I said. Then I hugged her one more time, to etch her warmth indelibly into my brain.

38

Escape

THE glowing of the skulls grows faint with the light of dawn. Hazy gray, it washes down, as one by one the sparks die away.

Until the very last ember fades, my fingers must race over the skulls, drawing in their glow. How much of the total light will I manage to read this single night? The skulls are many, my time short. I pay no heed to the hour as I ply my attentive touch to skull after skull. Her mind is at my fingertips, moment by moment, in distinct increments of heat. It is not a question of quantity. Not number nor volume nor ratio. There is no reading everything of a mind.

The last skull returned to the shelves, I collapse. I can tell nothing of the weather outside. A subtle gloom drifts noiselessly through the stacks, lulling the skulls into their deep slumber once more. I yet feel a glimmering of their warmth when I put my fingers to my cheeks.

I sit until the calm and cool has quieted my thoughts. Time is advancing with fitful irregularity, yet it is a constant morning that filters in, the shadows unmoving. Fleeting fragments of her mind circulate through my mind, mingling with all that is me, finding their way into my being. How long will it take to render these into coherent form? And then, how long to transmit that to her, to let it take root? I know I must see her mind returned to her.

I leave the stacks to find her sitting alone in the reading room. In the half-light, her silhouette seems somehow faint. It has been a long night for her, too. Without a word, she rises to her feet and sets the coffeepot on the stove. I go to warm myself.

"You are tired," she says.

My body is an inert lump; I can scarcely raise a hand. I have been dreamreading an entire night, and the fatigue now sets in. It is as she told me the first day: no matter how tired the body gets, one must never let the exhaustion enter one's thoughts.

"You should have gone home to rest," I tell her. "You needn't have stayed."

She pours a cup of coffee and brings it to me.

"It was my mind you were reading. How could I leave?"

I nod, grateful, and take a sip of coffee. The old wall clock reads eight-fifteen.

"Shall I prepare breakfast?"

"No thank you," I say.

"You have not eaten since yesterday."

"I feel no hunger. I need sleep. Could you wake me at two-thirty? Until then, would you sit here, please, and keep watch over me? Can I ask you to do that?"

She brings out two blankets and tucks them in around me. As in the past—when was it?—her hair brushes my cheek. I close my eyes and listen to the coals crackling in the stove.

"How long will winter last?" I ask her.

"I do not know," she answers. "No one can say. I feel,

perhaps, it will not last much longer."

I reach out to touch her cheek. She shuts her eyes, she savors the touch.

"Is this warmth from my mind?"

"What do you feel in it?"

"It is like spring," she says.

"It is your spring, you must believe. Your mind will be yours again."

"Yes," she says, placing her hand over my eyes. "Please sleep now."

She wakes me at exactly half past two. I don my coat, scarf, gloves, and hat.

"Guard the accordion," I tell her.

She takes up the accordion from the table as if to weigh it in her hands, then sets it back down.

"It is safe with me," she says.

Outside, the wind is slackening, the snow diminished to small flurries. The blizzard of the previous night has blown over, though the oppressive gray skies hang low still. This is but a temporary lull.

I cross the Old Bridge southward, then the West Bridge northward. I see smoke rising from beyond the Wall. Intermittent white swatches at first, gradually thickening into the dark billowing gray masses that burning corpses make. The Gatekeeper is in the Apple Grove. I hurry toward the Gatehouse. Everything holds its breath, all the sounds of the Town are lost under the snow. The spikes of my snow boots crunch into the newfallen powder with a disproportionately large sound.

The Gatehouse is deserted. The stove is extinguished, but it is still warm. Dirty plates litter the table. The Gatekeeper's pipe is lying there as well. It seems that at any moment he will appear and place a giant hand on my shoulder. The rows of blades, the kettle, his smell, everything undermines my confidence.

I carefully lift the keys from their wall hook and steal out the back door to the Shadow Grounds. There is not a footprint to be seen. A sheet of white extends to the one lone dark vertical of the elm tree in the center. It is too perfect, too inviolate. The snow is graced with waves written by the wind, the elm raises crooked arms in sleeves of white. Nothing moves. The snow has stopped, this whisper in the air but the afterthought of a breeze. Now is the moment I defile this peaceful but brief eternity.

There is no turning back. I take out the keys and try all four in order; none fits. A cold sweat seeps from my armpits. I summon an image of the Gatekeeper opening this iron gate. It was these four keys, there can be no mistake. I remember counting them. One of them must be the right key.

I put the keys into my pocket to warm them by hand; then I try again. This time, the third key goes in all the way and turns with a loud dry clank. The metallic sound echoes across the deserted enclosure, loud enough to alert everyone in the Town. I look nervously around me. There is no sign of anyone. I ease the heavy gate open and squeeze through, quietly closing it behind me.

The snow in the enclosure is soft and deep. My feet advance across the enclosure, past the bench. The branches of the elm look down with menace. From somewhere far off comes the sharp cry of a bird.

The air in the lean-to is even more chill than out. I open the trapdoor and descend the ladder to the cellar.

My shadow sits on his cot waiting for me.

"I thought you'd never come," say his white puffs of breath.

"I promised, did I not?" I say. "We need to get out of here, quick. The smell in here is overpowering."

"I can't climb the ladder," sighs the shadow. "I tried just

now, but couldn't. I seem to be in worse shape than I thought. Ironic, isn't it? Pretending to be weak all this time, I didn't even notice myself actually getting weaker. Last night's frost really got to my bones."

"I'll help you up."

My shadow shakes his head. "It won't do any good. I can't run. My legs will never make the escape. It's the end of me."

"You started this. You can't bow out now," I say. "If I have to carry you on my back, I will get you out of here."

My shadow looks up with sunken eyes. "If you feel that strong, then of course I am with you," says he. "It won't be easy carrying me through the snow, though."

"I never thought this plan would be otherwise."

I pull my exhausted shadow up the ladder, then lend a shoulder to walk him across the enclosure. The dark heights of the Wall look down on our two fleeing figures. The branches of the elm drop their heavy load of snow and spring back.

"My legs are almost dead," says my shadow. "I exercised so they wouldn't wither from my being prone all the time, but the room was so cramped."

I lead my shadow out of the enclosure and lock the gate. If all goes well, the Gatekeeper will not notice we have escaped.

"Where to from here?" I ask.

"The Southern Pool," the shadow says.

"The Southern Pool?"

"Yes. We escape by diving in."

"That's suicide. The undertow is powerful. We'll be sucked under and drowned."

My shadow shakes and coughs. "Maybe. But that's the only possible exit. I've considered everything; you'll have to believe me. I'm staking my life on it. I'll tell you the details along the way. The Gatekeeper's going to be coming back in another hour, and the ox is sure to give chase. We have no time to waste."

There is no one in sight. There are but two sets of footprints—my own approaching the Gatehouse and those of the Gatekeeper leaving. There are also the ruts left by the wheels of the cart. I hoist my shadow onto my back. Although he has lost most of his weight, his burden will not be light. It is a long way to the Western and Southern Hills. I have grown used to living free of a shadow, and I no longer know if I can bear the umbrage.

We head east on the snowbound roads. Besides my own earlier footprints, there are only the wayward tracks of the beasts. Over my shoulder, the thick gray crematory smoke rises beyond the Wall, a malevolent tower whose apex is lost in the clouds. The Gatekeeper is burning many, many carcasses. The blizzard last night has killed scores of beasts. The time it will take to burn them all will grant us distance. I am grateful to the beasts for their tacit conspiracy.

The snow packs into the spikes of my boots. It hinders my every step, causing me to slip. Why did I not look for a sleigh of some kind? Such a conveyance must exist in the the Town. We have already reached the West Bridge, however, and cannot afford to go back. I am sweating from the difficult trek.

"Your footprints give us away," says my shadow, casting a backward glance. I imagine the Gatekeeper on our trail, all muscle and no one to carry, charging over the snow. We must flee as far as we can before he returns to the Gatehouse.

I think of her, who waits for me in the Library. Accordion on the table, coals aglow, coffeepot steaming. I feel her long hair brush my cheek, her fingers resting on my shoulder. I cannot allow my shadow to perish here, cannot allow the Gatekeeper to throw him back into the cellar to die. I must press onward, onward, while the gray smoke still rises beyond the Wall.

We pass many beasts on our journey. They roam in vain search for such meager sustenance as remains under the snow. Their limpid blue eyes follow our struggle. Do they understand what our actions portend?

We start up the Hill. I am out of breath. I myself have been without exercise. My panting forces out white and hot into yet new flurries of snow.

"Do you want to rest?" asks my shadow from over my shoulder."

"Just five minutes, please."

"Of course, it's all right. It's my fault for not being able to walk. I've forced everything on you."

"But it *is* for my own good, too. Is it not?"

"You must never doubt that."

I let my shadow down. I am so overheated, I cannot even feel the cold. But from thigh to toe, my legs are stone.

"And yet," muses my shadow, "if I had said nothing to you and quietly died, you would have been happy. In your own way."

"Maybe so," I say. "But I am not sorry to know. I needed to know."

The shadow scoops up a loose handful of snow and lets it crumble.

"At first, it was only intuition that told me the Town had an exit," he says. "For the very reason that the perfection of the Town must include all possibilities. Therefore, if an exit is our wish, an exit is what we get. Do you follow me?"

"Yes. I came to understand that yesterday. That here there is everything and here there is nothing."

My shadow gives me a firm, knowing look. The flurries are picking up. Another blizzard is moving in.

"If there has to be a way out, it can be found by process of elimination," he continued. "We can count out the Gate, where the Gatekeeper would be sure to catch us. Besides, the Gate is the first place anyone would think to escape from; the Town would not allow an exit so obvious. The Wall is impossible to scale. The East Gate is bricked up, and it turns out there is an iron grating where the River enters. That leaves only the Southern Pool. We will escape where the River escapes."

"How can you be sure about that?"

"I just know. Only the Southern Pool is left unguarded, untouched. There is no fence, no need for a fence. They've surrounded the place with fear."

"When did you realize that?"

"The first time I saw the River. I went to the West Bridge with the Gatekeeper. I looked down at the water. The River was full of life. I could feel this. There is nothing bad about it. I believe that if we give ourselves over to the water, the flow of the River will lead us out. Out of the Town and back to a real world. You must trust me."

"What you say does make sense," I respond. "The River connects with whatever is out there, with our former world. Lately, I don't know why, I am starting to remember things about that world. Little things. The air, the sounds, the light. I am reawakened by songs."

"It's not the best of all worlds," says my shadow. "I make no promises, but it is the world where we belong. There will be good and bad. There will be neither good nor bad. It is where you were born and where you will live and where you will die. And when you die, I too will die. It's the natural course of things."

We look out upon the Town. The Clocktower, the River, the Bridges, the Wall, and smoke. All is drawn under a vast snow-flecked sky, an enormous cascade falling over the End of the World.

"We should be moving," says my shadow. "The way the snow is coming down, the Gatekeeper may have to stop and return early."

I stand up, brushing the snow from the brim of my hat.

rier after all the planes had flown.

"Not a cloud," I said.

"There's one," she said, pointing to a cotton puff above Hibiya Hall.

"Hardly counts," I said.

She shaded her eyes with her hand to take a better look. "Well, I guess not. Probably should throw it back."

We watched the cloudlet for a while. I opened a second can of beer.

"Why'd you get divorced?" she asked.

"Because she never let me sit by the window on trips."

She laughed. "Really, why?"

"Quite simple, actually. Five or six summers ago, she up and left. Never came back."

"And you didn't see her again?"

"Nope," I said, then took a good swig of beer. "No special reason to."

"Marriage was that hard?"

"Married life was great," I said. "But that's never really the question, is it? Two people can sleep in the same bed and still be alone when they close their eyes, if you know what I mean."

"Uh-huh, I believe so."

"As a whole, humanity doesn't lend itself to generalizations. But as I see it, there are two types of people: the comprehensive-vision type and the limited-perspective type. Me, I seem to be the latter. Not that I ever had much problem justifying my limits. A person has to draw lines somewhere."

"But most people who think that way keep pushing their limits, don't they?"

"Not me. There's no reason why everyone has to listen to records in hi-fi. Having the violins on the left and the bass on the right doesn't make the music more profound. It's just a more complex way of stimulating a bored imagination."

"Aren't you being a tad dogmatic?"

39

Popcorn, Lord Jim, Extinction

EN ROUTE to the park, we stopped by a convenience store to buy some beer. I asked her preference, and she said any brand that had a head and tasted like beer.

I had money to spare, but Miller High Life was the only import I could find.

The autumn sky was as clear as if it had been made that very morning. Perfect Duke Ellington weather. Though, of course, Duke Ellington would be right even for New Year's Eve at an Antarctic base. I drove along, whistling to Lawrence Brown's trombone solo on *Do Nothin' Till You Hear from Me*, followed by Johnny Hodges on *Sophisticated Lady*.

Pulling to a stop alongside Hibiya Park, we got out of the car and lay on the grass with our six-pack. The Monday morning park was as deserted as the deck of an aircraft car-

"Exactly what she said."

"Your wife?"

"Yes. 'Clear-headed, but inflexible'. Her exact words. Another beer?"

"Please," she said.

I pulled the ring on a can of Miller and handed it to her.

"But how do you see you?" she asked.

"Ever read *The Brothers Karamazov*?" I asked.

"Once, a long time ago."

"Well, toward the end, Alyosha is speaking to a young student named Kolya Krasotkin. And he says, Kolya, you're going to have a miserable future. But overall, you'll have a happy life."

Two beers down, I hestitated before opening my third.

"When I first read that, I didn't know what Alyosha meant," I said, "How was it possible for a life of misery to be happy overall? But then I understood, that misery could be limited to the future."

"I have no idea what you're talking about."

"Neither do I," I said. "Not yet."

She laughed and stood up, brushing the grass from her slacks. "I'll be going. It's almost time anyway."

I looked at my watch. Ten-twenty-two.

"I'll drive you home," I said.

"That's okay," she said. "I've got some shopping to do. I'll catch the subway back. Better that way, I think."

"I'm going to hang around a bit longer. It's so nice here."

"Thanks for the nail clippers."

"My pleasure."

"Give me a call when you get back, will you?"

"I'll go to the library," I said. "I like to check out people at work."

"Until then," she said.

*　　　　*　　　　*

I watched her walk straight out of the park like Joseph Cotten in *The Third Man*. After she'd vanished into the shade of the trees, I turned my gaze to a smartly dressed woman and her daughter throwing popcorn onto the grass, pigeons flying toward them. The little girl, three or four years old, raised both hands and ran after the birds. Needless to say, she didn't catch any. Pigeons are survivors by their own pigeonness. Only once did the fashionable young mother glance in my direction. It took her no time to decide that she wanted nothing to do with anyone lying around with five empty beer cans on a Monday morning.

I closed my eyes and tried to remember the names of the Karamazov brothers. Mitya, Ivan, and Alyosha—and then there was the bastard Smerdyakov. How many people in Tokyo knew the names of all these guys?

I gazed up at the sky. I was in a tiny boat, on a vast ocean. No wind, no waves, just me floating there. Adrift on the open sea. *Lord Jim*, the shipwreck scene.

The sky was deep and brilliant, a fixed idea beyond human doubt. From my position on the ground, the sky seemed the logical culmination of all existence. The same with the sea. If you look at the sea for days, the sea is all there is. Quoth Joseph Conrad. A tiny boat cut loose from the fiction of the ship. Aimless, inescapable, inevitable.

So much for literature. I drank the last can of beer and smoked a cigarette. I had to think of more practical matters. There was little over an hour left.

I carried the empty cans to the trash. Then I took out my credit cards and lit them with a match. I watched the plastic curl, sputter, and turn black. It was so gratifying to burn my credit cards that I thought of burning my Paul Stuart tie as well. But then I had second thoughts. The well-dressed young mother was staring at me.

I went to the kiosk and bought ten bags of popcorn. I scattered nine on the ground for the pigeons, and sat on a bench to eat the last bag myself. Enough pigeons descended upon the popcorn for a remake of the October Revolution.

"He's gone to Finland. Too many problems if he stayed in Japan. He'd never get any research done. He's going to set up a laboratory in Turku. Says it's nice and quiet there. They even have reindeer."

"And you didn't go with him?"

"I decided to stay here and live in your apartment."

"In my apartment?"

"Yes, that's right. I really like the place. I'll have the door fixed, put in a new refrigerator and video and stuff like that. Lots of broken things here. You wouldn't mind if I changed the sheets and curtains to pink?"

"Be my guest."

"I think I'll subscribe to a newspaper. I'd like to know what's on TV."

"You know, it might be dangerous there. The System boys and Semiotecs might show up."

"They don't scare me. They're only after Grandfather and you. What am I to them? Just now I sent away some gorilla and his little twerp of a trainer. Weird team."

"How'd you manage that?"

"I shot the big guy's ear off. Probably busted his ear-drum."

"Didn't people come running at the sound of a gun?"

"No," she said. "One shot could be a car backfiring. More than one shot would draw attention, but I know my stuff. One shot is all I need."

"Oh."

"By the way, once you lose consciousness, I'm thinking of putting you in deep freeze."

"As you see fit. I sure won't know," I said. "I'm going to head out to Harumi Pier, so you can come and collect me there. I'm driving a white Carina 1800 GT Twin-Cam Turbo. I can't describe the model, but there'll be Bob Dylan on the stereo."

"Bob Dylan?"

"He's like, standing at the window, watching the rain—" I started to tell her, but then dropped it. "A singer with a rough voice."

"With you in deep freeze, who knows? In time, maybe Grandfather will find a way to bring you back. I wouldn't get my expectations up, but it's not outside the realm of possibility."

"With no consciousness, I won't be expecting anything," I pointed out. "But who's going to do the freezing? You?"

"No problem. Deep freezing's my specialty. I've frozen dozens of live dogs and cats. I'll freeze you nice and neat and store you where no one will find you," she said. "And if all goes well and you regain consciousness, will you sleep with me?"

"Sure," I said. "If you still feel like sleeping with me by then."

"Will you really?"

"Using all available technologies, if necessary," I said. "Though I have no idea how many years from now that might be."

"Well, at least I won't be seventeen."

"People age, even in deep freeze."

"Take care," she said.

"You too," said I. "Good I got to talk to you."

"Have I given you hope for returning to this world?"

"No, it's not that. Of course, I'm grateful, but that's not what I meant. I was just glad to be able to talk to you, to hear your voice again."

"We can talk longer."

"No, I don't have much time left."

"Listen," she spoke. "Even if we lose you forever, I'll always remember you, until the day I die. You won't be lost from my mind. Don't forget that."

"I won't," I said. Then I hung up.

At eleven, I went to a park toilet and did my business, then left the park. I started the car and headed out toward the Bay, thinking about the prospect of being deep-frozen. Crossing Ginza, I looked for my librarian friend among the crowds of shoppers. She was nowhere to be seen.

When I got to the waterfront, I parked the car beside a deserted warehouse, smoked a cigarette and put Bob Dylan on auto-repeat. I reclined the seat, kicked both legs up on the steering wheel, breathing calmly. I felt like having a beer, but the beer was gone. The sun sliced through the windshield, sealing me in light. I closed my eyes and felt the warmth on my eyelids. Sunlight traveled a long distance to reach this planet; an infinitesimal portion of that energy was enough to warm my eyelids. I was moved. That something as insignificant as an eyelid had its place in the workings of the universe, that the cosmic order did not overlook this momentary fact. Was I any closer to appreciating Alyosha's insights? Some limited happiness had been granted this limited life.

I wanted to think I gave the Professor and his chubby granddaughter and my librarian friend a little happiness. Could I have given happiness to anyone else? There wasn't much time left, and I doubted anyone would dispute those rights after I was gone, but how about the Police-reggae taxi driver? He'd let us ride in his cab, mud and all. He deserved his share of happiness. He was probably behind the wheel right now, cruising around to his rock cassettes.

Straight ahead was the sea. Freighters, riding high in the water, their cargo unloaded. Gulls everywhere, like white smears. I thought about snails and *suzuki* in butter sauce and shaving cream and *Blowing in the Wind*. The world is full of revelations.

The early autumn sun glinted on the water, an enormous mirror ground to powder and scattered.

Dylan's singing made me think of the girl at the car rental. Why sure, give her some happiness too. I pictured her in her company blazer—green, the color of baseball turf—white blouse, black bow tie. There she was, listening to Dylan, thinking about the rain.

I thought about rain myself. A mist so fine, it almost wasn't rain. Falling, ever fair, ever equal, it gradually covered my consciousness in a filmy, colorless curtain.

Sleep had come.

Now I could reclaim all I'd lost. What's lost never perishes. I closed my eyes and gave myself over to sleep.

Bob Dylan was singing *A Hard Rain's A-Gonna Fall*, over and over.

40

Birds

SNOW is falling heavily by the time we reach our destination. The sky presses, thick and solid, upon us. The mass of swirling flecks gravitates toward the Southern Pool, an unblinking eye in a world of white. Or does the Pool beckon the flurries down, only to drink them under?

My shadow and I are speechless. How long we survey the scene, I do not know. The disquietive gurgling I heard the last time I was here is muffled under the moist air. The cloud ceiling sags so low, the darkened form of the Wall looms even higher, grim behind the snow. It is a landscape befitting the name the End of the World.

My shoulders grow white as we stand there. By now the snow will have concealed our footprints. My shadow brushes off the snow periodically and focuses on the surface of the water.

"This is the exit. It must be," proclaims my shadow. "Nothing can keep us in this Town any longer. We are free as the birds."

My shadow looks up, then closes his eyes to receive a blessing of snowflakes. And as if heavy shackles have lifted away, I see my shadow regain strength. He walks toward me, however feebly, on his own.

"There's a whole world the other side of this Pool," he says. "Ready to take the plunge?"

I say nothing as the shadow crouches to unlace his boots.

"We'll freeze to death standing here, so I guess we might as well do it. Let's tie our belts together end to end. It won't do us any good if one of us doesn't make it."

I remove my hat, this regimental issue from some past campaign, given to me by the Colonel. The cloth is worn and hopelessly faded. I brush off the brim, then put the hat back on my head.

"I have been thinking it over . . . ," I dredge up the words. "I'm not going."

The shadow looks at me blankly.

"Forgive me," I tell my shadow. "I know full well what staying here means. I understand it makes perfect sense to return to our former world, the two of us together, like you say. But I can't bring myself to leave."

The shadow thrusts both hands in his pockets. "What are you talking about? What was this promise that we made, that we'd escape from here? Why did I have you carry me here all this way? I knew it, it's the woman."

"Of course, she is part of it," I say. "Part, though not all. I have discovered something that involves me here more than I ever could have thought. I must stay."

My shadow sighs, then looks again heavenward.

"You found her mind, did you? And now you want to live in the Woods with her. You want to drive me away, is that it?"

"No, that is not it at all, not all of it," I say. "I have discovered the reason the Town exists."

"I don't want to know," he says, "because I already know. You yourself created this Town. You made everything here. The Wall, the River, the Woods, the Library, the Gate, everything. Even this Pool. I've known all along."

"Then why did you not tell me sooner?"

"Because you'd only have left me here like this. Because your rightful world is there outside." My shadow sits down in the snow and shakes his head from side to side. "But you won't listen, will you?"

"I have responsibilities," I say. "I cannot forsake the people and places and things I have created. I know I do you a terrible wrong. And yes, perhaps I wrong myself, too. But I must see out the consequences of my own doings. This is my world. The Wall is here to hold *me* in, the River flows through *me*, the smoke is *me* burning. I must know why."

My shadow rises and stares at the calm surface of the Pool. He stands motionless amid the falling snow. Neither of us says a word. White puffs of breath issue from our mouths.

"I cannot stop you," admits my shadow. "Maybe you can't die here, but you will not be living. You will merely exist. There is no 'why' in a world that would be perfect in itself. Nor is surviving in the Woods anything like you imagine. You'll be trapped for all eternity."

"I am not so sure," I say. "Nor can you be. A little by little, I will recall things. People and places from our former world, different qualities of light, different songs. And as I remember, I may find the key to my own creation, and to its undoing."

"No, I doubt it. Not as long as you are sealed inside yourself. Search as you might, you will never know the clarity of distance without me. Still, you can't say I didn't try," my shadow says, then pauses. "I loved you."

"I will not forget you," I reply.

Long after the Pool has swallowed my shadow, I stand

staring at the water, until not a ripple remains. The water is as tranquil and blue as the eyes of the beasts. I am alone at the furthest periphery of existence. Here the world expires and is still.

I turn away from the Pool and begin the walk back. On the far side of the Western Hill is the Town. I know she waits for me in the Library with the accordion.

Through the driving snow, I see a single white bird take flight. The bird wings over the Wall and into the flurried clouds of the southern sky. All that is left to me is the sound of the snow underfoot.

up one night and the two of them helped another adolescent girl run away, broke into a house, and bought $100 worth of marijuana from Mike.

Ordinarily, Eve says, her co-dependent pattern of behavior would have set in. "I don't like fighting with the kids. When there are problems, I try to explain away the issue at hand, I try to make everything right. I make excuses for the children, I keep them from paying the price that they should." This time, however, Eve and Mickey decided to hang tough, to act in a unified manner to confront the problem and connect Frank with the consequences of his actions.

"When Frank got caught, he looked at his situation as if he were an outsider," Eve says. "He wasn't upset about what might happen to him. He wasn't afraid of going to jail." Frank was sent away to Spring Creek Community in Montana, a boarding school that specializes in dealing with children who have emotional difficulties and who are drug abusers.

His exploits continued. "At the boarding school, Frank and some friends managed to swim the river near the school and then walk five miles to the nearest town to steal cigarettes, which he wrapped in plastic so that they wouldn't get soaked when he swam back across the river." Frank also tattooed himself extensively and learned how to use nutmeg to get high. "He would mix water with nutmeg and then drink it to get a flash high that lasts for about two minutes. He also smelled fumes to get high, and before he ran away from the school he dug out a smoking room under one of the cabins. The room was big enough to hold two and three people, and when it wasn't in use, that's where the booty [cigarettes] was stored." As described by Eve, "Frank is a high energy mover-and-shaker who will either end up president of the United States or the godfather in the Mafia. He's that type of person; he's got that type of drive."

Eve contrasts Frank with Mickey's son, Mike, introverted, quiet, reserved, yet who kept the house in an uproar in his own way. "He did so very passively through a hundred small actions a day. He would leave crumbs on the table and if you asked him to clean up behind himself he would say, 'No. I'm not going to do that,' and sit down. Or he might come in late and turn on the light that he knew would shine into our bedroom. If asked about it he would say, 'Why don't you close your door?'

"Mike's personality and mine are the opposite," Eve adds. "He's very self-centered. He does for himself only, although everything he does sounds logical to me but feels rotten." Up until Mike was about eight or nine he lived with his mother, who, Eve says, "taught the kids that the only thing you have to worry about in life is taking care of yourself."

When Mike was about 13, he went away to camp as a junior counselor and began to experiment with marijuana. When he returned he shared this experience with Eve and Mickey. "We told him that he should wait to experiment with drugs until he was older and in a more safe place. We told him that camp definitely was not a safe place and that using drugs was not a safe thing to do now." He didn't listen, and by the time he was 16, Mike was enrolled in the same boarding school that Frank eventually attended.

Eve and Mickey made the decision to send Mike to Spring Creek after his behavior became disruptive to the entire family. It took a lot of discomfort on everyone's part to draw such a rigid line, but by all accounts the decision has paid off for the entire family. "Mike ended up being the valedictorian when he graduated from Spring Creek. He now has self-confidence and he's learned how to motivate people. And what we really feel good about is Mike's acknowledgment of us. He toasted his dad and me for sending him to Spring Creek and for seeing what he needed even when he didn't know what he needed," Eve explains.

Eve is also pleased with the effect family counseling has had on her own personality, her marriage, and her relationship with the rest of the family. "I am less controlling and more willing to let people live their own lives nowadays. I am more willing to let my family see my hurt, not just my anger." In addition, Eve is excited about the progress her family has made. "The process that we have been going through has taken what was two family groups and made them into one. We are much more effective now. The kids get more of what they want, if it's appropriate, and we get more of what we want. Plus, my marriage is a whole lot better than it used to be, because we know now why we do what we do."

MICKEY

"Both of the boys have had general behavior problems. Mike couldn't relate to the family and to friends. He was very disruptive. Frank has had some problems with honesty and has been in trouble with the police," says Mickey, a pleasant man who repeatedly stated that Eve would be a better person to talk to about topics of this nature. "I think she can give you more of the emotional side of this than I." Still, Mickey was willing to offer his own theory about the source of Mike's problem. "Mike never quite coped with my divorce from his mother, Sarah. In fact, he saw a psychologist off and on for about seven or eight years before attending Spring Creek at the age of seventeen."

Moreover, when Mickey married Eve, Mike had trouble making the adjustment, although "Eve has been an excellent mother to the kids." Eventually Mike started using marijuana, and though shy and reserved outside the home, he was argumentative and aggressive among immediate family members. Explains Mickey: "There were a lot of arguments and fights and screaming matches provoked by Mike. Our family stayed in a constant uproar. We tried everything to help Mike, but he was on a dead-end street. Something had to change."

Mike was sent to Spring Creek and remained there for a couple of years. "They sent me back a new and improved kid, so I can't kick about that," Mickey says. Mike is currently enrolled in his first year of college. Frank, on the other hand, recently ran away from Spring Creek. He has lived with his grandparents in Savannah, Georgia, and with his birth father in Charlotte, North Carolina. Eve and Mickey will not allow him to return to their household. "Frank had had problems for years. He has used cocaine and LSD and got into trouble with the police. He would slip out at night and steal the family car. We would hide the keys, but he would steal the car anyway. Basically, we couldn't control him."

From time to time, Mickey thinks about how he could have done more for the children. "I didn't spend enough time with the kids; I pretty much had my plate full." He says that the counseling he received while trying to assist the boys has helped him overcome his longstanding, co-dependent habit of feeling guilty about the past. "I've pretty well worked through my guilt problem, but the family isn't perfect. Kids can manipulate the hell out of you. Kids really know where the buttons can be pushed," he says with a chuckle.

MIKE

Mike, now concentrating on math in college, says he will probably become a psychology major because he wants to help people, as he has been helped. His own problems began a number of years ago, though the escalation was gradual. "I guess from junior high on it just kinda got worse and worse. It wasn't a real drastic thing at all. Throughout much of the time I was fighting with my parents a lot. I totally did not get along with my family. I had like very little motivation for school. So I was getting poor grades and I was very angry. The bottom line was I had no confidence in myself.

"I fought with my parents all the time about typical teenage things, like clothes and grades and who I could see and all that stuff, except that it was really bad. I hated them. Then the summer before the tenth grade I started drinking a lot, and later on I started smoking pot to see what it was like. But then I was so unhappy with my life I started doing that like every day."

Mike used his allowance from mowing the lawn and income from a summer job to support his marijuana habit. He never used any other drugs; "I just did a lot of marijuana." Eventually his parents figured out that Mike was involved in some type of substance abuse as he began to return home from late Saturday night outings "messed up. So they knew I had done it [used drugs] a couple of times, but they weren't aware of the extent I was doing it. And every time I did it they would punish me or something, but I still did it anyway." Using drugs, Mike admits in hindsight, was a crutch he used to escape from life, to seclude himself.

Toward the end of his junior year in high school, Mike recalls, "Every night I would be screaming at my dad or Eve would be screaming at me. My house was like a battleground. I just can't explain how bad it was. I hated my life. I had very few friends. All I really cared about was getting stoned. I knew my life was pretty miserable. My parents were thinking, 'He's doing pretty bad in school, so we want to get him to a school that will turn his life around so that he will be happy.' I kinda agreed because my life was pretty miserable, plus I wanted to get away from my parents. I also agreed because I was too afraid to run away. I had nowhere else to go."

Meanwhile, about the time Mike started using pot, Frank started as well, although Mike didn't know it. "At first I didn't want Frank to know what I was doing because I didn't want to be a bad example. But then when we found out about each other we started getting high together. So we covered up for each other, we shared our drugs together, we did all of the same stuff, except he was kind of worse. He broke into houses and stole money and I never got into that. I was very careful about not getting kicked out of the house or whatever. Frank just didn't really care what happened."

Eve and Mickey brought up the issue of sending Mike to Spring Creek in the middle of his junior year. He knew for several months that his parents were looking for schools that might help him. "Every week they would tell me what schools they were looking at, and when they decided on Spring Creek they took me to see the educational consultant they had been working with, who explained the school to me. So I had a pretty good idea about what was going on."

Throughout this period Mike was getting further and further behind in his studies, but "I never skipped school. I went to school every day, but I never studied. I had like straight D's. I got F's all the time. I was at the bottom of my class, because all I cared about was getting high. I would go to school and sleep in class and walk around and sort of drift through life. It was pretty hopeless."

Once Mike landed at Spring Creek, everything opened up for him. "I liked Spring Creek. Most people really hate being there because you can't eat red meat and there's no television and you can't smoke. Most people hate it because of that type of stuff. Plus they're away from their friends and everything. But I liked it because for one of the first times in my life I was accepted for who I was. I started to feel better about myself and I felt confident enough to do things that I was afraid of before, like making friends, taking leadership roles in the school, stuff like that."

Toward the end of his two years at Spring Creek, Mike became the head of the honor society. "I had a lot of respect there. Before at my old school I talked to about two guys and no one knew me and no girls really liked me or anything. So it just felt pretty good. It's kinda like I got to start all over." When asked what was so different between the Mike who attended school in North Carolina and the Mike who was enrolled at Spring Creek, he offers the following observation:

"It was partly me and partly the school. I'm not really sure how this happened, but I just started off feeling comfortable to be open, to let people get to know me. I felt confident enough to just be myself, whereas at the other school I was so shy and insecure that I avoided people. I was so afraid that people would hate me, I didn't really try to get to know anyone. Plus at Spring Creek the students are a lot more accepting, because people are honest there and real and they care a lot about how you feel compared to your average school. People there are a lot more accepting, also."

Despite Mike's success at this school, a few of his actions were less than exemplary during his first six-month tenure. "I managed to sneak in some pot several times. The one big occasion that happened was when I went home for my first vacation. Even though I was doing pretty good at Spring Creek, I still had this big craving to get high. So I went home and smoked pot and I brought some back to the school and they found it. I got in trouble for that—I had to work at a mentally retarded center for a week. I actually liked my punishment, but it was my consequence. Then I got caught [again] about a month later."

This time Mike says that his "consequence" was a bit more difficult to cope with. "They have these things called compacts, where they put you out into the woods for a week with one staff member and depending on what time of the year it is, they work you. And since it was in February, I was cross-country skiing every day and sleeping in the woods and it was really hard."

Mike secured the marijuana that was responsible for his weeklong punishment at a racquetball club. He says that "some guy just gave it to me." He admits, with a laugh, that in those days he was "real open to finding it. I kinda kept my eye out, I suppose." That was the last time Mike has smoked marijuana—approximately 18 months ago as of the date of this interview. He does drink beer occasionally, he says, "but it's just college stuff."

Seven months after Mike arrived at Spring Creek, his stepbrother, Frank, joined him. "I was really looking forward to his coming, because we were pretty close. But when he got there it was different, because when we were friends in North Carolina we were like beer buddies, covering up our drugs and everything. But when he got to Spring Creek, we didn't *not* get along, we just didn't talk. We were pretty distant. We just never hung out. And, now, we get along okay but we're just very different people with very different goals in life, so we never really talk."

From Mike's point of view he and Frank differ in some significant ways. "I made it out of adolescence in one piece. . . . I've got some definite goals in life and some pretty strong values about what's right and wrong. As far as a career, I want to either be a therapist, some sort of social helping career, or I want to be an architect. I'm not really sure. I don't want to judge Frank or anything, but he just has this what-the-hell attitude about life. He doesn't seem to care about anything. He sort of has no sense of conscience at all about what's right or wrong. One time, for example, at Spring Creek he broke into the nurse's house and took her alcohol. It was like this big thing and he said he was sorry and he got punished for it, but then a week later he did the same thing to the same nurse. He just doesn't seem to have any idea of morality. He does stuff that it's so obvious that he's going to get caught, but he still does it. I don't understand where he's coming from." When asked if he thinks he can help Frank, Mike replies, "No. I don't know if anyone can."

In terms of his relationships with his younger sisters, Mike explains, "What I had done before Spring Creek was really isolate myself. I stayed in my room much of the time. I got along with them okay, I didn't really fight with them—well, sometimes I did, but they were in such a different world that I just didn't interact with them that much."

Mike says that he can "talk for years" about what he

got out of Spring Creek. During this interview, he manages to provide an abbreviated list of his gains. "I feel a lot better about myself—that's basically the biggest thing. I have a lot more confidence in myself and I know what I need to do to get what I want in life." So what does he need to do? "That's a big question. I just need to keep my goals straight and I need to discipline myself to go to classes. As far as emotionally, when I get depressed and stuff, I need to take care of myself and not just bottle up my feelings and I need to talk to someone and to remind myself that I'm still an okay person."

Mike says that his first month of college has truly tested the skills he learned at Spring Creek. "At Spring Creek, everyone is very honest with their feelings, very vulnerable. You can cry in front of thirty people and it's okay. But in college the guys are all macho and I really do not get into that at all. And it's been kinda hard because people are just really shallow. A lot of people are not willing to expose who they really are, and that kind of frustrates me. I like to talk about stuff, but a large chunk of the people here are into football and drinking beer. I like to have a good time, but there's more to life than that."

Loneliness has been a problem, Mike says. But he's been coping by forcing himself to remain social instead of retreating emotionally. "I've made myself keep going out there to meet people and not isolating myself. So I have started meeting a lot of people who I can talk to, but it's kind of frustrating. The people in the dorm, their priorities are just so different from mine. My roommate is the way I was three years ago. He and the guys in my dorm are not into expressing their feelings and any weakness is not accepted at all. They're into proving their masculinity and I don't think that's necessary. I'm comfortable with who I am, so I don't need to prove it to anyone."

Still, he admits that he has to struggle sometimes with his insecurities. "I have a fear of being alone. And so I've been kind of freaking out and going, 'Oh my God, there's no one here I can talk to.' So I write letters to people and I write a journal and I call my parents and talk to them and I have met some people here who I can be vulnerable with and tell them what's going on without them saying, 'Dude, you're a wimp.' "

To keep his head above water and not use drugs, one of the things Mike does is to give himself reassuring psychological strokes. "I wake up in the morning and I just keep telling myself, 'You're a nice guy. You should feel confident about yourself. You're likable.' "

Mike believes his insecurities can be traced to his parents' divorce. "My parents got divorced when I was eight years old. That was a real turbulent time. My mom [Sarah] was having a real difficult time, even before divorce, when I was six or seven. She kinda went wild for a couple of years. She was partying a lot, she had an affair with this guy, and then she left and went to Boston for a couple of years when I was seven. So she really wasn't there for me as a mother. And I had a lot of fear about being abandoned, because she left me and I had no mom. So that made me pretty insecure. . . . There was this point when one day I just woke up and I didn't like myself and I couldn't get rid of that feeling." He knows all this about his mother's past because she told him some years later. "We're like totally good friends now."

Mike didn't really like Eve when his father married her. "My real mom is really relaxed as far as authority and rules and stuff and she's just more like a friend to me. Eve was real strict about things. She is really authoritarian; she's kind of a dictator. It was a pretty drastic change. For eight years I had been able to do these things, then all of a sudden there's this strange woman telling me to cut my hair, what's appropriate and what's not appropriate. I really resented it." Nowadays, Mike gets along with Eve—with reservations: "She really irritates me sometimes. I think she has a big control issue. She has to get her way and that kind of frustrates me sometimes."

Mike says he still has not worked out all of the kinks in his relationship with his father. "We get along all right, but there's still some unresolved stuff. My dad's a perfectionist, so I've always felt that I was never good enough for him. I'll feel really good about myself and I'll feel like I'm doing great and then I'll come home and it's just like, 'Mike, go take out the garbage' from my dad. They [his parents] complimented me a lot at graduation and said they were really proud of me, but I don't know. When I lived at home I just didn't get the recognition . . . well, maybe I sort of did sometimes, but I don't know."

Mike admits that his father has changed a lot since he got involved with Spring Creek. In fact, his father tells him now that whatever Mike does with his life will make him happy if it makes Mike happy. After a bit, Mike is even willing to admit that perhaps some of the problem he has with his father may stem from voices from the past. "He doesn't have any expectations for me and stuff. And I know that logically, but I still hear the old voices."

"I get along with my real mom the best of all three of my parents," Mike says. "She had a lot of problems growing up, but ever since about two years ago she's been taking really, really good care of herself and this is like the happiest she's ever been in her life. So we really connect in terms of talking about stuff." Reaching this stage took some effort, Mike recounts. "I didn't see her for several years because there was too much tension. She didn't get along with my dad or Eve and they didn't like her and she had been gone for a couple of years, so I had not seen her. . . . I had some problems with her leaving, so we had a lot of stuff to work out, too." Mike and his mother started the process of sorting out their difficulties when one of the therapists at Spring Creek asked her to visit the school. "She was there for a couple of days, so we talked about our problems and, eventually, over the course of the two years I spent at Spring Creek things sort of smoothed out."

All in all, Mike feels like a great deal has "smoothed out" in his life, particularly since he feels he now has a handle on his own best self. "When I went to Spring Creek I found out who I really was; I really learned what I thought was important in life, what I wanted to do in life. I have this great desire to want to help people that have problems. I sort of took a look at the world and saw how unhappy people are and how bad people treat each other— there's just a lot of unfairness. So, it just seems to me that as long as we're going to live here we might as well get along."

POSTSCRIPT

"The difference between Mike and Frank, in terms of progress, was night and day," explains Gary Kent, Frank's counselor at Spring Creek Community. "The first contact that I had with Frank was with a young man who was very verbally compliant on the surface and in the presence of adults, though he became very angry when he couldn't get what he wanted." According to Kent, Frank had a history of psychiatric problems, including manic depression.

Kent viewed Frank as a very dependent person. "Frank would never do anything on his own. He needed people to direct him, to nurture him, to protect him. He would seek this typically in his relationships with women. While he was at Spring Creek he got involved with a codependent little gal who would take care of him." After some time at Spring Creek, however, Frank was beginning to try to take care of himself, but "his neediness was so overwhelming he could not succeed." Frank tried to establish some distance between himself and this girlfriend, for example, but his efforts to keep her away only lasted for about a week. Being alone, Kent says, "would create such an empty space, the pain would simply engulf him. There was a great deal of fear involved whenever he was feeling that he was by himself."

Frank was very pleasure oriented. "His mode of escape was to drink his pain away or engage in some type of sexual activity." One of the techniques Kent used to attempt to help Frank was to require him to engage in regularly scheduled self-reflection. He was to compile a daily journal and record what caused him to demonstrate poor impulse control. "He was moderately successful, but he didn't have the discipline to keep it up."

Kent estimates Frank's emotional age at about six or seven, though he possesses "some real fine intellectual capabilities to process information." Yet, the counselor notes, Frank is weak in linking up cause and effect. "We were also very suspicious of an attention-deficiency disorder." Kent believes that Frank ran away from Spring Creek because of his frustration in dealing over and over again with the same problems. "He felt helpless to change his behavior."

Eve was the primary enabler of Frank, Kent opines. She took the responsibility for Frank's behavior. As a result, Frank has had difficulty sorting out who he is, where he stops, and where other people begin. "In a way, if you look at Frank's activity over the past two months [running away from Spring Creek and moving from one relative's house to another], his behavior is an acting out of his anger that Eve is no longer willing to play that role. And Frank is really trying to say to her, 'Hey, I'm out here hung out to dry, by myself, and I'm scared.' "

Still, Kent adds, "As long as there's someone there to bail him out he will continue with dysfunctional behavior. The worst-case scenario for Frank is that he'll end up behind bars with a full-blown addiction. Right now what needs to happen is for Frank to really hit bottom to become painfully aware that there are some pretty big consequences for the choices he makes."

Are Eve and Mickey really helping Frank by barring him from their home since he ran away from Spring Creek? Will hitting bottom cause Frank to want to change his ways? Chapter Four, "Raising the Bottom, or Hanging Tough Phase Two," takes a look at such issues and more.

❧ 4 ❧

Raising the Bottom, or Hanging Tough Phase Two

My psyche has been tortured by images that friends recounted to me of how my sister fared once I decided to hang tough and she hit bottom. More than one person who saw her during the period immediately following her departure from my home reported that she roamed the streets in dirty clothes too small to cover a stomach that held a seven-month fetus. Even today I squirm when I think of what she experienced and what my role was in contributing to that experience.

Yet there is something good to be said about this time in my sister's life: She did find a drug treatment center and she did manage to stop using cocaine before her baby was born. What I have since learned is that most often a drug abuser has to hit bottom to want help and ask for it. The chemically dependent person will not face the problems caused by addiction until he's painted himself into such a tight corner that only two options remain: to take positive action to improve his situation or to give up on himself.

My sister, for example, was forced to sleep in shelters for the homeless because she had burned virtually all of her bridges to family and friends. She had to range the streets during the day because the shelters in Los Angeles insisted that the homeless population vacate the premises by a certain early-morning hour. She tells me now that she "saw it all" during that time and that what she saw and experienced was pretty horrible. But the squalidness of her circumstance, coupled with the fact that she was carrying another life inside her, finally caused her to dig deep and pull upon an inner resolve to survive. My sister reminisces:

> At some point I just looked around and saw that I had to change. I saw that my world was caving in on me, that I had to pull myself up and out of my situation. I thought a lot about my baby. And I cried a lot. For a while, I thought if the worst came to be, I might have to give my baby up for adoption. That's not something I wanted to do, but I knew that I had to start thinking about my child, I had to start thinking about what was the best thing for my child. I was scared, too. I thought about what the cocaine might be doing to my baby. I started praying that my baby would be healthy, that if I stopped using cocaine right now there would be no effect on my child. Well, I stopped using drugs and my prayers were answered. I have a really healthy, chubby baby boy—and I'm proud of that.

Hitting bottom happens differently for different people. But what cuts across all manner of adolescent drug abusers is this: A child in trouble will only reach out for help when she feels boxed in and believes that her options are limited to that of progress-or-perish. The same bottom line, however, can be attained when you, the parent, intervene and paint your child into a corner rather than waiting for her to do the same. When you hang tough you are drawing a line to protect yourself and your family members from the dysfunctional behavior of your chemically addicted child. When Eve and Mickey in Chapter Three's case study refused to allow 17-year-old Frank to return to their household, they were hanging tough by maintaining the integrity of their home and family. Once you refuse to enable your child and decide to look out for yourself instead, you have placed a mirror of sorts in front of your child. If you then provide your child with a way to receive help in a structured, therapeutic environment, you have engaged in a method of artificial intervention that's called raising the bottom, the second phase of hanging tough. Left to her own devices, your substance-abusing child can be expected to spiral downward in three stages.

THE DRUG-DEPENDENCY DOWNWARD SPIRAL

STAGE ONE:
IT'S JUST A PASSING PHASE

In the early stage of chemical dependency, the problems associated with the addiction are manageable. Your drug-abusing child doesn't feel she needs help. Moreover, if you, as a parent, are aware that your child is using drugs and the substances in question are gateway drugs—such as marijuana, beer, and cigarettes—which are considered the precursors to more hard-core substance abuse, you tend to feel no acute anxiety. Instead, you dismiss the problem. You tell yourself it will go away with time, your child is simply experimenting, doing what's natural to grow up. Some parents are so into denial during this phase that they don't even acknowledge strong indications that their child is using drugs—that she has become lethargic and her grades are beginning to slip, for example.

STAGE TWO:
THE MONSTER REARS ITS UGLY HEAD AND DOESN'T GO AWAY

During the middle stage of a drug-dependency cycle, the drug problem is noticeable to others, although the child continues to deny that there is a problem. Now you are worried, though you may be at a loss as to what to do. Often, parents attempt to help during this stage in ways that really hurt the child. By providing the wrong type of support—making excuses, hiring lawyers, offering trips, nice cars, and nice clothes to their child as a bribe in hopes of making the addictive behavior go away—parents enable their children to continue to abuse drugs.

STAGE THREE:
HITTING BOTTOM

During late-stage dependency, the drug-abusing child is out of control. He can no longer deny that he is in trouble. He may run away from home because of his shame and fear of what he may do next. Generally, he has become part of a cadre of "friends" who are part of the local community's drug culture. This group lies, steals, and cheats others as well as themselves. At some point (as with Jeremy, the teenager in Chapter Two's case study, who finally stole from a neighbor and was incarcerated), the child will do something that boxes himself in so tight that he has no choice but to accept that he has hit rock bottom. When that happens, the child will commonly "relent and repent," according to drug-abuse experts, and either desperately seek help or readily succumb to parents' efforts to intervene. Tony, one of the young people interviewed for this book, is a real-life example of this downward spiral, of hitting bottom the hard way.

Tony was introduced to marijuana by his neighborhood "buddies" when he was only 14. It was not long before his school attendance and grades began to decline. Both parents knew he was using drugs but did not take the practice seriously. They became Tony's staunch defenders in discussions with school officials. By the time Tony was 17 and had graduated from high school, his drug habit had developed into both a cocaine- and alcohol-dependency problem.

Tony had no desire to continue school or to work for a living. His parents opted to let him stay home. He received what was equivalent to an allowance with no responsibilities attached and, in general, basked in the certainty of shelter and overall financial support. Every now and then, over a three-year period, Tony's father would find him a job, but Tony rarely lasted more than a month at such employment.

During this period, his chemical dependencies led him to start stealing valuable items from his home. When confronted by his parents, Tony lied. His mother tended to quietly accept her son's version of reality; his father would rant and rave but would not push Tony to produce the missing piece of property. Soon Tony began to get into trouble with the law. He was arrested several times for disorderly conduct such as fighting in a public setting, for possession of small amounts of cocaine, for driving under the influence of drugs and alcohol, and for other motor vehicle infractions. In each instance, Tony's parents came to his rescue by bailing him out of jail, securing an attorney, and welcoming him home with no demands that he change his behavior.

Finally, Tony's run-ins with the criminal justice system led to fines that were too expensive for his family to pay. Faced with a prison term and no parental rescue in the offing, Tony hit rock bottom and at that moment decided he needed help with his cocaine and alcohol problem. At 20 years of age, he signed himself into a residential drug-treatment center, in lieu of serving a two-year jail term.

What happened to Tony is common in terms of his downward spiral and in terms of how and why he sought help. Just like Aaron, the teenager who used and sold cocaine in Chapter One's case study, Tony managed to avoid going to prison by volunteering to be admitted to a live-in treatment center. When the criminal offense of a young drug abuser does not involve the use of weapons, judges have a tendency to be lenient if there is an effort on the part of the child to correct the drug problem.

The situation with your child does not have to reach such a low point. You can successfully intervene to thwart this process of downward projection.

ARTIFICIAL INTERVENTION: THE ROAD TO RECOVERY

The method of intervention called "raising the bottom" at drug recovery centers lets parents connect children, directly and painfully, with the consequences of their addictive behavior without endangering their lives. Often, for example, such children are isolated from their family and friends and made to live in residential treatment centers where their every move is monitored. Frequently, these facilities impose a strict regimen that may not even allow the child to make an unsupervised phone call. One of the first punishments Aaron, of Chapter One's case study, endured at a treatment center was for phoning a friend without permission. Jeremy, the teenager highlighted in Chapter Two's case study, made the point quite clearly that Spring Creek took control of his life in a way that he found displeasing, though now he seems to understand the value of such a tough method. Basically, then, when parents raise the bottom they artificially induce a late-stage crisis that causes substance-abusing children to feel as if their life has closed in on them.

A number of the parents I spoke to said the decision to take such harsh action against their child was a tough one to make, but most shudder to think of the consequences if they had not done so. The parents in this chapter's case study took a chance and intervened when their son was only 13 by enrolling him in a residential school many hundreds of miles from home. Though the final verdict is still out as to how Alex, now 14, will fare in the years to come, neither parent regrets the decision. In fact, what has since happened to their son's drug-using friends bears witness to the wisdom of the difficult choice these parents made. Alex declined to be interviewed for this book.

CASE STUDY:
ROBBIE, PETER, AND ALEX

Alex is an adopted child who was brought into Robbie and Peter's home when he was seven weeks old. He was 2½ when they divorced 12 years ago. According to 44-

year-old Robbie, however, "We were one of the first couples in the Santa Barbara [California] area to insist on establishing joint custody." Though Peter, 44, has remarried, he and his current wife live only minutes from Robbie—an arrangement that has allowed the ex-spouses to try almost "every permutation possible" with their joint custody agreement, in Robbie's words. When they first divorced, Alex spent three-and-a-half days a week with his mother and three-and-a-half days with his father. Then the schedule changed to one week at a time with each parent, then two weeks at a time. Finally, by the time Alex was 6, Robbie and Peter had settled on a formula that they felt worked: a one-month rotation at each home. "We went to one month so that everyone had the time to deal with issues and not be tempted to sweep their problems with Alex under the rug to deliver to the other parent," Robbie explains.

Alex has always known that he was adopted. Robbie and Peter told him all they knew about his birth parents. Alex has focused very little on the fact that he's adopted, so neither parent attributes his subsequent problems to that. Peter's current wife, Jodi, believes that Alex's behavioral problems stem from something else: "I think in Alex's early years both Robbie and Peter were very career oriented. I just think that he was hustled from one thing to another, from one parent to another."

Both Robbie and Peter are busy professionals. Robbie is a university professor who has earned two master's degrees; Peter runs his own real estate and property management company. Over the years, the two parents have also been involved in many community activities. In addition, Robbie has routinely sought additional teaching assignments and consultant work to finance vacations every summer for Alex and herself.

ROBBIE

Robbie recalls that Alex's problems first surfaced when he was in the fourth grade. "It was when the 'Night Stalker' was killing people [a murderer who was breaking into homes in Southern California late at night]. Alex was very, very concerned with this. He was concerned about people kidnapping him or breaking into the house. He was so afraid, he wouldn't even walk to the library." At this time, Alex asked to leave a mentally-gifted-minors program in which he had been enrolled for two years. The school counselor agreed that Alex could attend regular classes to relieve the pressure, and suggested that the parents seek therapy for the family and for Alex individually.

Robbie took Alex to see an art therapist, to whom he became greatly attached. The therapist died of cancer before she and Alex could have their last scheduled session. "Alex handled it very stoically, and I say stoically because it was as if Alex shut down," Robbie recalls. The next semester, during his sixth-grade year, Alex began to act out in class, giving his teacher some problems. By the time he entered the seventh grade, Robbie says, "In my mind all hell broke loose. He was growing very fast—he was obviously going through puberty. He started behaving as the class clown. He was experimenting with cigarettes. He looked as if he was using dope. It was as if the floodgates had opened."

From Alex's point of view, things were not as bad as they appeared to Robbie. "I'm just a teenager," he told her, "and this is what teenagers do." But, according to Robbie, all was not normal. Alex started getting lower grades—C's and D's, and an F in English, his former best subject. "He would do crazy stuff. He would do his homework but then leave it at home and not turn it in." However bad Robbie thought the seventh grade was, "The eighth grade was as if we were going downhill at a hundred miles per hour."

Alex starting hanging out with a group of five boys. They would hang up when Robbie answered the telephone. "I should have suspected something was wrong, but I didn't." Then Alex, who was 13 at the time, asked to spend the night at the house of one of these boys. Robbie agreed and met the friend's parent to make sure the arrangements were as Alex described. When Alex did not return on time the following day, Robbie called the friend's parent and discovered that the boys had spent the night elsewhere. "When he got home the next day I was hysterical and grounded him for one entire week. 'Lying doesn't cut it with me,' I told him." He behaved perfectly for the next week.

Then Robbie had to go out of town. She arranged for Alex to spend the time with his father, but Alex pleaded for another chance to sleep over at a friend's house, and eventually Robbie succumbed to his pleas. When Robbie returned home a few days later, she noticed that the quilt on her bed was not in the position she had left it. She also noted that some of her drinking glasses were not where they were supposed to be. "We've always had the agreement that kids aren't allowed in my house when I'm not home, so I cornered Alex and said, 'What went on in my house while I was gone?' Alex looked real nervous and denied everything." Robbie knew better than to believe his story.

She let him go to school without giving her a satisfactory answer. By the end of the day, she received a telephone call from the school informing her Alex had ditched all of his classes after 1:00 P.M. "I called Peter at work, had him pulled out of a meeting and told him he had to meet me at my house immediately. I ran to my next scheduled class and wrote a message on the blackboard that class was cancelled that evening."

When Robbie and Peter arrived at her home, they found a note from Alex that said, "I have to get away for a few days. I'll be okay. Please don't tell Dad." Alex had drawn hearts at the bottom of the note. All of his friends had left their parents similar letters, so all of the parents got together that evening to compare messages and to worry. One of the boys required insulin injections three times a day to control diabetes, so they called the sheriff out of concern for this child's life. After 24 hours, the boys called and asked to be rescued—they were 20 minutes away.

"They came back tired, cold, and dirty. We hugged each child and told him how much we loved him. Peter took Alex to his house, and we didn't let them go to school for one day. Since the whole school knew they had run away, we didn't want to encourage the return of the conquering hero." The next day one of the fathers confronted the boys with an accusation that the group had been using drugs. They did not deny the accusation. Alex became belligerent. He told Robbie that "nobody could tell him what to do." Alex's new and more intractable attitude persuaded Robbie that she could no longer handle him and that it was time to send him to some type of therapeutic boarding school. Robbie and Peter sought the advice of an educational consultant and decided on Spring Creek Community in Montana.

"It was the hardest thing that I've ever done in my life, sending Alex away. Peter and I cried and cried about having to do it." However, the chilling events that have transpired with Alex's cohorts since he was enrolled in Spring Creek have helped assuage any feelings she and Peter may have harbored that their decision was a mistake. Two of these 14-year-old boys, for instance, stole a truck and drove to Tijuana, where they were arrested and reported to the U.S. Border Patrol. All five adolescents were involved in a drinking and drug-taking spree that temporarily landed the group in juvenile hall and may cost their parents $400,000 because of a fire they started that burned down the administration office at their local high school. One of the boys was remanded to the California Youth Authority; one was sent to live in a group home; the diabetic child was placed in a drug rehabilitation center. "I feel as if I don't need to have any more data to let me know I made the right decision sending Alex away," Robbie concludes.

PETER

According to Peter, Alex's downfall began during his sixth-grade year when he went away to science camp for a week during spring vacation. "Alex came back a completely different person. It was as if somebody had turned the switch. He went away a kid and came back a young-man-in-the-making, and he was much less willing to take any direction from anyone." By the seventh grade, "Alex was just not fitting into the world in any way. I started thinking about sending him away, but Robbie wouldn't do it. Then Alex decided that he wanted to live with Robbie full time. At first I was hurt, but then I found out that it wasn't that he wanted to be with Robbie, it was that he wanted to be with his friends, who lived closer to Robbie than to my house."

Alex's behavior took an even sharper turn for the worse during the eighth grade. "As we tightened up and tightened up, he would do his homework but then he simply wouldn't turn it in. He also starting dressing like the group of kids that you don't want your kid to dress like." The final cataclysmic event, Peter remarks, took place when Alex ran away. "Fortunately it rained and it was a very cold night, so the kids returned the next day very bedraggled.

"We learned, though, that Alex and his friends were using marijuana, and we felt that this was not the way a thirteen-year-old boy was supposed to behave." The next step was to get Alex away from this environment. "We arranged to have Alex spend a night at my house under the guise that he was going to see his grandfather who had come to visit for the weekend." The educational consultant hired by Robbie and Peter handled the rest. "He woke Alex up and informed him that he was going to be taken to Spring Creek. Alex didn't try to get away once. In fact, he almost looked relieved. Still, it was a difficult thing for me to do, but I felt I had to do it."

Since he's been at Spring Creek, Peter says, Alex has made "essentially no progress. He's decided the whole world is wrong and he's right and that he's going to prove it to the world. He told us he didn't want us to visit him a few months ago, so we told him, 'If you don't want to see us we won't come.' He's got to figure out who's going to bend here, Alex or the world." Alex is also angry with Peter because of the trouble Alex's group has gotten into since he's been at Spring Creek. "His attitude was that if he had been there this [the fire incident] wouldn't have happened. Here he was looking at me straight in the eyes and saying, 'I could have controlled the other boys.'"

No matter how Alex feels about things, Peter and Robbie have decided that he will remain at Spring Creek until he's 18 or until he "figures out how things work in the real world." But, Peter adds, "I miss him a whole lot and I think about him a whole lot. I really wish he would figure out how the world works so that he's not unhappy the rest of his life."

POSTSCRIPT

"Alex is a very angry boy," reports Gary Kent, his counselor at Spring Creek. "He has a huge issue of being rejected by his birth mother. Alex still has to go through a real grieving about the loss of his birth parents and the divorce of Robbie and Peter." It's easy for Alex to be verbally abusive, explains Kent. But the counselor's diagnosis is that Alex's aggressive behavior belies a latent and deep-rooted insecurity. "Alex does a lot of pushing away of people on the theory that he should push them away before they push him away, as he perceives it."

Alex has been vacillating between compliance and defiance at Spring Creek. When he's in his compliance mode, Alex is trying to get released from Spring Creek, Kent notes. So far the tactic has not worked. "Alex will have to honestly confront some of his issues. Compliance alone won't get it." Not long ago, to move Alex along the continuum of cooperation at a little faster pace, Kent forced Alex to spend a period of time on the physical and social perimeter of the school because "that's the choice he has made when he chooses to be disinvolved." Alex's isolation involved being housed in a cabin outside of the main complex, though still on campus. He was also restricted as to who he might see or talk to. Alex was not allowed back into the school's mainstream until he was willing to genuinely participate in the treatment program. He lasted eight days in exile. Alex will be monitored regularly by Spring Creek staff, Kent says, to keep tabs on his sincerity.

"Alex is a very, very little kid, really, who wants to crawl into his mother's arms and receive nurturing. Robbie has a real desire and need to establish a close and intimate relationship with her son but doesn't know how to do this. She very much operates from an intellectual level." Kent believes that Robbie will have to take some real emotional risks to be the person she wants to be, and it's going to be a scary undertaking—especially, Kent says, "if you've been hurt."

Peter has been trying to rebuild bridges to Alex that they both have burned, but for the most part his son does not trust what his father is trying to do. "Peter, in his own words, feels that in his need to overcome his own handicap [a harelip] he's probably overlooked the needs of both Robbie and Alex." Regarding Alex's rejection of Peter, Kent adds, "I also think that Alex feels that if he reestablishes a relationship with his father, his father might go away again, he may just die or leave."

Robbie recognizes that her co-dependent behavior plays itself out in her tendency to withdraw emotionally in times of great conflict. "I call it taking a little vacation in my mind," Robbie explains. "I like to be a good girl. Still, I am controlling, but in a manner that is not direct and hostile. I control through organizing a person's day, his life. I organized Alex's notebooks for him, I restructured his schedule for him. I tried to make everything all better so that there was no verbal violence." This tactic put her at odds with Alex, who is verbally combative.

By intervening and raising the bottom of Alex's life, Robbie feels she has worked against her co-dependent habits: She set up a situation where Alex could stand on his own and learn to become his own person without her manipulations. So far, Alex has resisted efforts to counsel him at Spring Creek, but he has not tried to run away. Robbie has faith that Alex will come out okay at the other end of the process. "The environment of Spring Creek is an opportunity. It's teaching Alex that it's possible to respond to your emotional needs no matter the environment. There's always a boss and there's a price to pay, good or bad, for not playing by the rules. This action of sending Alex to Spring Creek was a very drastic step. But I feel that once you have done it, you have to see it through."

Did Robbie and Peter make the right decision to raise the bottom of their son's life before he did something that landed him in jail or that caused him physical harm? Or did they jump the gun? The tough decision that this couple faced to send their child to a residential treatment center will be explored in the following chapter, which examines the many treatment options parents have to choose from.

✿ 5 ✿

Treatment Options

My sister was seven months pregnant, lacking in family support and without funds when she went in search of a treatment program that would help her overcome her addiction to crack cocaine. Her options were limited, however, because of her pregnancy, financial status, and lack of insurance coverage. She did eventually enroll in a program, but some of the circumstances surrounding the experience worked against her recovery in several important ways.

First, not one of my sister's family members, including myself, was willing to take part in her drug therapy program. I was still of the opinion that my enabling behavior had been of some help to her—or, at least, should have been of some help. As I saw the situation, it was time for my sister to go it alone; I had gone as far as I was willing to go. In truth, my so-called help had been limited to providing financial support, since it was already late in the game when I was able to accept the fact that my sister's drug problem existed.

Likewise, my mother and stepfather took a distanced approach primarily because of their history with my sister. Every effort in the past to help her youngest daughter, my mother has oftentimes repeated, had caused family dissension and inevitably led to my sister's unceremonious departure from home or an ugly breach of some kind that fueled a temporary estrangement on the part of all involved. My mother said that she simply did not want to go through the pain of a familiar pattern. What my mother and I did not discuss, however, was that neither of us had ever really addressed my sister's drug problem. We had never attempted to steer her toward a rehabilitation program, and we had never taken it into account that we—my mother, my stepfather, or myself—could have been a part of the problem.

Although my sister was in her mid-twenties at the time, family involvement in her treatment program could have increased her chances for recovery, according to the National Federation of Parents for Drug-Free Youth. This organization reports that family participation in a young person's treatment program improves chances of recovery by ten times. In the absence of family involvement, explains California psychiatrist Loren Woodson, the only path of recovery is for the substance abuser to be able to say, "I want to save my own life." This is a tough road for a child to go down alone.

Getting help for your child, then, means that you should be open to securing help for yourself also. In fact, Steven W. Cawdrey of Spring Creek Community reports that the key to successful and speedy rehabilitation of the substance-abusing child is the extent to which the child's parents are willing to take part in the program and try to sort out how they themselves might grow and change. "At Spring Creek, parents are required to attend monthly parent groups. We even have a full-time family counselor. All that person does is call parents and ask, What are you doing in terms of getting therapy for yourself?"

Cawdrey adds that "If the parents can say, 'I'm really

tired of living this way' to themselves and mean it, if the parents can do this, the kids one hundred percent of the time see the parent as a role model, and the child's progress picks up almost immediately." In essence, raising the bottom for your child should mean that you are willing to raise it for yourself as well. No one said it would be easy, but taking the initiative to help your child and yourself is far superior to the alternative—continuing to deny and enable. Once you have reached this point of view and are ready to move forward to help your child and yourself, you will find various treatment options available, depending on a number of factors: your income level, geographic location, type of insurance coverage (if any), and ability to critically evaluate what is appropriate for you and your child's circumstances.

GETTING HELP

There are literally thousands of drug rehabilitation programs located throughout the United States, and hundreds based in Southern California. Yet my sister, roaming the streets of Los Angeles, had a hard time getting help once she was finally willing to seek it. Her problems were primarily threefold: She was pregnant, homeless, and virtually penniless.

Despite the alarming increase in the number of young, pregnant substance abusers, treatment programs dealing with this segment of the population are few and far between. Few programs are willing to take on the responsibility and potential liability of helping a pregnant woman withdraw from drug addiction.

My sister's homeless status also worked against her enrolling in an outpatient program. Participation in any drug treatment program requires discipline, which includes the willingness and ability to show up at the appointed hour on a regular basis. When you are one of the homeless, your precarious circumstances work against your reliability.

Also, since my sister was homeless, participation in an outpatient program would not have protected her from a drug-infested environment—an environment she would have no choice but to return to following every treatment session. Remember how the counselor in Chapter One's case study recommended that Aaron not return to his former environment upon completion of his long-term residential treatment, because it would be easy for him to reestablish his drug connections. My sister's homeless status posed the same threat in spades.

Moreover, her lack of money and insurance coverage worked against her enrolling in any treatment program, residential or outpatient. Treatment of a drug problem can become a very expensive undertaking. Low-cost or sliding-scale treatment centers are in short supply and thus have long waiting lists. The shortage of affordable treatment programs is especially critical when parents face what has become a relatively common judicial option: the choice for the substance-abusing child between a jail sentence and enrollment in a drug treatment facility.

Although close to 85 percent of Americans carry some sort of medical insurance, help in covering the expenses related to drug dependency is not widespread. As recently as 1986, according to a report issued by the National Association of State Alcohol and Drug Abuse Directors (NASADAD), only ten states required private insurers to cover alcohol- and drug-dependency treatment, and only two states required that purchasable policies be offered to cover the expenses of drug-dependency programs. Even

Medicaid, a program administered by states to serve low-income families who cannot afford medical care, does not universally provide coverage for drug treatment. (For a state-by-state list of health-insurance statutes as they relate to coverage for alcoholism and drug treatment services, turn to Appendix A at the back of this book.)

Although the current picture is somewhat discouraging, hope is on the horizon. Legislative measures in the public sector are moving in a direction that will improve health-care coverage nationwide for chemically dependent patients. A 1988 legislative update published by NASADAD shows that some significant changes have taken place:

> The District of Columbia, Hawaii, and Kansas now mandate insurance coverage for alcoholism, drug dependency, and mental health services.
>
> New York state now mandates coverage for outpatient drug-dependency treatment services, as well as for outpatient alcoholism treatment services.
>
> Pennsylvania now mandates coverage for alcoholism treatment services.
>
> Utah now requires insurers to offer, as an option for purchase, the provision of coverage for alcoholism treatment services.

According to documents prepared by NASADAD in 1988, new totals for the numbers of states that mandate coverage, require the offering of coverage for purchase, or have no relevant legislation are as follows:

> Twenty-five states and the District of Columbia mandate that private health insurers provide coverage for alcoholism treatment service benefits: Connecticut,

District of Columbia, Hawaii, Illinois, Kansas, Maine, Maryland, Massachusetts, Michigan, Minnesota, Mississippi, Missouri, Montana, Nevada, New Jersey, New York, North Dakota, Ohio, Oregon, Pennsylvania, Rhode Island, Texas, Vermont, Virginia, Washington, and Wisconsin.

Thirteen states and the District of Columbia mandate that private health insurers provide coverage for drug-dependency treatment service benefits: District of Columbia, Hawaii, Kansas, Maine, Michigan, Minnesota, Montana, Nevada, New York, North Dakota, Oregon, Rhode Island, Virginia, and Wisconsin.

Thirteen states require that private health insurers offer, as an option for purchase, coverage for alcoholism treatment service benefits: Alabama, California, Colorado, Florida, Kentucky, Louisiana, Nebraska, New Mexico, North Carolina, South Dakota, Tennessee, Utah, and West Virginia.

Eight states require that private health insurers offer, as an option for purchase, coverage for drug-dependency treatment service benefits: Alabama, Florida, Louisiana, Maryland, Missouri, North Carolina, Tennessee, and West Virginia.

Twelve states, as of January 1, 1988, had not yet passed any relevant legislation either mandating coverage or requiring the offering of coverage for purchase of alcoholism treatment service benefits: Alaska, Arizona, Arkansas, Delaware, Georgia, Idaho, Indiana, Iowa, New Hampshire, Oklahoma, South Carolina, and Wyoming.

Twenty-nine states have not yet passed any relevant legislation either mandating coverage or requiring the offering of coverage for purchase of drug-dependency treatment service benefits: Alaska, Arizona, Arkansas, California, Colorado, Connecticut, Delaware, Georgia, Idaho, Illinois, Indiana, Iowa, Kentucky, Massachusetts, Mississippi, Nebraska, New Hampshire, New Jersey, New Mexico, Ohio, Oklahoma, Pennsylvania, South Carolina, South Dakota, Texas, Utah, Vermont, Washington, and Wyoming.

AVAILABLE TREATMENT PROGRAMS

Costs for the three basic types of treatment programs—outpatient, residential, and long-term therapeutic care—can range from as little as $100 for a one-time visit to $25,000 or more annually. To assist you in seeking professional help for you and your child in all three treatment categories, a list of drug-dependency centers throughout the United States can be found in Appendix B at the end of this book. Though the prices for such services can be expected to change, the following represents a reasonable estimate of costs as of 1988.

OUTPATIENT CARE

Typically, a four-to-six-week outpatient program can cost $3,500 or much more, depending upon the particulars of what is offered by the treatment center. Outpatient facilities can be found within hospitals and mental health clinics or can be freestanding operations like those of Phoenix House in New York and California. Outpatient care for teenagers ordinarily requires that the youngsters come to the clinic after school every weekday. You should expect to be involved in the treatment program. Often, with outpatient care, therapy sessions are of two types: group meetings that include other drug abusers, and multifamily meetings where both parents and children confront, openly and directly, what is happening to the drug-dependent children and their families. Drug-abuse expert Steven W. Cawdrey describes it this way: "Our view of therapy is that both the parent and child must be put in the position where they are being challenged to calmly and constantly identify what they see in themselves that is healthy and unhealthy."

Outpatient treatment programs usually begin with an extensive one-time evaluation, which provides background information and determines the child's current drug-use status in order to fashion an individualized recovery program. An evaluation usually consists of information gathered from the parents; self-reporting during an interview with the child; reports from other counselors where a history of therapy exists; school records; police records and probation department evaluations; and observations of the counselor at hand. The following is an example of some of the information requested from parents on an actual evaluation document used by Spring Creek Community. Many programs nationwide require parents to fill out similar questionnaires.

> This information will be extremely helpful to us in constructing a clear picture of the applicant and the family dynamics. Please be as detailed as you feel necessary. Use additional paper if necessary.
>
> Name any significant family members or friends who are deceased. Please describe circumstances.
>
> Describe the following relationships in which applicant is or has been involved: each parent and/or

stepparent, sibling(s), and any other significant relationships.

Describe your relationship with your spouse, ex-spouse.

Specify any family member(s) who have in the past or are presently abusing/using or abstaining from drugs, alcohol, or nicotine.

Detail of family history in regards to alcoholism or drug addiction.

If applicable, describe applicant's adoption history.

Has the applicant been held back/skipped a grade in school?

If no longer attending school, give dates and details.

Describe any suspensions or expulsions.

Has the applicant ever used any of the following: Drugs? Alcohol? Nicotine? If yes, please specify and describe circumstances (i.e., substance, began at what age, behavior when using, etc.).

Has the applicant ever run away? Describe.

Tell us of any and all arrests, convictions, and probations; including age at time of occurrence.

Has applicant been involved in any physical, verbal, or sexual abuse situations that she or he initiated or was on the receiving end of? Please detail.

Describe your specific concerns regarding applicant's behavior, overall development, role models (adult or other), specific changes in behavior (dates, situations), pronounced changes in moods, eating habits, age-specific problems, and academic-specific problems.

Please list all professional treatment (hospital, treatment center, therapist, psychiatrist, etc.) applicant has utilized.

Describe any efforts made to resolve your concerns/problems with applicant.

This particular therapeutic center also requires parents to sign a substance-test release, thereby allowing the treatment facility to administer, at random, tests to measure the patients' drug and alcohol use.

Such programs almost invariably include one-on-one counseling as well as family and group counseling. In group counseling, your child will be encouraged to talk about her history of drug use with other young people who have had similar experiences. The tone and tenor of the group often take a no-nonsense approach: Your child will be expected to own up to her problems. If she still denies that she is or was addicted to drugs, she can expect a tough and unyielding challenge by peers in the group and the counselor.

Spring Creek Community also works at developing self-esteem by requiring each student to complete two three-week courses called Survival and Challenger. As described in the school's literature, "the Survival course is a course like none other. Whether in the deserts of Arizona or the rocky crags of the Montana Rockies, students learn to survive using the same skills practiced by the ancient North American Indians." The skills demonstrated and taught include: Paiute bow-drill fire, shelter construction, water procurement, tracks and scat identification, edible wild plants, trapping with snares and deadfalls, and bow and arrow construction. The course covers 60 to 100 miles of varied terrain, with emphasis placed on individual achievement. The trips are led by certified survival instructors, male and female. Therapy is ongoing during the course and at weekly intervals in large groups facilitated by therapists.

Reports one teenager who had just completed the Survival course, "Three weeks ago I was certain I was a failure but now I feel I've accomplished a lot. I feel positive about myself and the way I look." According to Cawdrey, "This course helps those young people who need to discover and confirm their own capabilities as well as those children who are making a transition from a protective environment to one of choice and responsibility. . . . The Survival course is a form of artificial intervention, a form of raising the bottom. It's taking a tough stance with your child. It's creating situations for your child where realities must be faced."

The Survival course is a prerequisite for taking the Challenger course. Challenger is an adventure program designed to help students develop a healthy sense of interdependence, group communication, cooperation, and care for one another, as described in Spring Creek Community's promotional materials. The course is conducted in several of the high mountain ranges of Montana. The child is taught rock-climbing, backpacking, kayaking, cross-country skiing, snowshoeing, search and rescue, and canoeing, among other skills. Trust-building activities such as search-and-rescue and river crossings shift the focus from the individual to the group effort. Students are encouraged to reevaluate preconceived limits through activities such as rock-climbing and rappel (using ropes to descend cliffs). Through shared experiences in a physically and emotionally demanding environment, it is hoped that the children will come to realize that helping one another is the key to helping themselves. Parents are required to be present during the last four days of the Challenger course.

RESIDENTIAL CARE

The extra expenses associated with providing room and board, intensive counseling, and sometimes an educational curriculum are responsible for inpatient treatment costs of as much as $10,000 for a two-week stay. A candidate for residential care is typically a chronic substance abuser who has tried an outpatient program unsuccessfully. Given that scenario, parents and counselors tend to decide in favor of inpatient treatment programs when it is felt that a youngster needs to be removed from his environment. Again, the first procedure undertaken upon entering a residential facility is an extensive evaluation. If necessary, the youngster will embark upon a detoxification program, which can be gradual or cold turkey, depending upon the type of substance abuse, the child's health, and the policy of the treatment facility.

As with outpatient programs, the next step in the recovery program is usually individual, family, and group-therapy sessions to rebuild the child's self-esteem. For longer-term residential programs, nutritional education and planned physical activities are part of the overall treatment plan. Counselors also spend time with parents and the child in developing an aftercare plan to reduce the chance of relapse. Because the strains associated with returning to an unsheltered environment often become more than children or parents can handle by themselves, aftercare is a vital part of the recovery process.

LONG-TERM THERAPEUTIC CARE

If your child has been abusing drugs for a long time, you may have to consider a long-term treatment program, which can cost $30,000 or more per year. Montana's Spring

Creek Community, a 24-hour therapeutic boarding school designed for young people aged 13 to 18, offers programs that range from $7,000 for six weeks to $30,000 for one year. Treatment programs at facilities such as Spring Creek usually include a wide range of therapy modes.

Spring Creek emphasizes the development of emotional literacy skills. The students participate in eleven types of therapy applications that take up approximately 25 to 30 hours per week:

1. Individual therapy

2. Small group therapy, where the teenagers meet in groups composed of those who enrolled at Spring Creek at the same time

3. Large group therapy, where the entire teenage population focuses on a topic of concern to the therapeutic community. Prejudice against newly enrolled black and homosexual youngsters was one recent topic, for example.

4. Chemical dependency group therapy

5. Special boys' and girls' group therapy, where the children come together based on gender to explore issues of sexual identity

6. Leadership training group therapy

7. Immediate-response group therapy, which takes place when some type of disruption has occurred within the therapeutic community, such as a robbery, or when a child is in serious emotional pain

8. Family therapy/parent training

9. Individual crisis intervention

10. Recreation therapy

11. Daily living therapy, which takes place every morning and involves an evaluation of how the child is handling routine structure, chores, and interaction with the people he has to deal with in his daily living situation

In addition to the above therapeutic activities, children enrolled at Spring Creek Community attend classes from 9:00 A.M. to 3:00 P.M. and devote about 90 minutes per night to homework and preparation for the next school day. They are also required to engage in eight to ten hours of sports activities per week. "Our attempt is to create a model where there is an effort to teach balance," Cawdrey explains. "How do you take care of yourself on all fronts? Do you know how to ask for what you need?"

Even with the extensive counseling and schedule of activities, it typically takes a child approximately six to ten months to "move out of the honeymoon period and allow us to see the anger," Cawdrey says. "It takes about another eight months to a year before a kid finally sees the light." This schedule holds true most of the time no matter what treatment mode the child undertakes. Parents, Cawdrey adds, "typically take two years just to begin to unlearn the patterns of behavior they've acted out for so many years."

A positive as well as realistic interpretation of Cawdrey's prognosis is this: It has taken both you and your child a number of years to develop the problems that exist within your family unit; it will take some time to unravel what needs to be unraveled. But at least there is comfort in knowing that by seeking treatment for yourself and your child, you and your family members are spending your time wisely by building self-esteem and rebuilding fractured relationships, rather than acting out unhealthy behavioral patterns over and over again.

For the family in this chapter's case study, the willingness to try a number of treatment options for their daughter, Shana, over a three-year period has for the most part paid off. Shana is no longer using drugs; she is no longer acting out sexually; she has moved back into the home; and she is enrolled in school. However, an important problem this family faced—one you may have to face as well—has to do with the patience and persistence needed to identify treatment options that would best serve the family's particular dynamics and needs.

CASE STUDY:
LAEL, GEORGE, SHANA, AND SKYLER

Lael, 47, obtained her degree in social work from a major Ivy League college, but her experience in this field did not help her diagnose her daughter Shana's use of drugs, which began at age 15. "We were in a period of denial for a long time. We had no idea that Shana was involved with drugs and alcohol and [sexual] relationships," Lael explains. Her husband, 49-year-old George, has another explanation of why it took them so long to figure out what was going on: "Shana and I have always had an almost mystical relationship. We know what each other thinks. So she [Shana] kept up a pretty good face with me."

Lael and George have been married for 21 years. Lael, a director of planning and development for a nonprofit organization, prefers to describe her specialty as involving "the role of money in the public interest" rather than to be called a fund-raiser. George is an economic development advisor to the government of a country in Asia. They live in Washington, D.C., with Shana, who is now 17, and Skyler, 15. Both children were adopted.

LAEL

"When Shana was fifteen she ran away from home, and that just terrified us." Shana was gone for three days or so. Lael adds, "We didn't have any experience dealing with a runaway child. We were the family who all of the other kids in the neighborhood came to." From this point forward, the family "became a battleground of tremendous hostility against me after years of family togetherness. We went for a long time believing that this was just a normal period of adolescent obnoxiousness."

At first they thought a "good Quaker boarding school" was the answer, but then, "things went from bad to terrible." Shana attempted suicide, got caught shoplifting, and deliberately crashed her fist into a tree. Lael and George now know, but did not then, that Shana had started using drugs and alcohol in large quantities. "All the while, we were in therapy. Three and four days a week the family was seeing this top-notch therapist, yet we were being sucked into this vortex where nothing we did helped." Shana only lasted a couple of months at the Quaker school before the headmaster called Lael and George and told them to come get their daughter. School authorities felt that her emotional problems were too severe for them to handle. "Shana captivated people with her despairing behavior," Lael explains.

On Christmas day during Shana's fifteenth year, she told her parents that she had a drug and alcohol problem. "We were shocked. We were startled. For so long we had been telling our friends, 'We're sure Shana doesn't use drugs. There is absolutely no evidence that Shana is using drugs and alcohol.' "

During this period, George was approached by Harvard University to serve as a resident consultant, to advise the prime minister of an Asian country on international development issues. If he took the job he would have to spend a good deal of time away from home. Still, it was an opportunity of a lifetime. After some discussion, Lael says, he decided to accept the position.

"We had, up until this time, been living and breathing Shana, a child who had become a whirling dervish." The parents decided that the world "had to go on too." So George left for Asia and the family determined to start living its own life.

For a brief period, Shana appeared to be doing better. But then her behavior took a dramatic turn downward. She stopped going to school. She stayed in bed. "This was the first time she had done this. I was crying every morning on the way to work. 'I've done something to cause this,' I thought. 'I can make this child's life better,' I kept telling myself." Then on Shana's birthday, Lael found marijuana in her purse. The anti-depression medicine Shana's therapist was recommending could no longer be prescribed since she was using illicit drugs.

By this time, Lael winces to relate, "Shana was spending the night with boys, dressing like a mushroom in black, and sitting in her room that looked like a graffiti hellhole." Lael turned to educational psychologist Sidney Manning, who advised her she had three options: (1) Let Shana go out on the streets. (2) Write a contract with her daughter that outlined what Shana could and couldn't do, accompanied by agreed-upon sanctions. Given Shana's lack of resolve and discipline, Lael felt this option would be like "setting up an obstacle course for a paraplegic." (3) Establish an intervention process. Lael decided on the third option.

Meanwhile, Shana ran away to stay with a boyfriend but called after a few days to negotiate the terms of her return to the household. By then, Lael's brother had come to visit and to help while George was out of the country. "Shana actually had the nerve to call us and ask could she bring home this boy she had met who she wanted to come live with her at home. This kid was ten steps below Shana, but my brother and I pretended to go along with what Shana was saying, so she and the kid showed up at our door. Of course we grabbed Fu Manchu by the scruff of his neck and said, 'That's it, buddy,' and threw him out."

With the help of Manning, whom Lael refers to as Saint Sidney, it was decided that Shana would be placed in an adolescent drug treatment center called New Beginnings. "She almost seemed relieved when we told her there were no other options." To ensure that Shana did not run away again, Lael called upon some of the parents of a support group she was associated with to volunteer to guard the outside of Shana's bedroom door in two-hour shifts. Shana stayed put long enough to be escorted to New Beginnings a couple of days later.

Once enrolled at New Beginnings, Shana "was at first angry and into total denial. Then after a few weeks Shana called and said, 'Mom, I just want to be a normal teenager.' " Shana ended up graduating summa cum laude from the New Beginnings program after six weeks. Still, it was determined that Shana was not ready to return home, so Manning's advice was taken once again. This time, Shana was enrolled in Montana's Spring Creek Community. Shana accepted having to go to Spring Creek, her mother says, though she "groused a bit." She started by taking part in the school's three-week survival course wilderness experience. Immediately following Survival, Shana took the Challenger course.

In some ways it was harder for Lael to make the decision to send Shana to Spring Creek than it was for Shana to accept Lael's decision, because of the family's character.

"This is a very sort of democratically ruled family. We believe in consensus. Our democratic process, though, had to learn how to become very explicit and nonnegotiable." Six weeks after Shana entered Spring Creek, Lael saw her. "This kid had stopped smiling for a year or two. But when I first saw her after she had finished the Survival and Challenger courses, she looked great. Her eyes were bright. It was wonderful to see."

Shana stayed at Spring Creek from April 1987 to June 1988. During that period Lael visited the school four times. "I actually reached a point where I could look at Shana and say, 'You were so damn lucky to have me for a mother.'" Shana left the school because she wanted to attend her senior high school year in Washington, D.C. "We decided that there were some risks, but that they were well worth the risk." Shana is following an after-school care plan that includes therapy sessions with a psychiatrist, attending Alcoholics Anonymous meetings on a weekly basis, and participating in family activities.

GEORGE

"Shana has never been an easygoing person. She seems often to cut off her nose to spite her face. She exhibits a stubbornness that is difficult to deal with." Still, George adds, "We've had a special relationship, and she's held on to that through her darkest times." When she was 11 or 12, George says, Shana began to have annual blowups, cycles of explosions that usually took place around her birthday. "Shana had a tough adolescence. Among other things, she was raped."

As she progressed into adolescence, the signs that something was seriously wrong with Shana's life begin to pile up, but, George says, "We told everyone, 'At least

Shana doesn't drink, use drugs, or smoke. At least we know that she isn't doing that.' " Meanwhile, Shana had started running away from home. She changed her style to a punk look that included tattoos. When she was at home, she sat shriveled up in her room and had many sleepless nights. One time George caught her sleeping at 2:00 P.M. with her eyes dilated and barely able to lift her head, but still he told others, "Shana is not using drugs."

At the time, Shana was seeing a counselor who advised her against taking part in family therapy. George has some strong feelings about this counselor's competence. "There's so much bullshit surrounding the mental health profession. There's so much backbiting between the different schools of thought. We were shunted around in this whole mental health field—it was incredible. We knew our way around this profession, and as literate as we were, we were helpless throughout this period. At one point we had to just go in and say to the professionals, 'Now just a goddamn minute! We had to fight every step of the way."

Though Shana took her therapist's advice and resisted family counseling, she did indicate that she wanted to be removed from the home, where she did not feel safe from herself. The counselor suggested that Shana check into the Psychiatric Institute in Montgomery County, Maryland. The family complied, but, shortly thereafter, when the head of the Psychiatric Institute suggested family counseling, Shana "stonewalled because of the advice given her by her individual therapist," explains George.

Advice on what to do with Shana came from many fronts. "One schoolmaster said that the best thing we could do is just leave her [at his school]. Adopt the tough-love approach. Let her know that we meant business. When we enrolled her in that same school, she ran away within a day and turned herself in at the local police station. We picked her up and brought her back home on the basis of a contract we negotiated with her, a contract that committed her to go to school, participate with the family, and change her language.

"She did well that summer, so we enrolled her in another school . . . and thought the worst was over. But then she started using drugs and shoplifting. She was suspended and willfully did not abide by the rules. She was given a deadline to return the lipstick she had stolen to the store. She didn't return it. Our [Lael and George's] theory for why she didn't go along with such a simple request is that inside she knew she couldn't handle the drug scene. So she wanted to get out of that situation, but instead of dealing with the problem directly, she took the devious approach and got herself kicked out of the school."

George and Lael sent Shana to another school, but Shana soon ran away to move in with her "druggie boyfriend," George recalls. George was in Asia at the time. "I didn't feel badly that I was in Asia because we had done for years everything that we could do. It was time to let go and turn it over to someone else." That "someone else" eventually became the staff at Spring Creek Community, though Shana was first sent to New Beginnings to dry out. When she was released from New Beginnings, George received a call in Asia from Lael, who was terrified because Shana had reverted back to her "old stuff—sitting shriveled up in a corner."

But, as George later heard from Lael, "Lael and Shana got on a plane [to Spring Creek] and Shana went to sleep, and when Shana woke up she was a different person. Lael's firmness, Lael's clarity was a relief to Shana. Shana was determined to make her life work." While Shana was in Spring Creek, George talked to her regularly by telephone and visited her twice. "I had difficulties understanding and accepting the depth of Shana's problems." But during one of his visits, George felt that they became closer than they had been in years.

Shana's younger brother, Skyler, who accompanied his father, was not so impressed with Shana's progress. "Skyler is a very magnanimous fellow," George says. "He was understanding and thoughtful of Shana, almost too much and that was scary, but it seemed genuine. However, he was also angry and unforgiving."

Skyler demonstrated his frustration during this trip when he was asked to comment about his feelings. "I don't see any change [in Shana] at all; I don't feel one bit closer [to her]." When George tried to make excuses for Shana, Skyler followed up with yet another curt remark: "That's bullshit. She made the choices."

Essentially, George says, "Skyler saw what Shana's behavior had done to us and he hated what he saw. Skyler also probably guessed the price the family paid in purely monetary terms." (Because the family had minimal insurance, the final cost of Shana's treatment will be approximately $250,000.) Still, George confides that Skyler has handled the impact of his sister's drug abuse and related activities very well and has gotten over much of his resentment. Out of concern that Shana's problems could harm Skyler, George and Lael sent him to a therapist throughout the family's ordeal.

How did George and Lael's marriage fare under the stress of coping with Shana? "The common struggle did not bind us closer at first," George says. "Each of us wanted the other to solve it [Shana's problems with drugs]. Each of us tended to give lectures to the other, lectures that were really meant for ourselves. We blamed each other. We were used to being very compatible householders, yet during that period we were flailing around, grasping after theories of why this was happening, while phone calls from Shana's so-called friends interrupted our sleep in the middle of the night. We suffered tremendously."

Today, George says that his relationship with Lael has grown. "There's a richness for having experienced the vagaries of life . . . but it sure ain't fun," he adds with a quiet laugh.

SHANA

"At the end of the eighth grade, when I was thirteen, I was raped, and I covered it up for about a year," 17-year-old Shana says now in a matter-of-fact way. "The person who raped me was the brother of one of my good friends." Shana's parents had gone away for the weekend to do some white-river rafting, she recalls, and this guy rang her doorbell and "kind of pushed his way in, though he started off sort of friendly. I had been upstairs watching television, so I told him to come on up and watch the program with me. Once we got upstairs he raped me. I didn't want my parents to know that he had been over. I didn't want anyone to know what had happened. I felt scared and dirty, so I just kept my mouth shut."

Suppressing her feelings about the rape caused her to become depressed. Her grades started to drop, and "I started hanging out with a lot of hard-core skateboard punkers. I started getting into a lot of fights with my mom and dad. I was drinking occasionally, but nothing really bad—I just got drunk every now and then. I was fifteen years old and I wasn't using drugs yet."

Shana was dating a 15-year-old boy named Scott when she got into what she calls a "stupid big fight with my parents." Shana ran out of the house and Scott, accompanied by one of her friends, followed Shana to the Metro [subway] station. "Scott thought I was going to jump in front of a train, so he held me. I decided to run away and Scott said he wouldn't let me go alone." They caught a bus from Washington, D.C., to Myrtle Beach, South Carolina, and remained there for a couple of days. "Then we decided to go to Florida, so we started to hitchhike." However, before they could make it out of Myrtle Beach they were stopped by a man in his early twenties who invited them to stay with him.

"The place was horrible," Shana recalls. "Dogs urinated on the mattresses. The food was awful and there was another runaway kid who lived there. We couldn't stand it, so we rented a motel room." Then, Shana recounts, as they were walking around a shopping center, she fainted for lack of food. While she was being checked at a clinic, Scott was throwing up blood because he had a thyroid condition that had been aggravated by the harsh conditions they were living under. Eventually, Shana called her father and asked for help. George said he would have the police come pick them up; they ran instead. They only lasted a few hours, though, because of Scott's illness.

"When I went home I started seeing a shrink and was tricked into being placed at the Psychiatric Institute. I was pissed off for about a week, then I didn't want to leave." It was during this stay at the Psychiatric Institute that she mustered the strength to tell her parents she had been raped when she was 13. "When I told my parents, they were upset but acted kind of as if it was my fault. At least that's the vibes they were giving off to me. And at the time that I told them, I couldn't even say the fact that I was raped without breaking down and crying." Two months later when she was released from the Psychiatric Institute, things were so bad for her at home, she went to live with Scott.

Lael was a friend of Scott's mother, so she was able to live with this arrangement because the two mothers were working together, at least initially. "Scott's mom was like the mom I wanted," Shana says. "She talked to my mom, so it was okay that I stayed there." While living with Scott, Shana dyed her blond hair black and cut it Mohawk-style. "When I met my mother for dinner for the first time in a few weeks, my mom almost had a heart attack." Shana was sent to a school in Maine, but she ran away and went to a police station because she didn't have anyplace else to go. "So my dad came to pick me up, but I had to agree on a contract. The terms weren't harsh, although I thought at the time that they were harsh."

Shana spent the rest of that summer at the family's vacation home in Maine. During that period she started "getting drunk a lot, just to do it. I also started smoking marijuana." Her parents sent her to another boarding school, near Vassar. There she was introduced to marijuana that was laced with PCP and heroin. It was at this school that she attempted to commit suicide. "My new boyfriend cheated on me with my best girlfriend. When I found out I had a big fight with both of them." After the argument, she walked to a storefront area where the local teenagers hung out, seated herself in an alleyway, and swallowed "about forty Tylenol tablets with codeine." Another friend found her and took her to a teacher she was "close to." The teacher rushed her to a hospital, where she remained for a week. Both parents, she recalls, came and sat with her because someone had to be with her 24 hours a day.

Once she recuperated, Shana returned to the school, only to get caught shoplifting. "We would go on these binges to see how much we could steal, like lipsticks. I got kicked out for not returning the goods by the deadline that was set. I forgot [to return the stolen items] because it was around exam time and I was busy studying." Shana spent Thanksgiving of that year visiting a friend in Florida, where she got high and had sex without, for the first time, experiencing a flashback of the rape. "Then I thought, 'Oh, wow. I can have sex if I get high.'"

Shortly thereafter, Shana was enrolled in the Thorton Friends School in Silver Springs, Maryland. "Some of the student body used drugs like pot and drinking and took coke leaves." (Coke leaves, Shana explains, "are leaves of cocaine that you just chew up to make your mouth numb.") During her tenure at Thorton, Shana says, she also "did speed once." In the end, she was ditching school to get high and was suspended. Her parents got her reinstated at the school, but she kept skipping classes.

During January 1987, when Shana was about to turn 16, her father departed to go overseas. Shortly after he left she ran away with an old boyfriend, John. "My mom tricked me into coming home to sleep for a little while and then I was supposed to leave. Of course I was stupid enough to believe her. When I got there she got rid of my boyfriend and I was sent to New Beginnings. It is a forty-five-day program, but I stayed for sixty days. I was pissed off for the first two weeks, then I started to meet people and started to like it." Shana stayed in the program longer than usual because she had to make up for assignments she failed to complete during her initial period of rebellion. After completing the New Beginnings program, she was put on a plane to Spring Creek Community.

"I never liked Spring Creek. It was just another place where I was locked up. They control you." When asked how her stay there helped her, she answers, "I'm alive." She learned to appreciate the many therapy groups the school offers. "There's a lot of one-on-one therapy, there's group therapy, and there's family therapy. I dealt with my rape and my drug issue. I worked through a lot of stuff there during my first nine months."

Things went well for Shana when she came home from Spring Creek for Christmas vacation. She managed just as well during the following summer vacation with the family. At the end of the summer, a decision was made by her parents and the Spring Creek staff that Shana could return home.

Today Shana can identify what caused her to have such explosive fights with her parents, and she understands at least one reason she used drugs. "I've always been really impulsive, which was something I couldn't control. A lot of times the fight would be about me staying on the phone too long. If anyone said anything to me, I would get angry and walk off." She used drugs because "the flashbacks to the rape were not there when I was doing drugs. I did it [got high] so that I could sleep with boys and not think about the rape."

These insights and more have contributed to Shana's feeling good about herself. "I feel like I'm in control of myself now, like I know what I'm doing. It's just an overall feeling that I'm together and I'm me. When I go out and see drugs sometimes—and I do—I can't bring myself to use them. When I see people now who are drunk or stoned, I see how stupid they look." Shana reports that she has been completely sober one year and eight months and really enjoys how her life has changed. "I can play soccer and do physical things now; before I was too strung out. Now I can think straight."

She feels no bitterness now toward her parents for having "tricked" her at various stages in her recovery process. "I think my parents did absolutely remarkable considering what I did. If my mom hadn't put me in rehab and sent me to Spring Creek, I'd probably be dead right now. I'm happy that she did it." Shana is particularly pleased with what she learned about herself during the six weeks she spent in Spring Creek's Survival and Challenger courses.

"During the three-week Survival course you are starved for the first three days. You are in the Arizona desert and are allowed to carry a bare minimum of clothes wrapped in a poncho and blanket. You hike for about eighty-five miles during the course of three weeks. If you refuse to hike they drag you, they pull you along. People cut themselves to get out of it, but you don't get out of it, they just bandage you up and you have to still hike. You are taught how to make 'cold beds,' which is when you heat rocks and then dig up dirt to bury the rocks underneath to keep you warm.

"You make needles out of some type of animal bone. Finishing Survival makes you realize all of the things that you have. It makes you realize that life isn't so hard as you thought. I remember writing mom and saying, 'I'll eat anything you cook, just let me come home.' You also have a sense of accomplishment—you made it through this. It's like a one-day-at-a-time thing. I can't say that I'm glad that I did the Survival course, but to know that I made it through is good for my self-esteem."

Given her newfound strength, Shana offers a compassionate explanation as to why it took her parents a while to figure out what was going on with her: "My parents were naive at first. They believed that I wasn't using drugs. I hid it from them for a long time. They grew up in another era so they just didn't know. I'm grateful for them." Shana and her parents get along much better these days. "The way we communicate has grown a lot. My parents and I can talk about things now. And our fights don't escalate like they used to. When we get angry we just go away from each other.

"The only thing I'd like to know now is what my birth mother looks like. Until I get a good relationship going with my mom, I don't want to get into a thing of searching for my biological mom, and even then I just want to see what she looks like. A lot of people believe that an adopted child has to have problems with that [being adopted], and some do, but I don't."

Shana says she's trying to live by some of the values passed on to her by Lael. "She taught me to be my own person and she instilled in me that if you believe in something, [you should] stick with it, follow it, pursue it, and don't change your belief for someone else." Shana is currently in high school and attends meetings of Narcotics Anonymous and Alcoholics Anonymous. She plans to take a year off between high school and college. "I'm thinking now that I want to major in psychiatry. I would like to help others based on my past experience."

After Shana was raped, she says, "I didn't know what was going on. I was always down and upset. I even blacked out my childhood memories [from] before the rape. I forgot everything before that. Now I'm starting to figure out that I was a happy kid prior to the rape and that I'm happy now."

SKYLER

"In about the seventh grade I knew there were problems with Shana because she ran away on my birthday," explains 15-year-old Skyler. "I got really down when she didn't return. I stopped doing my schoolwork. I kept to myself a lot at that time. I was kind of distracted." On the other hand, all of the attention focused on Shana caused some resentment to well up in Skyler. "I felt ignored a lot. They [his parents] kept saying, 'Shana this, Shana that, will Shana ever turn around.' I got tired of dealing with it, hearing it, so I started moving on with my own life."

Skyler says he knew Shana was using drugs before his parents did, but he didn't say anything because "I didn't know how serious it could get." Why did he ignore her downward spiral? "I don't know. I didn't want to deal with it or her, so I just let it be." When his parents did find out about Shana's drug abuse, they asked Skyler to keep it a secret, but his friends already knew what was going on. "I've gotten into a couple of fights with guys who said something about Shana that I didn't like." He never told his parents or Shana about the fights, "because it's easy for me to hold things in." Lael tried to get him involved in Al-Anon (a branch of Alcoholics Anonymous for family members of alcoholics), but, he says, "I refused to go. I didn't think it was right for me. I didn't think I would get anything out of it." Skyler did go to family counseling, because "they made me go."

Skyler is not as confident of the solidness of Shana's recovery as is the rest of the family. "They think she's so-called cured. But it doesn't seem like a family to me. It seems like a movie, like somebody's writing lines for her to say. It's been a shock having her be good for a change. I think she's been busting her ass to be good, but Shana feels like a boarder to me. Half of me says, 'It's real,' but half of me says, 'Is it fake or is it real?' It's weird having her back home."

If Shana suffers a relapse, Skyler does not believe the family should invest any more money or time in her recovery. "The thing to say is put her back into treatment. But why put her through treatment again if she wants to mess her life up? It [more treatment] could change her, but I doubt it. It seems like a broken record to me for her to keep going through this [using drugs]."

Skyler's cynical assessment of Shana is tempered, however, by his final remarks: "I've always wanted to be close to Shana, to have someone to talk to besides my parents. I'm glad she's home. I'm going to work at being close, though I don't know how at this moment, but I'll just have to work that out along the way."

POSTSCRIPT

"I really grew up thinking that I could fix things and make people feel better. I spent lots of energy working the world around Shana," Lael explains. "I cannot say that we wanted to be victims, but we got locked into a kind of fear. We worried about Shana being out on the streets by herself. We worried about her use of drugs. There were times when we simply could not sleep because of the fear that some terrible thing might happen to Shana."

George echoes Lael's sentiments. "The three of us [Lael, Skyler, and George], at least, have determined that we are not going to live in that terror again. Shana's not going to live under this roof exacting the same toll. We can't make the difference if Shana doesn't want to live differently, but we are not going to live the way we did once before. We are concerned about family safety, and from now on we're going to take care of ourselves."

And, Lael is quick to point out, Shana will have to learn how to take care of herself. Lael believes, for example, that the "identity issue [dealing with the fact that Shana is adopted] is an important one for Shana, though she says it is not an issue." Now, however, instead of feeling that this is something Lael has to "fix," Lael believes the identity issue is something Shana has to cope with for herself. "I know now that that's a gap that she [Shana] has to fill."

Lael admits that some good things came out of her wrenching experience with Shana. "We're a much more explicit family now. We put the bad stuff right out on the table. I grew up not knowing how to express the angry stuff." Another plus: "My son and I got to know each other better." Indeed, she adds, "All of the members of the family are doing better as a result of this."

Have Lael, George, and Skyler reached the most healthy conclusions when they state that the family has gone through enough and now it is time to safeguard their own well-being? Are they being selfish or self-centered by drawing such a hard-and-fast line? If Shana is having trouble coping with her adoptive status, should she be left to her own devices to sort out any problems she may have with such a deeply emotional matter? You should already be able to answer the first two of these questions based upon what you've learned in Chapters Three and Four. You can find insight as to what might be an appropriate and healthy response to the last question in the final chapter, "Letting Go."

❧ 6 ❧

Letting Go

A close friend who felt she was doing a good deed brought my sister back into my life four months after she had delivered a healthy baby boy and seven months after she had unceremoniously exited my home. Up until that moment, I believed I had rid myself of my addiction to rescue my sister. I was confident I had my co-dependent behavior under control. I had faith that this time I had truly learned what it meant to let go and allow my sister to triumph over her own troublesome life.

It was the Christmas season, which is what prompted my friend to attempt a reconciliation between my sister and me. My friend called and asked if she could drop by since she was in the neighborhood. At the same time, she had picked up my sister, telling her that a mutual acquaintance wanted to see the baby. So we were both surprised to see each other. I wanted to hug her, but I would not let myself. I could tell she wanted to hug me, but she felt my reticence and refrained from reaching out. When she left I felt guilty and immediately began to devise ways to help my sister get on her feet, though I did not call it that.

At first I restricted my efforts to the baby. In my mind, it was okay to help my nephew because that would not count toward helping my sister; therefore, I would not be breaking my recently formed resolution to leave my sister alone. The memory was still fresh of how much money I had lost "helping" my sister, and I had not yet gotten over my resentment toward her for what I viewed as her abuse of my generosity.

On the other hand, I was afraid of what I might do once I saw my sister: I wasn't sure that I could trust myself to know just how far to go in terms of my new resolve. Perhaps what scared me even more was a nagging suspicion about myself: I wasn't sure I had the strength to stop myself from spending beyond a prudent limit. Why? In part I was unsure of myself because I felt guilty about having pressured my sister into leaving my home. Meeting with my sister to do some of the research for this book, I've come to an additional insight: I've also felt guilty about my sister's lot in life because I have been riding a tide of success that I didn't feel I deserved.

I was uncomfortable observing my very, very thin sister, who wore ill-fitting clothes, knowing that I had the money to upgrade her situation . . . especially after she told me she wasn't eating much in order to ensure that her cherubic-looking offspring ate as much as he desired. I accepted her explanation and started to purchase diapers and infant formula, believing that if I did this on a regular basis it would allow my sister to buy food for herself. There were a couple of critical circumstances, though, that I had chosen to ignore. First, I knew that my sister was living with the unemployed father of her child. Second, I knew that her boyfriend was using both alcohol and drugs.

My sister's weight did not pick up, even though my efforts to help did. In addition to buying diapers and formula, I offered my sister the job of transcriptionist and eventually paid her for services I never received. Finally, though, I exploded and decided, once again, that my role as helper simply had to cease. My sister was relieved because she saw my efforts as no more than patronage. She felt I had displayed a haughty pity for her rather than a genuine desire to help. Whether her assessment of me is correct I have yet to entirely sort out, but what I unequivocally gleaned from the experience is this: letting go is learning how to cope with chronic co-dependent and drug-dependent patterns of behavior. In essence, I supported my sister's relapse of sorts—her willingness to be rescued—and she supported my relapse—my anxiousness to be a rescuer.

These days, my sister and I have fashioned a very delicate relationship that entails keeping a respectful distance from each other. Occasionally we engage in long telephone conversations, but we rarely spend time together although she lives about a ten-minute drive from me. It is hard to break destructive patterns, but we are both finally ready to face that fact and rebuild our relationship carefully and with great caution.

SLOUCHING TOWARD RECOVERY

If there is a moral to be found in my personal experience, it is that letting go is an important part of the recovery process when dealing with a substance-abusing family member. It is also one of the more difficult parts of the recovery process to embrace, because it is often seen as abandonment rather than detachment with love. Parents who help their children overcome drugs are learning that they can only do so much; at some point parents must have faith in their child's ability to lead a productive life, although this may very well include periods of relapse.

Drug counselor Barbara Green of Pomona, California-based American Hospital explains why parents typically resist so strongly the concept of letting go: "Many times the need for a parent to let go is interpreted as indifference by the parent and by the child. It [letting go] brings out a lot of threatening issues, especially when dealing with a child. Parents are reinforced in so many ways for so many years that their role is to protect and to provide for the child. To detach, then, from their child is very hard for most parents."

Christy, Jeremy's mother in Chapter Two's case study, recounts how difficult it has been for her to let go and to accept her 17-year-old son's pattern of moving out over and over again to live with her ex-husband. "I've had to let go so many times, yet letting go has been a difficult thing for me to do. The first time I went through the process was when I made the decision to leave my husband, Richard. It was something I knew I had to do, so damn it, I was going to do it, but I didn't face what I was doing head-on. So it took years for me to really get over the experience.

"The next time I had to let go was the first time my son Jeremy decided he wanted to go live with his father. He was about eleven years old and I remember how he tried to help me let go by trying to talk with me, but I had a really hard time with it. It was really hard for me to let this happen gracefully. I just wasn't able to sit down with Jeremy and talk about what was happening. I don't think I helped Jeremy much during that move. When he left I sat down on the sofa and I drank a bottle of wine and I cried and cried and cried."

Currently, Jeremy lives with his father in another city. Jeremy calls her about once every couple of weeks and she writes him every week. Letting go is something she continues to struggle with, because "I still like to fix things, make things better for Jeremy, but now I can't do that, I just have to wait and see how it turns out for him."

Lael, the mother of Shana, 17, who provided testimony in Chapter Five's case study, says, "We're kind of letting go right now because Shana is in a lot of turmoil these days. We had a three-and-one-half month honeymoon with her [after her return from Spring Creek], and after a series of family gatherings she really crashed when her father left to return to his job in Asia. She's talking about wanting to leave home, but I think the turmoil is temporary. I think she's almost overwhelmed at her own success and she almost can't stand it. We've been bumping and grinding our way through this process for a while and what we've learned is that we can't coerce, force, fix, or change Shana. I can't make her happy."

Parents who help their children overcome drugs are learning that certain patterns of behavior displayed by both the co-dependent parent and drug-dependent child can work against the important step of letting go and can even lead to relapse for the entire family. This is so because of the interconnected symptoms of the parent and child. It is important that parents understand and recognize the three categories of warning signs that indicate the potential resumption of their co-dependent patterns of behavior, which can trigger a relapse of their recovering adolescent drug-abuser. The following lists are adapted from "Co-Alcoholic Relapse: Family Factors and Warning Signs," in *Co-Dependency: An Emerging Issue,* by Terence Gorski, president of Alcoholism Systems Associates in Hazel Crest, Illinois, and

Merlene Miller, director of education at Miller Intervention and Recovery Center, based in Olathe, Kansas.

EARLY WARNING SIGNALS

If you are experiencing five or more of these symptoms, there is reason to be concerned:

- Situational loss of daily structure, such as a sudden inability to get to work on time
- Lack of personal care
- Inability to set and stick to limits with your children
- Loss of constructive planning
- Excessive or sudden pattern of indecision
- Any type of sudden compulsive behavior
- Fatigue or inability to rest
- Return of unreasonable resentments
- Return of tendency to control people, situations, things
- Defensiveness
- Self-pity
- Overspending
- Eating disorders—overeating or loss of appetite
- Scapegoating

SIGNS OF A CO-DEPENDENT CRISIS

A co-dependent crisis is under way if you find yourself behaving in three or more of the following ways:

Sporadic attendance at formal support meetings or therapy sessions

Failure to maintain interpersonal (informal) support systems

Inability to construct a logical chain of thought

Confusion

Sleep disturbances

Behavioral loss of control

Uncontrollable mood swings

Feelings of loneliness or isolation

Emerging health problems

Use of medication or alcohol as a means to cope

THE DEBILITATION STAGE

You have reached the critical debilitation stage if you are experiencing three or more of the symptoms listed below:

An inability to change behaviors in spite of a conscious awareness that your actions are self-defeating

The development of an "I don't care" attitude

Complete loss of daily structure

Despair and suicidal thoughts

Major physical collapse

Major emotional collapse

LETTING GO WITH LOVE

The good news is that the worst-case scenario does not have to happen. Parents who help their children overcome drugs are learning how to detach from the symptoms of drug abuse exhibited by their offspring and to control their own symptoms of co-dependency. But, as Spring Creek's Steven Cawdrey points out, "Managing your symptoms is a forever program. You chip away at it a little every day. Since we are humans we are not perfect, so relapse on some level is inevitable."

Most treatment modalities in the area of drug abuse and co-dependency use, to some degree, the Twelve Steps of Alcoholics Anonymous as their practical under-pinning. The Twelve Steps program is, in fact, a pro-gram geared to handling relapse. Letting go with love means that you understand that relapse is possible, per-haps even probable, but that you have enough faith in your child and in yourself to not rush to her rescue —one of your old patterns of co-dependent behavior. Letting go with love also means that you realize you deserve to protect and take care of yourself. To that end, you can reduce the risk of your own relapse and the risk of your child's relapse by taking on the follow-ing adapted list of doable tasks, developed by Gorski and Miller:

1. Become informed about what it means for your child to be addicted to her drug of choice. Under-stand the nature of the drug and what its impact is upon the user. Going to the library or bookstore to secure copies of books listed in Appendix C, "References and Suggested Reading," can help you become educated in these matters. Setting up an appointment to talk with your doctor is another way to get information. You can also obtain such guidance by calling one of the local drug treatment centers listed in Appendix B at the end of this book.

2. Become informed about the symptoms that accompany your child's recovery from chemical addiction. Whether you have opted to place your child in an outpatient or residential treatment program, the program's personnel should be able and willing to sit down with you and explain what to expect and help you handle the inevitable. In addition, the "References and Suggested Reading" list at the back of this book provides some basic explanations and descriptions.

3. Accept and recognize the symptoms of co-dependency—your reaction to a drug-dependent family member—by becoming involved in a support group like Al-Anon or your own individual therapy or family therapy through your participation in your child's treatment program, where you will be helped to develop a plan for your recovery. Addresses and telephone numbers for treatment centers as well as Alcoholics Anonymous, Cocaine Anonymous, Narcotics Anonymous, Drugs Anonymous, Al-Anon and Alateen, Drug-Anon, and Families Anonymous can be found in Appendix B.

4. Recognize the relapse potential of the adolescent drug abuser and of your own co-dependent behavior. Getting involved with support groups such as the ones listed above, where you share your own experiences and learn about the experiences of other parents and their substance-abusing children, will help you to accept the human condition which, by definition, means that none of us are perfect.

5. Develop a plan to prevent your own relapse, and support relapse prevention plans for your recovering drug-dependent child. "Self-discovery and growth requires consequences, not reactions," Spring Creek's Cawdrey explains. He suggests that you should develop a contract with and for yourself that ties you to consequences if any of the aforementioned symptoms of co-dependent relapse become apparent. For example, if you are a co-dependent person who falls easily into the practice of scapegoating, you could require that you make face-to-face apologies to the people you've blamed. Also, a good treatment program should have a strong aftercare component that includes preparation for relapse—yours and your child's.

6. Be patient with your own recovery and the recovery of your child. Neither of you became ill overnight, so recovery will take some time. However, be assured that recovery is possible. With effort, faith, and perseverance, dysfunctional families can be made whole, and committed parents can help their child overcome drugs.

The final case study for this chapter really encompasses all that the book has strived to make clear about how parents can, in fact, help their children overcome drugs. What I hope this case study demonstrates is what I hope the book itself has demonstrated: There is more than one definition of success and good familial health, and the key to such accomplishments has more to do with your and your child's willingness to work hard to change than with your and your child's ability to achieve perfection.

CASE STUDY:
MARY ELIZABETH AND PHILLIP

A New Yorker, Mary Elizabeth, 46, has been divorced for 13 years. She spent much of that time going back to school and getting a degree to develop her own career. Then she got so involved in the troubles of her son that there was no continuity in that career. Nineteen-year-old Phillip, she reports, has had difficulties ever since the divorce. By the time he started using drugs at 13, he had already been in therapy for six years.

Mary Elizabeth works from her apartment as a free-lancer coordinating special events in the arts. She has another son, Gregory, 16, who has just gone off to boarding school. She remains single. Her ex-husband also lives in New York City and has remarried, and his wife for a time tried to help Phillip during his struggles with drug abuse. On the other hand, Mary Elizabeth believes that her ex-husband has done some nonsupportive things that have actually hindered Phillip's recovery. Phillip declined to participate in this book project. Gregory agreed but could not be contacted at his boarding school in time to meet this book's press deadline.

MARY ELIZABETH

"The real problems with Phillip set in when he entered the eighth grade. He was thirteen and showing all of the symptoms of a kid who was experimenting with drugs and probably abusing drugs." These symptoms included: withdrawal; a change of friends to children who were equally withdrawn, sullen, and passive; loss of his former interest in athletics; erratic eating behavior, where he would be either ravenously hungry or not hungry at all; change in sleeping patterns so that he would stay up late and then sleep late and have trouble getting up; and "tuning out" in general.

"In the spring of his eighth grade I found some paraphernalia in his room, pipes for smoking marijuana and the paper that they use to roll the marijuana cigarettes," she remembers. Her response was to "address it for a very short time in the therapy that he was in. I brought up the fact that I had found it. I had allowed for about three weeks—once the issue came up about drugs—to see if any headway could be made. In the therapy I saw that there was no mileage being covered. Even though the information was out, Phillip was still resisting, there was still no dialogue. So I started looking into other alternatives in order to try to treat this problem."

There were programs in New York City specifically targeted to adolescents and drugs, and one was Phoenix House. Phoenix House had an outpatient program where children were required to attend group and family meetings every night but continued to go to school. "It's a very stringent, very demanding kind of program, and that's where I decided that Phillip was going to go. So I enrolled him in this program with a tremendous reluctance on his part, because he said he was using drugs so infrequently this was really an overkill to get him into a program for substance abusers. The doctor that was treating him also agreed [with Phillip]. He said that this was a drastic measure. I doggedly pursued it. There was a tremendous fear in me that if I didn't do something right now, he could slip into using even more drugs, and I wanted to confront the issue from the very beginning."

Mary Elizabeth now recognizes that her inclination to act and to act fast had as much to do with her co-dependency as it did with her fears of what might happen to Phillip. "I am a very confrontational person and also a very controlling person, so that this sort of satiated my hunger to keep it [Phillip's drug abuse] under control and pick up the baton and do something about it. There's something very, very assuring when there's a clear-cut action that you can take, there's a program that tells you what to do and that has a very clear-cut message. A lot of these drug rehab programs have a sort of zealot approach, which has its advantages and its disadvantages." The disadvantage, according to Mary Elizabeth, is that such programs leave you with the impression that there is only one way—their way—to pursue help. "This approach, of course, feeds into a lot of parents who are floundering and want someone to come in and say, 'This is the way to do it,' which prevents some type of assessment about what would be the most propitious route for each individual kid," she explains.

Phillip was substantially younger than most of the children in his group, who were juniors and seniors in high school while he was still in the eighth grade. Also, he was not as far along in his drug abuse as the young people he encountered at Phoenix House. Phillip remained in the Phoenix House program for over a year but did not "graduate," meaning he did not complete the program. "He did not respond to Phoenix House's group methods, and there was the tremendous disadvantage Phillip suffered under, which was that any program worth its salt requires the full participation on the part of the parents and I had an ex-husband who was very resistant. He was resistant to Phoenix to begin with, and he was resistant to the kind of demands that were being asked of all parents, which is essentially to question your own responsibilities and to risk opening up and sharing and exploring some painful issues that you might have with yourself or with your ex-spouse or with your child.

"My ex-husband was unwilling to try that out or to attempt to do that out of fear, out of anger." At one point, Phoenix House actually asked Phillip's father not to attend any of the family meetings, because he was not participating in a healthy manner and was demoralizing the rest of the group. He made fun of other parents and sarcastically questioned the leader of the group. Eventually, his word battles with the leader took up a lot of time in the group. "His attitude of mockery was very demoralizing for a lot of people who really wanted to work in the group," Mary Elizabeth says. "His attitude also derailed a lot of parents who were initially ambivalent and who found an ally in my ex-husband. . . . He is very resistant to any type of questioning of roles that should be played. For him that is hard to do and he was unable to do it. Since Phillip did not have the full support of both parents, it allowed him to play one off against the other and to manipulate, which drains all of the energy away from any kind of positive route that you can take."

Phillip simply did not respond to the method that Phoenix House employs. Later, Mary Elizabeth learned that some programs may succeed with some kids and fail with others. Phoenix House is very confrontational. "The idea was to try to tear down that brittle facade that the kids had built up for themselves. You had to be very forceful and very, very confrontational to tear it away. But with some kids, in the process of tearing it away, they [Phoenix House staff] did a lot of scarring, because these kids came in with some very fragile egos." Thus, she adds, "Depending upon the maturity of the kid who is going through this process, sometimes it worked to the child's disadvantage."

The technique worked for other children in Phillip's group, but not for him. "Phillip was almost like damaged goods when he left," she says.

"There is a process where you have to diminish and then grow. Phillip left the program prematurely because it wasn't working for him, but that meant he left before he could sort of grow up and put things back together again. If you fall apart and you don't have that other subsequent [rebuilding] process, it can be very damaging. I, being a distraught parent, stuck with the program too long, I think. And I think that the program at Phoenix House was too slow to acknowledge that perhaps Phillip needed another kind of treatment, because there are many different types of treatment and if one doesn't work there's always others." During the get-tough periods of his group sessions, "Phillip would withdraw and quite literally bury his head in his lap. And he never broke down. He just balled up into a tight ball. They were never able to get through to him by either having him break down, cry, or explode with anger—some type of reaction where he could open up and be a bit vulnerable."

Eventually, Phoenix House staff decided to allow Phillip a three-month probation on his own since he wasn't responding to their method and since he wanted so much to get out of the program. What troubles Mary Elizabeth now, though, is the fact that Phillip was not "clean," free from drugs, at the time he was put on probation. "They take urine tests, and they did not tell me at the time that Phillip was not clean. I had assumed that he was clean and that was why they were willing to take the risk of giving him a three-month probation period."

So Phillip left on those terms and, not surprisingly, was not successful. With the support systems that he had rejected at Phoenix House unavailable, he was completely on his own. "Despite the fact that he had resisted the program, there were friendships that he had developed among the kids and there were one or two counselors that had been there to support him, and then suddenly there was no program at all," Mary Elizabeth recalls. "So he did decline rather quickly during the summer of his ninth grade. I made a point of calling Phoenix House and making a special appointment to say, 'I feel abandoned; I need some guidance; help me.' Basically, they said, 'Let's just see what happens after the probation period.'" With that, Mary Elizabeth left the program bitter.

Phillip, then 15, developed a pattern that summer of running away and coming back. "He would just hang out with his friends. They would just take off. Phillip would only stay gone for about two weeks and he would always keep in contact with me, he would always have a note saying he was leaving. He was very confused, but he never lost contact with me. He would always make a call. His father over that summer did what he did from then on, which was to essentially write Phillip off when he was acting out. The message was: 'When you get your life together you can call me again.'"

When autumn arrived and the new school semester began, Mary Elizabeth wanted to adhere to the regular schedule she had been accustomed to, rather than tackling the more difficult issues surrounding Phillip's use of drugs. She fell back on "all of the little pegs that delineate your year, such as school starting in the fall." So she and Phillip "went through the procedure of trying to get into the routine of school, but it didn't last long—I think it lasted two days and Phillip was kicked out of school." He was asked to leave his prep school for violation of its strict dress code. The school required that Phillip's hair be cut a certain length and he decided not to comply. "So he went to school the next day and the headmaster called and said Phillip could not return until he got his hair cut. That was a real red flag, so the following day Phillip arrived with his hair uncut and was barred from attending class." To get Phillip under some kind of control, the headmaster suggested that Mary Elizabeth should threaten to send him to a public school; that, she recalls him saying, "should scare the shit out of him." "The public schools here in New York are quite different from public schools in other parts of the country," she says. "They're very tough. Walking into most of them could terrify anyone. It's predominantly minorities and it's large, impersonal, and sometimes frightening. There's a lot of violence in the public schools."

She ended up taking him to the best public school available in her neighborhood, and Phillip decided that he wanted to attend this school. Within the first month, however, he was pretending to leave for school but not attending classes. "In a public school setting, because of the number of students, the parents really are not notified about absences until about two months afterwards." Even before she was notified, she had noticed changes in Phillip. "He'd sleep late, then he would sort of drag himself out to school. Sometimes I would have to fight to get him out of the door so that he could try to get to school on time. His appearance became more and more disheveled. More calls were coming in [for Phillip] that were sort of odd calls from strange people with names that I was unfamiliar with, and that was a new wrinkle. In the past I usually knew the kids who called. I might not like them, but at least I knew them. In a private school setting you have class lists, you have parent meetings, so that names become familiar. But when you are dealing with a public school system, it's wide open, so you don't have a clue who these kids are."

During that year of Phillip's tenth grade, he plummeted. "By November, by the time I had gotten word from the school [that he wasn't attending], I knew that we were in deep trouble and I had already surmised that he was not going to school and had confronted him with my suspicions. . . . I was in such despair because I didn't have a Phoenix House to turn to for any kind of guidance. The psychiatrist I turned to was totally inadequate in terms of dealing with the whole drug issue." She ended up asking a priest for help and was told of a support group called Toughlove, made up of families in similar crises. She went to a meeting and found the support she was in search of.

"Toughlove was very helpful during the time that I needed it. It helps a parent begin to regain some type of control, and I mean control in the best sense of the word. Most of the parents, like myself, felt so out of control—not even knowing what to do either for the kid or for oneself. Many of the parents in this group who had been there a little bit longer really served as a support to try to regain some type of control over the situation and proceed in a way that would be not only healthy for them as parents, but healthy for the kids."

By the time Mary Elizabeth sought out the Toughlove group, Phillip no longer even went through the pretense of going to school. He just slept late, sat around the house during the day, and came in at all hours of the night. "I would lock him out and he would end up slumping on the outside of the door and in the morning there he would be. He was totally out of control. He was experimenting with all types of drugs. Anything that was available he tried, PCP, cocaine, heroin. Indiscriminately, he tried absolutely anything and everything that was provided for him.

"His mood swings would be very violent—either they were extremely low where he would be so despondent he wouldn't even be able to do the minimum of washing or eating, or his mood could be very violent, where his anger could be quite explosive and intimidating." She remembers how Phillip used to tyrannize both her and her younger son, Gregory. "He would go through the procedure of strangling his brother. Or he would scream and yell at me and push me up against the wall. He never hit me, but he was very intimidating in his whole manner. He would throw a dish down to the floor. He also stole money from the household. And every time I would impose even the most minor restriction he would fly into a rage."

Gregory survived this period, according to Mary Elizabeth, "by retreating into his own life. Once I saw him typing methodically, 'Gregory is great. Gregory is great. Gregory is great.'" Gregory found it difficult to openly share what he was feeling inside. "That concerned me," his mother says. Also, she adds, "When Phillip went to Spring Creek Gregory became very fearful. He wanted to be with me all of the time and he didn't respond to any type of therapy." As Gregory became interested in girls, he snapped out of it and concentrated more on his hairdryer, his mother reports, than on any trauma associated with or provoked by Phillip.

Meanwhile, with Toughlove, Mary Elizabeth got the support she needed to initiate a very dramatic action to control Phillip—to get a PINS (Persons in Need of Supervision) petition. In a PINS petition, parents give the court authority to control their child. In New York, this can be done before the child turns 16, when the child is considered a minor. "It's a very dramatic gesture. Most parents who do it are the poor and uneducated. They are the ones who usually resort to this procedure. I intentionally used it to see if there was a way of using it as a leverage to be able to regain control for myself as a parent. I was not doing it in order to relinquish my control or my responsibilities.

Basically, I was using it as a scare tactic to see if I could then get Phillip back into some sense of control, and I needed help on it."

To get a PINS petition, a parent must go to family court, formally request a petition, fill out the forms, and wait for the courts to request a hearing at which the child has to appear. The child is provided a court-appointed lawyer, and the parent can either hire his or her own attorney or do without legal representation. Then a formal hearing takes place where the judge determines what will be demanded of the child. Legally, the child must comply with whatever is demanded. The child's attorney is given the charge of protecting the child's interests, but that can mean many things. In this case, Mary Elizabeth's situation with Phillip was not really adversarial from her point of view. "I had a meeting with Phillip's lawyer so that he could see that we were both trying to do the same thing for him [Phillip]." She did not hire an attorney for herself. "I didn't feel like I really needed one, particularly since Phillip's lawyer concurred with me on the basic principles of what we were trying to do." The goal was to provide Phillip with some sense of an authority that he could listen to. In general, Mary Elizabeth wanted Phillip to be to frightened enough to want to do something to help himself. "The whole court procedure is very intimidating. It intimidates me, you can imagine what it does to a kid."

Phillip was not living at home when this process was taking place. "He was hanging out and spending the nights with people I didn't know." In court, a determination was made that Phillip had to go to a testing place called Geller House. Geller House is a state-funded, nationally renowned residential facility where children are assigned for six weeks to be tested and evaluated to decide where the court should place them. "That was the beginning of Phillip's feeling that there was someplace he could be that felt safe." However, it took a scare tactic to make Phillip consent to go to Geller House, since it is a voluntary program. "The other alternatives were that Phillip could either be sent home, because there's always that option if the parent will receive you, or be sent to a shelter. That was one of the most painful times that I had to make a decision, because at first Phillip said, 'I will not go to Geller House,' and I said I will not take my son back.

"The shelters in New York are very dangerous. You don't send a white boy into a shelter. The lawyer said so too. He said, 'Please don't send him there; he just won't get through. He'll either be abused physically or sexually.' But I said I would not take him. So when I left the court I left him behind knowing that he would stay in the courtroom until the end of the day, knowing that they would round up the kids, put him in a bus, and send him to a shelter."

Phillip bolted en route to the bus and got away. He was out on the street for two days, terrified, and then he called his mother and agreed to go to Geller House. At the end of the six weeks he went directly from Geller House to court. "The evaluation said that Phillip was not appropriate for what's called a therapeutic community. The therapeutic community, referred to by Geller House counselors, is a residential facility that is run by the state of New York for troubled adolescents who don't have substance-abuse problems. Phillip's evaluation stated that he needed a combination of a therapeutic community and some kind of drug rehabilitation." The report also indicated that Phillip needed counseling and psychiatric attention.

The therapeutic community didn't have the drug program that Phillip needed, though it did have the psychological support systems that were indicated. On the other hand, the local drug rehabilitation programs did not have a sufficient counseling and psychiatric function. So a compromise was struck: Since the Geller House counselors felt that Phillip needed to tackle his drug problems first, they suggested he be placed in a drug treatment center immediately, though they did not feel that was the ideal solution. An ideal solution would have been a drug program that had a very strong counseling and psychiatric component. However, Mary Elizabeth was told that the courts could not legally remand a child to a drug rehabilitation program because state funding for drug treatment programs had been severely cut a few years earlier. The courts could force Phillip into foster care through her PINS petition. "But foster care was not an alternative that would help Phillip, since that simply meant that he would be going from one family to another and not dealing with the issues. So I rejected that idea because I would only proceed if I knew that it would help him."

The court advised Mary Elizabeth that there was really nothing else the court could do for her. But, within the context of the family court, she was told that the judge could make it sound as if Phillip had to do what he was being told to do, although legally he did not have to comply. "We walked into the final hearing, Phillip had to stand up, and then the judge stood up to say, 'You have to do what your mother thinks is best for you.' Phillip bought that line. On the way out of the courtroom I told Phillip he had to go to the therapeutic boarding school I had found for him. Phillip did try running away, but I reminded him that the [PINS] process would start all over again, and this time he wouldn't be able to get away before he was delivered to a shelter." The threat worked. She got Phillip safely ensconced in the boarding school within 10 days of his being released by the courts. When she dropped him off, their farewell was amicable. "It was almost as if Phillip was relieved to be able to turn his life over to someone else, because I think he'd really gone through hell."

Phillip, then 16, ended up staying at the boarding school—Spring Creek—for two years. He resisted the school's program during his entire tenure, however. He ran away three times, the last time six weeks before his scheduled graduation. Whenever he ran away, Mary Elizabeth told him, "I will not receive any calls from you. Get back to school and we can continue this dialogue, but I will not talk to you while you are out on the streets." Though he did not return to the school to graduate, she says that Phillip did get a lot out of the school's program in terms of learning how to connect with people. "He began to start trusting some adults. He made some friends with counselors. He made some friends with his peers. He had some really good breakthroughs in terms of how he perceived himself, his relationship with me, and also his relationship with his father. When he left he was capable of setting some goals for himself that were more than 'I want to leave tomorrow; I want to get the hell out of here.' "

Phillip never completely accepted the school's program, his mother reports, but through the everyday experiences of living there for two years and having responsibilities that he either lived up to or not—and suffering the consequences of success or failure—he was able to begin to learn how to live in a safe environment. The last time Phillip ran away, he hitchhiked to Los Angeles from the Midwest, where he had some very bad experiences. "He was accosted by some homosexuals; he found himself penniless in the airport; he was very frightened. He was resourceful enough to find a family to take him in—a janitor who had watched him get attacked in the airport." After getting nowhere with his mother in his requests for financial support, Phillip managed to track down a nurse who had taken care of him when he was young, and she sent him the money for busfare home.

When he arrived home, Mary Elizabeth told him, "You can't come home until you can somehow prove to me that you want to do something for yourself. I'll put you up at the YMCA for two weeks so that you can at least be in a safe place, but you have to find a job and you have to find a support group." Phillip did both within the time frame allotted, and Mary Elizabeth let him move back. For one year, a lot of positive things happened. "Phillip was almost like the prodigal son. He returned and reestablished a close friendship with his brother. We began to learn again how to function, on a daily basis, like a family, which essentially we really hadn't been doing for more than six years. It was a lot of work for all of us, because we were sort of new at it, and it was successful in many areas. Phillip, as well as Gregory and myself, had really hungered for that kind of interaction. What a lot of families take for granted, like having dinner together where we all stayed until dessert, was a novelty for us. It felt new and different and reassuring and safe."

Phillip had a hard readjustment in terms of reentering into the general scheme of things outside the home. He was determined, though, to attend high school rather than test to obtain a General Education Diploma. Attending school every day and doing assignments were difficult for Phillip, but he persevered. He did not, however, respond to the therapy group he had chosen. "I had taken the stand that attending his group sessions was a requirement to stay in the house, but once again the scene repeated itself: Phillip went because he was told he had to go, so he went and just took up space. He didn't take advantage of the group."

In the spring of 1988, Mary Elizabeth reassessed Phillip's involvement in this group and came to the opinion that to continue was pointless; the group itself agreed. So Phillip stopped attending the group. He did graduate from high school and attended summer school because he wanted to get into Fordham University. But Mary Elizabeth started to see subtle changes in the way he cared for himself. "He began to have a harder time getting up in the morning. He was less motivated and just barely got through his summer school class.

"In looking back on it, whenever something has happened where Phillip was slipping and I had to get him back onto the right track, I have always used the same leverage: What does he want most? As a parent, how can I manipulate him so that I can have him do what I want him to do? In this particular case, as I could see that he was beginning to slip again, I did exactly the same thing. I said, 'Phillip, I know you're on drugs, I know you're slipping back into drugs, and I, as a parent, will not support that. I will not support, financially, your going to Fordham unless you can first acknowledge that you have a problem and that you're going to do something about it, so therefore college is out until you come to that realization. And if you don't, you're not even going to be able to stay in the house.'"

Phillip's response was to feel betrayal, anger, rage. "He said, 'How can you take this away from me? I want to go to college. Okay, so I've taken some drugs. I'll try to work on it. I slipped, but I'll try to do better.' But I said, 'That's not good enough. You get yourself into a program or you're out.'" Mother and son came to an impasse when Mary Elizabeth realized that emotionally she wasn't prepared to kick him out of the house; also, she began to examine how appropriate that action would be at this point. She started to wonder if his behavior really warranted such drastic action. "I began to question how effective this whole stance was, because I envisioned that if I succeeded again in forcing him into some other group, it would probably just be one more time that he went through the motions to stay at home."

Besides, she adds, "I was getting totally depleted and I knew that I had to examine what my responsibility was in terms of what I should do for myself and what I should do as a parent. And that's what started a whole sequence of perceptions about myself, that started tentatively and in a very confused manner, and in many respects I'm still very confused. But there was an incident that catapulted me into Al-Anon."

As the battle lines were drawn, with Mary Elizabeth on one side insisting that Phillip seek help or be kicked out of the house, and Phillip on the other side refusing to comply or leave, Mary Elizabeth remembers sitting on her bed and feeling a great deal of pain. "That pain was more than just the pain of a parent witnessing a kid floundering. I didn't know why it was more, but I just knew that it was. And it was so intense that I said I've got to examine this. Then I realized that a lot of that pain was that I realized that there was nothing more that I could do to fix it for Phillip. The phone was sitting in front of me, I remember, almost mocking me saying, 'There's no other program that you can call, there's no other therapist you can call. It has to, at some point, come from Phillip.'" Then I started going to Al-Anon, and the message there was very clear: The responsibility has to fall on the individual who has the problem. And there has to be a responsibility for yourself to start taking responsibility for your own life and your own attitudes."

Mary Elizabeth had spent virtually the last six years of her life so preoccupied with what Phillip was doing that she lost track of her own personal goals. "When I look at where I am right now, I feel depleted. And when I realized that there was nothing more I could do with Phillip, I couldn't fall back on any other thing that was nurturing because I hadn't created that for myself. So there was a tremendous loss and mourning that I couldn't somehow fill my life with some more solutions for Phillip. I also realized that I had hinged my own energy and moods to the success and failure of someone else, in this case Phillip, who basically I had very little control over."

To help her handle these painful insights, Mary Elizabeth started seeing the therapist who had worked with her to weather the storm of going through the PINS petition process of a few years before. This therapist's advice was: "You have to allow Phillip to try to sort out his own problems and to try to sort out his own mistakes. However, if Phillip is directly abusing you or destructive of something in the house, then you should address that kind of behavior, but otherwise you have to allow Phillip to take on some responsibilities."

As Mary Elizabeth has changed, she admits that there has been a small change in Phillip as well. "I'm allowing that to happen, though it's really hard for me to do. I have told him that I think he has a problem; that I hope he addresses it; he can make something of his life, but he has to make the decisions about how he wants to approach it. I suggested my therapist, however, he did make the call on his own; he has gone to her twice. And he said that he does want to go to college next semester. I said that he could but that he had to work between now and when school starts. Also, I told him that if he needed any guidance, here's a person you can call to help you sort out which colleges you want; he went to see that guy. He is looking for a job and it looks like he has one of his own choice, not one that I had suggested or through my contacts. And, finally, I'm backing off."

Phillip is still sleeping late, watching a great deal of television, remaining in isolation, and not seeing any of his friends, but that's his way of trying to stay off drugs, his mother reports. "That's short-lived, I know, but he has to find that out for himself, whereas before I would have said, 'That's not good enough. This is what you have to do and here are the programs, and you had better sign up with any of those programs within the next two weeks or you're out of the house.' I didn't do any of that this time. That's a big change for both of us."

POSTSCRIPT

All is not perfect for Phillip and Mary Elizabeth, but they appear to be off to a solid start in developing a relationship with each other, and with themselves, that is healthy and can be sustained over the long haul. The measure of their constructive teamwork, and how it has evolved for the better over the years, is best exemplified by Mary Elizabeth's newfound point of view: "When Phillip slipped there was a tremendous rage and anger that he had failed and that after all I had done for him, why wasn't he doing well? Basically, I had the power as a parent and I wanted to wield it while I had the opportunity, because the older they [children] get the less they need you. If I look at Phillip's and my relationship as two people rather than as a mother and child, I would never have treated him that way. The message for me now is, any type of recovery is a process. So you are going to slip, but then you get up and try again."

Mary Elizabeth has changed dramatically and so has her son. In the process she has, in fact, helped her child overcome drugs. She has also provided herself with the opportunity to live a full and productive life, albeit much work remains to be done for both her and Phillip to maintain their successes. Still, it's reassuring to know that what they have yet to accomplish in no way diminishes the quality of their current achievements.

What has provided the most inspiration for me, the author, in preparing this book has been the validation that recovery is the result of gradual but persistent attempts to change. Your willingness to persevere is something over which you do have control. That is an exciting concept because it's a goal that is within everyone's reach no matter how dark your days may appear at this moment.

Epilogue

Very few experiences take place in a vacuum. Writing this book was no exception to that rule. As I researched, interviewed, and wrote chapter after chapter, my own life moved forward in ways that influenced my approach to the preparation of this book. In turn, what I was learning about co-dependency definitely changed the way I handled my child and household.

My journey began when I decided to observe a multifamily group therapy session. It didn't take long before the leader of the group warned me that continuing with this project would not be easy. "You won't be able to escape your own stuff," he explained. I politely nodded that I understood and immediately adopted an attitude of mixed amusement and uncertainty. Thinking back, I realize that I didn't know what he meant, and I certainly had no idea of what would eventually come to pass.

"My own stuff" turned out to be my co-dependent patterns of behavior. Figuring out in specific terms what some of my "stuff" was, though, took time and was an evolutionary process of sorts. At that first family therapy session, for example, I thought that the participants' practice of starting each session with a greeting and an admission that they were co-dependents was a hokey thing to do. I simply saw no value in a person saying, "Hi, I'm a co-dependent and I feel pretty good today." Discussions about the concept of hanging tough seemed extreme to me as well. Yet, as I wrote the chapters and listened to parents and children tell me their stories, my attitude slowly changed.

Nowadays, I will quickly admit that I am a co-dependent person who has attempted to control my sister through my efforts to enable and rescue. It's important to me to have the courage to own up to what I am and what I've done. To that end, I've decided to share something I haven't shared until now: My co-dependency extended to my son also. For years I have felt guilty about not raising him in a traditional fashion. To put it simply (though still painfully), I never allowed my status as a mother to intefere with my professional ambitions. My son spent much of the first few years of his life with baby-sitters, for instance, because I was driven by a desire to obtain my college degree, and I did so without the benefit of family or spousal support since I had left my first husband when my son was in diapers and moved three thousand miles away from my parents.

So, as the years passed, I carried around a guilt that translated into a compulsion on my part to rescue my son whenever the going got rough, even as he entered his early twenties. I paid his parking tickets; I agreed to help him make his child support payments when, at age 21, he decided to quit his job and return to school though he had recently sired two children out of wedlock; I covered his long-distance telephone expenses (does this sound familiar?); and I told lies to protect him from the wrath of girlfriends who mistakenly believed in his fidelity.

It all came to a halt when I discovered that my VISA card, which I had allowed him to take to college, had been charged almost to its limit. I was nearing the end of this book when I learned this. By then, I had the courage to break my long-time pattern of co-dependency; having been exposed to the wisdom shared by the parents and children

I had interviewed, I understood why it was so important to hang tough and protect myself. Still, it was hard to take action and call the bank to cancel my son's credit card privileges. To make what I considered such a drastic move, I had to come to grips with my feelings about my relationship with my son, and my feelings about myself in terms of what I deserved in life.

To live fully, I learned from one of the counselors I interviewed, I had to learn how to deal with emotional pain. "After a while, you begin to understand," this counselor said, "that if you can handle the depths of pain you can also experience the heights of joy. . . . You can't shut down the bad stuff without also shutting down the good stuff." This dictum was made very clear to me when I met with my sister during the writing of this book and explored areas of sibling strife, resentment, and confusion that we had never before shared.

My sister pointed out to me, for example, that she was not the only child in the family to emerge with an addiction. Indeed, she reminded me, I had a history of compulsive spending. Somehow, I had managed to forget that I had at one time struggled mightily with this problem. As we continued our dialogue, I noted that I was afraid to ask her tough questions about the role I had played in her life. I was able, however, to silently question my fear, and I finally discovered what was really bothering me: I did not want to risk unearthing any additional evidence of my imperfection. My sister, on the other hand, seemed comfortable disclosing where she had fallen and where she had failed. I was shaken by her confidence and, at that moment, placed my co-dependent behavior under a brighter, more revealing light.

This experience allowed me to return to my manuscript with a more compassionate view of parents and their mistakes and why it is so hard for many mothers and fathers to move beyond denial toward recovery. My breakthrough with my son proved to me that this book was valuable, that what I had written could help others since I knew it had already helped me. What I hope, then, is that my story will help you step forward with faith and confidence to tackle the difficult process of recovery; in truth, by reading this book, you have already begun the process.

Appendix A
Summary of State Health-Insurance Statutes for Alcohol and Drug Treatment Programs

This list is derived from information provided by the National Association of State Alcohol and Drug Abuse Directors. It sums up the legislative requirements for coverage for alcoholism and drug-dependency treatment services on a state-by-state basis. If your state is not listed it means that, as of January 1988, your state had not passed any relevant legislation either mandating insurance coverage or requiring the offering of coverage for purchase of substance-abuse treatment benefits.

ALABAMA requires that alcoholism and drug-dependency coverage be offered by insurers and health maintenance organizations (HMOs).

CALIFORNIA requires that alcoholism coverage be offered by insurers.

COLORADO requires that alcoholism coverage be offered by insurers only.

CONNECTICUT mandates that inpatient treatment for alcoholism be provided by insurers and HMOs; also requires that outpatient alcoholism coverage be offered by insurers and HMOs.

DISTRICT OF COLUMBIA mandates coverage for alcoholism and drug-dependency services by insurers and HMOs.

FLORIDA requires that alcoholism and drug-dependency coverage be offered by insurers and HMOs.

HAWAII mandates coverage for alcoholism and drug-dependency services by insurers and HMOs.

ILLINOIS mandates coverage for alcoholism services by insurers only.

KANSAS mandates coverage for alcoholism and drug-dependency services by insurers only.

KENTUCKY requires that alcoholism services be offered by insurers and HMOs.

LOUISIANA requires that alcoholism and drug-dependency coverage be offered by insurers and HMOs.

MAINE mandates that alcoholism and drug-dependency coverage be provided by insurers and HMOs.

MARYLAND mandates that alcoholism coverage be provided by insurers and HMOs; also requires that drug-dependency coverage be offered by insurers.

MASSACHUSETTS mandates that alcoholism coverage be provided by insurers and HMOs.

MICHIGAN mandates that residential and outpatient alcoholism and intermediate drug-dependency coverage be provided by insurers and HMOs; also requires that coverage for inpatient alcoholism and drug-dependency programs be offered by insurers and HMOs.

MINNESOTA mandates that alcoholism and drug-dependency group coverage be provided by insurers and HMOs; also requires that alcoholism and drug-dependency individual coverage be offered by insurers only.

MISSISSIPPI mandates that alcoholism group coverage be provided by insurers only.

MISSOURI mandates that alcoholism coverage be provided by insurers and HMOs; also requires that drug-dependency coverage be offered by insurers and HMOs.

MONTANA mandates that alcoholism and drug-dependency coverage be provided by group insurers only.

NEBRASKA requires that alcoholism coverage be offered by insurers and HMOs.

NEVADA mandates that alcoholism and drug-dependency coverage be provided by insurers and HMOs.

NEW JERSEY mandates that alcoholism coverage be provided by group and individual insurers only.

NEW MEXICO requires that alcoholism coverage be offered by group insurers only.

NEW YORK mandates coverage for outpatient alcoholism and drug-dependency services by insurers and HMOs; also requires that inpatient alcoholism coverage be offered by group insurers and HMOs.

NORTH CAROLINA requires that alcoholism and drug-dependency coverage be offered by group insurers and HMOs.

NORTH DAKOTA mandates that alcoholism and drug-dependency coverage be provided by group insurers and HMOs.

OHIO mandates that alcoholism coverage be provided by group insurers only.

OREGON mandates that alcoholism and drug-dependency coverage be provided by group insurers only; also requires that alcoholism and drug-dependency coverage be offered by individual insurers only.

PENNSYLVANIA mandates that alcoholism coverage be provided by insurers and HMOs

RHODE ISLAND mandates that alcoholism and drug-dependency coverage be provided by group insurers and HMOs.

SOUTH DAKOTA requires that alcoholism coverage be offered by insurers and HMOs.

TENNESSEE requires that alcoholism and drug-dependency coverage be offered by insurers and HMOs.

TEXAS mandates that alcoholism coverage be provided by insurers and HMOs.

UTAH requires that alcoholism coverage be offered by insurers only.

VERMONT mandates that alcoholism coverage be provided by insurers and HMOs.

VIRGINIA mandates that inpatient alcoholism and drug-dependency coverage be provided by group and individual insurers only; also requires that outpatient alcoholism and drug-dependent coverage be offered by group and individual insurers only.

WASHINGTON mandates that alcoholism coverage be provided by insurers and HMOs.

WEST VIRGINIA requires that alcoholism and drug dependency coverage be offered by group insurers only.

WISCONSIN mandates that alcoholism and drug-dependency coverage be provided by insurers and HMOs.

Appendix B
Substance-Abuse Programs Nationwide

This list is not all-inclusive but is meant to give you at least a start in finding help in your community.

NATIONAL REFERRAL AGENCIES AND SELF-HELP GROUPS

COCAINE HOTLINE
Fair Oaks Hospital
19 Prospect Street
Summit, NY 07901
(800) COC-AINE

NATIONAL INSTITUTE ON DRUG ABUSE
Drug-Referral Helpline
5600 Fishers Lane
Rockville, MD 20857
(800) 662-HELP

THERAPEUTIC COMMUNITIES OF AMERICA
54 West 40th Street
New York, NY 10018
(212) 354-6000

NATIONAL CLEARINGHOUSE FOR DRUG AND ALCOHOL INFORMATION
P.O. Box 2345
Rockville, MD 20852
(301) 468-2600

AL-ANON/ALATEEN
1372 Broadway
New York, NY 10018
(212) 302-7240

DRUG-ANON
P.O. Box 473
Ansonia Station
New York, NY 10023
(212) 874-0700

FAMILIES ANONYMOUS
P.O. Box 528
Van Nuys, CA 91408
(818) 989-7841

TOUGHLOVE
P.O. Box 1069
Doylestown, PA 18901
(215) 348-7090

ALABAMA

BIRMINGHAM

The University of Alabama
   at Birmingham
   Substance Abuse
   Programs
3015 Seventh Avenue South
Birmingham, AL 35233
(205) 934-2118
Program: Outpatient

DECATUR

Charter Retreat Hospital
P.O. Box 1230
Decatur, AL 35602
(205) 350-1450
Program: Inpatient
   short-term (45-day)

MOBILE

Charter Southland Hospital
5800 Southland Drive
P.O. Box 9699
Mobile, AL 36691
(205) 666-7900
Program: Outpatient and
   short-term (four-week)

ALASKA

ANCHORAGE

Charter North Hospital
2530 Debarr Road
Anchorage, AK 99514
(907) 258-7575
Program: Inpatient
   short-term (30-day);
   outpatient short-term
   (four-week)

ARKANSAS

FAYETTEVILLE

Charter Vista Hospital
4253 Crossover Road
Fayetteville, AR 72702
(501) 521-5731
Program: Outpatient
   short-term (60-to-90-day);
   inpatient short-term
   (four-week)

CALIFORNIA

ACTON

Acton Rehabilitation Center
P.O. Box 25
Acton, CA 93510
(805) 947-4191
Program: Inpatient
   short-term (90-day)

AUBURN

Sierra Family Services
219 Maple Street
Auburn, CA 95603
(916) 885-0441
Program: Outpatient

CORONA

Charter Oak Hospital
2005 Kellogg Street
Corona, CA 91719
(714) 735-2910
Program: Outpatient and
   inpatient short-term
   (30-day)

COVINA

1161 East Covina Boulevard
Covina, CA 91724

(818) 915-8711
Program: Outpatient and
inpatient short-term
(six-week)

GARDENA
South Bay Chemical
Dependency and Family
Treatment Center
15519 Crenshaw Boulevard
Gardena, CA 90249
(213) 679-9031
Program: Outpatient

HOLLYWOOD
Hollywood Community
Recovery Center
1857 Taft Avenue
Hollywood, CA 90028
(213) 461-3161
Program: Outpatient

INGLEWOOD
Inglewood Community
Recovery
279 Beach Avenue
Inglewood, CA 90302
(213) 673-5750
Program: Outpatient

LONG BEACH
Charter Hospital of Long
Beach
6060 Paramount Boulevard
Long Beach, CA 90805
(213) 408-3100
Program: Inpatient
short-term

LOS ANGELES
East L.A. Chemical
Dependency and Family
Treatment Center
3421 East Olympic Boulevard
Los Angeles, CA 90023
(213) 262-1786
Program: Outpatient

EL SERENO CHEMICAL
DEPENDENCY AND FAMILY
TREATMENT CENTER
4837 Huntington Drive
North
Los Angeles, CA 90032
(213) 221-1746
Program: Outpatient

MOUNTAIN VIEW
Comadres
Family Service Association
655 Castro Street
Mountain View, CA 94041
(415) 968-3371
Program: Outpatient

PASADENA
Impact Drug and Alcohol
Treatment Center
1680 North Fair Oaks Avenue
P.O. Box 93607
Pasadena, CA 91109
(213) 681-2575
Program: Outpatient

POMONA
American Hospital
2180 West Valley Boulevard
Pomona, CA 91768

(714) 865-2336
Program: Inpatient long-term

ROSEVILLE
Sierra Family Services
424 Vernon Street
Roseville, CA 95678
(916) 783-5207
Program: Outpatient

SAN FRANCISCO
Haight-Ashbury Free Medical
  Clinic
529 Clayton Street
San Francisco, CA 94117
(415) 621-2014
Program: Outpatient

SAN JOSE
Comadres
Family Service Association
55 East Empire Street
San Jose, CA 95112
(408) 288-6200
Program: Outpatient

SANTA ANA
Phoenix House
1207 East Fruit Street
Santa Ana, CA 92701
(714) 305-0170
Program: Inpatient

SANTA MONICA
Delancey Street Foundation
1344 16th Street
Santa Monica, CA 90404
(213) 393-2657
Program: Outpatient

TARZANA
Tarzana Treament Center
18646 Oxnard Street
Tarzana, CA 91356
(818) 996-1051
Program: Outpatient and
  inpatient

TORRANCE
Charter Pacific Hospital
4025 West 226th Street
Torrance, CA 90509
(213) 373-0261
Program: Inpatient
  short-term

VENICE
Phoenix House/Tuum Est
503 Ocean Front Walk
Venice, CA 90291
(213) 392-3070
Program: Inpatient adolescent

COLORADO
LAKEWOOD
Cenikor
1533 Glen Ayr Drive
Lakewood, CO 80215
(303) 234-1288
Program: Outpatient

CONNECTICUT
NEW HAVEN
Connecticut Mental Health
  Center
APT Foundation
Substance-Abuse Treatment
  Center

285 Orchard Street
New Haven, CT 06511
(203) 789-7387
Program: Outpatient

NORWALK
Connecticut Renaissance
83 Wall Street
Norwalk, CT 06850
(203) 866-2541
Program: Outpatient

STAMFORD
Liberation Clinic
125 Main Street
Stamford, CT 06901
(203) 324-7511
Program: Outpatient

DISTRICT OF COLUMBIA
Second Genesis
1320 Harvard Street, N.W.
Washington, D.C. 20009
(202) 234-6800
Program: Outpatient

FLORIDA
FORT LAUDERDALE
Spectrum
Financial East Building
2801 East Oakland Park
    Boulevard
Fort Lauderdale, FL 33306
(305) 564-2266
Program: Outpatient

FORT MYERS
Charter Glade Hospital
3550 Colonial Boulevard

Fort Myers, FL 33912
(813) 939-0403
Program: Inpatient
    short-term

JACKSONVILLE
Gateway Community
    Services
4814 Lexington Avenue
Jacksonville, FL 32210
(904) 384-8669
Program: Outpatient

MIAMI
Charter Hospital of Miami
11100 N.W. 27th Street
Miami, FL 33172
(305) 591-3230
Program: Outpatient
    short-term

New Horizons Community
    Mental Health Center
1469 N.W. 36th Street
Miami, FL 33142
(305) 635-0366
Program: Outpatient

Spectrum
11055 N.E. 6th Avenue
Miami, FL 33162
(305) 754-1683
Program: Outpatient

OCALA
Charter Springs Hospital
3130 S.W. 27th Avenue
P.O. Box 3338
Ocala, FL 32678
(994) 237-7293

Program: Outpatient and
  inpatient short-term

ORLANDO
Straight
2400 Silver Star Road
Orlando, FL 32804
(305) 291-4357
Program: Outpatient
  long-term; inpatient
  short-term

ST. PETERSBURG
Straight
3001 Gandy Boulevard
St. Petersburg, FL 33702
(813) 577-6011
Program: Outpatient
  long-term

TAMPA
Charter Hospital of Tampa
  Bay
4004 Riverside Drive
Tampa, FL 33603
(813) 238-8671
Program: Inpatient
  short-term

GEORGIA
ATHENS
Charter Winds Hospital
240 Mitchell Bridge Road
Athens, GA 30604
(404) 546-7277
Program: Inpatient
  short-term

ATLANTA
Charter Brook Hospital
3913 North Peachtree Road
Atlanta, GA 30341
(404) 457-8315
Program: Outpatient and
  inpatient short-term

AUGUSTA
Charter Hospital of Augusta
3100 Perimeter Parkway
Augusta, GA 30909
(404) 868-6625
Program: Outpatient and
  inpatient short-term

COLUMBUS
Turning Point
1220 Third Avenue
P.O. Box 2299
Columbus, GA 31993
(404) 323-3167
Program: Inpatient
  short-term

MACON
Charter Lake Hospital
3500 Riverside Drive
P.O. Box 7067
Macon, GA 31209
(912) 474-6200
Program: Outpatient and
  inpatient short-term

MARIETTA
Straight
2221 Austrell Road
Marietta, GA 30060
(404) 434-8679

Program: Outpatient
long-term; inpatient
short-term

SAVANNAH
Charter Hospital of Savannah
1150 Cornell Avenue
Savannah, GA 31404
(912) 354-3911
Program: Outpatient and
inpatient short-term

ILLINOIS
BELLEVILLE
Gateway Foundation
409 East Main Street
Belleville, IL 62220
(618) 234-9002
Program: Outpatient

CHICAGO
Charter Barclay Hospital
4700 North Clarendon
Chicago, IL 60640
(312) 728-7100
Program: Inpatient

Gateway Foundation
3162 North Broadway
Chicago, IL 60657
(312) 929-1865
Program: Outpatient

EAST ST. LOUIS
Gateway Foundation
1509 King Drive
East St. Louis, IL 62205
(618) 397-9720
Program: Outpatient

SPRINGFIELD
Gateway Foundation
815 North 5th Street
Springfield, IL 62702
(217) 522-7732
Program: Outpatient

INDIANA
FORT WAYNE
Charter Beacon Hospital
1720 Beacon Street
Fort Wayne, IN 46805
(219) 423-3651
Program: Inpatient
short-term

KANSAS
TOPEKA
C. F. Menninger Memorial
Hospital Alcohol and
Drug Abuse
Recovery Program
P.O. Box 829
Topeka, KS 66601
(913) 273-7500
Program: Outpatient and
inpatient short-term

WICHITA
Charter Hospital of Wichita
8901 East Orme
Wichita, KS 67207
(316) 686-5000
Program: Outpatient and
inpatient short-term

KENTUCKY

LEXINGTON

Charter Ridge Hospital
3050 Rio Doso Drive
Lexington, KY 40509
(606) 269-2324
Program: Inpatient
short-term

LOUISVILLE

Charter Hospital of
Louisville
1405 Browns Lane
Louisville, KY 40207
(502) 896-0495
Program: Outpatient and
inpatient short-term

LOUISIANA

LAKE CHARLES

Charter Hospital of Lake
Charles
4250 5th Avenue South
Lake Charles, LA 70605
(318) 474-6133
Program: Inpatient
short-term

St. Patrick Hospital
524 South Ryan Street
Lake Charles, LA 70601
(318) 433-7872
Program: Outpatient and
inpatient short-term

NEW ORLEANS

Odyssey House Louisiana
1125 North Tonti Street
New Orleans, LA 70119

(504) 821-9211
Program: Outpatient

SHREVEPORT

Charter Forest Hospital
9320 Linwood Avenue
Shreveport, LA 71108
(318) 688-3930
Program: Inpatient short-term

MARYLAND

ROCKVILLE

Second Genesis
14701 Avery Road
Rockville, MD 20853
(301) 424-8500
Program: Outpatient

MASSACHUSETTS

BOSTON

Family Services Association
of Greater Boston
34½ Beacon Street
Boston, MA 02108
(617) 523-6400
Program: Outpatient

SPRINGFIELD

Marathon House
5 Madison Avenue
Springfield, MA 01105
(413) 733-2178
Program: Outpatient

MICHIGAN

DETROIT

Family Services of Detroit
and Wayne County

Family Trouble Clinic
11000 West McNichols Road
Detroit, MI 48221
(313) 862-0330
Program: Outpatient

PLYMOUTH
Straight
42320 Ann Arbor Road
Plymouth, MI 48170
(313) 453-2610
Program: Outpatient
long-term; inpatient
short-term

WEST BLOOMFIELD
Maplegrove Youth Treatment
Center
6773 West Maple Road
West Bloomfield, MI 48033
(313) 661-6507
Program: Inpatient short-term

MINNESOTA
PLYMOUTH
Hazelden Pioneer House
11505 36th Avenue North
Plymouth, MN 55441
(800) 559-2022
Program: Inpatient
short-term

MISSISSIPPI
JACKSON
Charter Hospital of Jackson
East Lakeland Drive
P.O. Box 4297
Jackson, MS 39216

(601) 939-9030
Program: Outpatient and
inpatient

MISSOURI
COLUMBIA
Charter Hospital of Columbia
200 Portland Street
Columbia, MO 65201
(314) 876-8000
Program: Inpatient
short-term

KANSAS CITY
Renaissance West
425 East 63rd Street
Kansas City, MO 64110
(816) 444-0733
Program: Outpatient

ST. LOUIS
Magdala Foundation
4158 Lindell Boulevard
St. Louis, MO 63108
(314) 652-6004
Program: Outpatient

MONTANA
THOMPSON FALLS
Spring Creek Community
1342 Blue Slide Road
P.O. Box 429
Thompson Falls, MT
59873-0429
(406) 827-4344
Program: Therapeutic
boarding school

NEVADA
LAS VEGAS
Charter Hospital of Las
    Vegas
7000 West Spring Mountain
Las Vegas, NV 89117
(702) 876-4357
Program: Inpatient
    short-term

NEW HAMPSHIRE
DUBLIN
Marathon House
Box C
Dublin, NH 03444
(603) 563-8501
Program: Outpatient

NEW JERSEY
NEWARK
Integrity House
103 Lincoln Park
P.O. Box 1806
Newark, NJ 07101
(201) 623-0600
Program: Outpatient

PARAMUS
Fair Oaks Hospital
Outpatient Recovery Center
Bergen Medical Center
   Building
One West Ridgewood
    Avenue
Paramus, NJ 07652
(800) 872-3864
Program: Outpatient

SUMMIT
Fair Oaks Hospital
19 Prospect Street
Summit, NJ 07901
(201) 522-7000
Program: Inpatient
    short-term

NEW MEXICO
ALBUQUERQUE
Charter Hospital of
    Albuquerque
5901 Zuni S.E.
Albuquerque, NM 87108
(505) 265-8800
Program: Outpatient and
    inpatient short-term

NEW YORK
BRONX
Daytop Village
16 Westchester Square
Bronx, NY 10461
(212) 822-1217
Program: Outpatient

BROOKLYN
Daytop Village
401 State Street
Brooklyn, NY 11202
(718) 625-1388
Program: Outpatient

Phoenix House
55 Flatbush Avenue
Brooklyn, NY 11201
(718) 852-3150
Program: Outpatient

JAMAICA
Daytop Village
166-10 91st Avenue
Jamaica, NY 11432
(718) 523-8288
Program: Outpatient

LONG ISLAND CITY
Phoenix House
34-25 Vernon Boulevard
Long Island City, NY 11101
(718) 274-4213
Program: Outpatient

MANHATTAN
Daytop Village
132 West 83rd Street
New York, NY 10024
(212) 595-7855
Program: Outpatient

Odyssey House
309-11 East 6th Street
New York, NY 10003
(212) 477-9639
Program: Outpatient

Phoenix House Riverside
    Center
164 West 74th Street
New York, NY 10023
(212) 595-5810
Program: Outpatient

STATEN ISLAND
Daytop Village
1915 Forest Avenue
Staten Island, NY 10303
(718) 981-3136
Program: Outpatient

NORTH CAROLINA
GREENSBORO
Charter Hills Hospital
700 Walter Reed Drive
Greensboro, NC 27403
(919) 852-4821
Program: Inpatient
    short-term

RALEIGH
Charter Northridge Hospital
400 Newton Road
Raleigh, NC 27615
(919) 847-0008
Program: Outpatient and
    inpatient short-term

WINSTON-SALEM
Charter Mandala Hospital
3637 Old Vineyard Road
Winston-Salem, NC 27104
(919) 768-7710
Program: Inpatient
    short-term

OHIO
DAYTON
Project Cure, Inc.
1800 North Western Avenue
Dayton, Ohio 45427
(513) 262-3500
Program: Residential and
    outpatient

MILFORD
Straight
6074 Branch Hill
Guinea Pike
Milford, OH 45150

(513) 575-2673
Program: Outpatient
long-term and inpatient
short-term

PENNSYLVANIA
ERIE
Abraxas II
348 West 8th Street
Erie, PA 16502
(814) 459-0618
Program: Outpatient
short-term

HARRISBURG
Guadenzia Concept 90
Harrisburg State Hospital
P.O. Box 10396
Harrisburg, PA 17105
(717) 232-3232
Program:Inpatient short-term

PHILADELPHIA
The Bridge
1912 Welsh Road
Philadelphia, PA 19115
(215) 969-8990
Program: Outpatient

Charter Fairmount Institute
561 Fairthorn Street
Philadelphia, PA 19128
(215) 487-4000
Program: Outpatient and
inpatient short-term

PITTSBURGH
Supervised Independent
Living

241 Amber Street
Pittsburgh, PA 15206
(412) 441-5233
Program: Inpatient short-term

RHODE ISLAND
PROVIDENCE
Marathon House
131 Wayland Avenue
Providence, RI 02906
(401) 331-4250
Program: Outpatient

SOUTH CAROLINA
WEST COLUMBIA
Charter Rivers Hospital
2900 Sunset Boulevard
P.O. Box 4116
West Columbia, SC 29171
(803) 796-9911
Program: Outpatient and
inpatient short-term

TENNESSEE
MEMPHIS
Charter Lakeside Hospital
2911 Brunswick Road
Memphis, TN 38134
(901) 377-4700
Program: Outpatient and
inpatient short-term

TEXAS
AUSTIN
Charter Lane Hospital
8402 Crosspark Drive

Austin, TX 78761
(512) 837-1800
Program: Outpatient and
    inpatient short-term

CORPUS CHRISTI
Charter Hospital of Corpus
    Christi
3126 Roddfield Road
Corpus Christi, TX 78414
(512) 993-8893
Program: Outpatient and
    inpatient short-term

DALLAS
Help Is Possible
723 South Peak
Dallas, TX 75223
(214) 827-2870
Program: Outpatient

FORT WORTH
Charter Hospital of Fort
    Worth
6201 Overton Ridge
    Boulevard
Fort Worth, TX 76132
(817) 292-6844
Program: Inpatient and
    short-term

HOUSTON
St. Joseph Hospital
1919 LaBranch
Houston, TX 77002
(713) 757-1000
Program: Outpatient and
    inpatient short-term

LUBBOCK
Charter Plains Hospital
P.O. Box 10560
Lubbock, TX 79408
(806) 744-5505
Program: Inpatient and
    short-term

SAN ANTONIO
Charter Real Hospital
8550 Huebner Road
San Antonio, TX 78240
(512) 699-8585
Program: Outpatient and
    inpatient short-term

UTAH
MIDVALE
Charter Summit Hospital
175 West 7200 South
Midvale, UT 84047
(801) 561-8181
Program: Outpatient and
    inpatient short-term

SALT LAKE CITY
Odyssey House of Utah
625 South 200 East
Salt Lake City, UT 84111
(801) 363-0203
Program: Outpatient

VIRGINIA
ALEXANDRIA
Second Genesis
1001 King Street
Alexandria, VA 22314

(703) 548-0442
Program: Outpatient

NEWPORT NEWS
Charter Colonial Institute
17579 Warwick Boulevard
Newport News, VA 23603
(804) 887-2611
Program: Inpatient short-term

RICHMOND
Charter Westbrook Hospital
1500 Westbrook Avenue
Richmond, VA 23227
(804) 266-9671
Program: Outpatient and
    inpatient short-term

WEST VIRGINIA
WAVERLY
White Oak Village
Route 2
P.O. Box 56A
Waverly, WV 26184
(304) 679-3621
Program: Outpatient

WISCONSIN
KENOSHA
Meridian House Ltd.
6755 14th Avenue
Kenosha, WI 53140
(414) 654-0638
Program: Outpatient

WYOMING
CHEYENNE
Pathfinder
803 West 21st Street
P.O. Box 1604
Cheyenne, WY 82001
(307) 635-0256
Program: Outpatient

Appendix C
References and Suggested Reading

The Twelve Steps of Alcoholics Anonymous. Interpreted by the Hazelden Foundation. New York: Harper and Row, 1987.

Ashley, Richard. *Cocaine: Its History, Uses and Effects.* New York: Warner Books, 1975.

Barun, Ken, and Philip Bashe. *How to Keep the Children You Love Off Drugs.* New York: Atlantic Monthly Press, 1988.

Black, Claudia. *Children of Alcoholics: As Youngsters, Adolescents and Adults.* New York: Ballantine, 1981.

Co-Dependency: An Emerging Issue. Pompano Beach, Florida: Health Communications, Inc., 1984.

Kinney, Jean, and Gwen Leaton. *Loosening the Grip: A Handbook of Alcohol Information.* 3d ed. St. Louis: Times Mirror/Mosby College Publishing, 1987.

Macdonald, D. I. *Drugs, Drinking and Adolescents.* Chicago: Yearbook Medical Publishers, Inc., 1984.

Smart, R. G. *The New Drinkers: Teenage Use and Abuse of Alcohol.* 2d ed. Toronto: Addiction Research Foundation, 1980.

Index

About the Author

Born in West Philadelphia in 1950, Barbara Cottman Becnel still remembers how local gang members trampled freshly mowed grass and multicolored flower beds as they chased their rivals through the gardens of her middle class neighborhood. As a child, she watched and wondered about such sights; as an adult, she has devoted much of her professional life to developing public policy and programs that help children in trouble.

She has traveled throughout the United States and abroad giving lectures and conducting workshops about the complex factors that help perpetuate youth unemployment and crime; she also has provided testimony for Congressional committees in Washington, D.C., about these matters. With the writing of *Parents Who Help Their Children Overcome Drugs,* she has developed a set of guidelines for parents that will help prevent their children from becoming or remaining involved in the nation's drug culture.

Barbara Cottman Becnel moved to Los Angeles in 1980 from Washington, D.C., and has lived there ever since. Currently she spends her days employed as a consultant for the County of Los Angeles developing employment and training programs for the hardcore unemployed, including gang members, youth exoffenders, former drug users, teen parents, and high school dropouts. During the evenings (and sometimes early morning hours) she writes books. Her only child, a son, attends college in Sacramento.